SOLAR FLARE

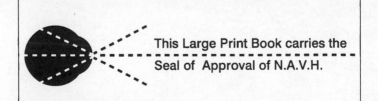

This Large Print Book carries the Seal of Approval of N.A.V.H.

SOLAR FLARE

LARRY BURKETT

Thorndike Press • Thorndike, Maine

Published in 1998 by arrangement with Northfield Publishing.

Thorndike Large Print ® Christian Mystery Series.

The tree indicium is a trademark of Thorndike Press.

The text of this Large Print edition is unabridged.
Other aspects of the book may vary from the original edition.

Set in 16 pt. Plantin by Minnie B. Raven.

Printed in the United States on permanent paper.

Library of Congress Catalog Card Number: 97-91275
ISBN: 0-7862-1323-X (lg. print : alk. paper : hc)

*To my lifelong friend, companion,
and wife, Judy*

ACKNOWLEDGEMENTS

*I would like to thank my editor, Adeline Griffith,
a dedicated servant of the Lord;
Greg Thornton at Moody Press, who
patiently endured every delay;
and my faithful readers, who
allow me to do these fun things.*

PROLOGUE

Jason jumped up from his chair, nearly stumbling in the process. What he was witnessing was incredible. The chart on the radio telescope was pegged off the scale.

The solar eruption Jason was observing was of staggering proportions. The plume of invisible radiation stretched nearly three million miles into space. Within 90 hours the explosion of trillions of tons of supercharged cosmic particles would bombard Earth.

In the meantime, Jason knew the eruption had to be observed by the Japanese SOHO satellite. His friend, Dr. Onera of Tokyo Observatory, had to be notified immediately. The world had to be warned — and quickly. The stream of supercharged energy streaming from area 403 on the solar surface was headed toward Earth at more than a million miles an hour. In less than three days the greatest threat to Earth's survival would be upon them.

Would Earth's magnetic shield deflect this great solar wind, as it had lesser solar flares in the past? Jason doubted it. His thoughts shifted back to the hundreds of lectures he had given his students about the effects of solar flares on planet Earth.

During a solar eruption, the sun spews out streams of plasma, which form into solar winds. These winds hurtle through space at over a million miles an hour, disrupting everything in their path. Periodically the sun will spew out plasma through coronal holes in the sun's surface. These coronal holes are what pose the greatest threat to Earth's inhabitants. If one of the holes happens to be pointed toward Earth, instead of outer space, the electrically charged winds strike Earth's magnetic field, often bending the magnetic lines of force and penetrating to Earth's surface.

When this happens and the magnetosphere fluctuates wildly, the millions of wires strung across the planet become electromagnetic generators. The currents created can short out electrical equipment and cause massive power grid dropouts like those experienced in the West in the late nineties.

The last major solar eruption occurred in the late nineteenth century, so no one really knows the effects that will be felt on Earth in our modern electronic era. Jason Hobart was widely known and just as widely ridiculed for his insistence that a major solar flare would disrupt global communications and, worse, could destroy sensitive electrical systems through "cosmic ray overload," which is what the media called his theory.

Jason knew the theory was sound, even if

his timing was errant. Dr. Edmond Carrington had first presented the theory in the nineteenth century and had correctly demonstrated that these solar flares were, in fact, the cause and origin of the aurora borealis, or northern lights. The greater danger of the flares were unknown to the nineteenth century population because they didn't have the modern electronic measuring devices available today. Jason shuddered as he looked at the data before him. Trillions of tons of cosmic matter was aimed in their direction. It was his firm belief that a total global burnout could occur. Were that to happen, the planet they lived on would be plunged back into the nineteenth century, as the modern electronic era would be brought to a screeching halt.

Jason breathed a sigh of relief that the president had been willing to listen to his theory. President Houston had promised that he would consider grounding all civilian aircraft until the extent of the pending flare was known.

Jason looked up in horror as the big commercial jet roared overhead. "No," he shouted as he rushed to the telephone on his desk. The president had to believe him or lives would be lost when the flare struck Earth. This eruption could cripple Earth and kill millions, perhaps billions. The president had to listen!

1

"Well, a disastrous solar eruption certainly is possible," Professor Jason Hobart replied defensively to one of the students in the freshman astronomy class he had been teaching for the last twenty years. "It is conceivable that a violent enough magnetic storm on the sun could affect Earth's weather."

"You mean, like it could cause tornadoes and stuff, Professor?" the bespectacled student with a bushy shock of reddish hair asked in a mocking tone — as if his professor had just suggested that Darth Vader was real.

"Probably not," Jason gruffed over the audible snicker that crossed the room. Jason Hobart was well aware of the disrespect for him among some of the other staff at Rockford College. Inevitably, it always worked its way into his classroom as well. More than once he had been treated to their snide remarks. No doubt the red-haired freshman also had been treated to a session on the nutty professor's "solar disaster theory" by some of the upperclassmen in his dorm.

For nearly three decades Jason Hobart had been consumed by his personal study of a phenomenon known as solar magnetosphere dislocation. In lay terms: solar flares.

The study of solar flares was neither controversial nor unusual; in fact, virtually every country with any scientific capabilities had a solar observatory where flares were catalogued and recorded. In this age of modern electronics, the study of solar activity is particularly important.

A large solar flare could disrupt vital communication links, especially satellite communications, for hours — and sometimes even for days. More recently, the viewing of the northern lights, a phenomenon created by the charged particles thrown out by a solar flare striking Earth's upper atmosphere, had become a growing tourist industry in the northern hemisphere, especially for the nations with outposts at the North Pole. Wealthy tourists paid big money to fly to the arctic region to watch solar storms light up the night sky. So, solar flare observation was a growing business.

But Jason Hobart had taken solar flare observation a step further when six years earlier he predicted a massive solar eruption that could (although the media had quoted him as saying *would*) disrupt communications on Earth and, according to the media, "bombard the planet with death-dealing X rays."

His predictions had been based on previous studies by nineteenth century astronomer, Sir Edmond Carrington. With little more than a crude six-inch telescope and some logical reasoning, Carrington had been able to accurately predict several solar eruptions during the early nineteenth century. He also had been able to conclusively prove the link between solar eruptions and the aurora borealis, or northern lights, although initially he also endured great ridicule for his ideas.

In the twentieth century, when solar flares were normally observed by sensitive X-ray equipment and spectral analysis, Carrington's accuracy in predicting eruptions still had not been matched. Jason Hobart had studied Carrington's techniques and formed some theories of his own, leading him six years earlier to predict a massive eruption, similar to one that Professor Carrington observed in 1872.

A Rockford television station had heard about his predictions and picked up the story. Through one of those flukes that frequently affect our lives, the story was fed to the network, where it was carried as a sidebar on the NBC evening news. Instantly Professor Hobart was a national celebrity and was in great demand for other interviews.

Unfortunately he also was the object of jealousy and scorn by members of the established scientific community, many of whom disagreed with his conclusions and most of whom envied his recognition.

Just as he had predicted, a solar eruption occurred, sending a billion tons of charged particles through space and toward Earth. For three days the northern lights treated the inhabitants of the arctic region to a celestial display unlike any that had been seen in the previous 50 years.

Professor Hobart became an icon on national television. Based on Carrington's formula, the professor predicted even greater eruptions, communications shutdowns, and worldwide chaos.

Unfortunately for Jason Hobart, and fortunately for the rest of mankind, instead, the solar eruptions subsided and within two weeks dissipated totally. Professor Hobart went from being a national celebrity to being a national goat. He became the object of ridicule and bad jokes, which is so typical in a fickle society.

Six years later he still bore the brunt of the academic society's cardinal rule: Kill all the wounded. Professor Jason Hobart had broken one of the commandments of academia: Don't make a wave without the blessings of the elite first. He paid the price in his career. Only tenure, that old tradition of academics protecting their own jobs, kept him employed as an assistant professor of astronomy at Rockford College.

Jason sighed softly as he stuffed some student papers into the old tattered briefcase and walked out of the classroom. Snapping the door lock behind him out of habit, he made his way to the faculty parking area, where his 200,000-mile Volvo awaited him — like one more unruly student.

"Start, please," Jason pleaded as he turned the key.

As if sensing that Jason had endured enough for one day, the tired old engine wheezed and then fired up. He relaxed a little and then slouched into his defensive driving position. An outside observer would have thought Jason was a good 10 years older than his 45 years.

Jason Hobart had been a widower for nearly five years. He and Nancy had been married 12 years before cancer took her life. Jason had never really recovered from his wife's death. They had been childhood sweethearts and were married during their last year of college. Jason's entire life, prior to her death, had revolved around three things: his wife, his daughter Wendy, and his work on solar flares, though not necessarily always in that order.

After Nancy's death, Jason had poured himself into his work, involving his daughter Wendy in every aspect of his life. Jason's older sister Karen had come to live with them right after Nancy's death. At the time, Wendy was nine years old. Jason knew there was no way he could adequately care for a young daughter and be involved with research and teaching at the same time.

14

At one time Jason had a very promising career as an astrophysicist, and although he worked for a small school, Rockford College, he was known in academic communities as one of the brightest upcoming astrophysicists in America. It was clear that, given enough time, Jason Hobart would make an impact on the scientific community and would be offered a major position at a large university.

Jason had chosen Dr. Carrington's work as a PhD project and had perfected many of the theories the nineteenth century astronomer had postulated. He was invited to virtually every symposium on solar flares held throughout the academic world. Unfortunately, after the aborted flare episode, all of that abruptly ceased.

It was not so much that Jason had been discredited in the scientific community, because his ideas were still widely accepted by many astrophysicists; it was that the media had presented him as the sacrificial lamb. He had been made the laughingstock for the sake of a few rating points in the national media. And in the fiercely competitive academic environment it was clear that many of his colleagues would never let him live down his reputation. Dr. Jason Hobart was made to seem a dunce when, in truth, he was working at far below his intellectual abilities.

The ridicule made little or no difference to Jason, because he was content in his world.

He had his daughter, and he had his work; and, although they rarely got along these days, he had his sister. Jason sighed lightly as he thought about Karen. She never had forgiven him for the humiliation he had heaped upon himself and, indirectly, upon her. It was clear now that Jason would never rise above the level of an associate professor, and his sister never failed to remind him that it was entirely his own fault.

Now, Jason thought somberly, *there is another solar flare developing in area 403. Should I speak out?* Then, for the hundredth time, he told himself, *No, keep your mouth shut this time, Hobart. Unlike a baseball game, professors don't get three strikes and you're out. In academia, two "strikes" and I'll be gone!*

He shifted the Volvo into gear, grinding slightly as it engaged; backed out of his parking space; and headed toward home.

At the Palo Alto Observatory, Drs. Camp and Moore were deeply engrossed in their work. Annette Camp could hardly contain herself. She was only two years out of her doctoral studies in astronomy, and she had made a significant discovery: an asteroid, dubbed Atlantis by the observatory team. Unbelievably, she had confirmed that Atlantis was definitely cutting a path through their solar system. In fact, if her calculations were correct, and she was certain they were, there was a very good chance that Atlantis, or more correctly asteroid 4001, would actually pass between Earth and its sun — at a mere 300,000 miles, which was a near miss in celestial terms.

"What if your calculations are wrong and old Atlantis there decides to hit this planet," her colleague, Dr. Gene Moore, said in jest. Although he wasn't nearly as certain about the path of asteroid 4001 as his lovely colleague, he knew it would miss by a quarter of a million miles or more.

"Don't even joke about that," Annette grimaced. "That's a billion ton hunk of rock and ice traveling at over 30,000 miles an hour. It would obliterate half the life on our planet, not to mention kicking up a dust storm that would plunge us back into the ice ages."

"Well you found it," Moore said with the respect he genuinely felt, in spite of the grin on his face. "You'd better keep it on the right course or it will be called the 'collision de Camp.' Heck of a thing to be known for," he chuckled as he sauntered off down the hall.

"Right," Annette mumbled to herself as she ran the figures again. Sure she had lucked out and found it during her brief assignment as the observer on one of the Hubble telescope's deep-space probing missions. But luck was only a part of it. Several other observers had missed it. Now Atlantis was her baby. It would attract a lot of attention, and it was her job to determine its exact trajectory. Her calculations said it would pass through the solar system with little more than a spectacular nighttime exhibition, missing Earth by slightly more than 300,000 miles, more or less. She shuddered to think of what an asteroid that size would do if one ever actually hit Earth. She gathered her notes and headed off to see the director — a task she dreaded.

"Dr. Camp, how can you be absolutely certain the asteroid poses no danger?" Dr. Paul Gamble, the director of the Palo Alto facility snapped in his normal demeaning tone.

She wanted to reply, "Elementary astronomy, you idiot," but she contained herself and answered as politely as her irritation with Gamble would allow.

"No one can say with absolute certainty where such a large asteroid will go once it enters our solar system," she responded coldly, "but all of my calculations show that it will miss this planet by several hundred thousand miles."

Annette was well aware that Gamble was still fuming over the fact that she had not allowed him to be listed as the joint discoverer of Atlantis. *But right is right,* she told herself again.

She had found the asteroid, and the pompous Gamble would not intimidate her into giving him half the credit. Of all the people on the project, he would be the least likely to find anything that was not firmly attached to the coattails of Dr. Robert Frasier, the current head of the National Institute of Science in Washington and former director of the Palo Alto Observatory.

Dr. Gamble was more of a politician than a scientist and would have been more than willing to take the credit for discovering Atlantis. And he might have, except that initially he had ridiculed the very idea that there was a large, undetected asteroid approaching the solar system or that an upstart like Annette Camp had discovered it.

No way, Annette thought determinedly. *If you want an asteroid, Mister, you go find your own.*

"Dr. Frasier said we should keep him informed so he can update the president on this crisis," Gamble growled.

"There is no crisis, Doctor," Annette said with more impatience than she wanted to show. "There is absolutely no indication that the asteroid will come closer than 300,000 miles of Earth. And, even if it were headed toward us, there is no way hydrogen bombs would alter the direction of an object that large."

She still had a hard time believing that Frasier or Gamble had suggested using rocket-launched hydrogen bombs to "bump" the asteroid off trajectory. In the first place it was far too large to be affected, and in the second place there probably was more danger from the launch of nuclear weapons than from the asteroid. "That kind of stuff makes for great science fiction, but it's not good science," she had told them after hearing about the idea.

"Well you keep me informed," Gamble groused and then hoisted his sagging trousers for the hundredth time that hour. He headed out the door in a waddle that reminded her of a wounded hippo.

One day! Gamble thought as he hustled out. *One day Miss High-and-Mighty! I hate pretty women — especially young ones,* he reconfirmed. But experience had taught him that it was better to get even than to get mad. *Today she's a star, but stars have a way of fading — at least the human ones do.*

Jason turned his tired old Volvo into the driveway of his very average suburban home. He had lived there three years longer than Wendy's fifteen years — something his sister Karen frequently reminded him about whenever the subject of his lack of promotions came up. He knew he probably never would be promoted. That really wasn't the problem though. They could live on his current salary, but that didn't keep Karen from picking at him.

It really isn't her fault, he rationalized once again. *She isn't the resident wacko of Rockford, Illinois. I earned that title all by myself.*

Jason shrugged his shoulders as the Volvo's engine rattled to a stop. The knowledge he had hidden away inside nagged at his sense of right and wrong. He knew he was right this time. *The sun is poised for a major eruption that could very likely alter life on this planet as we know it. We made it through the last sun cycle, but this one.* . . . He involuntarily gritted his teeth as he dropped his worn leather pouch on the side table.

"Did you talk to the dean about the chair being established in your department, Jason?" Karen asked as soon as he walked into the room.

"Yes," he lied. "Dean Thomas said he would take it up with the committee."

"Well keep after him," Karen said irritatedly. "You need that promotion. After all it's been ten years since you got a raise." She suspected Jason hadn't really approached the faculty dean about that promotion. She knew her brother would never stand up for himself — not if he could get around it.

Karen Hobart had convinced herself that she had given up a very promising career to help her brother Jason. She had always envisioned herself as a concert pianist of world renown. In reality, she had only mediocre talent and, at best, would have remained a high school music teacher. Perhaps the knowledge of that, without admitting the truth of it, was what gnawed at her and caused her to perpetually nag her brother. She had long since stopped feeling remorse about it. It was now her vocation, in fact, her lifelong duty, to never let Jason forget how he had failed his family, and her, since she was a part of his family.

"Hi, Wendy," Jason chirped with a quick smile as he passed his daughter's room. She was the delight of his life. Her smile and wit made everything else bearable for him.

Wendy felt the same way about her dad. Although she and her aunt were barely cordial anymore, she lived for her father's return each day, knowing that if the sky was clear that evening they would spend hours together in his makeshift observatory, tracking the paths of the heavens' little bright lights. Almost since she could walk she had been interested in astronomy, as was her best friend and father. She hurt for him whenever someone ridiculed his work. He was a brilliant man, and she believed that, with a little support, he could do great things in astrophysics.

After supper Jason and Wendy cleared the table, and after loading the dishwasher they went out to the greenhouse that doubled as their personal observatory. The little observatory was deceptive, except to the trained eye. Jason had scrimped for many years, doing without lunches and dependable cars to buy his own 10-inch reflector telescope, the lens of which he and Wendy had meticulously polished themselves.

And the radio spectrometer he owned, although purchased from government surplus, was as good as any found in the best observatories. Unknown to Karen, it had cost him virtually all of his retirement funds, but he simply could not pass up a bargain like that. When NASA had the spectrometer made, it had cost nearly half a million dollars; he had bought it for a mere $50,000.

Its very existence put him into the same league with other much more extensive scientific facilities. In fact, once it was known that he had unlimited access to a 10-inch telescope and a spectrometer, colleagues around the world called on him to verify many of their findings. Jason Hobart might be known as the nutty professor in his community, but to his closest colleagues he was respected as a top-flight astronomer and physicist.

"Daddy, what about area 403?" Wendy asked as they entered the observatory.

Jason's protective facade melted away as soon as they entered their own private world. Away from all the wagging tongues and antagonists, he knew he could be totally open with his daughter. For several weeks they had been tracking a large area of sunspot activity known as area 403. Using the spectrometer and its motorized tracking system, he was able to record any activity throughout the day.

It was area 403 that Jason believed could potentially erupt into the biggest solar flare of the last 100 years. *But that's what I thought the first time,* he was quick to remind himself.

"Well, let's see, Honey," he replied as he plucked the wax-coated paper from the machine. He was running out of the tracking paper he had gotten with the initial purchase. Soon he either would have to convert to a digital recorder, something he could never afford, or he would have to start searching all the old government storage depots for paper to feed his ancient recorder. The spectrometer was state of the art, but the recorder was 1960 vintage — indicative of the typical government-run facility that had owned the spectrometer at one time: spend half a million for one machine and $10,000 for another to record its output.

"Look at this," Jason said excitedly waving the strip of paper in his daughter's face.

"Sure, Dad," Wendy grinned as she grabbed his arm. "But it's a little hard to read with you waving it around that way, you know."

"Oh, sorry," Jason replied sheepishly as he held the paper steady so his daughter could see it. "But it's right there! Area 403 has had a coronal flare. This could be the beginning of a major eruption, Honey!"

"Take it easy, Dad," Wendy said lovingly. "You know what happened last time you said that."

Jason stopped as if struck in the face. His countenance dropped. Wendy had struck a sore nerve.

Seeing his expression, Wendy realized that she had made an unintentional mistake.

"I'm sorry, Dad. I only meant you should keep this low-key until you're sure."

Seeing the hurt look in his daughter's eyes, Jason responded quickly. "It's okay, Honey. I know what you mean, and you're right. Besides, I doubt I could get many people to take anything I might say seriously anymore."

"Daddy, that's just not so and you know it. You have lots of colleagues who trust your observations."

Jason knew his daughter was probably right, but in the real world one ignorant reporter was worth a thousand trained observers.

"I'll keep my quack ideas to myself this time," Jason responded with a grin. "But, between you and me, I'll bet we see some terrific northern lights out of this one — certainly a visible solar eruption. Now wouldn't that be something?"

Few laypeople knew that most solar eruptions are invisible to the human eye. Sure, the Discovery Network showed a flaming eruption every time a solar flare was mentioned. But those eruptions represented less than one percent of all flares. Most were visible only in the X-ray range. Such was the case with the current flare from area 403.

Inside, Jason was a lot more disturbed than he was willing to let on. If he was right about this, they would see a lot more than just northern lights before this eruption ended. With five billion people on this planet, what would be the effects of a major solar eruption? He shuddered involuntarily.

In about three days this flare would hit Earth.

2

After Wendy went to bed, Jason studied the flare data for several hours. He was disturbed. This eruption was larger than he initially had thought — a level 2 flare. He decided it was time to share his observations with someone who would listen objectively. He knew that Lewis Singer of Cambridge not only would listen but, more importantly, he would keep his confidence. Jason was well aware of the court of public opinion that stalked him just outside his door as he placed the phone call.

"Dr. Singer, please. Jason Hobart here," Jason said to the pleasant English accent on the other end of the line.

Jason had spent a sleepless night after seeing Wendy off to bed. The more he had reviewed the data, the more convinced he became that area 403 was a potential coronal hole — a major breach in the sun's surface. But, once the initial excitement had worn off, common sense took hold. He told himself several times, *Slow down Jason, or you really will be the fool others think you to be.* He decided that he certainly wouldn't go public this time; instead, he would simply share his factual observations with another trained scientist.

"Professor Singer here," the strong voice on the other end of the line responded in a perfect English accent. Singer was a classic example of a Cambridge professor. Short and robust, Lewis Singer was in his mid-60s, with a sagging middle. He perpetually wore a crumpled tweed jacket over worn trousers held in place by red suspenders. He always had a great curved leather pipe, which was hardly ever lit, stuck in his mouth. And he had the respect of all who knew him. He was one of Jason's few real friends in the world of astrophysics. It was clear he still believed in Jason's abilities as a solar physicist.

When the receptionist told him that Dr. Hobart was calling, Singer thought back to the first time he'd heard from the American scientist. *What was it — maybe five or six years ago now?* Dr. Hobart had called to ask his opinion of what he termed "an impending solar flare of immense proportions." Singer had been observing the same area, identified on solar charts as area 403, and he concurred with Dr. Hobart's analysis that a solar flare was developing.

Though the sun had not been in its most active phase, Singer had concurred that it certainly was possible to have a major solar eruption during a calm cycle. When Jason had shared some of his calculations about the potential intensity and duration of the solar flare, Singer had been duly impressed. He knew the man had a well-thought-out theory.

Singer himself was familiar with Dr. Edmond Carrington's work and, although he had not done a great deal of research on the subject, he believed Carrington had been a man of great insight and a brilliant scientist — well before his time.

Singer had encouraged Jason to go public with his information, believing, as the American scientist did, that if a major solar eruption occurred it would, at minimum, affect communications worldwide. He also knew that if the media had not picked up on Professor Hobart's error in regard to the magnitude of the eruption, the American might well have received international recognition for his work — perhaps even a Nobel Prize. Instead, the quiet professor who had now become one of his closest friends had been ridiculed and disgraced.

He sighed as he responded to the receptionist's message. *Too bad, my friend,* he thought quietly, *but that really is life.*

"Lewis," Jason said in an upbeat tone, "have you been following 403 lately?"

Lewis Singer smiled at the question. His friend had alerted him and many others in the international scientific community to the renewed activity of Sun area 403 weeks before even the most sensitive instruments in their own observatories had spotted it. He wished he understood all of Hobart's model, but he didn't. He believed the American scientist was a genius when it came to solar flares.

Perhaps, Singer concluded, *that was why Hobart received so much flack from the other members of his fraternity: Academics have to ridicule what they can't comprehend or they would feel smaller than their egos would allow.*

So as not to hurt his friend's feelings, Singer replied with careful deliberation. He knew how sensitive Jason was to perceived acceptance within the scientific community.

"Yes, Jason, I have been following 403 carefully. It seems to be building, just as you predicted."

Jason winced at the term "predicted," and he quickly corrected his friend. "Guessed!"

"Ah yes, guessed indeed, and I trust it is an inspired guess, my friend."

"Inspired or demented," Jason added, loosening up a little as he caught the inflection in his friend's voice. "So what do you think?"

"I think you are justifiably concerned," Singer replied very matter-of-factly, his voice carrying the message of respect he intended.

"No, I mean what do you think about the first-stage flare?" Jason interjected. His face blushed slightly at the thought that his friend might perceive that he was fishing for a compliment.

"I think it may help tourism in the northern latitudes in a few days," Singer said.

"The first flare is at least a level 2, and I

believe we may see a level 6 or 7 eruption," Jason blurted out in spite of himself. He instantly regretted his comment.

But before he could say anything further, Singer replied, "You could be very right, my friend. Our findings confirm that the latest eruption is at least a 1.8. The next one could be higher."

Jason was a little taken back. He wasn't used to people, even Lewis Singer, agreeing with his predictions so readily.

"I'm flattered," Jason responded with some degree of surprise obvious in his voice. "But why the sudden agreement, Lewis? You're always so skeptical."

"Because, my friend," Singer replied, "we're seeing major activity in the extreme X band."

"Are you sure?" Jason asked excitedly. He thought to himself, *Activity in the extreme X band means a highly unstable coronal area. It's the coronal areas that erupt, throwing super-charged gases at nearly a million miles an hour into space. If we're actually seeing extreme X-band activity, it could be an indicator that area 403 is ready to eject huge volumes of supercharged hot gases directly at Earth itself.*

Jason was excited, because this would be a confirmation of his observations and of his theory. "What do you project, Lewis, in terms of magnitude?"

"I don't," Singer replied. "I leave such

things to younger, braver men."

Or stupider, Jason thought.

Singer hastened to correct his thoughtless comment: "Jason, I didn't mean to imply that you . . ."

"That's okay," Jason responded, once more in control. "You're probably right. We younger guys tend to jump to hasty conclusions."

"Jason," Singer scolded, "just because you made a mistake once, you can't let that rule your life. I have known you for many years now and have seen you make excellent analyses of sunspot activities. You must learn to put the past in the past."

"I wish I could, Lewis," Jason sighed. "I wish I could. Can you send me the data on the X-band activity? I'd like to factor it into some of my equations."

"I'll be glad to," Singer replied. "Keep me informed of any ideas you might have, will you?"

"You know I will, Lewis," Jason replied warmly. "Thanks for being such a good friend. They aren't so easy to come by these days."

"I know what you mean," Singer agreed. "Keep in touch."

As Jason hung up the phone, he had a feeling of dread that he hadn't felt for a long time. *No way,* he told himself resolutely, *no way I'm going to get involved this time. I'll just stand back and observe like all the rest . . . absolutely!*

Jason waited impatiently for the data Singer had promised. Fifteen minutes later the data from Cambridge was transferred to his own computer. Jason cringed as the data flow continued for more than 30 minutes. *Karen will have a fit when the phone bill comes,* he thought. His sister usually had fits about anything he did with astronomy that cost money.

As soon as the transfer was complete, the modem beeped twice and Jason began to print out the data. It was obvious that someone, perhaps more than one, had spent a great deal of time and energy monitoring area 403.

Jason knew the potential damage a major solar eruption could do if it hit Earth. Billions of tons of supercharged particles buffeting Earth, at the very minimum, would disrupt communications.

As a scientist he knew the probability of a large plasma eruption actually striking Earth's surface was extremely remote. The planet's magnetic shield deflected most solar storms. *But area 403 is aimed right at Earth,* he thought. *Could this be the big eruption that occurs every 140 years or so? If it is, what will be the effects?* His head hurt from too much thinking and too little sleep. He decided to check the figures one more time.

Jason had run the numbers a dozen times during the last three hours: the size of area

403, its mass, the direction a coronal eruption might take, the mass of Earth, and each time the machine came up with the same answer. There was more than an 80 percent chance that the flare would occur while Earth was in its direct path. "Eighty percent," Jason said aloud. "Unbelievable!"

When he thought about the one-in-a-million possibility that such an eruption would ever occur at all during his lifetime, the odds seemed incredible.

"Daddy, aren't you ever going to bed?" Wendy asked her father as she poked her head into the observatory. "What are you working on?"

"Oh, nothing, Honey," Jason answered as calmly as his tense mood would allow. "Just running some computer programs. Sorry, I lost track of the time."

Wendy knew something more had distracted her father. He often worked late but not until 3:00 in the morning, and certainly not on a school night.

"Well, please stop, Daddy," she pleaded. "You'll be dead tired for school tomorrow."

Jason knew she was right, but he hated to stop. He had that feeling of impending disaster; but he wasn't sure if it was the flare or his reputation, if he announced his findings. "Okay, Honey, I'll stop in just a minute."

"I'll just wait out here with you then," Wendy said emphatically, as she drew her robe around her and stepped inside.

"Okay, okay, you nag. You win," Jason quipped as he closed out the computer program he had been running. "But I'll bet your old man will beat you out of bed in the morning."

"Promises, promises," Wendy wisecracked as she hugged her father and they left the room.

Jason tossed and turned in his bed until nearly 5:00 A.M., when he finally dozed off. He was remotely aware of something like a fire alarm clanging in the distance. He squeezed his eyes shut tighter, trying to block out what obviously had to be a bad dream.

"Wake up, Jason," Karen scolded. "You're going to be late to work."

"Huh?" Jason muttered, trying to clear the cobwebs from his head.

"That's the second time the alarm has gone off," his sister snapped. "Don't punch it off again. You wouldn't be so tired if you went to bed at a decent hour."

A little more awake now, Jason vaguely remembered slapping at the snooze button on the very loud alarm clock. The clock had been a present from Wendy the previous Christmas for just such days as this. Sleeping late was a characteristic both he and his daughter shared and one that was greatly resented by his early-to-rise sister.

He stumbled out of bed and toward the

bathroom. Looking back, he saw Karen pulling the covers up over the spot where he had just been laying. She was still grumbling that if he had any common sense he wouldn't stay up so late that he couldn't get up in the morning.

Jason splashed his face with cold water and tried to focus his thinking, but some nagging, subconscious thought seemed to cloud his consciousness. Then, suddenly, it came back to him and his mind was focused again on area 403. Disaster! Why did he keep thinking disaster? He had an ominous feeling but he couldn't put his finger on exactly why.

Somewhere in his subconscious he knew this wasn't just some academic problem he was trying to work out. Out there somewhere was a solar flare headed toward Earth and maybe a bigger one just waiting to happen. Area 403 was enormous; it covered an area on the Sun 10,000 times the surface area of Earth. The probabilities of a major eruption happening anywhere on the Sun were extremely low, but the probability that the planet would be lined up with the path of a coronal hole was a phenomenon so rare that the odds were incalculable. But, here it was.

That's what Jason had been trying to put together. An eruption that only happened every 140 years anywhere on the Sun's surface, and this one was aimed directly at Earth!

Get hold of yourself, he chastened. *You're do-*

ing it again. In the first place, solar eruptions are not all that rare, and there is nothing to say this one will be any bigger than most others. Remember, a major flare from 403 looked certain before, but it didn't happen. Maybe you're wrong now too.

But what if it does erupt? he pondered. *What would the effects be?* The anxiety returned. *What can I do about it anyway?* He shrugged as his thoughts made the full circle again. He wasn't sure. The only thing he was sure of was that he was going to be late to class again and the administration would be on his case if they found out.

He continued to get ready as quickly as he could and hurried out the door, heading for the old Volvo that sat waiting — like a rebellious child just looking for an opportunity to irritate him.

Much to Jason's surprise, the usually stubborn vehicle fired up on the first try. *You're always trying to keep me guessing,* Jason thought as he dropped it into gear and backed out of the driveway.

He had missed the morning staff meeting, but he actually made his first class on time, and the day was going reasonably well by the time lunchtime rolled around. Several of his worst students hadn't showed up for class that day. Later he found out they were participating in an intermural football game with another school. Jason didn't really understand the fascination with a sport that resulted in bloody noses, broken bones, and a variety of cuts and bruises, but he assumed it was a throwback to some ancestral need to do battle. *Well,* he thought with a sly grin, *it's an ill wind that blows no good.*

He made his way down the stairs toward the teachers' lounge, marveling again at the well-worn hand rails leading down the stairs. Seasoned hardwood had been smoothed and grooved by the constant contact with much softer human skin. *There's an object lesson in that somewhere,* he mused. *Numbers are more important than strength.*

Once in the teachers' lounge, he opened the lunch Wendy had fixed for him that morning, as she always did. Inside, on the sandwich, he found her handwritten note: "Dear Daddy, have a great day. I love you very much. Wendy"

He felt a tug at his heart as he shoved the note into his shirt pocket. He had every note she'd ever written him. He wasn't sure why he had kept them all, except that he couldn't force himself to throw them away.

"Nasty note from a student?" John Harley asked sarcastically.

"No, from a beautiful young woman," Jason replied just as sarcastically.

Although usually polite to everyone, Jason could not stomach Harley. He had been the instigator of many student insults about him.

A bumbling, incompetent teacher himself, Harley was one of those people who always had to put down others in order to feel their equal. Jason suspected that, in reality, Harley had no equal — at least not where stupidity was concerned.

"Any new flares threatening Earth?" Harley asked and then snorted like a pig at his own worn-out joke.

"Not really," Jason said in a sarcastic tone. "If I find one about to destroy it, Harley, I'll let you know."

"As if anybody would listen," Harley retorted. "What about that comet? Think it's going to hit Earth?"

Just the tone of Harley's voice grated on Jason's nerves. Every inflection was like fingernails scraping a chalkboard. But this time he did catch Jason a little off guard.

Jason had been so absorbed in his own study of the pending solar flare, he hadn't even bothered to turn on the television, so he had no idea what Harley was talking about. But he was not about to let Harley know that, so he answered, "Well, in the first place, it's not a comet, Harley, it's an asteroid. I should think that you, as a geologist, would know the difference."

Harley's face turned red. It had been a good guess on Jason's part. He had no idea what Harley was talking about, but he knew the difference between comets and asteroids.

Comets were small and difficult to trace, but asteroids were normally much larger and easier to observe. So he assumed that if somebody had found a new object in space, it would be an asteroid and not a comet.

"Don't worry, Harley," Jason said in a matter-of-fact tone. "It probably won't hit us. And even if it did, I suspect you'd be okay. The last time that happened, I understand the dinosaurs were wiped out, but rodents did pretty well."

Jason hadn't realized that he was talking loud enough for others to overhear, but a snicker went up around the teachers' lounge. Many of the other teachers thought Jason was a little strange, but virtually all of them considered John Harley to be a loud-mouthed irritant.

Harley's face turned red and he got very angry, but he tried to contain himself. Not to be outdone, Harley quipped in a loud voice, "Well, it's kind of strange that the government didn't ask for your opinion. After all, you *are* Rockford's most famous astronomer, aren't you?"

Jason started to correct Harley again, since he was an astrophysicist, not an astronomer, but once more a snicker went around the room. Jason was cut to the quick. No matter how hard he tried to ignore the opinions of his colleagues, he was still vulnerable to their lack of respect for him.

"I was certain you had been in on the meetings about that asteroid, Professor," Harley continued, sensing Jason's vulnerability. "After all, it is in your area of expertise, isn't it?" And with that, Harley dumped his tray and sauntered toward the men's room with a stupid grin on his face, chuckling as he walked. With a man like Harley, any small victory was great satisfaction, and he thought he had at least outdone Jason Hobart in their mental combat.

"Harley's a horse's patoot," Jim Benifren said as he sat down. "Don't let him get to you, Jason."

"Harley doesn't bother me," Jason replied with as much gusto as he could muster. But silently he reminded himself, *Unfortunately, Harley probably represents the majority view around here.*

As if reading his mind, Benifren said, "Harley doesn't speak for all of us, Jason. We've seen your work and know you're a top-notch teacher."

"Thanks," Jason replied as he lowered his automatic defenses a little. He knew Benifren was a good guy and was one of the rare real friends Jason had at the college. Benifren had stuck by him during the earlier episode and had supported him in every faculty meeting. As the chairman of the math department, Benifren's support had been crucial at the time.

"What was Harley talking about?" Jason

41

asked, confessing that he had no idea what they had been debating.

"Haven't you been watching the news? It's everywhere. There's a big asteroid that's on track to make a swing through our solar system. But the best estimate is that it'll miss Earth by about 300,000 miles," Benifren said, handing Jason a copy of the latest paper.

Although not the lead article, the asteroid had made the front page of the *Chicago Tribune*. Jason quickly scanned the article. "Whew," he muttered, "300,000 miles is a near miss by astronomical standards."

"Yeah, apparently there were even some discussions in the government about using rocket-launched hydrogen bombs to bump that asteroid off course and make it fall into the Sun."

"What idiot would propose an idea like that?" Jason asked in disbelief. "Surely no one in scientific circles would agree."

"Apparently someone does, because the inside article says there are still some discussions about it going on in Washington even now. On the *Good Morning America* show this morning, Dr. Frasier, head of the National Institute of Science, suggested that the idea had some support in the scientific community."

Frasier, Jason thought, *he's about as qualified as Harley to make that kind of call.* Jason remembered Frasier from the earlier debacle when Frasier had headed the Palo Alto Observatory. He'd been one of the leaders in the scientific community to discredit Jason — but only after the big solar flare failed to materialize. His attack, especially on the talk show circuit, had been personal and vicious.

But, Jason recalled, *Frasier went on to head the National Institute while I barely kept my job as an associate professor. So, who's really the idiot?* he asked himself.

"Well, hopefully no one is taking that idea seriously," Jason commented. He knew enough about physics to know that intercepting a fast moving object in space was a nearly impossible feat. Changing the trajectory of an asteroid 30 miles in diameter, moving at 30,000 miles an hour, was virtually impossible. It might happen in science fiction but not in real science.

"Well apparently the latest public opinion polls this morning show 74 percent of the public wants government action."

"Public opinion polls!" Jason scoffed. "Our government is run by opinion polls now! Even so, there is no way anyone is going to use nuclear weapons on an asteroid," he said. "Besides, an asteroid is the least of our problems." As soon as he said it, Jason regretted making the comment.

Benifren asked, "What do you mean, Jason?"

Jason's inner sense told him to let it drop,

but he was so caught up in his anxiety about the solar flare he simply needed to talk about it with someone. He knew that Benifren was a good guy and wouldn't ridicule him. But what he didn't know was that John Harley was listening intently just behind the wall leading to the men's room.

"Can I share something with you — confidentially?" Jason asked in a whisper.

Harley could just barely hear what Jason had whispered, so he moved a little closer.

"I know what you've been through these last few years, Jason," Benifren assured him. "Whatever you say will stay right here."

Jason began to share his observations of area 403, telling Benifren his concern about a major solar eruption. "There's no telling what the effects of a really big flare might be," Jason said, as he paused for breath. Only then did he realize that he had not stopped to breathe for nearly a minute.

"How serious do you really think this is?" Benifren asked as he caught some of Jason's excitement.

"I don't honestly know," Jason said reflectively. Inside he felt his tension ease. Benifren wasn't ridiculing him. He was genuinely concerned, or so it seemed.

Reading the look on Jason's face, Benifren asked, "But what do you think, Jason? Is there any danger?"

"Area 403 is aimed directly at Earth. It's

like having a loaded gun pointed at us. The last time this area erupted was in 1872," Jason explained, slipping effortlessly into his teacher role. "But that was well before modern communication and air travel, naturally. Even then there was evidence of a shift in Earth's magnetic field and a major shift in weather patterns. There is some geological evidence that a major solar eruption shifted the magnetic poles just prior to the last ice age."

"Do you honestly think that could happen because of a solar flare?" Benifren asked with obvious sincerity.

"Yes I do," Jason replied, almost in a whisper. "I've been watching area 403 for a long time now, and I believe it's ready to erupt. And, if it does while Earth is in its direct path, I think it's going to drastically alter life on Earth."

"What do you mean?" Benifren exclaimed.

"Well, in the first place, we're going to have some major communications problems. I think even the first flare that's headed our way right now will disrupt some satellites, and it's just a level 2. A major eruption will do a lot more than that, if it's as big as I think it's going to be."

"How big is that?" Benifren interrupted once more.

"I believe area 403 will yield at least a level 6 flare."

"What's that mean?"

"Well, according to Dr. Carrington's scale, solar flares are graded the same way as earthquakes, from a 1 to a 10, each point increase being a magnitude of 100 percent greater than the previous, so a level 6 would be on the order of 500 percent greater than the biggest flare we've had in the last century. But even more important is the fact that we're right in its path! It's possible that an eruption of this magnitude could set off another ice age, or global warming, or who knows what else."

"Whew!" Benifren whistled. "And you think that's going to happen?"

"I think something is going to happen," Jason hedged, "but I can't say anything. You know what happened the last time I spoke up about a solar flare."

"I understand," Benifren said, "and I promise I won't say anything. But . . . when do you think the big eruption will occur?"

"There's no way to tell for certain," Jason said, "but probably it's going to be in the next few weeks — maybe days."

"What does that *really* mean?" Benifren asked tensely.

"Disaster maybe," Jason said. "I just know I wouldn't want to be in space during an eruption of that magnitude or in a high-flying aircraft either for that matter," he added.

Even as he was voicing the words, Jason was bringing all of his thoughts together at one time — for the first time. He also knew that if any word of what he just said leaked out, not only would he be the laughingstock, he probably would lose his job for violating his gag order with the school.

"Please don't say anything to anyone," Jason pleaded, even before Benifren could speak. "After what happened last time, any word of this would really make me look like a fool."

"But if what you say is true, you have to tell somebody," Benifren argued. "Even if you think it's only a possibility, you have to say something, don't you?"

"Who do you think would listen to me now?" Jason said more gruffly than Benifren deserved. "I'm the wacky professor from Rockford. Remember?"

Benifren nodded in agreement, but he was clearly shaken. "But what if you're right this time, Jason? Shouldn't the public be warned?"

Jason found himself caught in one of those proverbial catch-22s. If he shared what he believed, he would almost certainly be made a laughingstock, and he'd probably lose his job. But if he kept silent and he was right, he would be guilty of gross negligence. In his mind's eye, the one image he saw was Wendy and the ridicule she would suffer if he spoke out.

"I can't do anything," Jason said resolutely.

"Please promise me that you won't say anything either."

Benifren agreed reluctantly. "I gave you my word, and I won't break it. But I do think you're wrong, Jason." As he got up to leave the table, he added, "However, I do understand your dilemma."

Jason purposely didn't look up as Benifren left the room. He knew inside his friend was right in what he said. But he also knew he had no stomach for all the grief such a pronouncement would bring on him. *No, I'll keep my observations to myself. Somewhere out there, there will be another physicist who will see things the same way and will speak out.*

Unnoticed by Jason was the squat figure of John Harley, exiting by the door next to the men's room.

"Don't you worry, Professor Hobart," Harley muttered with a dark grin. "I'll tell the world for you."

3

John Harley was ecstatic, as only someone of Harley's warped nature could be. *I've got him now,* Harley chortled. He knew what he had to do: call Emily Hart, the investigative reporter at WNN affiliate WJLL in Rockford — the station that had covered the original solar flare story. She was by no means Harley's friend, but he had met her when the original story broke. In fact, it had been Harley who had fed her confidential personal data on the nutty professor. In turn, she had been assigned by WNN headquarters to do the piece.

If someone had asked John Harley why he felt compelled to vilify Jason, he wouldn't have been able to explain it anymore than he could keep from doing it. Harley had been hurting people all his life. It was the one thing he was really good at and, for Harley, any successes were to be coveted.

He could barely contain his enthusiasm as he dialed the station's number. In fact, he cursed as he redialed the number for the third time. He was so nervous with excitement he dialed it wrong twice. Finally, he got it right.

"WJLL," the pleasant voice on the other

end of the line said. "How may I direct your call?"

"Emily Hart!" Harley snapped. He hated it when people pretended to be nice. He knew it was all an act. People were never really nice — certainly not to him.

"Ms. Hart is not available," the receptionist replied with well-rehearsed poise. "Could someone else help you?"

"I've got some important information," Harley growled. "Let me talk with Emily Hart!"

"Are you a friend of Ms. Hart, Sir, or is this a news-related item?" the young woman asked subtly.

"Yeah, we're friends," Harley lied. "From way back."

"If you would like to leave a message, I'll be sure Ms. Hart gets it," she countered with a practiced assurance.

"I have critical information she'll want!" Harley shouted at the unseen, arrogant young woman.

"I'm sure you do, Sir," the receptionist replied, a little less courteously this time. She had correctly identified the caller as no one of importance to her career at the station, so she didn't bother to sugarcoat her words. "If you'll just explain what your information is, perhaps I can help," she replied in her most professional tone of voice.

"I don't want to talk to a receptionist,"

Harley spat rudely. He made the word "receptionist" sound like a four-letter word.

Unruffled, the young woman retorted in a soft voice, "Are you *trying* to be rude, Sir, or is this your normal approach?"

Harley's eyes flashed with fire as he started to call her several choice words from his library of vulgarity, but then he thought about why he had called in the first place: to destroy haughty Professor Hobart, the town idiot. He decided that his ends would be better served by tact at this time.

"I'm sorry, Miss," he almost crooned over the phone. "It's just that I have some information that's very important. It's about a major solar flare headed for Earth."

She was still angry, but clearly her interest suddenly was piqued. She, like most others at the station was well aware that the solar flare story several years earlier had been the only nationally syndicated news story to come out of Rockford in the last 20 years.

"Please hold while I try Ms. Hart," she said, once more switching to her professional tone. She dialed Emily Hart's private line.

"Yes, Robin, what is it?" Emily snapped, as her attention was redirected from C-SPAN-4, which provided 24-hour-a-day coverage of the White House meetings. Hart, as with many other news hawks across the country, scoured the White House meetings for any faux-pas she might pick up from

51

President Houston's office.

As a devout liberal, Emily Hart detested the conservative trend the nation had taken since the ouster of the democratic majority during the last elections. "Three years without leadership," she was prone to exclaim during staff meetings when they were engaged in political discussions, "and Houston represents the worst of what has happened to this country!" Often she would rant on for several minutes at a time. Clearly, her views on conservatives in general, and President Houston in particular, were well-known.

In fact, Emily Hart's views parroted those of Neil Farmer, news director at WNN headquarters in Atlanta. Farmer was an avid liberal who also detested the conservative President Houston. Most of the WJLL staff assumed Emily Hart and Neil Farmer had a thing going since the big solar flare story broke nearly a half a decade ago. They also assumed Hart would kill to get a news job at WNN in Atlanta, but Farmer was smart enough to keep her well away from his suspicious wife.

"Ms. Hart," Robin said, with a coldness borne out of many tongue-lashings from the abusive reporter, "there's a Professor Harley from Rockford College who says he knows you . . . says he has vital information about another solar flare. Would you like to talk with him?"

Emily clicked off the television. *Nothing much to pick up anyway*, she grumbled silently. *Houston is about as exciting as a choirboy.* The asteroid thing was something she and Farmer had been hoping might turn out to be an issue they could use against the administration, but so far they had nothing of great interest.

She thought for a moment, *Harley . . . oh yeah. He's that slimy little professor from Rockford College. But he was helpful on the solar flare story a few years ago.* Hart had nearly parlayed that story into a network job. *But that other moron, Hobart . . . yeah Hobart, screwed up and the story fell apart. That debacle is what trapped me in this hick town*, Hart thought angrily.

"Put him on," she commanded, as only a news reporter with exaggerated self-importance can do. The receptionist connected Harley.

"This is Emily Hart," she said with only slightly shaded politeness. "What's this about, Harley?"

For a moment Harley was irritated with the younger woman's tone. *Who does she think she is anyway?* But he held his temper.

"Some very critical information that's just come to my attention."

"What kind of information?" she snapped. She remembered not liking Harley earlier. He was a fat little weasel with greasy hair who made her skin crawl.

53

For a moment Harley hesitated again. It was one thing to be a rat; and it was quite another to be known as one. "Will my identity be kept confidential?" he whined.

Idiot! Emily thought, and almost said, but instead she responded with a practiced lie, "Of course."

Harley caught the ring of phoniness in Hart's voice, but he had come too far to back out now.

"It's about Hobart. Remember him?"

"Of course I do!" *As if I could forget him!* "What about him?"

"At lunch today I overheard Professor Hobart talking about another solar flare," Harley said haughtily.

"So what?" Hart replied. "Big deal. He talked about a solar flare once before, and nothing happened." Her ears still burned when she thought about the tongue-lashing she'd gotten when the story fell apart. Six years and she was still a hick town reporter.

Harley was taken back. He thought surely Hart would jump on the story. "But don't you understand?" Harley said. "He's doing the same stupid, crazy things he did before. He's saying that a solar flare is going to erupt and threaten Earth."

"I'm not interested," Hart snapped, although somewhere deep inside her news-hungry mind, her interest was piqued slightly. But she wasn't about to step out on that branch

54

again. The last time she had done so, it had been sawed off under her.

Harley was scouring his mind for anything that might attract Hart. He knew he couldn't let her get off the phone or she'd never talk to him again. He added, "I also heard him say that if President Houston used nuclear bombs on that asteroid it would endanger millions of lives."

Hart stopped. Hearing Houston's name again piqued her attention. *Probably nothing to the story. This is a know-nothing professor at a know-nothing little college. But what the heck? I have nothing better to work on.* "Tell me more," she said.

Harley went on to outline the conversation he'd overheard between Hobart and Benifren, embellishing any point that he thought might pique the newswoman's attention.

There might be a story here, Hart decided. *Who knows? Maybe along the line of "The nutty professor who predicted a solar flare that never happened warns the president about an asteroid." Hum . . . may be a story.*

"Okay, Harley," she said. "I'll look into it. Give me as much information as you can. And I'm going to need to have a direct quote from you."

Even though she knew she didn't need a quote from Harley, she thought she'd give him a passing shot so he'd keep his mouth shut, lest he call some other news organization and give the story to them as well. The story might not amount to anything, but the last thing she wanted was to be in competition with one of the other local stations.

Hart was already buzzing the research staff to come into her office. *Even if this Hobart is a nut case,* she reasoned, *Neil might be able to use it against that blundering do-gooder president. We'll make it sound like the president is getting advice from the nutty professor of Rockford College. It's not much,* she decided, *but it's better than nothing.*

As the conversation ended, the research team entered her office. Hart filled them in on her conversation about Professor Hobart's latest prediction, including his warning to Houston. She left out the small detail that Houston hadn't heard of it yet.

"Who's the source?" one of the staffers asked. "Is he credible?"

"I'll worry about the source," Hart snapped. "Besides, I want a personal, on-camera interview with Professor Hobart."

"Say, I know him. Yeah, he's the professor who raised such a stir a few years ago," Jake Young, the senior member of the research team said.

"That's right," she responded. "That story made national news."

"You know I researched that story when I was at Fox. I always thought the press was too hard on Hobart. He called that flare right on time. It just wasn't as big as he predicted," Jake said.

"Well, he's made another prediction now," Hart said sarcastically. "And right or wrong, we're going to play it up. I want all the data on the asteroid, Hobart, and that flare he's talking about. I want Houston linked to Hobart. You got it?"

Jake knew Emily Hart well enough not to challenge her. They were going to link some rumors and some lies together and make a story out of it. It was tabloid journalism at its slimiest, and he hated it.

Hart was the station's prime time investigative reporter. She was still young, chronologically, but too old by network standards to break in as an anchor. She needed that one big break, and Farmer owed her.

When the research team left her office, she dialed Neil Farmer's private office in Atlanta.

Farmer picked up the phone. "Yeah?"

"Neil . . . Emily," she cooed with all the warmth she could muster. She didn't really like Farmer. He was rude, uncouth, suggestive, and considerably past his physical prime. She considered their affair necessary if she was going to further her career.

Farmer, on the other hand, didn't consider her important at all. She was a convenience to him from time to time — one of many. She was pushy, but so were a lot of others. At least she was a good reporter.

"What's up?" he asked.

"Maybe a story. It seems to have potential, anyway." She filled him in on Harley's call and told him her idea of sabotaging the president.

"I don't know how we can tie Houston into this," Farmer said. "I doubt the president will call on Hobart for counsel."

"Hobart is, or was, a well-known commodity," Hart argued. "You know the public. They won't remember if it's good or bad. If we put this together right, I think we can link Houston. I'll play up the asteroid thing. We'll have Hobart warning the president not to use the rockets on it. We know he's not going to anyway, so we'll make it sound like he took Hobart's advice. You know: Wacky Professor Warns the President."

"It's pretty weak," Farmer said, "but put it together and hotline it to me. We'll see what you have."

"Great!" she exclaimed. "I'll get right on it." Then she realized he had already hung up.

She buzzed Jake's desk and snapped, "Jake, I want everything you've got on Professor Hobart — pronto! And Jake, I want you and the camera crew ready to roll in 20 minutes!"

"You got it!" Jake growled. *Objective reporting,* he thought to himself. He didn't know what Hart was up to, but he had no doubt

58

that Hobart would get the sharp end of the stick.

When Hart emerged from her office, the film crew knew she was in her attack-and-destroy mode. They just hoped they wouldn't be the target if this thing fell apart.

Within the hour, the Channel 2 news crew was swarming the Rockford campus, searching for Professor Hobart.

As soon as he learned of the TV crew, Dwayne Thomas, faculty dean, stormed out of his office and demanded, "What do you want with Professor Hobart?"

"We need to verify a statement he made earlier today," Hart replied, as she glanced around at the growing circle of students and faculty.

"Say, aren't you Emily Hart from the nightly news?" one of the students asked.

"That's right," she replied haughtily. To local TV viewers she was known as "Sweet Hart," but off camera the sweet-faced reporter was known to her colleagues as "Emily Hart-less."

"What kind of statement did Professor Hobart make?" the agitated Thomas demanded. He had a sinking feeling that somehow Hobart was out on a limb again. Anger simmered inside. Hadn't he warned Hobart repeatedly over the last six years not to make any more wild predictions? The college had gotten all the bad press it could stand. Academic institutions in general were in bad repute with the conservative mood of the country, and a small college depended on bequests and donations to keep its doors open.

"I'm not at liberty to discuss the issue," Hart replied curtly. "Are you refusing to let the media interview one of your teachers?" she added in a veiled threat.

"N . . . nn . . . no," Thomas stammered, "but just be sure you make it clear that Professor Hobart does not speak for the school."

"No problem," she lied. She was already planning her story around the discredited scientist who was advising the president. It didn't matter that the president knew nothing about it. She knew from experience: the public will make the connection and forget the facts.

"I'll call Dr. Hobart to my office. You can interview him there," Thomas offered in a conciliatory tone.

"No, I don't think that will work," Hart replied brusquely. "I need to do the interview in the observatory."

Thomas blanched. *Oh no,* he thought as his knees went slack momentarily. "I'm sorry," he stammered, "but that won't be possible. The observatory is being repaired right now."

Hart detected his obvious lie and sensed his fear. She drew from her reserve of dirty tricks: "Does this school receive any taxpayer money?"

"Why, yes. Certainly," Thomas muttered, "but all schools . . ."

"Well, this station is a public facility too," she threatened. "I would hate to have to tell our viewers that Rockford College is trying to deny access to the press."

"All right," Thomas said as his nerve collapsed. He knew he was cornered. Better to dump this whole thing in Hobart's lap, he decided. "But I want to be present at the interview — to protect the school's interests," he added.

"Fine," she said. "Just stay out of the way." Grabbing her notebook, she snapped her fingers for the camera crew to follow her.

Jason was seated at the well-worn desk in his office next to the observatory. Normally an associate professor's office would have been located in the new faculty building. However, in the opinion of the administration, Jason didn't rate a better office. In reality, he didn't mind the shun. His professional life consisted of studying the Sun and its many complexities — not its politics. Unfortunately, his separation simply added to his image around campus as an outcast.

Jason was engrossed in studying the data Dr. Singer had sent him the night before, when the door to his office burst open and Emily Hart walked in, followed by Dean

Thomas and the WJLL camera crew. Hart was positioning the camera crew even as she approached the desk. The cameras were rolling as they crowded into the room.

Jason was so startled he just sat there with his mouth open. Emily Hart spoke first.

"Professor Hobart, I would like to ask you some questions about your warning to President Houston about the danger of using nuclear rockets on the asteroid; and, oh yes, about the impending solar flare."

Jason stammered, "Uh . . . uh . . . I'm not sure what you're talking about." His thoughts flashed back to the conversation he had had at lunchtime. *Benifren! But why?* Before he could ponder the question very long he heard. . . .

"Come now, Professor, don't be so modest," she said in a very professional but persistent manner. "One of your colleagues reported a conversation you had today, in which you were describing the potential calamity from a solar flare, much like the one you predicted previously. Is that correct?"

Emily Hart was a clever reporter. While she was talking she was also redirecting the camera crew to take in the observatory, which could be seen through the window in Jason's makeshift office. Hart already had set the agenda by connecting the president, the mention of another solar flare warning, the asteroid, and the nutty professor.

Jason was dumbfounded. *How does she know about my lunchtime conversation? Why is she insisting the president knows anything?* His head was spinning.

"I don't have anything to say," Jason replied through clenched teeth.

Hart knew she had him. He was scared. All she had to do was lead him a little bit. She decided to take an entirely different tack.

"Professor, I'm not here to ridicule your work. To the contrary, my news director has followed your work for a long time and is concerned about the asteroid and the potential of a dangerous solar flare. As I understand it, you have some new information."

"I have nothing to say," Jason repeated, although his defenses were lowered a little by Hart's comment.

"Well, I'm certainly not here to pressure you into saying something you don't believe," she said in a condescending tone, trying to draw Jason in.

"I do believe it," Jason blurted out defensively. Suddenly he was sick and tired of being forced to keep his mouth shut about things that should be made public.

They say that most life-changing decisions are not really planned. They are made impulsively. Certainly that was true in Jason Hobart's case. If he had been able to look a few hours into the future he probably would have bitten his tongue and swallowed his pride one

63

more time. But he didn't.

He was a good physicist and he had confidence in his observations. Sure, he had been wrong before about the magnitude of the flare, but his prediction of the timing was correct, and area 403 was much more unstable this time. People needed to be warned. He was going to tell his story, even if it cost him his job. He spent the next half hour detailing his study of area 403 and explaining to the now attentive reporter why he felt the area could yield a solar flare of enormous severity.

Hart kept slipping in comments about the asteroid and whether he would recommend the use of nuclear rockets to divert it.

"No one with any common sense would even consider that," Jason said.

"And you would advise the president not to do so?" she asked.

"He hasn't asked," Jason replied. "But if he did, yes, I would tell him."

Good, Hart thought. *With a little creative editing it will sound like he did advise Houston.*

While Jason was talking, Jake Young, from WJLL, was taking notes. He didn't have the background to evaluate all the professor was saying, but he knew enough to realize that this shy, unassuming college professor had information that those in power should listen to. But he also knew that Hart had absolutely no interest in Professor Hobart's

64

theory, outside of how she could use it to bash the president.

"Are you saying then, Professor, that the president should act immediately to warn Americans about this flare or he will be risking the lives of millions of people?" Hart asked, pretending to be shocked.

"N . . . nn . . . no," Jason stammered. "I didn't mean that exactly. I don't know." Jason realized the reporter had trapped him by his own words.

"Now come on, Professor," she bantered sarcastically, "you either believe the flare is a threat or you don't. Which is it?"

"Of course I do," Jason said defensively, and he tried to add that he hadn't talked to the president, but he never got the chance to make that point. By that time Hart was off into her commentary. Even if he had been able to tell his story, she would have edited it out in the final copy anyway. She had her story: President Consults Discredited Scientist on Asteroid Threat to Earth and Impending Solar Disaster.

In one of those twists of irony, a meeting was going on at the White House at almost the same time the interview was taking place in Rockford. The president was meeting with his chief of staff, Warren Butts; his press secretary, Allen Dean; Dr. Robert Frasier, director of the National Institute of

Science; and Gen. Floyd Boland, head of the Joint Chiefs of Staff.

"Mr. President, the whole idea is totally asinine," Gen. Boland said, commenting on the plan just presented by the head of the NIS.

"I agree," Butts added.

"Not so," Frasier said angrily as he stood up in protest. "It can be done."

"Sit down, Dr. Frasier," the president said calmly. "Let's hear what General Boland has to say. Go ahead, Floyd."

"Well, in the first place, Mr. President, I'm not at all sure we could even hit the asteroid — if we tried. Remember, those rockets were designed to launch a warhead from one spot on Earth to another spot on Earth. It's a whole different ball game when you're talking about intercepting a moving object in space."

"My scientists think it will work," Frasier interrupted irritatedly.

"Yes, given enough time and enough money, both of which are in short supply in this administration," the general countered, not bothering to hide the contempt he felt for the administrator-turned-scientist, or vice versa.

"Give us the go-ahead and we'll hit that asteroid, Mr. President," Frasier said smugly.

"Even if you could," the general interrupted, shaking his big finger in the face of his smaller civilian counterpart, "it would be like sending a sparrow up to divert the path of a 747." He stopped before adding, "You political pimp!"

"What do you mean, Floyd?" the president asked.

"I mean that rock is so big, my guys say it would take at least five 100-megaton bombs to budge it. And even then it might just break up into pieces.

"Besides," Boland added, "the best data our guys can gather says there is no reason to worry; it will miss us by at least 300,000 miles. Not exactly a crisis, Mr. President."

Frasier glared at the general. "Mr. President, our scientists believe the asteroid does pose a threat. What if we do nothing and the asteroid hits Earth? Millions, perhaps billions, could die."

"Nonsense," the general countered. "I told you that asteroid will miss Earth by 300,000 miles!"

"Can you guarantee that, General?" Frasier asked in an icy tone.

"You know that nothing is guaranteed when it comes to astrophysics, but . . ."

"Exactly!" Frasier exclaimed. "Our latest figures show a slight shift in trajectory. Look for yourself, Mr. President," and with that he shoved a bound copy of the NIS report at Houston.

Glancing briefly through the huge stack of

papers, the president looked over at Gen. Boland and asked, "Have your people reviewed this, Floyd?"

"No, Sir," the general growled. "Dr. Frasier has not provided our people with his data."

"Is that true, Doctor?" the president asked angrily. He could tell by the look on Frasier's face that it was.

"This is not a game being played for the benefit of your career, Doctor," the president said angrily, nervously clicking the ballpoint pen he was holding.

"I want all, and I mean *all* the data available to General Boland's team immediately." Without waiting for Frasier's response, he continued, "General, I want your analysis by 0800 tomorrow."

"Yes, Sir," the general snapped. He glanced out of the corner of his eye at a red-faced Frasier, and a slight grin curled his mouth.

As the group got up to leave, Houston said, "Just a minute, Doctor Frasier. I want to talk to you alone."

General Boland pulled the door shut behind him as he exited the Oval Office.

"I want you to turn this investigation over to a real scientist — one of your top physicists will do." Glancing over at the report, Houston caught the name of the originators: Drs. Annette Camp and Gene Moore. "Bring in

Drs. Camp and Moore to take over the project," he commanded.

"But, Mr. President . . . ," Frasier started to protest.

"No arguments," Houston snapped. "Just do it!"

If the president could have read the mind of the NIS director, he might have called in his Secret Service. It was pure hate.

At Rockford College things were quickly going from bad to worse for Jason. As soon as Dean Thomas could do so, without all the press around, he called Jason into his office.

"Dr. Hobart, your actions today will most certainly result in ridicule for the school — once again," he spat out, his face flushed with the anger he felt inside. "Professor, as you may know, I thought the administration should have demanded your resignation long ago, and now I know they will. You can either submit your resignation, effective immediately, or you will be put on administrative leave — without pay — pending a meeting of the executive committee to dismiss you."

Jason felt a flush of panic as he heard the words he had long dreaded. *What will I do?* he thought. Then, suddenly, in one of those inexplicable reactions, Jason felt a surge of self-confidence that he had not felt in a long time.

He knew he was right. He also knew he

had not done anything wrong. He had simply told the truth as he saw it when asked. He didn't call the TV people in, but he wasn't going to lie either. After talking with Benifren, he was convinced his associate had not called the station either. He suspected Harley, but it didn't matter now anyway.

"Dean Thomas," Jason answered calmly, "I won't resign. If you think you can get me fired, then so be it, but I have not done anything wrong. And I think this is still a nation that believes in free speech. If you want to get rid of me, you'll have to do it yourself," he said with finality as he slammed the papers Thomas had handed him back on the desk and left the room.

The dean was so shocked at the outburst from the normally placid Hobart that he couldn't respond. The best he could do was to shout after him. "Hobart, you're suspended!"

Jason raised his right hand and waved to Thomas without ever looking back. He had worried for six years for nothing. He felt like the cares of the world had been lifted off his shoulders.

As Jason walked down the hall and out of the administration building, he felt great! *No more hiding and skulking around,* he promised himself. *At least the whole thing's out in the open now. Karen! What will Karen say?* he thought.

Well, it's a little late to worry about that now, he decided. *Besides, I didn't really have any control over the circumstances anyway.*

He tried to think of something pleasant. *Wendy will be okay. Didn't she tell me to stand up for what I believe a million times before? I know I can count on Wendy.*

4

Jason returned to his office, repacked his tattered leather briefcase, and went down the steps leading from the observatory to the faculty parking lot. He climbed into the old Volvo sedan that, by its very being, spoke volumes about its owner. The original forest green paint had long since faded to a dull, dusty color — the shade of September leaves. The broken antenna sported a twisted wire coat hanger, placed there by Wendy after the car's fourth antenna had been snapped off in the college parking lot. The cotton stuffing showed through the back seat covers, where years of ultraviolet sun rays had baked the vinyl to a hard plastic feel. The one thing Jason knew he didn't have to worry about was car thieves.

Jason voiced a rehearsed prayer as he turned the key in the ignition: "Please . . . please." He breathed a sigh of relief as the engine roared to life. He backed out of the parking space and headed home.

Strange, he thought, *I should be feeling anxiety but I don't. Maybe it's just having this thing out in the open. But what will I do?* he wondered. Then he put it out of his mind. *Done's done,* he reminded himself. *Nothing I can do about it now.*

He eased into the driveway and switched off the ignition. The engine wheezed, coughed, and bucked a couple of times and then shut down with a clatter. As Jason slipped his key into the front door, someone from inside pulled it open, and the key flew out of his hand. Jason tripped over the threshold as his momentum carried him through the doorway.

"Jason, what are you doing home?" Karen demanded.

He took a deep breath. "Well, there's been some difficulty at the college."

"What kind of difficulty?"

Not knowing exactly where to start, Jason stammered a little bit. "Well, uh. . . ."

Reading the look in his eyes, Karen answered her own question. "You've done it again, haven't you, Jason? After all the warnings, after all this time, you've done it again, haven't you?"

"Done what?" Jason said innocently.

"You know exactly what I'm talking about, Jason Hobart! It's about that stupid sunspot again, isn't it?" she shouted. "You've shot your mouth off again, and now you're in real trouble. Am I right?"

Jason gathered his courage and responded defiantly: "Karen, I only did what I believe is right. Somebody told the television people that I was observing an unstable area on the Sun."

"Television people!" Karen shouted. "What do you mean, television people? You don't mean you said something like that on television *again,* did you?"

"I guess so," Jason hedged, "but I just told them the truth. I'm not going to be silent any longer. I know my theories are right!"

"Jason, it doesn't matter whether you're right or wrong," Karen voiced through gritted teeth, her eyes flashing back and forth. "People think you're a fool and everything a fool says becomes more foolish. Don't you realize that? Whatever you say, they're going to use against you. What about the college?"

"What do you mean?" Jason asked, hedging again.

"Dean Thomas! That's what I mean. You don't think he's going to let you get away with this, do you?" Karen demanded. "Not likely, Jason. You and I both know better than that."

"He did ask for my resignation," Jason replied defensively, "but I refused, because I've done nothing wrong."

"Jason, you're unbelievable sometimes!" Karen said, glaring at her younger brother. "You're a smart man in some ways, but you're so naive. Don't you know that they've got the power, and you don't. If they want to fire you, there's nothing you can do about it. Nobody's going to come to your defense, not after the last time. Exactly what did you tell these TV people?" she demanded.

"I didn't say anything I don't believe," Jason said defiantly.

"What exactly does that mean?"

"It means that I believe there's going to be an eruption on the Sun, and the president should be advised."

"So you told them, like you did before, that the president needs to shut down the country," Karen said incredulously.

"Not exactly," Jason sighed, "but that's the essence of it."

"Jason . . . *really!*" Karen sputtered, shaking her head. She turned and stormed into her bedroom, slamming the door as she went.

Jason shrugged his shoulders slightly as he put his old briefcase down in the hallway. He was feeling a lot less defiant now and a lot less confident than he had back at the school. All the years of browbeating had taken its toll on his self-esteem.

It was nearly 8:30 that evening before Wendy came home from the meeting she'd been attending with her high school drama group. They were getting ready to do a musical at the school and she was engrossed in learning the songs and her supporting role in the play. She came in the door, dropped her backpack on the table, and made her way through the house to the observatory.

"Daddy!" she shouted excitedly. "Have you seen the news?"

Jason glanced down at his watch. *Eight thirty!* He could hardly believe it. He had been so engrossed in his thoughts that he hadn't even noticed the time. "No I haven't, Honey," he replied. His heart did a flip-flop as he remembered the TV crew. "Tell me about it."

"Oh, Daddy. I think it's terrific. I saw you on the news giving your analysis of the solar flare, and I thought it was FANtastic!"

What Wendy didn't say was that the reporter had made him look like a wild-eyed fanatic. The news clip included scenes from her father's earlier episode with the national media. She knew what would happen if WNN national picked up the interview.

Jason felt a warmth go all over him. He could care less what the others thought. As long as Wendy was for him, it was okay.

"Thanks, Sweetheart, but I don't think the administration at the college sees it the same way."

"Aw, they're just a bunch of old fogeys," Wendy said, giving him a hug. "Who cares? Daddy, you can do anything that you want. You're a genius. People will be after you all over the world once your theories are proved."

"Dr. Carrington's theories," Jason corrected his daughter. "They were his theories.

All I've done is try to adapt them."

"Sure, sure, Daddy," she replied with a soft pat on his hand, "but, remember, it took you to put them into modern terms. *You're* the genius. What about Aunt Karen? How'd she take it?"

"Not very well, I'm afraid," Jason replied with a sigh. "She was pretty angry. She's afraid I'll lose my job."

"I wish you would, Daddy. I hate it that you work at that stodgy old school. They don't appreciate you. I just hate it!"

"Well, thanks, Honey. I appreciate your support, but unfortunately, it's the only job I have at the moment."

"You can get another one, Daddy. I *know* you can. What are they going to do?"

"In all honesty, I don't know, Wendy. Dean Thomas asked me to resign. I refused, but he said something about suspension when I was leaving."

"Good for you, Daddy. You're right and they're wrong and everybody will know it. Then *they* will look like fools."

"Well, right now, unfortunately, your ole man looks like the fool, Sweetheart. The media wants a fool, and the politicians need a scapegoat, and I rather suspect that I'll be chosen for both."

Jason worked late into the evening, running new calculations. He concluded that a solar eruption in the range of 6 or more was quite possible — maybe within the next few days or weeks at the most. With the initial burst of solar winds headed toward Earth at a million miles an hour, Jason knew, or at least believed, that most of the communications and navigation satellites should be shut down until this flare passed. Unfortunately, he knew that the majority of the scientific community wouldn't agree with his notion.

He wished Wendy were still up so he could share this information with her, but she'd already gone to bed. She had been dead tired from her activities of that day. Jason knew that he should go to bed as well but, first of all, he wasn't tired and, second, he dreaded another confrontation with his sister if she was still up.

In reality, he didn't have to worry about confronting Karen because, earlier that evening, two suitcases in hand, she had stormed out the front door, slamming it behind her. She'd left a note on his bedroom dresser that said it all: "Jason, I'm through. I can't take this any longer. You and Wendy will be fine without me." There was no "Love, Karen," or "Hope everything works out" or anything of the sort — just "Karen."

Later that evening, when Jason went into his bedroom, he found the note. *What will we do without her?* he wondered. But then he realized that he was actually relieved. He'd feared the confrontation he knew would be coming when he saw her again, and he really was tired of the continual battering she put him through.

So he found himself with mixed emotions as he laid down on the bed fully clothed. He loved his sister and he did not want her to leave but, at the same time, he was glad that he didn't have to face her wrath this evening.

Now to tell Wendy, he thought. *No, I'll just wait until tomorrow. No sense disturbing her.* Little did Jason know that Wendy had already gone into the bedroom to talk to her aunt and found that her stuff was gone. *Good!* she told herself. *If you can't support Dad, he's better off without you.* Wendy had known for a long while that her aunt resented her. Karen was a controlling person who wanted total domination over her brother. Wendy would never allow that, and Karen knew it.

When he fell asleep exhausted that evening, or more correctly the next morning, Jason was oblivious to the swirl of events taking place across the country that would grab and enmesh him.

Once the interview had aired on local television, Emily Hart transmitted it to WNN headquarters in Atlanta. Neil Farmer reviewed it and then called her. "Emily, this piece on the flare is excellent," he said in uncharacteristic praise. "You did a great job in making the transition from the asteroid piece to the solar flare 'crisis.' We tested the story on a focus group and they assumed the president was involved too. Great work! We'll run it as the lead story at 8:00 tonight."

"Thanks, Neil," Emily replied. "What about that interview for the morning program director's slot?"

"Yeah, sure," Farmer said, instantly irritated. "I'll get back to you on it."

Neil Farmer had no intention of allowing any one of his many bimbos close to his wife — especially Emily. She was too bright and pretty. His wife would make the connection. She might tolerate his occasional wandering, as long as she and her women's club friends didn't know, but he didn't want to push his luck.

Hart never had a chance to respond. When she heard the line go dead she knew Farmer had hung up on her. She slammed down the receiver. "He'll get his!" she vowed.

Shortly after WNN aired the interview that evening, the other networks picked it up and were in the process of making the solar flare and President Houston a national issue. Farmer was busy contacting many of his colleagues across the country and convincing them to pick up the story.

By the time the late night news aired, the trap had been set. The networks appeared to be neutral on the issue, but they questioned the president's wisdom in seeking counsel from a discredited scientist.

"What's this nonsense the networks are carrying?" the president asked Allen Dean, his press secretary. "I don't even know this Dr. Hobart, and I haven't heard anything about a solar flare danger."

"I don't think there's much to it, Mr. President," Dean replied. "If you remember, Professor Hobart was involved in a fiasco a few years ago when he predicted a major solar flare on the Sun that would create chaos in the satellite communication systems."

"I recall that," Houston said reflectively. "Pretty big stir at the time, wasn't it?"

"Yes, Sir. Probably even more so for Dr. Hobart when the crisis failed to materialize."

"You were with the *Times* then; what was your take on Hobart, Allen?"

"Well, the professor wasn't entirely wrong. The flare did, in fact, occur right on schedule. Pretty remarkable prediction actually. And there was some disruption in communications — mostly some power grid problems and AT&T lost a satellite — but not much else."

"Do you think we should talk to this professor now?" Houston asked, with an uncanny ability to cut through chaff.

Dean was a bit taken back; he hadn't even considered the idea.

Allen Dean had done a great deal of checking on Dr. Jason Hobart since the interview broke on national television the previous evening. He had been thoroughly briefed by the president's chief of staff, Warren Butts, on what the networks were maneuvering to do: trap the president.

"The best advice I can give, Mr. President, is to wait this one out. You've already dealt with the asteroid thing."

"You're probably right," Houston agreed. "The reports from Doctors Moore and Camp pretty well put that one to bed. It's not a threat to Earth."

"Right, but Frasier will certainly kick up a fuss about it. He's bound and determined to launch those missiles."

"Frasier's got a one-track mind," Houston said with an uncharacteristically negative expression.

"Maybe a half-track," Dean quipped. "He can't stand to be out of the media's limelight."

"Warren," the president said to his chief of staff, who had just walked in. "Have those two scientists from Palo Alto — Moore and Camp — contact Professor Hobart and give me their opinions, will you? And posthaste!"

Butts responded, "I think that could be very hazardous to your political career, Mr. President. If you even appear to consult Professor Hobart, the media will make you look like a nut case."

"Probably right," Houston agreed. "The

percentage call probably is to ignore this altogether. But you know I've never been one to play the percentages. I want an honest evaluation of Hobart and this solar flare."

"Mr. President, if the press catches wind of it they'll crucify you," Dean warned.

"Well, I guess they've crucified better men than me," Houston said resolutely. "Just do what I said."

5

Annette Camp could not remember a time when she wasn't fascinated with astronomy. As a young girl, her father had bought her a telescope, and she had spent countless hours in her backyard staring into the sky. An avid reader, she consumed all of the information in her local library on astronomy and navigation. By the time she was in high school, she was dazzling officials at the Science Fair with her discussions and displays on gravitational interrelations. Her early star maps still grace the walls of San Jose High School.

She had dedicated her life to becoming an astronomer and, to that end, she had invested more than 10 years in education and internship at a variety of major universities. Unfortunately, all along the way she had to fight the "ole-boy" clubs — first at Stanford, then at UCLA, and later at USC. The tenured professors of astronomy at those institutions simply refused to let a bright young woman into their ranks, even one with earned PhDs in astrophysics and mathematics.

When the position at the Palo Alto Observatory became available, she had reluctantly made application. She was convinced that only the deadbeats and dropouts went to work for the government, and Palo Alto was funded primarily by government dollars. But as she considered it she came to the conclusion that the universities, in fact, were funded by government money too — both state and federal — so she would be no worse off at Palo Alto. It might even be a new step in her career direction.

Shortly after joining the research team at Palo Alto, she had changed her opinion. She discovered that once she got beyond the political hacks at the top there were some top-notch scientists working at Palo Alto; and her associate Gene Moore was one of them. The research team at Palo Alto, she found, had no "ole-boy" club mentality. She was readily accepted as a legitimate scientist. There she was judged solely on the basis of her contribution to the team's efforts.

It was almost purely by luck that she had spotted the asteroid during the team's brief interval with the Hubble telescope. Rarely did a scientist have the opportunity to discover anything new in the heavens, because there were thousands of people peering up into the skies virtually every night. Most of them had as their primary motivation the discovery of a new space object that would make them famous and wealthy.

When she had first spotted the asteroid, she

went to Gene Moore for confirmation. After verifying that it actually was a new asteroid, never before identified, Moore made a big deal out of it, as did the rest of the team. Dr. Annette Camp had made a major discovery in only her second year of service at Palo Alto.

Because of the discovery, she was given additional time on the telescope to make more detailed observations. Once she determined that the trajectory of the asteroid would take it through the solar system and near Earth, the excitement at Palo Alto really began to build.

Word of a "near miss" never should have gone beyond the observation team, once it was determined that the asteroid posed no threat to Earth. And it probably would have died there except that Dr. Gamble, current director of the facility, called his friend and former director, Dr. Robert Frasier at the National Institute of Science, to inform him of the asteroid. He tried to claim as much credit as he could for the discovery.

Frasier then made the announcement to the press, implying that the asteroid would be passing "near Earth," and the rest of the story was history. The press made the asteroid into front-page news by alarming the public over the "near-miss scenario." Once the word was out, the exaggerations began to grow, and soon the near miss — 300,000 miles —

turned into a grave threat for the earth and its inhabitants.

When the first hint of the "impending asteroid crisis" was made public, Drs. Camp and Moore, as well as many of their associates, immediately went to Gamble to protest.

"There is no threat to the earth," Annette argued vehemently. "This asteroid poses absolutely no threat to the inhabitants of this planet." To Gamble that made little or no difference. The fact was, he and Frasier had an issue and they were going to milk that issue for all of its publicity value.

Then when an article appeared in *The Washington Post,* that officials at the National Institute of Science were considering recommending to the president the use of nuclear weapons to divert the asteroid, Annette was livid. She went to Gamble again, armed with reams of computer printouts that showed the trajectory of the asteroid.

"The asteroid presents no threat to human beings," she argued, but to no avail. Gamble simply turned a deaf ear. He explained to her that, in the collective wisdom of Washington, it had been determined that the asteroid perhaps would represent a threat and that moving it further off course would be the recommended course of action.

Annette grabbed all of her data and stormed out of the director's office, mumbling so that he could hear her, "Madness!

The whole organization has gone mad!"

Ultimately, Drs. Camp and Moore had their day in court, because it was impossible for Gamble or Frasier to present any scientific evidence to the president and his advisors without revealing the source of their data; hence, the president saw the report from Drs. Camp and Moore.

Dr. Frasier had amended the report to recommend the use of the nuclear weapons to alter the trajectory of the asteroid, but Gen. Boland and his team had quickly seen through that ruse, because the data showing the actual trajectory of the asteroid had been complete and thorough. Armed with that information, the president concluded that the asteroid posed no threat and, therefore, there was no reason to consider using nuclear weapons to change its direction.

When the president directed his chief of staff to ask Drs. Camp and Moore for their opinion about the pending solar flare, Annette was surprised by the request.

"Solar observation is not my specialty, Gene," she protested to her colleague.

"It's not mine either, but apparently the president liked the report we sent him and would like for us to take a look at this issue as well."

"Well, I don't pretend to be an expert in flares," Annette protested once again. "Do you know anything about Dr. Hobart?"

"All I know about him," Moore said as he reached back on his desk for the report one of his staffers had provided, "is that Dr. Hobart has a PhD in astrophysics and is an associate professor of astronomy at Rockford College in Rockford, Illinois. However, there's one additional pertinent fact. About six years ago, Dr. Hobart predicted a major solar eruption that was picked up by the media. If you remember, that's back when we had the power grid drop-outs in the western states."

"Oh yes, I do remember that," Annette said. "I remember something about a solar eruption, but as I recall it didn't happen. Did it?"

"Well, yes and no," Moore said. "A flare did occur, but not on the scale Dr. Hobart predicted and, as a result, he received a lot of bad publicity."

"Oh great," Annette moaned. "And here he is, making another prediction. Is this guy some kind of a publicity hound, Gene?"

"Probably," Moore said. "But the president has asked us to look into it, and I guess it's our responsibility to make an evaluation for him."

"Okay," Annette groaned. "But I really don't have any desire to get involved with some political hack from academia again."

Moore replied, "Well, as Shakespeare said, 'I think thou dost protest too much.' Where shall we begin, Madame?"

"Well," Annette said, drumming her pencil on the desk. "I would say we ought to go to two of the best solar physicists that we know and ask their opinion about Dr. Hobart."

"Good idea! For sure, Lewis Singer would be one," Moore said.

"I agree," Annette confirmed. And the other would be Dr. Onera at Tokyo University. The Japanese have had their SOHO satellite up for several years now. Certainly they're some of the foremost solar flare observers in the world, wouldn't you say?"

"Probably so," Moore agreed, rolling his chair toward the desk.

"Good. I'll take Dr. Onera if you'll take Dr. Singer," Annette offered.

"Agreed."

Annette went back into her office and called up WordStar on the Internet. When the inquiry came back, "What data is requested?" she typed in, "solar astrophysics." Immediately the computer responded, "Name?" and she typed in, "Dr. Ito Onera, Tokyo University." Less than a second later, the machine responded with the data.

"Dr. Ito Onera: Professor of Astronomy and Solar Physics, University of Tokyo." It also provided his e-mail location, telephone number, and fax code. Annette printed out the information and decided it would be more efficient to e-mail Dr. Onera, because if he operated like she did he rarely took phone calls. She would, however, regularly sort through her e-mail, pick out the people she wanted to talk to, and call them back.

She typed a memo:

To: Dr. Ito Onera
From: Dr. Annette Camp, Palo Alto
**   Observatory**
I have been commissioned by the president of the United States to investigate the potential of a solar flare, predicted by Dr. Jason Hobart at Rockford College, USA. Request any information you have available on Dr. Hobart and solar flare.

She then hit the send key on her computer and the data was transferred through the Internet to Dr. Onera's e-mail location.

That responsibility ended, Annette decided that she would query the Internet for any additional information. Following the same sequence again, she typed

Dr. Jason Hobart, Rockford College
Request info on the most recent solar flare solar activity.

Almost immediately, her screen filled with information. As she began to read through the data being transmitted to her screen, Annette was impressed. *Certainly, Dr. Hobart is no hack. He has provided detailed analysis of his observation of solar surface area 403.* Annette was no solar physicist, but she knew enough to understand that his data was thorough and complete.

As soon as the last page of information had been transmitted to her computer, she pressed the print key and her laser printer began to zip off the data that had been transmitted.

It was nearly lunchtime, so she decided to get something to eat. She was turning to leave her cubicle when she glanced at the screen and saw the message light flashing. She sat back down and typed in "ready." Almost immediately, a message appeared.

To: Dr. Annette Camp, regarding inquiry on Dr. Jason Hobart
From: Dr. Ito Onera, University of Tokyo Solar Observatory
Dr. Hobart is a close friend and colleague. I consider him to be the most knowledgeable astrophysicist in the world on solar predictions. I have studied data from Dr. Hobart on area 403 and concur with his initial evaluations. I suggest that if President Houston has commissioned you to evaluate Dr. Hobart's work you should do so thoroughly. If I can be

of further help, please do not hesitate to contact me.

Annette decided as she printed the message, *If Dr. Onera believes Dr. Hobart is credible, he must be worth investigating.*

She tore the last page off of her computer printout and headed out the door. On the way down to the cafeteria, she met Moore on his way to her office. "Annette, I believe we're on to something here," Moore said.

She started to tell him about Onera's message when he interrupted again, "I just talked to Lewis Singer of Cambridge, and he thinks Dr. Hobart is a topflight solar physicist. He says that if Hobart predicts a solar flare of any magnitude everybody should stop and listen to him. He filled me in on the details of what happened in the earlier episode. It seems that Hobart predicted the solar flare correctly. Apparently, the only error was in the magnitude of the flare. He had predicted the flare would continue to build and, instead, it dissipated after the initial cycle. Singer says that's not an unusual characteristic for solar instabilities and in no way detracts from what Hobart did in accurately predicting the flare."

"Interesting indeed," Annette said. "I didn't get that detailed a report from Dr. Onera, but what I got confirms what Lewis Singer says. Dr. Onera believes that Jason Hobart is the premier solar physicist in the world when it comes to predicting flares."

"Interesting," Moore said reflectively. "Now what?"

"Well I would say, first, we need to go through Dr. Hobart's data thoroughly. Apparently he has provided a detailed analysis of this projected solar eruption. Then I would say we need to contact Dr. Hobart directly." Having said that, Annette turned and hurried back up the stairs, forgetting her plans to eat.

Moore followed her to her office, where they spent the next several hours pouring through all the data provided via the Internet.

"Very thorough. I'm impressed," Moore told his colleague.

"I certainly concur with that. This man is no hack. Whether or not he can predict solar flares, he certainly knows his physics and coronal activity."

"No doubt about that," Moore agreed.

"I think it's time we tried to contact Dr. Jason Hobart," Annette said, picking up the telephone and punching in the number provided from the Internet data.

The automated answering service responded. "You have reached the Rockford College administration office. Office hours are from 8:30 A.M. to 6:00 P.M." The message droned on and on before Annette hung up.

"Ah, it's past office hours at the college. Obviously that's his office number," Annette said.

"Oh, apparently you haven't been watching the news. You just aren't up on the latest information, are you, Dr. Camp?" Moore teased.

"What do you mean?" Annette asked.

"Well, most of the networks have been carrying news about Dr. Jason Hobart. It seems that he has been suspended from his position at Rockford College, as a result of his latest prediction."

"What's that mean?" Annette asked. She had long made it a habit not to watch television. She rated the network news on a par with soap operas.

"It probably means that he irritated somebody in the college administration, and they're trying to get rid of him," Moore said.

"You know," Annette responded with a grin, "I'm beginning to like this Jason Hobart more and more. Now the next question is, how do we get his number?"

"Have you tried calling information in Rockford, Illinois and asking for his telephone number?"

"Good thought," Annette admitted, blushing slightly. She called the long-distance information number and heard "What city?"

"Rockford, Illinois," Annette replied.

The automated answering service said, "What name?"

"Dr. Jason Hobart."

"One moment please." Almost immediately, the computer voice came back with the number of Dr. Jason Hobart. Annette made a note of it and then called it.

Jason heard the phone ring, first in the house and then half a second later on the portable in his observatory study. When it rang the fifth time, Jason stopped what he was doing. *I forgot to put the answering machine on,* he thought irritatedly. He decided to ignore the telephone, and after five more rings there was silence again.

"Nobody home," Annette said to her colleague.

"Or at least no one answering," Moore countered. "If you were Dr. Hobart and you were being hounded by the press, would you answer your telephone?"

"Probably not," she agreed, "but now what do we do?"

"If somebody wanted to reach you and you weren't answering your telephone, what would they do?" Moore asked.

"They would e-mail me, of course," she said, slapping her forehead with the heel of her hand. She immediately went over to her computer terminal, called up the Internet one more time, and requested the e-mail address for Dr. Jason Hobart, Rockford, Illinois. Immediately, the screen provided the address. She sat down and typed in a note.

To: Dr. Jason Hobart, Rockford, Illinois

From: Dr. Annette Camp, Palo Alto Observatory

I am interested in the information you provided on the pending solar flare. I have been commissioned by President Houston to evaluate this solar activity. I would appreciate a response at your earliest convenience.

Annette then left her e-mail address, telephone number, and fax number.

Jason had been sitting at his desk for several hours, pondering what he was going to do and had come to the conclusion that there was really nothing he could do. He had said what he believed and provided the information to the people who should know. From that point, it was out of his hands.

Earlier in the evening he had shut down most of his equipment. For the time being, he simply didn't have the heart or the will to do anything further. But he was a scientist to the core, and as he got up to leave his little study he decided that the least he could do was to take one more look at the latest activity. He switched on the small tracking recorder attached to the X-ray spectrometer. The device beeped twice as it began to power up and, as a part of its calibration cycle, the needle swept from the zero X axis to the zero Y axis and then traveled back to the center position.

Jason punched up the tape drive that had been storing pertinent information over the last several hours since he had powered down. Almost immediately, the needle registered two sharp spikes and then settled back down again at the bottom of the X axis. Jason was suddenly alert. If the data he just printed was accurate, there had been a second coronal burst from area 403. He quickly flipped on the S-band spectrometer and rewound the tape to the beginning one more time. As soon as the device had warmed up, it also beeped twice and went to the zero axis. Jason punched on the digital tape and the same two spikes appeared.

A second flare from area 403! Jason realized. By now the two spectrometers were fully operational and were scanning the sun's current activity. "More activity," Jason muttered as he looked at the data coming from the two devices.

Some eight hours earlier area 403 had had a second flare in both the S- and X-band ranges. Jason made a quick calculation. *In two days the first flare will hit, followed a day later by this second flare! Two flares, less than a day apart. What will the impact be?* He wasn't sure yet.

He needed more detailed calculations from the computer. The first thing to come on the screen was his e-mail prompt. He noticed that he had some new correspondence. That wasn't unusual. Almost every evening scientists from around the world traded information.

He clicked on the e-mail scan. The very first message caught his attention. It was from a Dr. Annette Camp at the Palo Alto Observatory. Jason searched his memory. *Camp . . . Camp.* He knew that name from someplace. *Of course.* He'd seen some of her asteroid data on the Internet. He'd been very impressed with its thoroughness and also with her analysis that the asteroid posed no threat to Earth. If he remembered correctly, Dr. Camp had discovered the asteroid. His curiosity piqued, he punched up her message. What he saw caught his undivided attention.

The president? The president of the United States is interested in my theory? Then he thought, *Maybe it's another hoax.* Jason had been around the media long enough by this time to know not to take anything for granted. Reporters would do virtually anything to get a story and to continue the story once they got it. Then he noted the address on the e-mail from Dr. Camp: It was from the Palo Alto Observatory.

She had left her e-mail address and telephone number. Jason started to type in her e-mail address and send a reply; then he thought better of it. *No,* he thought, *first I need to evaluate this latest flare.* So he called up his primary program.

By this time he had rewound the digital tape and once more was feeding that data through his computer. Within a few seconds, information began spewing out of the machine, detailing the second flare from area 403. It had occurred eight hours and twelve minutes previously and was a magnitude of approximately 1.6, which meant, based on Dr. Carrington's formula, that another several billion tons of cosmic matter was now hurtling its way toward Earth.

Jason quickly ran through some more calculations, which predicted the impact of the dual solar storms hitting Earth's magnetic shield. He whistled aloud. *This one will get some attention,* he said to himself. *We'll not only have a show of the northern lights, we're going to lose some expensive satellites if they aren't powered down.*

As soon as he had the data stored, Jason switched back over to the Internet. He typed in Annette Camp's e-mail address and wrote a note.

To: Dr. Annette Camp, Palo Alto Observatory
From: Jason Hobart
Received your e-mail and will call you in five minutes.

Five minutes later the telephone in Annette Camp's office rang. She almost dropped it in her haste to answer.

"Dr. Camp?"

"Yes, this is Annette Camp."

"This is Jason Hobart."

"Oh, Dr. Hobart. Thank you for calling."

"My pleasure, Doctor," Jason responded. "If I understood your e-mail correctly, you're investigating my much notarized prediction of a solar flare. Is that correct?"

"Yes," she responded warmly. "Also, I've reviewed your Internet data, and my colleague Gene Moore and I have talked to Drs. Singer and Onera, both of whom have given you glowing recommendations."

"Tell them thanks," Jason said as he began to relax a little. "They're probably the only people in the world who'd give me a good recommendation at this point."

"I understand," Annette replied. She could sense the hurt in the ex-professor's voice. Maybe she simply felt some of her own rejection from the academic society. "The academic world can be pretty brutal; and the media is even worse, isn't it?"

"That's for sure," Jason agreed. "But, Doctor, that's not what I called you about. Your e-mail was providential. I've been reviewing some data from area 403 and I need to contact somebody in authority," Jason said as matter-of-factly as his sense of urgency would allow.

101

"Is there a problem?"

"I think so," Jason said. "About 20 hours ago area 403 experienced a level 2 coronal eruption, and eight hours ago it had a second, smaller flare and . . ."

"I'm sorry, Doctor," Annette interrupted. "I'm not that familiar with solar physics. Can you clarify?"

"Yes," Jason said. "A level 2 flare means that there has been a major eruption from a coronal hole. A level 2 flare is not all that uncommon in a high activity cycle. But in the case of area 403, the coronal hole is pointed directly at Earth. The first flare will impact our atmosphere in about two days. The second is 12 hours behind."

Annette caught two things: Jason's intensity and his anxiety in discussing it. "What will be the effect of these flares?" she asked.

"That's hard to say with any certainty," Jason hedged, the old caution resurfacing. Then he decided, *What the heck!* "Want an educated guess?" he asked. "Off the record?"

"Sure," Annette responded.

"A level 2 flare can destroy the more sensitive satellites. Probably GEOs and the high orbit stationary communication ones. Back-to-back flares can really disrupt satellite communications."

"What would you advise?" Annette asked as matter-of-factly as her surprise would allow.

"Shut them down until these flares pass," Jason replied. "Probably Earth's magnetic shield will divert most of the high energy particles, but anything in high orbit is at risk."

"Anything else, Professor?" Annette asked, sensing he wanted to say more.

"The second, smaller flare, although it is less intense, is troubling. Having two successive flares back-to-back is a bad sign."

"How so, Doctor?" Annette asked.

Jason then decided to level with Dr. Camp. *After all,* he thought, *what do I have to lose now?* "Dr. Camp," he continued in a more solemn tone, "I believe we are seeing the early stages of a phenomenon known as a coronal displacement. If so, this planet's inhabitants are in grave danger."

Annette didn't know exactly what to say. She had expected a wild-eyed fanatic looking for publicity, but she sensed that the man on the other end of the line was neither a fanatic nor wild.

"Tell me, Professor, what should I do with this information?" she said for lack of anything else to say.

"Well," Jason answered, returning to his normally placid manner, "I'd say that the president and his scientific advisors should at least be advised of these flares. One thing about it," he commented, "we should get a graphic demonstration of the power of a solar flare in about two days, plus or minus a few hours. When the solar winds reach Earth's magnetic field, the high altitude satellites are at extreme risk."

"Can you send me some data on the most recent observations?" Annette asked.

"Already done," Jason said. "I've loaded it on the Internet. You can download it anytime you'd like."

"Thank you, Professor. We'll be in contact with you, and I sincerely appreciate your professionalism."

"Thanks," Jason said warmly. "It's very good to know that at least one person doesn't think I'm deranged."

"Don't worry," Annette said as warmly as she could. "All of us have been subjected to the same treatment at one time or the other. The only difference is, yours got spread further and wider than most of ours."

When Jason hung up the telephone, he decided, *I don't know the lady, but I certainly do like her.*

After hanging up, Annette relayed the information to Moore. Turning around in his chair, he activated his terminal, located Jason's Internet site, and began to download the information. A quick review of the data told both Camp and Moore that, in fact, Dr. Hobart was correct. There had been two flares separated by some 12 hours, more or less. When the first solar winds reached Earth, in about two more days, they would have a firsthand display of its effects. A lesser flare in 1996 had disabled two high altitude communications satellites.

Annette stuffed the printout into her oversized briefcase. "It's time to tell the powers that be about Dr. Hobart and his theories — in person," she said to Moore. "Let's throw a few things in a bag and catch the next flight for Washington, D.C."

Moore started to protest, but the determination on Annette's face told him that he could either go with her or she would go alone. He shrugged and grabbed his coat. She had already starting making arrangements for their tickets on the Internet.

During the flight to Washington, Annette kept thinking about the WNN newscast she had seen in the airport. WNN reported that the president had decided not to interfere with the asteroid, having been advised that it posed no threat to Earth. She was glad to see that some common sense and reason still existed in Washington. The broadcast later went on to show Professor Hobart and suggest that he had advised the president on the impending solar flare. She knew that it wasn't true. *The media!* she thought disgustedly.

She could imagine the pressures that the president had been under from pseudoscientists like Dr. Frasier. The utter stupidity of even suggesting the use of nuclear weapons on an asteroid the size of Atlantis caused her to shake her head.

"What's the problem?" Moore said, glancing over at his associate.

"Oh, nothing," Annette mumbled. "I'm just thinking about Gamble and Frasier and the insanity of thinking that somehow they could bump that asteroid off its projectory with nuclear weapons, even if it *had* been a threat to the world."

"I agree," he said. "However, I guess if it had been headed for Earth, you and I both would have been cheerleaders behind the launching of those rockets. I mean, even if it could not help, at least it would have been something to do. Right?"

"Well maybe," she responded with a smile. "But, fortunately, greater wisdom seemed to have prevailed. What do you think about Professor Hobart's solar flare theory?" she asked.

"Well, I've been reviewing the data pretty thoroughly, and I'm not sure that I can follow Dr. Hobart's logic in predicting the magnitude of solar flares. But certainly, he's called this one pretty close. He predicted that the first solar flare would be a magnitude of 1.8. It was a 1.6. Based on the flare in '96 that was a 1.5 on the Carrington scale, some of the unprotected satellites may be in harm's way. He's suggesting that these satellites be powered down."

"I know," Annette said. "However, trying

to convince AT&T or GEOs to shut down their $40 million satellites won't be all that easy. And trying to convince them that they should leave them off for another two days will be near to impossible, I suspect."

"You're probably right," Moore concurred. "All we can do is pass along this information to the president. Anyway, by the time we get to talk to anyone in authority it may be a moot point for the first flare. Let's hope the professor is wrong about even bigger flares — for the world's sake."

"For sure," Annette said halfheartedly, "but somehow I don't think he's wrong."

After their plane landed at Dulles, they were approached by two men in dark suits.

"Doctor Camp? Doctor Moore?" the first man said. "We're from the president's office."

"But how . . ." Annette started to ask.

"Let's just say we're paid to know these things."

The other Secret Service agent seemed much less formal. He said with a grin, "You can call me C.C."

At six-feet-five inches and nearly 250 pounds of lean muscle, C.C. was an imposing figure. He was the largest man Annette had ever seen up close and personal. Next to him she felt like a midget.

6

Doctors Camp and Moore were led to the waiting limousine by the two Secret Service agents. Annette had several questions she wanted to ask, but she kept silent until they were well on their way. Then she turned to the friendly one who called himself C.C., "How in the world did you know that we were on our way to Washington?"

"It was really pretty simple," C.C. responded. "The president asked his chief of staff, Mr. Butts, to contact you, so he called your offices, found out that neither of you were there and that nobody had seen you for the last couple of hours. So he pulled a few strings, checked the airlines reservations, and found that you both had reserved flights to Washington, D.C. So here we are."

"Where are we headed?" Annette asked.

"All I can tell you is that we were instructed to bring you to the White House. From there it will be in someone else's hands."

"Well, all that certainly solves the problem of how we're going to get in to see the president," Moore responded with a big grin.

"For sure!" Annette agreed.

The rest of the trip was made in silence,

except for the normal street sounds of the city. When they pulled up to the gate at 1600 Pennsylvania Avenue, they were checked through security, the gates were opened, and in they went.

The White House, Annette thought. *Well, I've always wanted to tour the White House. Now's my opportunity.*

When the limousine stopped, C.C. stepped out, opened the door, and helped Drs. Camp and Moore out of the limo. From the parking garage they went down the stairs to a steel door. C.C. put his security card in the scanner and the door opened. Once inside they got on an elevator guarded by another security agent. C.C. cleared the four of them with the guard on duty, and the elevator door closed. Under automatic control the elevator went up to the second level. When the doors opened, Annette knew immediately where they were: the presidential office level.

"This way please," C.C. directed. They entered the reception area and C.C. motioned for them to sit on the couch.

The security guard behind the desk said, "Doctor Moore . . . Doctor Camp, the president will be right with you. May I offer you some refreshments? Perhaps some coffee or tea? I know you've just flown in. With airlines being what they are these days, you're probably hungry. Would you like a roll or coffee?"

"I could use a cup of coffee," Gene Moore responded.

"Decaf for me, please," Annette said.

"Would you like cream or sugar?" the guard asked, to which both replied no. He pressed a button on the desk, spoke to someone on the other end, and in less than five minutes two coffees on a silver tray arrived. The tray was passed to C.C., who then offered the coffee to the two guests.

While she sat sipping her coffee, Annette mulled over everything that had happened over the past several days. One thing for sure: her life had certainly changed since she discovered the asteroid, and now the asteroid had paled into insignificance. It would pass through their solar system in a couple of weeks on its way to the great open reaches of space and wouldn't be seen again for more than a hundred years.

The solar flare was an imminent reality. She went back over the details in her mind: What was it about Jason Hobart that made her believe him so readily when she was such a skeptic about everything else? Obviously he was a good scientist and very thorough, but it was something more than that — a feeling she could not put into words. She just knew the man was honest.

But then she reminded herself, *Even honest scientists can be wrong.* She was staking both her reputation and Gene Moore's on the fact that Dr. Hobart was not wrong, because she knew that she was here to defend Dr. Hobart's position. *Why?* she asked herself again.

Just then the guard spoke up, "Doctor Moore . . . Doctor Camp, the president is ready to see you now."

Annette put her thoughts out of her mind for the time being, stood up, and walked into the room. As she entered, her eyes swept across the room where presidents from George Washington to the current Philip Houston carried on the daily activities of the most powerful nation in the world. She knew the desk was Abraham Lincoln's. The chairs were George Washington's. The rocker in the corner, John F. Kennedy's.

As they crossed the room, three men stood up to greet them. The first introduced himself as Allen Dean, the press secretary; the second as Warren Butts, presidential chief of staff; and the third man was recognized by both scientists: Dr. Robert Frasier, head of the National Institute of Science. The scowl on Frasier's face clearly reflected his disdain for the meeting.

Even before all of the introductions were finished, the president strode into the room wearing a big smile. He walked over to the two scientists and reached out his hand, first to Annette. "Doctor Camp, I presume," he said.

"Hello, Mr. President," was all that Annette could muster at the time.

"And Doctor Moore," he said warmly, reaching out his hand.

"Glad to meet you, Mr. President," Gene Moore responded.

"Please, sit down." The president glanced momentarily in Robert Frasier's direction. The scowl on his face was still quite evident, which irritated Houston to no end.

Frasier's still resisting. He thought to himself, *I've got to do something about that man.*

"Well, Doctors, I can't tell you how glad I am to see you," Houston said warmly. "You must have read my mind, because I had just put the word out that I wanted the two of you to come here. I want to say how much I appreciated the report that you made on the asteroid. It really got me out of a bind."

Directing his attention to Annette, he continued, "I concur with your analysis, Doctor Camp, that the asteroid poses no threat to Earth and that the use of nuclear rockets would be a frivolous waste of taxpayers' money and a fruitless effort to boot." He glanced once more at Frasier, who had hardened the scowl on his face even more, if that were possible.

"Well, Doctors, I presume what brings you here is Dr. Hobart and his solar flare. Correct?" Houston said.

"That's right, Mr. President," Moore said. "I would like to defer to Doctor Camp. She will brief you on our analysis of Dr. Hobart's latest observations."

"Please do," the president said as he settled back into his chair.

"Well, Sir," Annette said. "I have all the data from Dr. Hobart here with me. I'd be glad to share it with you if you'd like."

Houston waved his hand. "That won't be necessary, Doctor. Just bottom line it for me if you will."

Annette went on to outline what she and Dr. Moore had found, noting that they had reviewed all of the data from Professor Hobart and found it scientifically accurate and, in large part, they agreed with his analysis.

"What does 'in large part' mean?" the president asked Annette.

"Well, neither of us are particularly well versed in solar physics. We've reviewed Doctor Hobart's data, and we believe that his findings are correct. In terms of the danger of a major solar eruption, Sir, we have no way to know. We've checked with two other scientists in whom both Dr. Moore and I have great confidence, and without reservation both of them gave Dr. Hobart resounding recommendations."

"Who are they?" Robert Frasier spat out. "What scientists did you check with? The ones I checked with think Hobart is a lunatic."

Houston held up his hand and looked in

Frasier's direction. "That's enough, Frasier," he said bluntly.

Annette continued, "We checked with Dr. Fred Singer, Cambridge Observatory; and Dr. Ito Onera, Tokyo University. Both of these men are considered to be top solar physicists," she said.

"And what did they find?" Houston asked.

"Both of them agreed that Dr. Hobart's theories on solar predictions were unique and remarkable in the world of science, and both also concurred that if he said there was going to be a solar eruption, they had great confidence that there would be."

"In all honesty," Dr. Camp said, "both of them also mentioned that there was no way they could know whether Dr. Hobart's predictions of a major solar eruption were correct or incorrect. They simply had insufficient data to understand his and Dr. Carrington's theories. However . . . ,"

The president interrupted, "What is it, Doctor? Just give it to me straight."

"Well, Sir, according to Dr. Hobart, there was a minor flare more than a day ago. The solar winds from that flare are due to strike Earth's atmosphere in a little less than two days from now. Dr. Hobart is recommending that high-orbit satellites be powered down. He says that when the solar winds strike some of these satellites could be disabled."

Warren Butts and Allen Dean looked at

each other and then back to the president.

"What satellites are we talking about?" the president asked.

"Basically, Sir, it would be any geosynchronous satellites; those are positioned about 22,000 miles above Earth's surface. These would include communication satellites, television satellites, and the geo-positioning satellites."

"Impossible!" Frasier spouted out. "Shut down the high-orbit satellites? Mr. President, that is insanity."

Houston didn't stop the irate professor this time. He thought, *Shut down all those satellites? I wonder how much that would cost. It would shut down half the communications in the United States.*

"That's about 90 percent of our communications system," Allen Dean offered, as if reading the president's mind.

"That's not a doable thing," Houston said.

"I understand your dilemma, Sir. However, I have to tell you that I do believe that Dr. Hobart is sincere and that his theories are sound," Annette argued.

"Well thank you, Doctors. I appreciate the input, but at this point there is no way we can shut down the satellites. I'd be the laughingstock of the world. I guess we'll just have to sit this one out and see what happens."

"I understand, Sir," Annette said, with her colleague nodding his head in agreement.

"Oh, there's one more thing, Mr. President."

"Yes, what is that?"

"The professor detected a second solar flare that will strike Earth's atmosphere about 12 hours after the first flare. He said such an event is extremely rare. And, Sir . . . ," Annette said, pausing.

After a long wait, the president said, "Go ahead. We're not here to play politics. We're here to get your evaluations. Give me what you have."

"Well, it's just that Dr. Hobart is convinced that the magnitude of subsequent flares will continue to increase and, without adequate preparation, it was his opinion that the people of Earth are in grave danger."

"What kind of preparations?" the president asked.

"He didn't elaborate," Annette said, "and I didn't explore it any further. I felt that what we had learned should be passed on, so that's when we caught the flight here to see you."

"I understand," the president said warmly. "Well, Doctor Camp . . . Doctor Moore, I want to thank you both and ask you to stay here in Washington for the next few days. If, in fact, what the professor predicts is correct, we're going to need a lot more counsel about this thing."

"Yes, of course," Annette agreed. "But, Mr. President, I have to emphasize what Dr.

Hobart told me. He recommends that all high-orbit satellites be powered down for the next several days until the solar flares are past Earth."

"But unfortunately, Doctor, that's virtually impossible," the president repeated. "Even if I decided to do that, I doubt that I could convince private industry to do so. Remember, as president I have only limited authority over the private citizens of this country and, unlike some of the previous presidents, I don't intend to expand that authority any further than the Constitution allows."

Annette responded, "I understand fully, Mr. President. I just wanted to make Doctor Hobart's recommendation clear."

"Well thank you, Doctor Camp. I do appreciate that. Doctors, we've arranged for some of our staff to escort you to Andrews Air Force Base, where we've provided facilities for you."

The meeting was adjourned and they were escorted out of the White House and into the waiting limousine.

After both scientists were out of the office, the president turned to Butts, "Warren, I want you to alert NORAD about this solar flare. I also want the people at NOAA to be aware of it. I want reports as quickly as possible on the effects of this first solar flare, specifically on how it affects our high-altitude satellites."

"Yes, Sir," Butts responded. "I'll get it done."

Glancing over to Dr. Frasier, the president said, "Doctor, I also want you to alert all the people at the NIS. I want a complete monitoring of the communication satellites throughout the world. Have your people contact all of the NATO countries. I want as much feedback on this solar flare as I can get before I make a decision."

Frasier quietly nodded in agreement.

"Thanks," the president said. "We'll get back together if and when this thing develops any further."

As they started to get up to leave, the president signaled Dean. "Stay for a second, Allen. I'd like to chat with you."

"Yes, Sir," Dean responded.

When the other group filed out, the president said, "Allen, if this thing develops as Doctor Hobart has predicted, I want you to contact him immediately."

"But, Mr. President . . . ," Dean started to say when the president cut him off.

"Allen, I know the political risks, but you and I both know I've never been one to play the odds. I'll let you know but, if I give you the signal, I want you to contact Professor Hobart and get him here to Washington. Understood?"

"Yes, Sir!" Dean said with a slight grin. He had worked with several presidents from the media side of the table. Most were percentage players — but not Houston. He was a man of conviction and, as he said, he rarely played the odds — certainly not the Washington odds. He sincerely respected Philip Houston.

At 11:13 A.M., 46 hours after the president's meeting with Drs. Camp and Moore, all the lights in the White House went off. Those people who had been working on the White House computer system watched as their terminals went blank. "Oh no, Washington power failure again," one of the secretaries muttered under her breath.

At the Oval Office, the president saw his lights blink and then go out. The lights were off for perhaps 45 to 50 seconds, and then they came back on as soon as the backup power system was functioning. The president punched the intercom, calling his personal secretary. "Mary, what happened?"

"I don't know, Mr. President," the older woman responded. "Could just be a power failure."

"Find out as soon as you can, if you would, please."

"Yes, Sir," she responded.

The president walked over to his television and flipped it on, only to discover that there was nothing but static on the screen. Apparently whatever had affected the White House power had also dropped the local cable system off the air. *Peculiar*, he thought to himself. He walked back over to his desk, pressed the intercom button and said, "Mary, get Allen on the line for me, please."

"Yes, Sir," she said. She called Allen Dean's office. He wasn't there. His secretary said he had gone down to the communications room. So she called communications, identified herself, and asked for Allen Dean. The receptionist put her on hold momentarily while she called Allen over to the telephone.

"Yeah, what's up, Mary?" Dean said.

"It's the president, Mr. Dean. Hold on please."

She connected the president's office and said, "Mr. President, Mr. Dean is on the line."

"Thanks, Mary."

"Allen, what's going on?" the president asked.

"Well, Sir, it would appear that we've had a power-grid dropout."

"How extensive?"

"It's hard to tell at this point, but the entire eastern United States grid has apparently overloaded, and we're getting similar reports from across the country. Sir, it seems to be related to the solar storm that struck the upper atmosphere. And, Mr. President . . . ,"

"Yes?" he responded.

"It would appear that we've lost at least six birds."

"Which ones?" the president responded.

"Two from the global tracking systems and at least four from our global communications link. And, Sir . . . ," Allen said in a somber tone.

"Yeah, Allen. What is it? Give it to me, bottom line."

"Apparently we're having some difficulties with the low-altitude satellites. Some of them have been knocked off-line, and others just aren't functioning properly. Apparently when this solar storm hit the ionosphere it created so much static interference that virtually all of our satellite communications were disrupted."

"What's the extent of it?" the president asked.

"Hard to tell yet, Mr. President. It's still too soon. But I would say this thing is pretty widespread. Looks like the professor called this flare right on time, and it's by far the worst interference that our people have ever seen in our satellite communications."

"Understood. Keep me informed, Allen."

"I will, Mr. President. Just as soon as we have the information, I'll pass it along."

The president leaned back in his chair. As was his custom, he propped his feet on the desk, wrapped his fingers together behind his head, and leaned way back. *Well,* he thought to himself, *maybe Dr. Hobart isn't the nut everybody's made him out to be.*

Within the hour, reports were pouring into Washington from all over the country and around the world, describing massive power dropouts. Power grids throughout the U.S. had been overloaded when the first wave of solar winds struck the ionosphere.

One of the power engineers explained to Allen Dean and Warren Butts that long electrical wires operate much like a power generator, and when strong solar winds strike Earth, the magnetic field fluctuates. The fluctuation of these magnetic lines of force across the power lines creates an electrical surge. That surge, in addition to the normal power flowing down the line, is what overloaded the circuits, causing them to drop out. He explained that because of the wide scope of this particular power outage it would take several hours, or even days, to get all of the grids back up and operating again.

In the meantime, the country was in chaos. All over Washington, D.C. the street lights were out. Hospitals were operating on backup generators, as were some of the other essential government services; but everyone else was out of power and probably would be until late that evening.

Dean gathered up as many of the reports as he thought were essential and headed for the Oval Office again. Mary ushered him right in to see the president. "He's waiting for you," she said.

As he walked in, Houston said, "Well, give me the bad news, Allen. I can see by your face that there's very little good news to go along with it."

"It's probably about as bad as it can be. We've had power-grid dropouts throughout the nation, and most of the major cities around America are without power right now, including D.C. It looks like it's going to be several hours before they get back on line."

"Well let's just pray that they get the power back up before dark," the president said. "I wouldn't want to be in this city, or any other big city, if the lights are out."

"No doubt about that," Dean agreed.

"What about communications, Allen?"

"Some communications have been reestablished. The solar storm is apparently still wreaking havoc in the atmosphere; so most of our satellite communications are either out or very undependable. Several of the high orbit satellites were fried. Our surveillance birds are still operational because they are shielded, but the transmissions are useless right now. Television networks are screaming because their satellite systems are down."

"Well, it's an ill wind that blows no good," the president said with a grin.

"Right," Dean agreed. "However, we've reestablished land-line communications, Mr. President, so most of the telephone systems are back up and operating again."

"Allen, I want you to contact Dr. Hobart, and I want him here just as soon as you can get him here."

"Yes, Sir. Understood," Dean said, without argument this time.

In his small home study, Jason knew what had happened. The first cosmic wave from the flare had struck. When the power dropped out it had been no great surprise to him. He just wondered how widespread the blackout was.

Twice he had gone into the house for something and, out of habit, had stuck a glass in the water dispenser on the refrigerator — to no avail. *Funny the habits you develop,* he thought. *No power, no ice.* He hadn't even bothered to buy any bottled water. *And I knew this might happen,* he chided himself.

He tested the phone and found it was working. *Of course,* he reasoned, *the telephone company has backup generators.* For lack of anything else to do, he went out to his observatory and just sat there, staring out at the trees and flowers. *Funny,* he thought, *the birds and bees don't even know there is a problem. It's only our artificial life that's disrupted.*

Jason was sitting at his desk when the phone rang. "Hello," he said.

"Dr. Hobart?"

"Yes it is," Jason replied with little energy. It had been a rough week thus far.

"Dr. Hobart, this is Allen Dean. I work with President Houston."

"Wh . . . wha . . . what?" Jason stuttered, trying to decide if it was somebody trying to put him on. "Who are you with?"

"I'm President Houston's press secretary," Dean responded again cordially.

Jason was taken back. *The president of the United States. Is that possible?*

"Professor?" Dean continued, "the president is interested in your theory regarding the potential solar eruption."

"What?" Jason stammered. His mind returning to his earlier conversation with Dr. Camp. "The president really is interested in what I have to say?"

"It would seem so, Professor, based on today's events," Dean said cordially. "President Houston would like to know if you can come to Washington immediately. But Professor," Dean added, "this must be totally confidential. Please don't talk to anyone, especially the press."

"I understand," Jason replied, "but that may not be too easy. I guess you've seen my interview."

"Yes, I have," Dean answered. "Well, do the best you can to avoid them. Just don't say anything about this conversation. Okay?"

"Right," Jason agreed.

"Professor, are you available to come immediately?"

"Yes," Jason responded hesitantly, "but I'm not sure exactly how I would get there. How long will I be there, and what about my daughter Wendy . . . ?"

Dean interrupted politely, "Professor, we'll set up everything for you. We already have booked you on a flight out of Chicago. The tickets for you and your daughter will be taken care of. You just need to get to O'Hare International. Your flight is American Airlines, Flight 103 to Washington Dulles Airport. Someone will meet you there. Is that clear?"

"Just a minute," Jason said, recovering his wits. "I'd really rather not fly. Would it be okay for us to take the train?"

"Take the train? It'll take you a whole day to get here by train. You can be here in two hours by air."

"Yes, but the effects of the solar flare may disrupt air travel," Jason argued.

"The airlines are fine, Professor," Dean said. "All of the essential functions are up and running, and Chicago was not hit by the power grid dropout. You should have no problems."

"Well, okay. In that case, I'll fly. Thanks!"

The president! Jason thought. *That's mind-boggling.* Putting the phone down, he went over the conversation with Dean again. *I'm not really afraid of flying,* he concluded, although he wasn't crazy about it either. Flying could become hazardous at some point during the next few days. *I'd rather not be in the air if, in fact, a major solar flare hits. It would be tough to find the way down in an airplane without navigational or communication equipment. But probably this one won't be that bad.*

He shuddered slightly as he thought about it. *Hopefully President Houston will listen,* he reasoned. *If not, a lot of people are going to be at risk when the big one hits.*

Later that afternoon President Houston called a staff meeting with Dean, Butts, and Frasier. "I want everything discussed at this meeting to be held in the strictest of confidence," Houston said. "I have invited Professor Hobart to Washington to discuss his ideas about the solar flare."

Houston could see the irritation on Frasier's face. Frasier started to speak, but Houston stopped him with a wave of his hand. "Never mind, Doctor," he said abruptly. "It's not a matter for discussion at this point. Professor Hobart is coming and we're going to listen to him and weigh what he says before I make any kind of decision."

"There's a lot of political risk in this, Mr. President," Dean reminded Houston. He knew the president had made up his mind, but it was his job to warn him one last time.

"I understand all that, Allen. We're still going to talk to the professor. Just try to keep this thing as quiet as possible."

"You know Washington," Dean responded. "As soon as Hobart picks up his tickets, I'll guarantee you the press will be on top of it."

"If they are, they are," Houston said. "In the meantime, Allen, I want you to do some investigation. Get Doctors Camp and Moore over here for our meeting."

"Mr. President, I don't think that's necessary," Frasier interrupted.

"If I say it is, then it is, Doctor," Houston snapped back. "I want some objective feedback."

Frasier bit his lip, trying to keep his anger from showing. *Don't get mad; get even,* he reminded himself silently. "I understand completely, Mr. President," he replied as politely as his dark mood would allow.

"What time will Professor Hobart be here?" the president asked Dean.

"He should be here in about eight hours," Dean replied with a frown on his face.

"Is there a problem?" Houston asked.

"Probably not, but the professor thinks that the solar flare could disrupt air traffic, and he was a little shaky about getting on an airplane right now. He's a little strange, I'd say."

Houston thought about that for a second; then he chuckled, "Well let me ask you this Allen. If you thought he was right, would you get on a plane and fly to Chicago?"

Dean paused, "When you put it that way, maybe not."

"Okay," Houston said, "that settles it. We'll wait for Professor Hobart and I want the other scientists available also. I want this to be a fair and impartial evaluation. Understood?"

"Understood," Frasier muttered under his breath.

7

When Jason put the telephone down his heart was racing. *Washington! The president!* Then he paused. *Am I being set up again? Is this just going to be one more fiasco?* Then he shrugged. *It can't get much worse. I've lost my job, and I have no prospects for the future. What have I got to lose?*

If Jason Hobart had been able to see into the future, he might have stopped and questioned more carefully what he had to lose. Instead, he threw on his jacket, grabbed his keys off the desk, and headed out the door. He was going to see his favorite person: Wendy. *She'll be thrilled!*

True to its unpredictable nature, when Jason turned the key the old Volvo just went *click*. "Come on," Jason pleaded, "give me a break." He turned the key again: nothing. Just a click, click, click. "Now what?" Jason said aloud.

Getting out of the car, he slammed the door and gave the old Volvo a firm, but loving, kick on the side of the door. The scuff mark he left perfectly matched the dozens of others that testified of previous frustrations. He was pondering what to do when a little two-door red Toyota turned into the driveway. The booming music was nearly deafening — even where Jason stood. The passenger door opened, and when Wendy stepped out the sound level rose another 20 decibels.

"Hi, Daddy," she yelled over the loud music. "Where you going?"

"I was just coming to see you. What are *you* doing home?"

"Nothing going on since the power failed earlier. We've just been hanging out. The principal sent everyone home for the day. Besides, I can't stand to hear the other kids ridicule you. They're all talking about the interview."

Jason started to shout that he was sorry, but he stopped. Instead, he had some exciting news about the president's inquiry.

"Thanks for the ride, Sarah," Wendy said as she slammed the door, closing out some of the sound.

"Is that Sarah Bower?" Jason asked his daughter as the Toyota backed out of the driveway.

"Yes."

"Since when is she driving?" Jason asked.

"Dad—dy," Wendy replied with a look of chagrin on her face. "Sarah's been 16 now for almost a year. She's got her own car."

"Well, she'll need a hearing aid if she keeps playing that music so loud."

"Oh, that's not loud. Anyway, what's up, Daddy?" Wendy asked with a grin. "Heard anything from Aunt Karen?"

"No, haven't heard a thing," Jason said with an unexpected sense of relief. "But I know she'll call when she gets things sorted out."

"Yeah, right!" Wendy said in undisguised relief. "What's up?"

"Honey, you're not going to believe this," Jason exclaimed as he hugged his daughter tightly. "I just got a call from the president's office."

"You mean the president of the college? What did he want?"

"No, I mean the president of the United States."

"Right, Daddy," Wendy said sarcastically, rolling her eyes. "And they want you to be secretary of state. Right?"

"No, really, Honey. I got a call from Allen Dean in the president's office — he's the president's press secretary — and they want both of us to come to Washington immediately. In fact, we're leaving this afternoon."

"No way!" she said, knowing her dad was prone to kid her.

"I'm very serious, Honey."

"What do they want?" she asked in a more cautious tone.

"Mr. Dean said the president wants to hear my theory on solar eruptions."

"Daddy, you know how that went before. What makes you think the president will care one way or another? Is it possible this is a setup — just to get you there?"

"That's always possible, but I have to go. They have tickets for us. We're leaving out of Chicago today."

"Well, okay," Wendy said more enthusiastically. "But we're not going to Chicago in your old heap, are we? Let's rent a car. Okay, Dad?"

When Jason thought about it for a minute, his spirits perked up. "You know what, Honey? You're absolutely right. We'll go in style."

Outside the president's office, a heated discussion was taking place between Allen Dean and Dr. Robert Frasier.

"The man is not competent to give counsel to the president of the United States," Frasier argued. "If the president wants information on solar flares, there are many more eminent scientists around the world who could provide that counsel," he shouted.

"Doctor," Dean said with finality in his voice, "the reason we're bringing Professor Hobart to the White House is that the president ordered it. It's not a subject for discussion any further."

"Calm down," Houston commanded the two men, stepping into the hall after overhearing the conversation. "Doctor, I appreciate your perspective on Professor Hobart, but

I've read the reports from Doctor Camp and she's convinced the man has a valid theory. Certainly his ideas are worthy of discussion."

Frasier didn't say anything further, but he was seething as he clenched and unclenched his fists.

Dean wasn't convinced that bringing Professor Hobart to the White House was a good idea either, but he wasn't about to let the arrogant Frasier off the hook at this point.

"Doctor, maybe a scientist from a little town in Illinois might have some fresh ideas," he quipped. "After all, all we've gotten out of the National Institute so far is a lot of mumbo-jumbo." Frasier shot a dagger-like stare over at Dean, but he held his tongue. The decision was made. He'll have his shot, once Hobart had been heard by the president.

"I just hope both of you know what you're doing," Frasier said as he stuffed some papers into his briefcase. "Hobart has been thoroughly discredited by the scientific community, and relying on him for information is very ill-advised."

"Your counsel is appreciated, Doctor," the president said with a note of irritation, "but as Harry Truman once said, 'The buck stops here.' It's my responsibility and with the lives of nearly 300 million people on the line, I'm going to take all the counsel I can get."

"Allen, block out two hours for the meeting when Professor Hobart arrives."

Wow! Dean thought. *Two hours! He's really serious about this solar flare thing!*

Jason and Wendy packed their bags and were on their way to Chicago in little more than an hour. They had taken a taxi to the rental agency, where Jason had rented a car. He was marveling at the way it handled. "This thing's got a lotta pep," he quipped as he passed another car on the interstate.

"Daddy, anything would have pep compared to the old Volvo 'tank.' After all, technology has advanced over the last 20 years or so."

"Yeah, I guess that's right, Honey." Jason sighed. "But mine's all paid for, and you know what they say, 'The cheapest car to drive is the one you're driving.'"

"Sure," Wendy answered with a smile, "but they also say, 'It's a wise man who knows when to quit.'"

"Goodness, I can't believe the traffic," Jason commented as they approached the city. "I'll bet half the people in Chicago are on the streets."

"Probably so, Daddy, but maybe you just need to get out more often. After all, Rockford is not the center of the universe."

"You're probably right," Jason muttered, slowing as a car cut in front of him. "But we also don't have this kind of traffic." Driving in on Interstate 90, Jason began looking for the signs that would direct him to O'Hare. "Wouldn't you know it?" he grumbled as he began to maneuver the car from the far left lane over to the far right. As he did so, there was a chorus of honking horns behind him.

"Dad—dy! Watch out! You're going to get us killed!" Wendy exclaimed.

"Did you see what that sign said, Honey?" Jason asked, trying to miss the buses and automobiles that were merging into his lane.

"Yes, it said American Airlines, gates A through C. Stay in this lane and we'll be okay."

"Right," Jason said with a sigh of relief as he slowed down to enter the parking lot. "Wow," he said. "I'd sure hate to go through this very often. Can you imagine the people who fly in and out of O'Hare every day?"

"No, I can't," Wendy agreed. "I think I like Rockford better."

Jason pulled up to the automated attendant, pressed the button, and the machine spit out a ticket. As he retrieved the ticket, the bar raised and he drove into the parking area. Locating the nearest empty space, he killed the engine and consciously relaxed.

"Well, phase one. Made it alive," he sighed.

"Just barely," Wendy quipped. "I'm driving back, Daddy."

"Worrywart," Jason teased, as he unlocked the trunk. "Admit it! Your old Dad's a pretty good driver."

"Only if you didn't observe traffic from my side," Wendy said, holding out her hand and feigning a nervous shake.

"Coward!" Jason chuckled, grabbing their bags and slamming the trunk shut. They hurried toward the entrance and made their way through the various counters, locating the American Airlines reservation counter.

After a 10-minute wait in line, they made it to the counter. "Do you have reserved tickets for Doctor Jason Hobart and Wendy Hobart?" he asked the young woman.

"One second, Sir," she said as she tapped lightly on the keys of her computer terminal. "Yes, we do, Doctor Hobart. Your tickets have been prepaid."

Although their flight was delayed two hours, once they were airborne the flight from Chicago to Washington was uneventful, until they reached the D.C. traffic control area. Jason sensed the big plane beginning a slow arc to the left.

"Ladies and gentlemen, we have just been informed by Washington Air Traffic Control that all flights in and out of the airport must observe visual flight rules due to a previous power outage," the captain announced. Then he added, "What it really means, folks, is that the traffic control system is screwed up and we'll be at least another 30 minutes getting clearance to land."

So the power grid problem is widespread, Jason

137

thought. *That's not a good sign.*

As it turned out, the delay was slightly less than the predicted 30 minutes. With many cities still without power and most flights either canceled or delayed, the air traffic was exceptionally light.

It was nearly 7:00 P.M. when the big plane thumped down on the runway.

When they deplaned, there was no doubt about who their escorts were. Waiting for them at the end of the passenger ramp were two somber-looking men in dark suits. The earpieces with the curly wires coming out of them clearly bespoke of Secret Service.

Also waiting for them were several reporters with their camera crews. Although they had not caught up with them in Chicago, the news had leaked out by the time Jason arrived in D.C.

"Professor, I understand that President Houston sent for you. Is that correct?" one of the reporters yelled above the group noise.

"No comment," one of the Secret Service men said for Jason as he pushed their way through the crowd.

"What are you going to tell the president?" another shouted.

By that time they were in the hallway, where an electric shuttle car picked up Jason, Wendy, and the two security men. They sped away to the shouts of irritated reporters left behind.

"Whew!" Wendy said. "I'll bet they can get hostile."

"You bet," the big Secret Service man who identified himself as C.C. agreed.

When they stopped at ground transportation, their bags were already waiting. "Follow me, please," C.C. said firmly but politely. Wendy fell in behind Jason and the second Secret Service agent fell in behind Wendy.

Wow! Wendy thought to herself, *Just like on TV!*

When the pneumatic doors sprung open, the big limo was waiting at the curb. The first agent moved to the back of the limo and opened the door. Without verbalizing, his mannerism said, "Get in."

Jason paused to let Wendy pass in front of him and climb into the back seat; then he climbed in beside her. As the door shut, the opposite side door opened and the two Secret Service men climbed into the seat facing them. The driver dropped the car into gear and they were on their way.

As they traveled through the city, Wendy began recognizing some of the landmarks. "Look, Daddy. There's the Lincoln Memorial!"

"Right, Honey. I wish we had time to see some of the city."

"It's okay. We're going to see the White House — from the inside. Not many people get to do that," she added with her usual optimism.

Most of the power had been restored to the D.C. area, but traffic was still stop-and-go, as city workers tried to make their way to the suburbs. The limo driver knew the back streets well and avoided much of the heavier traffic.

As they turned onto Pennsylvania Avenue, Jason got his first glimpse of the White House. He'd been there before, but it had been many years earlier, and at the time he was just one of the thousands of tourists standing outside the big iron gates, peering at the house where the president lived.

Now here he was, in a government limo pulling up to those big iron gates. The gate guard checked the driver's credentials, then pressed a button, allowing the bomb-proof gates to roll back. The limo sped inside and, in spite of himself, Jason couldn't help looking back to see the big iron gates rolling shut once more. They were inside the president's compound now. *Just think, I, Jason Hobart, have a meeting with the president of the United States!* Suddenly his old insecurities resurfaced.

The president . . . and we're going to talk about my solar flare theory, he thought. *What if I'm wrong? What if this is all another wild goose chase — another false alarm?*

As if reading his thoughts, Wendy reached

over and squeezed his hand. "Daddy, you're the best solar physicist in the world and I've got confidence in you. It's going to be okay."

Jason could have hugged his daughter. She always knew exactly what to say and when. Wendy knew him well. His fears subsided and his confidence began to rise again. Was he absolutely certain he was right? No, nobody could be absolutely sure, but all the signs pointed to a looming disaster and the consequences of doing nothing would be disastrous.

For better or worse, here he was — Professor Jason Hobart from Rockford, Illinois — driving up to the White House entrance. It was nearly dark and when they stepped out of the limo Wendy exclaimed, "What is that?" pointing toward the darkening horizon. In the sky overhead were streaks of red, blue, and purple. Vivid flashes illumined the moonless sky.

"Wow!" C.C. said.

"That is the aurora borealis," Jason said. "The northern lights."

"Over Washington?" C.C. asked.

"It's part of the solar flare that caused the power outages," Jason explained.

"Well, we'd better get you inside," C.C. declared, "or the president will light up just like that sky," he chuckled.

As soon as they were inside, C.C. said, "I'm to take you to the Oval Office. Would you like to freshen up first?" he asked Wendy.

"No, I'm fine," Wendy replied. She wasn't about to miss anything.

"I'd like to use the men's room," Jason said. His nerves were so on edge that he felt like his bladder might let go at any time.

"This way," C.C. said and headed down the hall. "There's a men's room right here," and pointing to the next door, "the ladies' room is right there."

"Thanks. Maybe I will go comb my hair," Wendy said.

A few minutes later, Jason emerged feeling quite relieved, at least physically. Mentally he was still in a state of turmoil. *The president of the United States . . . ,* he kept saying to himself silently. Then he reminded himself, *Well, done's done. I'm here. Let's make the best of it.*

Wendy came walking up to Jason with a big smile. She was feeling lots of butterflies in the pit of her stomach now that they were actually going in to see the president.

"I'll need my briefcase," Jason said to C.C.

"Of course," he replied. "It will be in the waiting room when you get to the Oval Office."

They were led down the hall toward the elevator. Stepping into the elevator, C.C. punched the single white button and Jason realized that this elevator was used only for the president's personal guests. When it stopped and the door opened, they were staring at what was obviously another Secret Service agent.

The man said hospitably, "Professor Hobart . . . Miss Hobart, glad to see you. The president's waiting."

"I'll need my briefcase," Jason repeated.

The other man responded, "Certainly." He reached down by his side and handed it to Jason. "I took the liberty of opening it, Sir, to verify the contents."

Jason hadn't even thought about it, but obviously everything that came in and out of the White House would be searched.

"No problem," he said, taking the briefcase. Then he and Wendy headed toward the open door where C.C. was standing.

As they entered the room, they saw four men and a woman seated at the table. One of the men rose and walked over to offer his hand. "Hi, Professor. I'm Allen Dean, press secretary to President Houston. Hi, Wendy," he said very casually, as if her being there were the most natural thing on earth.

Jason and Wendy glanced at each other with one of those "wow" looks, and Wendy decided that Allen Dean was as handsome as he was polite.

"Wendy, you're more than welcome to wait in the outer lobby and we'll provide you with a tour of the White House while your father's in the meeting," he offered cordially.

"No, thank you," she said. "I'm here to be

with my father and I'd like to stay with him, if it's okay."

"I'm sorry," Dean said more formally, "but it won't be possible for you to attend the meeting." Wendy had a dejected look on her face and Jason started to intercede when Dean added, "I'm sorry, Professor, but it's the president's policy and I can't do anything about it. You're welcome to take it up with President Houston, if you'd like."

"No, that won't be necessary," Jason said, glancing over at Wendy. "I'm sorry, Honey, but rules are rules I guess."

"I understand, Daddy. I'll be fine. You just take care of yourself and tell it like it is!"

"I will, Honey. Thanks! I love you."

C.C. escorted Wendy from the room, closing the door behind them.

Dean said, "Professor, I'd like to introduce you. This is Mr. Warren Butts, the president's chief of staff." Butts stood up, offered his hand, and Jason shook it. "This is Dr. Gene Moore, a scientific advisor." The smallish man with a balding head stood up and offered his hand.

"And this is Dr. Annette Camp."

Jason put his hand out to shake Annette Camp's hand and said, "Are you the Dr. Camp of Palo Alto Observatory?" Jason was struck by two impressions: how strikingly beautiful Annette Camp was and how warm and friendly her eyes seemed. For a woman in her mid-30s, she looked more like 25. Her auburn hair was still without any gray, and her glowing skin was smooth and unblemished. Then he realized he had not released her hand and he suddenly let go, fearing his face might be as red as it felt.

"Yes, I am," she said, amused at his obvious discomfort. *Well, it's been a while since I've had that effect on anyone,* she thought.

"I appreciated your call," Jason said, recovering his composure. "I assume I'm here because of your recommendation. Thank you."

"You're welcome, Professor," Annette said with just the slightest grin showing through her expression.

"These last two gentlemen are General Floyd Boland, chairman of the Joint Chiefs of Staff, and Dr. Robert Frasier, the head of the National Institute of Sciences."

"Glad to meet you," Jason said, extending his hand to each of the men. "I'm honored to be a part of this group."

Gen. Boland spoke. "We're glad to have you here, Doctor. I've reviewed your work and think it's very interesting."

Jason felt the sincerity in the man's attitude as he shook his hand, and although his response was reserved that was to be expected. However, a glance at Dr. Frasier told him that he could expect no cordiality from the head of the NIS. Frasier wore a scowl on his face that told Jason he was definitely not an ally. He also didn't extend his hand.

"I believe that's everybody," Dean said. "Why don't we sit down."

They had no more than sat down when the door leading into the Oval Office opened and in walked the president.

Jason and the others stood. "Sit down, please," Houston said with his usual informality. "Make yourselves comfortable." Instantly Jason knew that he liked Houston. *If ever a man could be called a born leader,* he decided, *he certainly fits the description.*

The president extended his hand and said, "Welcome to Washington, Professor."

Jason mumbled a thank you and shook the president's hand.

"Let's get started, Warren," the president said as he nodded toward his chief of staff.

As he did so, Butts lifted the cover of the folder sitting in front of him marked "Most Secret."

Butts began to speak. "Mr. President, I have the FBI file on Professor Jason Hobart. I've reviewed it thoroughly and I have to be very honest with you and Dr. Hobart when I say that I have some reservations about his qualifications."

"I know all about that," Houston said with a wave of his hand. "I've read the file too, Warren, but I want to give the professor every courtesy. According to Doctors Camp and Moore, several other eminent scientists share

146

a concern about the potential dangers of a solar flare. Is that correct, Allen?" the president asked his press secretary.

"Yes, Sir," Dean replied without further elaboration. He knew Houston's style; he preferred only the facts.

Jason glanced over at Frasier and was startled by his glare. His face reflected pure hatred. Not knowing the man, Jason could only guess that his hostility had something to do with White House politics. He was very familiar with politics; Rockford College was replete with politics. He could only assume that in Washington it was infinitely worse.

Frasier's expression was not lost on Houston either. He knew the head of the NIS was irritated that Dr. Hobart was in Washington. Almost imperceptibly Houston shrugged. *He's willing to risk the lives of millions of innocent people, rather than swallow his pride. How do these people live with themselves?* he wondered. He knew he couldn't. *Well, we'll see, Doctor.*

"Professor Hobart, share your theory with us, if you would, please," Houston said, settling back in his chair. "I think we have all seen the evidence of the first flare."

Boy, you can say that again, Allen Dean thought. The whole National Security Network was still down. He and the president had been standing at the window earlier, taking in the nighttime display. Unbelievable! He

147

knew the professor had the president's undivided attention.

As soon as the president placed his interlocked fingers behind his head, Dean broke out in a big grin. He was glad to see the president had also picked up on Frasier's foul mood. Dean's grin helped Jason immensely. Before that he was afraid that if he stood up his legs would buckle under him.

Pushing his chair back a little, Jason reached down and retrieved the package of statistical data from his briefcase and laid it on the table. It contained all the detail on area 403. He was just about to hand the information to the president when, in one of those periodic strokes of genius that hit people, he caught himself and said, "Mr. President, I have all the statistical data backing up my theory and, if you would like, I'll provide that material to your experts. However, it's also been made available on the Internet, and I'm sure most of them have access to it. So, rather than bore you with the minutiae, I'd like to ask you a question instead."

"Fire away," Houston said. "This is an open meeting, not an inquisition. You ask anything you want, and I'd like to reserve the right to do the same."

"Please do, Mr. President," Jason said. *Yes, I definitely like this man,* he decided.

Houston had already sized up the professor as being a straight shooter, and Houston liked that. He wasn't from Washington, and that was definitely in his favor. And he had listened in when the professor and his daughter had first come in. *I trust people whose kids trust them. That's a good sign.*

"Sir, I'd like to know how much you really understand about solar flares and the theory behind them."

Houston was caught off-guard and he paused for a moment, the wheels in his mind turning. He replied, "You know, actually, Professor, I don't know a whole lot. Lately I've heard discussions about the effects of flares disrupting communications and such, but I guess I don't know a lot about them."

"Well, with your permission, Mr. President, I'd like to give you a brief course in solar flares, because I think it's essential to understanding the theory that I propose and the imminency of the problem."

Frasier started to object but Houston silenced him with a sweep of his hand. "Let's hear about solar flares." Houston said, shifting forward in his chair.

"Well, Mr. President," Jason began, slipping easily into his teacher role, "solar flares have been around a long time. In fact, they've been around as long as the universe. In the past, outside of the obvious manifestations, such as the northern lights, they've been pretty much ignored — mostly because they didn't affect the lives of the people on Earth a great deal. Or, if they did, nobody understood what the effect was. However, over the last century, with the development of modern communications, and certainly over the last half century, with the development of satellites and intercontinental air travel, solar flares have come under intense scrutiny because they do affect our lives now.

"Solar flares are actually huge gas bubbles that develop on the Sun's surface — or corona. When these bubbles pop, so to speak, they throw out streams of charged particles into space. The bubbles are developed during geomagnetic storms on the Sun. During these storms, the Sun spews out enormous streams of supercharged plasma. When the plasma streams are large enough, they're actually visible to the naked eye. In 1872 one eruption extended almost a million miles into space."

Jason glanced over at Dr. Frasier, who rolled his eyes, as if to say "This is kid's talk," but Jason knew, as a teacher, that it was important to make it simple for people who weren't into science and he knew not to presume anything. So he continued.

"These big streams of plasma are ejected at extremely high speeds — speeds up to a million miles an hour or more, and when they strike our planet they push charged cosmic particles through Earth's magnetosphere with an unusual amount of force. During solar maximals, when the Sun is the most active, these streams come from openings in the Sun's magnetic field called coronal holes. Gas spews out of these holes like water from a fire hydrant, and if that hose happens to be pointed at Earth, the planet is showered with tremendous magnetic particle storms. It is my belief that plasma from one of these coronal holes, designated area 403, crippled two communications satellites in the mid-1990s and more recently in the latest storm to hit Earth."

Jason could see the attentive look on Houston's face. Clearly, no one on his staff had made the effort to explain solar flares to him. Houston shot a glance at Frasier. Frasier quickly looked away.

"Well," Jason continued, "in the mid-1990s the Japanese launched the solar heliospheric observatory, or the SOHO satellite. This satellite's function is to take digital pictures of solar eruptions so that we can have better information about geomagnetic storms — or solar flares.

"The danger from a geomagnetic storm is heightened during a maximal period, such as we are in now. Billions of tons of plasma can explode from the surface of the Sun like guided missiles hurtling their way toward Earth. If the total mass of these plasma storms is great enough, Earth's magnetosphere can be contracted. In other words, Earth's magnetic shield is bombarded with such force that it bends and shifts.

"It's important to remember that major eruptions occur during these cyclical maximal periods of the Sun, but once every nine maximal periods we have a *super* maximal period. According to Dr. Carrington's calculations, we are now approaching such a time and there is a danger of severe communications disruption on Earth during this period — or worse."

"What do you mean, 'or worse'?" the president asked.

"In my opinion, spacecraft in near-Earth orbits, as well as high flying aircraft, are in danger. Theoretically, when these cosmic storms hit the magnetosphere and it contracts, these aircraft will be exposed to high energy protons. A direct hit by these protons could conceivably disable our space shuttles and the near-Earth space labs. If we have a solar flare large enough to actually collapse the magnetosphere, it is conceivable that high-flying aircraft could also be damaged or disabled."

"Are you saying that people in airliners could be in danger?" the president asked, sitting upright. He didn't know what he had expected from the mild-mannered professor, but it was not what he was hearing. Jason Hobart was certainly no fool and he believed what he was saying. That much was clear.

"Nobody really knows, Mr. President, including me. But, in my opinion, based on

Dr. Carrington's calculations, it is conceivable that Earth's magnetosphere could collapse during an extremely violent magnetic storm. In fact it was Dr. Carrington's belief that this actually happened back in 1872. If it happened today, Sir, it would have catastrophic consequences."

"But we don't know that," Frasier responded brusquely, "and, let me remind you that Doctor Carrington's theories are by no means accepted by scientists today."

"I've heard your opinion, Doctor!" Houston snapped. "I'd like to hear the professor's now."

Frasier plopped back in his seat, closed his eyes, and leaned his head against the back of the chair; but the scowl on his face clearly revealed his attitude.

"Well, Mr. President," Jason continued, "the most violent storms of all occur when, upon rare occasion, the sun's magnetic field connects with Earth's magnetic field. If this happens, it's like a giant funnel is created between the Sun and the Earth that channels huge quantities of plasma into our atmosphere. This is an extremely rare occurrence that takes place only when a whole series of events occur at one time.

"First, Earth is in its apogee — or closest point to the sun. Second, Earth is directly over a coronal hole in the Sun. And third, an eruption occurs at precisely that time. As of now, two of the three are in place.

"If we have a major solar flare between now and the next several weeks, massive quantities of charged ions would surge through the high altitudes of our atmosphere, basically blocking broadcast signals and other forms of communications — destroying sensitive electronic equipment. Understand, we're talking about billions of tons of charged particles moving at a million miles per hour. Without Earth's magnetosphere protecting us, we would be totally defenseless during this period of time.

"And, Mr. President, in my judgment it appears that area 403 is getting ready for this kind of an eruption."

"Are you saying, Professor, that you believe a solar flare of the magnitude you just described is now imminent?"

"Yes, I do," Jason said with as much confidence as his weak legs would allow. "I've run the calculations numerous times, and I still come back to the same basic conclusion: The stage is set for a massive solar eruption."

"Didn't you also predict such an eruption once before, Professor?" Frasier asked sharply. "And weren't you proved wrong then?"

"Yes," Jason admitted, glancing downward. "And I'm well aware that nothing in solar physics is a certainty, but this situation is classic according to Dr. Carrington's theory . . ."

Frasier interrupted, "A theory never proved

and generally discounted in the scientific community."

"Yes, but . . ." Jason sputtered, losing his poise a little.

"But, nothing!" Frasier spat out. He started to say more but the president stopped him again.

"That's enough! Sit down and shut up, Robert!" Houston commanded with uncharacteristic anger.

Frasier stopped, surprised, but with a look that could kill. He thought about storming out of the meeting with a dramatic flare, but common sense told him to stay put — for the time being.

Jason continued. "Dr. Frasier could well be right, Mr. President. I wish I could tell you absolutely at this point. It's possible that area 403 will not erupt, but I believe it will and, in doing so, will create widespread chaos throughout the earth. I believe it will disrupt communications and celestial navigation and will pose a danger to commercial aviation: a potential danger that is too great to ignore."

"And what would you have us do, as a result of this?" Houston asked bluntly.

"Sir, until we know if an eruption will occur, I would ground all aircraft — commercial, military, and private — and call the leaders of every major nation in the world and ask them to do the same thing. And at the first sign of an eruption I would be ready to power down all electric equipment, including all satellites during daylight hours."

"For what period of time, Doctor?" Houston asked incredulously.

"It's hard to say, not knowing the magnitude of this eruption. I would say for not less than a week — perhaps longer."

"Shut down all power and ground every aircraft on Earth for two weeks?" Houston repeated, leaning forward in his chair. "Are you serious, Doctor?"

A smirk developed on Frasier's face. He knew that Hobart was losing the president. *Shut down all industry for weeks? Madness,* he thought angrily.

"Well, Mr. President, I can only tell you what I believe. In my opinion, it is imperative to be ready. You will have less than three days warning."

8

"Well, Professor, you've certainly given us something to think about," President Houston said, rising from his chair and extending his hand.

"Sorry to be the bearer of bad tidings, Sir," Jason responded humbly.

"That's okay," Houston said with a slight shrug of his shoulders. "Better to be honest. Honesty seems to be a lost art in this city. Thank you, Professor. I assure you, I *will* think on what you have said."

"Thank you, Sir," Jason said. He turned and followed C.C., who had opened the door in response to an unseen signal.

Once Jason was out of the room, the president motioned to the others to sit back down. Glancing around the room, he could read the expressions on almost every face. If he had to put it into words he would have said "discomfort" or "disbelief."

There were only two exceptions. One was Frasier; he had a smirk on his face. Houston could only guess what was going through Frasier's mind, but he doubted it would be good for either the nation or for his administration. The other person who had a different expression was Annette Camp.

Houston prided himself on being able to read people. More than once it had helped him to avoid the traps liberals tried to set for him. Reporters were keenly aware of his discernment when they asked him leading questions.

He decided that Dr. Camp was an intelligent woman and also a straight shooter. Her report had been clear and precise and had shot holes in Frasier's obsession to use rocket-launched nukes on the asteroid. It was clear that she had formed a definitive opinion of Professor Hobart.

Houston said, "Dr. Camp, give me your evaluation of Dr. Hobart and his theory."

Gene Moore showed ever so slight a grin on his face. The president was pretty astute. If there were one scientist in the room who would give a totally objective opinion, no matter what the circumstance, it would be Annette Camp. Houston apparently had sensed it too.

Annette hesitated, choosing her words carefully.

"Doctor Camp," the president said looking directly at her, "bottom line . . . give me your opinion."

Somehow Annette had been expecting the question. She had already seen that the president's method was to be very straightforward and direct. She had been pondering in her own mind what Professor Hobart had said. *What is my opinion? I'm not totally sure.* She decided that with President Houston it would be far better to be totally honest.

"Well, Mr. President, honestly, I don't know. I'm confused. One side of me says that what Professor Hobart outlined here could not possibly happen — that it's beyond the imagination to think that a major solar eruption on the Sun, regardless of the magnitude, could wreak such havoc. I can accept that it would interrupt communications, because we've seen that before, but there's nothing in my background that would suggest that such a solar eruption would pose a serious threat to air travelers, astronauts, the space lab, and even destroy land-based electronic installations."

Dr. Frasier, picking up on Dr. Camp's negative comments, saw his opportunity to speak. "It's madness! The man's a lunatic!"

With an icy stare, Houston silenced Frasier once more and the disgruntled head of the NIS slumped back into his chair in a pout.

"Let me hasten to say, however," Annette continued, "that Dr. Hobart is not a lunatic; nor is he mad. I've reviewed his most recent work and also that from his earlier prediction, and I can tell you that it is brilliant. Just because he was wrong once is no reason to discredit him, Mr. President. Who among us has not been wrong?"

"That's for sure," Houston said. "Well, it's a dilemma. If he's right and I do nothing, I could endanger the lives of thousands, perhaps millions of people. On the other hand, if he's wrong and I ground all the airplanes and shut down our industry, I'll be the laughingstock of the world, and mine would be the shortest administration since Richard Nixon's second term," Houston chuckled. Then, turning serious, he asked, "What's your advice, Doctor?"

Annette said nothing for a good 30 seconds. Then she took a deep breath. "Well, Sir, in good conscience I could not advise you to ground all the aircraft in America, but I would advise you to notify NASA of the potential danger, and I would suggest you remove the Sky Lab personnel and ground the space shuttle until this danger is over."

Frasier bolted upright in his chair, "What? Evacuate the Sky Lab and ground the space shuttle? That's crazy!" he shouted at Houston. "We'll be the laughing stock of the scientific community if you do that!"

Houston hardly glanced in Frasier's direction. Instead, he smiled at Annette and said, "Doctors, I want to thank you for your help. I know you have come a long way and I sincerely appreciate it. If you don't mind, I need to meet with my staff for a while. I'd like for you both to be my guests in Washington for a few days, if you can."

Both scientists nodded in agreement as the door opened and C.C. appeared again, as if by magic. Once they had left the room Houston motioned to his chief of staff and asked, "Warren, what do you think?" Houston knew his old friend would have come to the meeting well prepared. He wasn't a scientist, but in his former role as CEO of Packard-Bell he would have many contacts in the scientific community.

"Well, Sir," Butts began carefully, "I wish we had more scientific evidence one way or the other. I've checked with some friends and I have to be honest when I say that sentiment is running about 9 to 1 against Dr. Hobart. Most of them aren't really familiar with his work and, therefore, what input they had came from scientific articles and newsletter clippings that we dredged up from the Internet. But I had an old friend, Dr. Cooper, the current head of the Hubble deep space project, review the professor's data, and he thinks it's top drawer."

"Bottom line, Warren," Houston said, resting his chin on his hand in his characteristic "thinker" pose.

"Boy . . . bottom line," Butts muttered, thinking out loud. "The bottom line, Sir: I guess I would probably evacuate the Sky Lab and ground the space shuttles. If you don't, and Hobart is right, those people will have no chance."

"Madness!" Frasier shouted dramatically. "Don't listen to him! This is madness!"

"That's enough, Doctor!" Houston said between gritted teeth. He plopped back in his chair, trying to weigh what he had heard. Nobody said anything.

Dean spoke up. "Mr. President, the politically safe thing to do is nothing. Dr. Hobart does not have the general support of the scientific community and it would certainly be within the privy of the president to ignore his counsel and go with the majority opinion."

"I know that would be the politically safe thing to do," Houston agreed. "But, somewhere in my gut I have this nagging feeling that Dr. Hobart makes sense."

Houston said, "Warren, I want a report on my desk by 0800, detailing how long it would take to evacuate the Sky Lab; and, after that's accomplished, I want all the shuttles grounded until further notice."

"Right," Butts responded with a sigh of relief. He knew that in a similar situation a lesser man might not have made the same decision. The politically correct decision would have been to do nothing and let the astronauts take the risks. He respected Houston more now than ever before in his life.

"This meeting is adjourned," the president said, pushing his chair back. Without waiting for a response, he strode out of the room. As soon as he was gone, the room was abuzz again.

Frasier glared at Butts. "I can't believe you would support the position of this hick professor from a no-name college."

"Well, I have to be honest with you," Butts responded with the contempt he was feeling. "I just happen to believe that hick professor from the no-name college is a whole lot smarter than you." He added mentally, *And that wouldn't take a lot.* "I don't know if his theory is correct or not, but I do know that if I were an astronaut I would want a president exactly like the one we have: who will do what's right and not what's politically expedient."

"Like the president we had . . ." Frasier muttered, slamming the papers into his briefcase. "Like the president we had!" and he stormed out of the room.

After leaving the meeting, Frasier went back over to the National Institute building. The staff still at work could tell when he entered the office that he was in a foul mood. Nobody said anything to him as he headed into his office. He slammed the door and dropped the blinds.

Insane! he muttered to himself. *Completely insane! Time to make some changes,* he decided. Picking up the phone, he made a call to Neil Farmer at WNN.

Farmer was still in his office, going over data for a special on how the ever-growing conservative movement in America was sacrificing the well-being of children in the inner cities. Welfare mothers, who once could count on the government to help them with their children, were now being forced to accept low-paying jobs, leaving the children abandoned to the streets of every major metropolitan city in America. This was something that Farmer felt passionate about. Society had created these kids and now society was abandoning them. He was irritated when the phone rang. He punched the button with the flashing light and snapped, "Yeah, Farmer here."

"Neil? It's Frasier," Frasier said, almost whispering into the mouthpiece.

"Oh yeah, Doctor. What's up?" Farmer replied in a more civil tone. Frasier had been a good source of inside information. He didn't know why Houston kept him on as head of the NIS. Personally, he couldn't stand the little wimp, but that was one of Houston's downfalls: he believed in loyalty — giving the benefit of the doubt.

"The president believed Hobart," Frasier said disgustedly. "He's planning to evacuate the Sky Lab and ground all the space shuttles for at least the next two to three weeks."

"Great!" Farmer nearly shouted into the mouthpiece.

"There's something else," Frasier growled. "That nutty professor told the president that he should ground all the commercial aircraft in America and recommend to the rest of the world that they should follow suit."

"Unbelievable!" Farmer exclaimed. "Is he going to do it?"

"No, I don't think so — at least not right now," Frasier said, in a little bit better spirits now. He had an ally on the other end of the line who could really wring the tail of this president.

"Although he believed Hobart, apparently he's not willing to go that far."

"Give the guy credit for a little common sense," Farmer said sarcastically.

"Doctor, can you tell me who was at the meeting?"

"I'd really rather not," Frasier said pointedly. "If word of this leaks back to the president, he'll know where the information came from."

"Listen, Doctor, you know that's inevitable, because once I publish this story, the president is probably going to be on your case anyway."

"Understood," Frasier said, "but, somebody has to stop this madness. And I think, once the word gets out, Houston is going to have a hard time retaining the confidence of the American people."

Frasier decided to put it all on the line.

"The meeting was attended by both the president's personal advisory staff and by two members of the scientific community, Doctors Annette Camp and Gene Moore."

"What was their advice to the president?"

"Well, Dr. Camp, who by the way is a junior member of the scientific community, having only recently received her doctorate in physics, recommended to the president that he follow Hobart's counsel, even though she admitted that he erroneously predicted the same kind of a solar eruption previously."

"Thanks, Doctor, but I'll do the byline to the story. We've got all the information on Dr. Hobart we need. By the way," he said as he made the connection, "is this the same Annette Camp who discovered the asteroid?"

"The same," Frasier answered.

Fantastic! Farmer thought to himself. We'll be able to tie Houston, Hobart, and Camp together.

Frasier continued. "Warren Butts is gathering information right now on how long it will take to evacuate the Sky Lab and the impact of grounding the space shuttle flights."

"Where do you think the rest of NASA will stand on the idea of evacuating the Sky Lab and grounding the shuttle?" Farmer asked.

"According to Butts, 9 out of 10 don't believe what Hobart said."

"Great!" Farmer chirped. "We've got him! Thanks for the information, Doctor. You'll

166

be hearing from me." With that, Farmer hung up the phone.

Frasier leaned back in his chair and put his feet up on the desk. *Well, all in all,* he thought, *not a bad day.* He decided that even if Houston fired him, the publicity he would receive from all this would guarantee him a job somewhere else in the scientific community. *I'd be on the Democratic team,* he thought to himself. *Yeah, why not? Once Houston's gone, the next administration will almost certainly be Democratic.*

When Jason came out of the meeting, Wendy was sitting there, waiting for him with an expectant look on her face. "Well, Daddy, what happened?"

"I don't know," Jason answered. "The president heard what I had to say and was very courteous."

"Well, what's he going to do?" she asked excitedly.

"I guess that's up to him. We've done all that we can. From this point on, the ball is in his court."

"What do we do now?" Wendy asked, noticeably let down.

"Well I guess we hop in a limo, go to the airport, and take a plane back to Chicago," Jason said with a big grin.

"Oh, Daddy, you know what I mean. What are you going to do?"

"I have no idea. I've done what I believe is right. From now on, the decision is somebody else's."

"What are you going to do for a living, Daddy? Have you given that any thought?"

"Actually, Honey, even if the college terminates me I'll get enough severance pay to last us for a few months. I'm going to take that severance pay, sit on my front porch, and rock."

"Yeah right, Dad," Wendy said with one eye squinted. "This from a guy who gets up at 6:00 in the morning and stays up until 12:00 at night? You're going to sit on the front porch and rock? Right, Dad!"

Jason reached out and grabbed his daughter by the shoulder, giving her a big hug as they walked down the hallway to where C.C. was holding the elevator. "I love you, Sweetheart," Jason told his daughter.

"Ditto, Dad," Wendy said with a big smile. "You're about the best dad in the world, even if you are unemployed," giving him a big hug as they walked together.

Less than an hour later they were back at the airport boarding the plane that would take them to Chicago. Deep inside, Jason had the same mixed feelings he had been having since this whole episode started. He knew he had done what he thought was right. *But what if I've just been fooling myself,* he thought. *Well, it's a little late to worry about that, Professor,* he scolded himself one more time. *The die is cast, for better or for worse, and what's done is done.*

Settling into his seat on the plane, Jason was finally able to focus his thoughts. *How much do I believe what I told the president?* he thought somberly. *Do I believe a major flare could erupt while we're on this airplane?*

The more he considered it, the more he decided, *Yes, I do believe it!* It frightened him. It frightened him, not for himself, but for the young woman sitting next to him that he loved so much. *And what about the thousands and tens of thousands of people who would be flying over the next two weeks? Would their lives be at risk?* Again, he decided yes. He was convinced they would be.

From that point he knew he would have no more doubts about Dr. Carrington's theory on solar flares. Something inside, some inner premonition, told him the next two weeks would be a nightmare for millions of people. He hoped silently that he would have favor with the president, because only President Houston could avert the crisis.

9

Jason and Wendy arrived back in Chicago physically and emotionally exhausted. Jason was tense throughout his body from the strain of what he'd been through. It was still unreal to think that he, Jason Hobart, had had a face-to-face meeting with the president of the United States. He was wondering what decisions the president would make. As he thought about the enormity of it all, he himself was confused, so he had no doubt about how the president was feeling.

Almost as if she could read her father's mind, Wendy said, "Daddy, you've done all you can do. Nobody could expect more of you. If the president accepts what you said, fine, and if he doesn't that's okay too. You did your part."

"But . . . all the people?" Jason stuttered.

"I know, Daddy, you care a lot about people, but remember that's not your responsibility. Remember what you always tell me: we are only held responsible for what we can do — not what we can't do."

Jason reached over and gave his daughter's hand an affectionate squeeze. She was mature far beyond her 15 years. She always knew the right things to say at the right time.

As they weaved their way through the maze of people at Chicago's O'Hare Airport and out to the shuttle that took them to the parking lot, the irony of it all hit Jason. *Here I am — an unemployed, and perhaps unemployable, professor of astronomy. I've just had a face-to-face meeting with the president of the United States, and now I've come back to no job and no real prospects.* "I have a strange life," he said aloud.

"What do you mean, Daddy?" Wendy said.

"Well, most people who go see the president are in positions of power and authority. Me? I'm unemployed and nearly broke."

"You're just available for greater things," Wendy chided her father lovingly.

The shuttle dropped them off with their baggage, and Jason said, "Honey, you wait here and I'll go get the car."

"Okay, Daddy," she said trying to be as enthusiastic as possible. She knew that her father was greatly troubled and that hurt her more than anything else.

Wendy's mind wandered back to the events that had taken place over the last few days and she found the resentment boiling up inside over her Aunt Karen's leaving. At the very time when her father needed his family the most, she'd abandoned him. Wendy made a vow that she would never do that to him, no matter what.

171

Where can Dad be? she wondered. Then she frowned. Even with all of his brains, the truth was, he had no sense of direction. He had been known to wander around in a parking lot for hours looking for his automobile, only to find out that he'd parked it in a different lot. She knew they were in the right lot, so eventually he had to find the car. But she wondered if he remembered that he was driving a rental car.

Jason had gone to the very spot he remembered parking the car but couldn't find it. He walked back and forth, up and down the aisles, even going to an adjacent aisle to search for it. After a few minutes of frustration, he sheepishly remembered something: he didn't have his old Volvo; he had a rental car. He went back to the original spot, and there it was. He verified it was the correct car by sticking the key in the door and hearing it respond with a pleasant click. In the past when he had lost his car, he had promised himself he'd bring a red flag and put it on his old Volvo's antenna. This time, he vowed that the next time he came to the airport he would write down the parking space and put it in his wallet.

He got in the car and turned the ignition key, felt the car respond with a pleasant hum. *It's great to have a reliable car,* he decided. After all the years of struggling with his old Volvo, he was not accustomed to a car re-

172

sponding without complaint. He had left the radio on and, even before he put the car into reverse, he heard the newscast. He felt weak as he listened.

"According to credible sources at the White House, it has been reported that Professor Jason Hobart, recently of Rockford College, had a meeting with President Houston. You may remember that this is the same Professor Hobart who predicted a massive solar flare six years ago — the one that never materialized. His pronouncement spread panic throughout America and was widely reported on the national news for several days. Well, Professor Hobart's at it again! He's recommended to the president that all U.S. aircraft be grounded until after the looming solar flare that he predicts strikes. But that's not all, folks. Professor Hobart also warned the president to shut down all industry in the country. Now how about that?

"Sources within the White House reported that President Houston has decided to evacuate the Space Lab and discontinue all space shuttle flights for the foreseeable future, based upon the warning from Dr. Hobart.

"Dissension within the president's own ranks is growing. WNN news recently reported that Dr. Robert Frasier, head of the National Institute of Science, strongly disagrees with Professor Hobart and recommended to the president that no actions be taken. In response, our sources tell us that President Houston is considering asking for the resignation of Dr. Frasier. However, several members of Congress have voiced their support for Dr. Frasier and are insisting that he stay on as the head of NIS."

Shifting into his role as commentator, the announcer said, "Now listen, folks, let me see if I can put this into commonsense English. Dr. Hobart, a professor from Rockford College with a track record, so far, of 0 and 1 in predicting solar flares, has recommended to the president that all aircraft be grounded, the space program scuttled, and industry crippled, all on the basis of his prediction. Dr. Robert Frasier, a scientist of renowned reputation, objected to this piece of advice to his boss, the president of the United States, who then threatened to fire him. Leaves you to question the credibility of the leadership of our country, doesn't it?" The announcer chuckled.

Jason turned off the radio. He had no doubts about his credibility at this point. As far as the American people were concerned, he was a nut case. He pulled up to the passenger waiting area, put the car into park, and popped the trunk lid. After he loaded the bags in the back, he slammed the trunk twice as hard as necessary and climbed into the driver's seat beside Wendy.

As they were driving out of the airport,

Wendy said, "Okay, Dad. Now what's the problem?"

"What do you mean, Honey?" Jason said, the false smile masking his hurt.

"Don't try to kid me, Professor Hobart. I've known you too long," his daughter quipped. "When you slam a trunk lid like you just did, something's wrong."

"Well, I guess it's better you know now rather than later," Jason sighed. "It's on the news — our meeting with the president — and as you would imagine they made me sound like the village idiot and the president like the keeper of the village idiot. Nobody believes anything that I've said. I was a fool to even open my mouth."

"No way, Dad," Wendy responded. "And stop degrading yourself! You're a brilliant man and I believe in you. The question is, do *you* still believe in you?"

Jason thought for a minute. *Do I really believe there is going to be a major solar eruption?* Yes, he concluded he did believe it. "Yep. I still do, Honey, but that doesn't make me seem less of a fool."

"Daddy, if you really believe it, time is on your side. I just trust that it won't be too late for people to listen by then."

"That's really one of those catch-22s, I guess," Jason responded. "If I'm right, we'll have a disaster on our hands that none of us want and, if I'm wrong, I'll have a personal disaster on my hands that I don't want."

Wendy didn't say anything. She just reached over and patted her dad's arm.

The trip back to Rockford gave Jason plenty of time to think about what had happened over the last few days. Less than a week ago he had been an obscure professor at a little-known small college in central Illinois. Now, he was a ridiculed national figure without a job and with a questionable future. Anger and resentment boiled up within.

The media doesn't even consider that one solar flare has already hit or that it destroyed several satellites and shut down all satellite transmission? That doesn't seem to make any difference to the media one way or the other, Jason thought bitterly. *All they want is a story — any story.* By nature Jason was not a pessimist and, as he began to think about it, a smile curled his lips. In spite of himself, he couldn't help chuckling.

Wendy glanced over and asked, "What's so funny?"

"Oh, nothing," Jason said, "But fame does come at a high price, doesn't it, Honey? Here I am, an unemployed professor but with great national exposure. How do you suppose we can use that?"

"Oh, I don't know," Wendy replied lightly. "Maybe you'll get a syndicated television program, Dad."

"Maybe," Jason said, smiling. "We'll see."

The trip to Rockford was uneventful and Jason eased the rental car into the parking lot, stopped, and transferred their bags to the curb. "Stay with the bags, Honey. I'll pay the bill and call a cab," Jason said.

"Okay, Dad."

Once inside the rental car office, Jason stood in line behind two other people waiting to check in their cars. While he was waiting, a special alert came on the overhead television that carried WNN news. Jason glanced up as he heard the announcement of a special bulletin from the White House. His heart leaped into his throat.

"President Houston announced the firing of National Institute of Science head, Dr. Robert Frasier," the announcer said. He went on to explain that it was in direct response to a disagreement between the NIS chief and the president over what the announcer called "the dubious predictions of Professor Jason Hobart of Rockford College." The screen flipped to a photograph of Jason that was taken six years earlier, but there was no mistaking the image.

"Six years ago," the announcer continued, "Professor Hobart predicted a similar solar flare and warned of disruptions on Earth and, even though his predictions proved to be false, President Houston has relied on the professor's prediction of another solar flare."

Jason tuned out the rest of what was being

said. He knew the pattern it would follow — ridicule the president for listening to a wild-eyed fanatic like Professor Jason Hobart.

"May I help you, Sir?" the attendant said. When Jason didn't respond, he said a little more emphatically, "May I help you, Sir?"

Jason snapped back to reality. "Yes, I'd like to check in my rental car," and he handed the rental agreement and keys to the agent.

"Say, aren't you the guy they're showing on television: Professor Hobart?" the attendant asked in surprise. Jason didn't say anything, and the man continued. "Why sure you are. You're that professor from Rockford College, aren't you, who says a solar flare's going to destroy Earth?"

Jason started to correct him, but then took a deep breath, sighed, and decided against it. "Yeah, I guess I am," he responded.

"Wow," the young agent responded. "Is all that stuff true — about the solar flares?" he asked incredulously.

"Yes, it is," Jason responded curtly, trying to break the conversation. "Now, would you please check me out?"

"Oh, yeah . . . yeah, sure. Give me a minute to figure it up. You wanta charge it to this credit card number you gave us?"

"Fine," Jason responded, signing the papers that the young man thrust before him.

He folded the receipt, put it in his jacket pocket, and headed toward the door. Just as he opened it, the young man shouted loud enough for everybody in the room to hear, "Better watch out, Professor. The sky may be falling out there! You wouldn't want to get hurt *now*, would you?" and he hawed at his own joke.

Jason neither stopped nor looked back. He just opened the door, and with shoulders slumping ever so slightly, he strode outside. He walked over to the taxi stand, where he flagged a cab. "Thank you," Jason said after the cab driver had stowed their bags. With one glance Wendy knew something had happened while her father was checking out, but she didn't say a word while they were in the cab.

All the way home, Jason was silent. As they pulled into the yard Wendy knew what the problem was. There were several vehicles parked out along the road, and their lawn was full of press people with cameras and microphones. Jason stepped out of the car and Emily Hart stuck a microphone in his face, "Professor, are you serious about the solar flare this time and what else did you recommend to the president? Do you know the president has evacuated the Sky Lab and grounded all shuttles?"

Jason started to respond, to defend himself; then, he realized it would be fruitless to do so. Instead, he shrugged his shoulders and said, "No comment." He pushed his way through the gang of reporters to his front door, put the key in the door, and opened it. Wendy slipped inside and Jason stepped in behind her, closing out the reporters left shouting and yelling in his front yard.

"Sorry, Daddy," Wendy said, slipping under his arm and giving him a hug.

"It's all right, Honey. It's to be expected."

Almost before her eyes, Wendy saw her father's demeanor change. Almost miraculously, Professor Jason Hobart was not defeated, discouraged, or embarrassed. Suddenly he was angry. *What right do these people have to harass me? What do they know about solar flares? They have no concept of the infinite power that we're dealing with,* Jason thought. He knew that he had done the right thing and, whether or not he had a job or friends or the approval of the press, it didn't matter anymore. He knew he had done the right thing.

He reached down and gave Wendy a hug. "Honey, I'm going to be all right now. They're the fools, not me."

Wendy looked up at her dad with a smile. "Good for you, Dad!"

All the next day, every time Wendy flipped on the television, the same news blared out at her: Dr. Jason Hobart, Professor of Astronomy at Rockford College, had once again warned of impending doom and the president of the United States, in an unprecedented

180

move, had fired his chief executive in charge of the National Institute of Science and had shut down the U.S. space program. Neil Farmer's campaign to discredit the president was working well.

Then in one of those twists of fate that occurs from time to time, as Wendy was flipping through the channels, she came across the Discovery channel that was running an old documentary on solar flares. The camera had caught one of the largest solar flares in modern history, and it was a truly impressive spectacle with a huge plume of super-charged energy flaring out from the Sun nearly 100,000 miles into space and then looping its way back onto the surface of the Sun. The area it covered was hundreds of times larger than the entire surface area of the planet they lived on.

Again, Wendy was reminded that what her father was warning the nation about was not an academic principle of astronomy. It had the potential of a major catastrophe that, at minimum, would disrupt communications on Earth and, at worst, might well cause massive chaos throughout this planet; and, for those foolish enough to be exposed in space, it could mean death.

At the end of the documentary, Japanese scientist Dr. Ito Onera, from the University of Tokyo, discussed the concept of solar flares. In doing so, he mentioned an obscure fact that the media had totally overlooked — that solar flares tend to run in cycles, that the last major solar flare cycle occurred in the 1870s, and that another major outbreak of solar flares was due. The documentary had been made a year ago.

How peculiar, she thought, *that not one of the major media outlets has mentioned that many of the world's leading scientists also believe that solar flares are a potential hazard to the world, particularly in this electronic era, but they never fail to mention that some of the world's leading scientists think Professor Hobart represents the lunatic fringe of science and has been discredited. Totally biased reporting,* Wendy thought angrily.

Throughout the day, as she watched various news programs, the media made President Houston their primary target, courtesy of Neil Farmer's grand smear plan. Most of the other media, wittingly or unwittingly, had picked up on it.

A very interesting thing happened later that evening on a couple of the news broadcast programs. When the opinion polls began to appear, they showed that the American public supported President Houston's decision to evacuate the Sky Lab by a margin of nearly 8 to 1. The public apparently agreed with the president's decision to take some preventative measures in the event that the solar flare proved to be a reality. Shortly, Fox news took the high ground and jumped on the president's bandwagon, praising him for his foresight in minimizing the risk to the astronauts.

But, instead of suggesting that her father might be right in his solar flare analysis, he became the object of their disdain. The media claimed that Hobart had given the president misleading information, and every detail of his previous prediction was paraded before the public once again. Wendy grimaced and tears filled her eyes as she realized that the media would never admit they were wrong or that her father might be right.

Unknown to any viewers, Drs. Onera and Singer sent faxes to the major networks stating that they supported Professor Hobart. No news of this was carried on any of the networks. After the Rockford College trustees' meeting, the 11:00 news announced that Professor Hobart had officially been fired from his job by the administrative officials. No further interviews with Jason were attempted. As far as the media was concerned, he had been accused, tried, and convicted — all without the benefit of representation.

At the White House, things were definitely heating up. President Houston was coming under heavy criticism from many of the more staid members of the scientific community, demanding that he renounce Professor Hobart's theories and calm the fears of the

American people. The majority of the president's cabinet and staff also urged him to do so.

Allen Dean told the president, "Sir, it is the politically correct thing to do. Distance yourself from Professor Hobart, and the media likely will drop this whole issue."

"You're probably right, Allen, but I've never been one to be politically correct," Houston replied.

Just then there was a strong rap on the door. "Come in," Houston said.

It was Warren Butts. "Mr. President, we've just gotten word that the Japanese have reported a big solar flare."

"How big?" Houston asked.

"I don't know, but apparently a lot bigger than the last one."

"Well," Houston said reflectively, "maybe the professor isn't as outrageous in his beliefs as some seem to think."

Jason was unable to shake the doldrums that haunted him. The trip to Washington and the meeting with President Houston had been exhilarating, but now he had to face the real world again. He learned of his dismissal while listening to a late news broadcast. Finally he fell back on his longtime refuge: work. He went out to his observatory and powered up the spectrometer and the recorder.

As the calibration cycle ended, the recorder pegged at the high end. "What the . . ." Jason said, punching the recorder to "run" mode. The needle stayed pegged out on the X-ray monitor. Jason cycled it over to S band. Same results.

He quickly rewound the digital tape recorder and fed the previously recorded signal into the spectrometer. The indicator fell to near zero, so he advanced the tape and again fed the spectrometer: still zero. He advanced the tape twice more before he found where the indicator pegged out. He noted the time: nearly three hours ago!

"This is it!" Jason shouted. He slipped the sun filter over the telescope lens and peered out at the Sun. "Unbelievable," he exclaimed. What he saw shook him to the core: The gigantic plume stretched out from the Sun's surface at least 200,000 miles and was still expanding.

Jason's first thought was that the sunspot might be evolving into a nova, where it would balloon out and engulf its neighbors. But then he noticed that already the great plume had started to curl. It was an eruption. *But what an eruption*, he thought. Then he decided, *I've got to contact the president.*

He pulled out his wallet and retrieved the card with the president's personal office number on it. He was so nervous he had a hard time punching in the right number. Finally he got it right.

"President Houston's office. This is Mary," the pleasant voice said.

Jason wondered, *If the president's in, will he even take my call?*

"This is Doctor Hobart," Jason said. "I was at the White House recently."

"Yes, I know who you are, Doctor," Mary replied. "What may I do for you?"

"I need to talk with the president. It's very urgent," Jason said.

"Hold a moment, Doctor," the receptionist replied, and she put him on hold.

To Jason the time seemed an eternity before he heard, "This is the president, Professor Hobart."

Jason blurted out, "It's happening, Sir. Area 403 is erupting."

"Hold on, Professor," the president interrupted. "I just received confirmation of a large solar flare from the Japanese. Is this the flare you predicted?"

"No," Jason replied more calmly. "There may be an even bigger one, and you will have precious little time, Mr. President."

"Stay where you are, Professor, and I'll call you back in a couple of hours. Hold on while Mary gets your number."

Houston told Dean, "Get Morgan in here!" Daniel Morgan was the president's choice to replace Frasier at the NIS. Houston and Morgan had been boyhood friends and had attended undergraduate school together at Arizona State University. After college, Houston had gone into business and Morgan had gone on to graduate school, later to receive a PhD in aeronautical engineering from MIT. After an illustrious career at Fillmore Labs in California, Morgan had been called to head NASA; he had held that position for the previous five years. When the president was forced to remove Frasier as head of the NIS, he had immediately called on his old friend to take the job on an interim basis.

Five minutes later there was a knock on the president's door. "Come in," Houston said. It was Dr. Morgan: a tall, handsome man in his mid-50s who still had a full head of hair, although it was streaked with white by this time. His very nature spoke of a calm, assured personality.

Houston considered Morgan to be one of his closest friends. Their common bond extended to the fact that both men had lost their wives to cancer. Houston had lost his wife Betty nearly 15 years earlier and, within two years after that, Morgan lost his wife. Morgan had since remarried. Houston regretted dragging his old friend into the middle of the biggest controversy of his administration, but he needed a good man in charge of the NIS who would give him honest counsel.

"Sit down, Dan," Houston said.

Morgan could see that Houston was upset, and little wonder. Based on what he had just heard from the NIS he would be upset too.

"Dan, have you been following the latest solar flare news?"

"Yes, I have, Mr. President," Morgan said without elaboration.

"Give me your opinion, and don't hold anything back."

"Well, I've just gotten an update. As you probably know, we've now gotten faxes from several of the leading astrophysicists in the world, including one of the men I trust most: Doctor Lewis Singer of Cambridge. I called Lewis and asked his opinion of Professor Hobart's prediction. He confirmed that area 403 is highly unstable and that two eruptions so close together is highly unusual."

Almost imperceptibly, the president took a breath. "You've read the professor's report, Dan. Tell me, do you believe this latest flare could be as dangerous as Hobart predicts?"

Morgan paused for a minute as he considered his answer. He wanted to be very precise. "Mr. President, I believe Professor Hobart could be right."

"That's not the answer that I want, Dan. I want a definitive answer. If you were the president of the United States and you were sitting in this chair right now with the information you have at hand, would you ground all the aircraft in America?"

"Whew!" Morgan said, running his fingers through his hair. "That's a tough question. I'm just glad that I'm *not* the president and *don't* have to make that decision. All I can tell you is, based on what I have heard, I would give a lot of credibility to what Professor Hobart says, but I can't call the shots for you, Phil . . . I mean, Mr. President." After so many years it was easy to slip back into the informality of friends.

Of course, Houston knew that would be Morgan's answer. If the situation were reversed, he would have said exactly the same thing. But what was he to do? Grounding all the airlines was a drastic move that would cost billions of dollars and inconvenience millions of people, and he knew he would bear the brunt of the biggest negative campaign ever launched in the media if he was wrong.

"Well thanks, Dan. I'm going to have to give this a lot more consideration and some prayer. It's a hard call."

"You're right about that. I wish I could help. I will be praying for you."

With that, Dr. Morgan left the room. Houston dropped his head into his hands. He felt like his head was ready to explode. *What should I do? If the Professor is right, not taking any action will risk thousands of lives, but if he is wrong . . .* Houston got up, went over to

189

his desk, and punched the intercom button decidedly.

"Yes, Sir," the receptionist said.

"Call Allen and Warren back in here as quickly as possible," he ordered.

"Yes, Sir," the receptionist said.

Five minutes later there was a knock at the door. Houston said, "Come on in."

Dean and Butts strode in.

"Have a seat," the president said, a little more emotionally than they were used to. "Gentlemen, I've made the toughest decision of my life. Effective at 8:00 A.M. Thursday, all commercial and military aircraft in the United States will be grounded until this latest flare passes."

"But, Mr. President," Dean protested. Houston shook his head.

"It's already decided, Allen. I know all the arguments. I've been through them a thousand times myself. The risk of not doing it is just too great."

Dean slumped back in his chair. His dejected look was understandable. As press secretary, his job would be to make the announcement to the media.

"They're going to crucify you. You know that don't you?" Butts said to his longtime friend.

"I understand exactly," Houston said. "My mind's made up. I'll have to live with the decision."

"What about the international flights coming into the U.S.?" Butts asked.

"No flights over U.S. territory until Professor Hobart gives the 'all clear,' " Houston said.

Dean slumped down a little further.

"It'll be hard to sell to our friends," Butts said.

"We're not going to try and sell this one, Warren. We're just going to tell them. All U.S. domestic flights will be grounded. All international flights will be grounded, and there will be no aircraft movement over the United States until this office notifies them."

"Allen, go out and tell them."

"Yes, Sir, but you know they'll want a press conference."

"No conference," Houston said. "I don't even want to discuss it. We'll just wait this one out."

"How long, Mr. President?" Dean asked in a dejected tone.

"I don't know right now, Allen," the president responded, "therefore, I won't tell you, so you can't tell them."

"Yes, Sir, I understand. I'll spread the news."

"Stand by for the wave!" Butts said with a frown.

"That's for sure," Houston agreed. "I just hope we're on top of this wave instead of under it."

The two men left.

Houston decided he had one more thing he had to do. He punched the intercom one more time. "Yes, Sir," the receptionist responded.

"Get Professor Hobart back on the line."

"Right, Sir," the answer came back.

Jason was still sitting at his desk in the observatory. It seemed like hours since he had called the president, but when he looked at his watch he was surprised to see it had only been 40 minutes.

When the phone rang Jason snatched it up. "Jason Hobart here," he said, and then he thought how stupid that must sound. If it was the president, he obviously knew who he was calling.

But Houston in his strong voice said, "Professor, I thought you should be the first to know. I've grounded all aircraft in the country until this latest flare passes, beginning Thursday morning at 8:00."

"Say that one more time, Mr. President."

"You heard me correctly, Professor. I've weighed all the facts and I believe the risk is too high to ignore it. I'm officially grounding all aircraft in the United States until the flare is past."

Jason was both elated and terrified at the same time. The president had believed his evaluation. He realized what a huge risk the president was taking. His entire political career was being gambled on the word of a discredited professor from Rockford, Illinois.

"Mr. President, I really don't know what to say," Jason stammered.

"You don't need to say anything, Professor. I'm dispatching a military aircraft to the Rockford airport. It should be there within two hours. I would like for you and your daughter to come back to Washington. I want you to spearhead our preparations."

"But . . . but . . . , Mr. President, there are many more qualified . . ."

"I don't care about that," Houston interrupted. "It's your call, Professor. You're the expert. Do you still believe what you said?"

"Yes, Sir, I do."

"Now, I'm asking you to come here and head up my team."

"Yes, Sir," Jason responded, in a subdued tone. He was overwhelmed and humbled.

"I'll see you in a few hours," Houston said. "Godspeed."

"Thank you, Sir . . . ," Jason mumbled as the phone went dead. He looked at Wendy who had just walked in. She had a broad smile on her face.

"The president believed you, didn't he, Daddy?"

"He did, Honey, and guess what? He wants us to come to Washington again. He asked me to head the scientific team that will prepare for the flare."

"I knew it!" Wendy said, elated. She ran over to her father and threw her arms around him. "I just knew it!"

10

To say the events of the next few hours were interesting would be a gross understatement. Even with the news that another flare had occurred, as soon as the press got the word that President Houston was shutting down all air traffic in the United States, on the basis of a recommendation by Professor Hobart, the lid blew off. Neil Farmer almost wept with joy when he heard the announcement. It was his life's dream to destroy the conservative Houston, and he had stepped right into the trap.

Farmer instructed his news team to run clips of Hobart's earlier prediction and to emphasize that the majority of the established scientific community thoroughly disavowed any relationship with the discredited professor. By the time the clips were produced, President Houston was depicted as an alumni of a mental institution, and Professor Hobart was characterized as the nutty professor. The saving grace was that neither Jason nor Wendy had time to look at any news, national or otherwise, while they were making their way back to Washington.

Jason tried to slip out as quietly as possible, but every step he took he was shadowed by the media. When Jason finally pushed his way to his car, the press was still yelling at him for a quote. He said nothing. But when he headed toward the Rockford airport, the press was right in tow. Cameras were rolling when the Lear jet bearing the insignia of the State Department touched down at the airport. Two Secret Service men pushed the reporters back to the entrance gate. The late news carried the image of Professor Jason Hobart and his young daughter boarding the sleek, twin-engine plane and being whisked off into the darkness.

The WNN news team in Washington, D.C. interviewed House Minority Leader Dick Gerstner to ask his opinion. "It is time for the Congress to act," Gerstner said. "Clearly, the president is being irresponsible, and his actions will cost tens of thousands of jobs and countless millions of dollars."

Gerstner informed the press that it was his intention to call a special session of Congress to consider impeachment proceedings against President Houston, who obviously was "mentally unstable." He indicated enough support was building in the Senate to support his position.

The furor caused by President Houston's decision went far beyond the Oval Office. Neil Farmer was ecstatic. He couldn't have wished for a more perfect scenario, and he made the most of the situation by running news specials all day long.

Fortunately, Jason still was oblivious to most of the controversy. All he knew was that President Houston had asked him to return to Washington to oversee the preparations for weathering the solar flare he had predicted.

When the State Department jet touched down at Andrews Air Force Base, Jason expected to see a gaggle of reporters awaiting their arrival but, instead, all he saw were some Air Force staff people awaiting their flight. Clearly, the president had sidetracked the press by diverting the jet to a military base instead of flying into Washington National or Dulles, as the press obviously expected.

On the way to the limo that was to transport them to the White House again, Jason prayed silently — initially, that he would be vindicated and, after chastening himself for that, he prayed that he would be wrong. He feared what a violent eruption on the Sun might do to millions of Americans — and perhaps billions of people around the world.

Driving through the streets of Washington for the second time in two days gave Jason an eerie feeling. He thought, *This city has been home to countless politicians throughout the ages, including presidents I have only read about in history books: Lincoln, Washington, Roosevelt, and Kennedy.* It left him awestruck. He could

197

appreciate the power that emanated from this city.

As the limo turned onto Pennsylvania Avenue, Jason was startled by the huge crowds at the White House gates. There were the reporters and film crews screaming and shouting to be noticed; and there were crowds of people carrying the usual signs predicting the end of the world: "Repent and Be Saved, The End Is Near"; "Heathen Babylon To Be Destroyed"; and many others. *Just what I need,* he thought, *to further my image. People already think I'm crazy.*

As the limo turned toward the gates, armed security people stepped from the guard house and brushed the reporters and camera crews back. However, many of the news people were persistent, and it took several minutes to clear a path wide enough for the limousine to drive through the gates. Once inside, the crowd of reporters was pressing to get inside, and the security guards literally had to shove them aside in order to close the gates. Jason heard the driver comment, "Wow, there hasn't been this much excitement in Washington since Richard Nixon resigned."

Jason started to respond but couldn't think of anything to say, so he just grunted in response. He wished the man had used a different example.

"Wow, pretty exciting, huh, Dad," Wendy exclaimed.

"Yes, to say the least," Jason agreed. "Maybe a little too exciting, Honey. What if . . ."

But Wendy cut him off. "Don't think, what if, Dad. You're here, you're committed, and from this point you have to go forward."

"Right," Jason responded, with a forced grin. "Arm the torpedoes, and full speed ahead," he said.

"Well, something like that, I think, Dad," Wendy agreed with a grin.

The limo pulled into the White House parking garage and, as soon as it stopped, C.C. stepped out of the shadows and opened the door.

"Welcome back, Professor," he said with an impish grin.

"Well, thank you, C.C." Jason replied. "Say, what is your actual name?"

"Calendar Collins," he replied affably. "My mother believed in naming her children after the first thing she saw after they were born. In my case it was a calendar. I opted for C.C."

Jason smiled. "C.C. it is then."

"Follow me, Professor. I believe the president's waiting for you. You too, Miss," he added politely with a warm smile.

They made their way through the corridor to the elevator that Jason remembered had delivered them to the Oval Office last time. C.C. stepped inside, punched the hold button, and waited for Jason and Wendy to enter.

Wendy said, "Oh, our bags."

"Don't worry about them," C.C. said. "Somebody will get them for you."

"Oh, okay. Cool!" Wendy replied. She really was impressed that there were people to do everything for the guests at the White House.

Once off the elevator, Jason followed C.C. down the hall. Before they got to the meeting room, C.C. said, "Don't worry, Professor, I'll take good care of the little lady for you. We're going to go see some sights."

"Thank you, C.C. See you later, Honey. Have a good time."

When Jason entered the meeting room, he recognized some of the participants. President Houston was already there, along with Warren Butts, Doctors Annette Camp and Gene Moore, Allen Dean, General Floyd Boland, and a man introduced as Daniel Morgan, the acting head of the NIS. Surprisingly, Jason saw someone he never expected to see at the White House: Dr. Lewis Singer from Cambridge University. He had been flown in at the request of the president, even before Jason had been called.

When Jason saw Dr. Singer, his face lit up. There were several other attendees he didn't recognize, including some high-ranking military staff.

"Come in, Professor," the president said warmly.

As Jason took his seat, the people in the room identified themselves. Jason noted that the group was comprised of people from the political world, the military, and science.

"Well, Professor," the president said after all the introductions were made, "you certainly have made an impression."

Jason hesitated and started to say something when the president broke in, "No need for false modesty, Professor. You're here because I believe what you said."

"Thank you, Mr. President," Jason said. His face was flushed, but he was flattered.

"Professor, we want to put aside all formalities. We're here to do a job. You no longer have to convince me that what you've been predicting is correct. If it is, we need to prepare for it. If it isn't, well, we'll all probably be out looking for new jobs," the president said with his characteristic grin.

"Tell us what to expect, Professor, in terms of magnitude and in terms of potential damage from this solar flare," Houston said.

Jason leaned back in his chair, reached down, and retrieved some papers from his briefcase.

"Well, Mr. President, according to my calculations, the flare that will strike Earth in the next two days may be a level 6."

"Translate what that means, if you would,

Doctor," the president said. "I need to know what it means in terms of potential damage."

"It's very difficult to say with any real certainty, Mr. President, but I would say the flare will result in great damage, unless we power down sensitive electronic equipment during daylight hours. But the remaining high-altitude satellites must be powered down at all times. I believe we'll have interruptions in all communications systems, both airborne and ground based. But let me repeat that all sensitive electrical systems, such as the power grids, must be powered down during daylight hours when the level 6 flare hits."

"Earlier, Doctor, you suggested that I ground all air traffic. Explain why."

"Mr. President, all air traffic is dependent on airborne communications, obviously. This flare will disrupt most communications and will make it impossible, or at least very difficult, for ground controllers to communicate with their aircraft. I think you would agree, Sir, that it wouldn't be very much fun to be in a commercial or military aircraft without being able to communicate with ground controllers."

"I'd say that would be a pretty accurate statement, Professor," the president agreed.

Annette Camp interrupted. "Dr. Hobart, how long do you anticipate that these solar flares will affect communications?"

"Again, it's very difficult to say with any

degree of certainty," Jason said. "We just don't have enough historical data to make any accurate calculations. But I would say this: When the United States has cycled onto the dark side, meaning that the mass of Earth is between us and the Sun, our communications should be marginally operable except for the high-altitude satellites. But when the country is cycled into the bright side, facing the Sun, our communications will be disrupted. I believe the flares will continue to build in magnitude. As unstable as area 403 is, we can anticipate another larger flare imminently."

"What then, Professor?" the president asked.

"Once the next eruption occurs, we will have approximately 90 hours until its effect is felt on Earth."

"Tell me, Professor!" Houston said, leaning forward and putting his elbows on the table. "Do you expect more flares?"

"Without question," Jason replied. "We're in a maximal period. Area 403 will continue to build pressure. The analogy is very much like a volcano, Sir.

"In a volcano, if the lava plug persists for any long period of time, the pressures inside the volcano build to an explosive level; then you have a major explosion like what happened at Mount St. Helens back in the '80s and Mount Penetubo in the '90s. Similar events happen on the Sun's surface. As the pressure builds, the flares will increase in magnitude."

"Are you sure, Professor? I want your bottom line," the president said.

Jason hesitated. *What is the bottom line?* He was so used to apologizing for any statement he made, he wasn't sure he was able to express what he felt. He paused for what seemed like an eternity, gathering his thoughts. Then he said, "I'm certain, Sir, that we are going to have a very large eruption — perhaps a level 8 or greater."

Jason saw the response on Dr. Camp's and Dr. Moore's faces; shock would be the only way to describe it.

"Do you have a question, Dr. Camp?" the president asked, seeing her expression.

"Well, not exactly, Mr. President. But a class 8 solar flare is almost beyond imagination. I don't purport to be a solar physicist, but a class 8 eruption is unheard of. According to the data Dr. Moore and I reviewed, the most severe flare recorded prior to the current one was no more than a class 4 or 5. If there hasn't been a flare of this magnitude since we've been keeping records, Professor, what makes you think that we're going to have a class 8 solar flare?"

Jason felt his heart rate increase, but he replied calmly, "Because area 403 is highly unusual. This area erupted twice before, and the last time it fizzled into a series of minor flares. But in 1872 Dr. Carrington recorded what he calculated to be at least a level 8 flare. And there is some evidence, at least according to Dr. Carrington's records, that area 403 erupts violently approximately every 130 to 140 years, give or take a few years. Only this time the coronal hole is pointed directly at Earth."

"Clarify these levels for me please, Professor," the president said. "Is there a difference between Dr. Camp's description of a class 8 and what you call a level 8?"

"No, Sir, no difference," Jason replied. "It's merely a matter of terminology. Every point on the Carrington scale indicates a magnitude of at least 100 percent greater than the previous point. In other words, a 2 is twice as large as a 1, and a 3 is four times as large, and a 4 is eight times as large, and . . ."

"I get the picture," the president broke in. "Then we're talking about some pretty big flares. Right?"

"Very," Jason said. Then he added, "Assuming I'm right."

"Granted," the president replied. "Tell me what to expect as a result of these flares, Professor . . . assuming you're right, of course."

"Well, Sir, it's really difficult to define because, as I said before, the last time such eruptions occurred we had virtually no modern instrumentation on Earth. We certainly had no electronics. All we had were visual observations through telescopes and mathematical calculations. According to Dr. Carrington's notes, in the period following the solar eruption in 1872, he observed some tremendous variations in Earth's magnetic field, including what he described as a temporary reversal of the magnetic poles."

"But there never was any proof to verify that," Dr. Singer interjected.

"That's true," Jason agreed. "Because in those days the use of magnetics was basically limited to compasses. There's no telling what effect such an event would have today."

"Absolutely true," Dr. Singer agreed. "With virtually every aspect of the industrialized world dependent on electromagnetic devices, the effect would be devastating."

"Okay, I understand," the president said. "So, we need to shut down all electronic equipment during the big flares. Is that correct?"

"That's correct, Mr. President," Jason said. "We will need to protect essential systems."

"Define 'protect,' " the president said.

"Turn everything off during daylight hours — at least until the initial wave of solar winds is past. The greater long-term problem, though," Jason continued, "is that since we are now so dependent on modern electronics in our society a solar flare of this magnitude could conceivably cripple an industrialized country. Think of what our life would be like without electricity for a month or more."

"Is that possible, Professor?" Warren Butts blurted out. "That seems farfetched — even alarmist."

Jason paused to consider his words carefully. He was ultrasensitive to the label of "alarmist."

"Perhaps you would allow me," Dr. Singer said, seeing Jason's discomfort.

"Thank you, Dr. Singer," Jason said with relief.

Singer began, "First, let me say that I'm not sure about the magnitude of this or any future solar eruptions. But if, in fact, we had a level 8 solar eruption, it is a near certainty that the electromagnetic pulse induced by the charged ionic particles hitting the atmosphere would overload electronic equipment and could conceivably destroy satellites and even their ground stations. Aircraft would be at particular risk, I would think. If a series of these flares struck one after the other, it is quite possible that life, as we know it today, would be greatly altered." With no further comment, Singer sat back down.

"I heard that the last time the professor was here," the president said. "And obviously, based upon the decision I made, I concur that the risk is too high."

"The problem is, Mr. President," Jason added, "we can't wait until the flare hits before the decisions are made."

"Okay, then I think we need to make adequate preparations," the president said. "Listen, I'm getting a lot of flack from the Congress about grounding all aircraft, and it's pretty clear that the Democrats aren't going to stand idly by and allow me to do this — Republicans either, for that matter — so we can anticipate some interference from the Congress.

"Is there any doubt about my constitutional authority to declare an emergency?" he asked, looking toward his chief of staff. Jason could see the frown on Butts's face, and he guessed that there probably was a doubt. Butts shrugged his shoulders.

"Well, until the Supreme Court rules or the Congress stops me, I guess I have that authority," the president said. "How much time do we have, Professor?" Houston asked.

"Three days at most, Mr. President, before the next flare hits. The difficulty is, it's not an exact science," Jason said.

"Well, I hope you're better at predicting solar flares than the weather forecaster is at predicting the weather," the president said with a chuckle. "For better or worse, the die is cast," Houston said.

"General," the president said, directing his attention now to Gen. Floyd Boland, chairman of the Joint Chiefs of Staff, who had been quiet up to now. "We need to be ready. I want all the elements in place so we can establish some kind of security in our cities. The last thing we want is panic, so I want you to activate the Emergency Broadcast Network, inform all the law agencies that we'll give them sufficient warning, and when the big flare hits I want travel limited. Ask the people to stay home until it passes and we can get some semblance of order." Houston paused a moment. Then looking at the general he said, "Okay, let's get it done."

Boland nodded his head ever so slightly. He thought his president had gone nuts, but he was the president, and he knew from experience that once Houston's mind was made up, that was it. You either went along, or you left.

"Yes, Sir," Boland said.

"Okay, folks, I guess this is the last meeting we'll have for a while," Houston said.

"Unless it's in court," Butts muttered. The president did not respond. He knew that his chief of staff didn't agree with his decision, but he was a loyal friend and would do exactly what he was told.

11

After the meeting Jason and Wendy were led into the president's private study. When the door closed, President Houston turned and extended his hand to Jason.

"Professor, I want to thank you for dropping everything and coming so quickly. Also, I want to thank you for your courage."

"No, Mr. President," Jason responded with a smile. "It's really *your* courage. It was easy to drop everything since I didn't have anything to drop. Besides, it's you who has the great job."

President Houston chuckled, "Well, I guess you're right, Professor. I do enjoy working here, but it's hard to hang onto this job. What I wanted to tell you is, we have set up a communications and solar observation facility at Andrews Air Force Base to track the progress of the solar flare. All the equipment and staff you'll require are assembled there. Doctors Camp, Moore, and Singer all have agreed to work with you to coordinate this effort."

"Thank you, Mr. President," Jason responded. "I'm humbled. Each of these scientists is eminently more qualified to head this group than I am though."

"No! It's *your* idea — your call," Houston said, putting his hand on Jason's shoulder. "For better or for worse, you're the man. Right, Wendy?"

"Right!" she said with a smile.

"Thank you, Sir. I appreciate your confidence," Jason said.

"Keep me informed, Professor," the president said as he shook Jason's hand once more, signaling an end to the meeting.

Jason nodded in agreement as C.C. stuck his head in the doorway.

"We're ready to go, Professor," the big man said.

This time Jason and Wendy were not shuffled into the limo. Instead, C.C. led them down the elevator and out onto the White House lawn. Waiting there was an enormous Marine helicopter. Already on board were Drs. Camp, Moore, and Singer, and as soon as Jason and Wendy boarded the craft and the door was slid shut, it lifted off the ground. As they lifted up, Jason could see the front gate leading to the White House and the huge ensemble of press that were still assembled there.

"Some kind of adventure, huh, Dad," Wendy said cheerfully.

"That's for sure. A lot of changes have taken place over the last few days," Jason said with a smile. "I went from a small town professor to unemployed to now being an unpaid volunteer for the United States government."

The others inside the helicopter responded with knowing smiles. Jason Hobart's career was on the line, not to mention President Houston's. Either he would be a hero or the biggest fool of the century; and that decision was totally in God's hands now.

The media was going crazy. Word of the special meeting had leaked out, as it always does, and long before the press conference was held by Allen Dean the press had released their twist on things. The president had appointed Professor Jason Hobart as head of the special committee to advise him on the status of the so-called disaster that was predicted.

Much was made of the fact that the president had overstepped his constitutional authority by ordering all commercial aircraft to be grounded and by prohibiting flights in and out of the country by other nations. Each new special bulletin carried the question, "What next?"

On the 6:00 P.M. news the WNN reporter said, "I wonder if the president is considering declaring martial law and ordering all private citizens to remain in their homes until the professor tells us that it's okay to go outside again."

Early editions of *The Post* portrayed the president as a radical fundamentalist, intent on usurping the Constitution. The headline story in *The Post*, as well as *The New York Times*, showed a caricature of the president's head on the body of a chicken and the caption reading, "The sky is falling! The sky is falling!" From that point, instead of referring to him as President Houston, he was consistently referred to as the "chicken-little president."

Congressman Gerstner, unrelenting in his attack on the president, was interviewed by every major network. "In my opinion," he said, "the president is mentally unstable and should be removed from office. What he is doing is irrational and unconstitutional."

The momentum was growing, even inside the Republican Congress, to sanction the president. Many members of Congress were questioning the president's authority to declare a national emergency when, in reality, nothing had happened to warrant it. Dr. Frasier and several other scientists testified that the latest solar flare "crisis" was significantly exaggerated.

The president issued an executive order, directing that the Emergency Broadcast Network be alerted and tested. All of this contributed to the nervousness of the American people and provided the president's enemies plenty of ammunition with which to hammer him.

At Andrews, the staff monitoring the Sun's activity had a real shock waiting for Jason.

After the latest eruption, area 403 had calmed down and was actually stabilizing. Jason felt a wave of panic. *Oh no,* he thought, *not again. I was so certain area 403 would continue to build. Could I be wrong again?*

This information already had been relayed to Warren Butts and he immediately appeared at the president's suite. "Tell him I'm here," Butts directed the receptionist at the desk outside the president's study.

"Yes, Sir," she replied, sensing his foul mood.

"Mr. President, Mr. Butts is here to see you."

"Is he in a good mood?" the president asked.

"No, Sir."

"Well, have him come in anyway," the president replied, slipping his shoes on.

When Butts stormed into the office, the president knew something was obviously wrong. "Sit down, Warren. Would you like some tea?" Houston said, pouring some for himself from the eighteenth century French teapot.

"No, I don't want any tea. Mr. President, I think you've got a political disaster on your hands here."

"How so?"

"I just got a call from Andrews and it seems the solar flare crisis is over. The scientists monitoring the equipment verified that the area is stabilizing."

"Great!" Houston grumbled. "Just what I needed. What does Dr. Hobart say?"

"I don't know," Butts replied gruffly. "He just arrived at Andrews."

Jason had recovered his wits after hearing that area 403 had settled down. He chided himself, *Don't be too hasty. That wouldn't be inconsistent with coronal eruptions, and it doesn't necessarily mean the danger is past.*

He concentrated his attention on the data that was streaming in from the solar X ray, gamma, and S-band monitors. Clearly, in the last three or four hours the activity from area 403 had begun to calm. Activity in the S-band range had dropped precipitously; gamma-ray activity was still up, but dropping; but the X ray output remained as high as ever. Something about that triggered a memory. It was one of those frustrating thoughts that he knew was important — but hidden from his conscious mind.

Annette asked, "What do you make of this, Doctor?"

"Look, we're going to be working together for who knows how long, so please call me Jason. Now, to answer your question, I really don't know. There is something familiar about this pattern, but . . ."

Suddenly it clicked: a memory, an idea, a concept that had been hidden in the back of his mind. In some of Dr. Carrington's papers he remembered a similar scenario when an unstable area on the Sun had stabilized and then erupted suddenly and without warning. Then it struck him like a bolt of lightning. *It was just before area 403 erupted in 1872!*

Turning to Annette, Jason exclaimed excitedly, "I believe 403 is about to erupt violently — probably in the next few days!"

"What makes you think so, Doctor?" Annette Camp asked, looking at the data herself.

"Jason," he reminded her. "This thing is building up pressure for a big bubble. The same thing happened before the eruption in 1872! We have to get to the president."

Jason hurried across the room to where the guard sat. "I've got to get hold of the president," Jason said breathlessly, "and quickly!"

The guard pressed a button and said, "Access to the president." With prearranged precision, the call went directly to the receptionist outside the president's study. In less than a minute the president was on the line.

"Yes, Professor," the president said curtly. Butts had clearly shaken his confidence.

Jason didn't notice. He said, "The activity from area 403 has dropped off significantly and . . ."

"Yes, I know, Professor. I heard," the president said, glancing at Butts, who sat there fuming. He could read Butts's mind. Not only had he sunk his own administration, but

216

he had brought his chief of staff and all the other team members down with him.

"Let me finish. I believe area 403 is about to erupt again — violently."

A little more attentive now, the president asked, "Why do you think that?"

"Because the same thing happened before the 1872 eruption," Jason explained. "And Doctor Carrington documented it. It's like the calm before the storm. Mr. President, you need to take immediate action! Put out an announcement over the Emergency Broadcast Network as quickly as possible. When the next flare hits the atmosphere, it will very likely disrupt communications. By the time it clears, an even larger eruption may already have occurred. There may be no time to send out another warning."

"Thank you, Professor. I'll take it under advisement," Houston said politely.

But before he could get off the line, Jason shouted into the phone, "Mr. President, if you ever trusted me, trust me now! Area 403 *is* going to erupt!"

"Thank you," Houston said abruptly as he hung up the phone.

Turning back to Butts, he said, "Professor Hobart believes that this is the calm before the big storm," the president said. "He wants me to put out an announcement over the EBN."

"Mr. President, I've gone along with you

so far," Butts said, "but this is nuts! You're going to ruin your administration; we're going to be the laughingstock of the world. That man is a dyed-in-the-wool, genuine wacko!"

"You could be right, Warren," the president said reflectively.

"I don't think the president believed me, Doctor," Jason said to Annette.

"If you want me to call you Jason, then you call me Annette," she corrected him. "You have to admit, Jason, from the president's perspective, it is pretty hard to believe."

"No question about that," Jason agreed. "Number one, I was wrong once before and was ridiculed for it; and now, here we are with the president's reputation — and job — on the line and the solar activity seems to be dropping off. But look at this, Doc . . . I mean Annette," he said, pointing to the graph. "As you can see, the gamma ray activity is dropping and the activity in the S-band range is dropping; but look at the X ray."

She glanced down at the chart. "Why, it's actually increasing!" Annette exclaimed.

"Right," Jason said. "And that's the dead giveaway. The thing is building pressure, and the more pressure it builds the higher the X ray output. It's a precursor to a coronal hole developing."

Annette looked at Jason. "As you know, I

don't understand all the theory behind Dr. Carrington's calculations, but I have to believe that you do. What are you going to do about it?"

"I've done all I can," Jason said, shaking his head.

Just then Wendy walked into the room, and when she saw her dad she instantly recognized something was wrong.

"What's the problem, Dad?"

Jason took a minute to bring her up to date.

"Well it's pretty obvious, isn't it, Dad? You need to go see the president."

"I've already talked to him," Jason protested.

"It doesn't matter, Dad. If you really believe you're right, you have to go *see* the president, face to face."

"You're right," Jason agreed. "I just don't want to face President Houston right now. Thanks, Honey. You're a treasure."

"I'd like to come along," Annette said.

"You're more than welcome," Jason replied appreciatively. He reached down and tore the strip of paper off the printer, folding it as he walked out the door. He had just entered the corridor when C.C. appeared.

"What's the trouble, Professor?" he asked.

"I have to see the president," Jason said. "Do you think I can get the helicopter, C.C.?"

"Sorry, Professor. The helicopter is already gone."

"I *have* to go see the president — now!" Jason said firmly.

"Well, my orders are to stick right with you, Professor. So I guess if you're going, I'm going too."

"Got any ideas?" Jason asked the big security man.

"Well, I'll just bet you there are some military vehicles around here somewhere," C.C. said. "Follow me." C.C. knew where the security compound was and headed directly toward it. Once there, he went inside and talked to the sergeant on duty.

"Sergeant, I need a vehicle immediately to transport Dr. Hobart to the White House."

"You've got it, C.C.," the young soldier replied. "My instructions were to do whatever you say."

"Thanks."

"Would you like an escort?"

"Can you get us there in a hurry?" C.C. asked with a chuckle.

"You betcha," the sergeant said. "Just follow our dust."

Within five minutes, two vehicles pulled up to the front of the compound. C.C. slid into the driver's seat of the second vehicle, and Jason, Wendy, and Annette slid into the back seat. The driver in the lead vehicle flipped on his blue light, and away they roared. From Andrews a drive into the city usually would take a good hour. However, with the escort much of the traffic was bypassed; so, with the lights flashing and the siren blasting, they made great time.

Steering the car through the city, C.C. had to smile. He had grown up in this city, but on the wrong side. He was a product of the D.C. ghetto. As dangerous as the Secret Service assignment was, it paled in comparison to everyday life on the streets in the poorest areas of the nation's capital.

His mother had died when he was a baby and he was adopted by his grandparents. They did their best to protect him, but he had been shot twice before his 16th birthday. His size, even as a teenager, made him a tempting target. He had been a tough young hood until a rival gang member's bullet left him bleeding in the street with a punctured lung. He survived only because a passing motorist saw what happened and called 911.

After that episode he no longer felt bullet-proof, as he had before. He and his grandmother moved to Philadelphia, where he reentered high school. He won an appointment to the Naval Academy because his grandfather — his adopted father — had been killed in action in Vietnam. After a five-year tour, which included the Navy Seals, he left the service and applied for the FBI. Instead he was chosen to join the Secret Service. He loved it.

C.C. knew enough about what Jason was saying to realize that if even half of it was true no city in America would be safe. He shuddered when he thought about what it would be like in the gang-controlled ghettos if all the power went off.

He refocused on what he was doing when he pulled up to the White House gates. The security guard, when he saw it was C.C. driving the vehicle, signaled and the troopers cleared a path while the gates rolled back. Five minutes later they were all in the elevator headed up to the president's suite. The president, not knowing Jason was on the way, had assembled Warren Butts, Allen Dean, Gen. Boland, and Dr. Morgan to discuss the latest events. Butts was arguing vehemently that the president should issue no emergency warning. Daniel Morgan stood neutral on the subject, and Dean supported Butts's position.

"Mr. President, the political hazards are just simply too high. And now that the evidence is showing that we will not have the big flare the professor predicted, I don't believe you can make this move. It's time to cut our losses and try to get out of this," Butts argued.

There was no question that Houston was waffling a little bit for the first time. Now he wasn't sure himself.

"You've got to buzz him," Jason argued

with Mary, sitting outside the president's door.

"But they're in a meeting, Sir," she countered.

"I don't care," Jason said. "They're meeting about me. You need to buzz him."

Reluctantly, Mary punched the intercom.

"Yes, what is it?" Houston snapped. He wasn't accustomed to being interrupted during a meeting.

"I'm sorry, Sir, but Doctors Hobart and Camp are here, and they insist on talking with you."

Houston was surprised. He stopped for a moment, and the slightest trace of a smile crossed his face. "Ask them to come in please," the president said.

Everyone in the room had heard the receptionist, and the scowl on Butts's face showed that he wasn't impressed at all.

Houston decided, *Well, professor, you are pretty gutsy, if nothing else.*

Jason and Annette came into the room while Wendy stayed outside with C.C.

"Okay, Professor, why are you here?" the president asked bluntly.

Jason didn't hesitate. "Gentlemen, I'm convinced that we're still going to have a major eruption of area 403."

"What makes you think . . ." Butts started to say, but the president cut him off.

"Let him have his say, Warren," the president ordered.

Butts leaned back in his chair, an irritated look on his face.

"Well, look at this," Jason said, laying out the graph on the table. "As you can see, the X-ray output from area 403 has not declined. In fact, it's increasing. I believe it is continuing to build even as we speak."

"Can you confirm that, Jason?" the president said, lapsing into the informality he felt comfortable with.

"Yes, Sir," Jason said, having prearranged a phone call before he entered. "I believe C.C. has Dr. Moore on the line from Andrews."

The president punched the intercom and said, "Is Dr. Moore on the line?"

The receptionist answered, "Yes, Sir. He is. He's standing by."

"Put him through," the president directed, punching on the speakerphone.

"Gene Moore here," came the response from the other end.

"Dr. Moore, this is Jason Hobart. Can you tell us what the X ray looks like on the spectrometer?"

"Yes, it's really remarkable," Moore said. "X-ray output is rising significantly. It's higher than it was an hour ago."

"Thank you, Doctor," Jason said.

"Do you have any questions for him, Mr. President?"

"No," Houston responded. "I think I've

heard enough. What do you recommend, Professor?"

Jason thanked Moore and hung up. "The same thing I said before, Mr. President. You should put out an emergency message, warning the American people; then notify the other nations of the danger. Sir, when this next eruption occurs, we may not have the opportunity to give a warning."

"I don't agree, Mr. President," Butts interrupted. "The risk is simply too high."

"I respect your opinion, Warren, maybe more than anybody else I know. You and I have been friends a long time, though, and as you know, I've played my hunches before, and my instincts tell me to go with the professor. Put out the word."

"Mr. President, because of our friendship I'll stick with you through this, but if this flare thing fizzles we're all going to look like fools."

"No doubt," Houston agreed, "and thanks. I've got a gut-level feeling about this flare and I'm willing to take the chance."

"All right. You're calling the shots."

"How long before the next flare hits, Professor?" Houston asked.

"Two days — a little less perhaps."

"That's not much time," the president said. "Pull out the stops, Warren. Allen, tell the media. Ask for their help."

"Oh, they'll spread the word all right,"

Dean quipped as he exited the room.

Within 30 minutes the message was going out over the Emergency Broadcast Network: that the president of the United States had declared an emergency and was asking Americans to stay in their homes until the emergency had passed. He announced that all federal facilities were officially closed and military personnel had been put on ready alert.

Neil Farmer and his associates in the media went ballistic. The president of the United States had declared an emergency warning of an impending solar flare when, in fact, they had just gotten word from other solar monitoring stations that flare activity actually had dropped off.

Farmer was preparing another editorial, declaring Houston to be mentally unstable and unfit to be the president. Congressman Gerstner was recommending that immediate action be taken by the Congress to remove him from office, until a panel of medical advisors could determine his psychiatric condition.

We've got him, Farmer noted smugly. *We've got him. The man really is a nut case. Houston will never get out of this trap. This time I'm going to see that man is put out of office. There won't be another conservative president elected in this decade.*

At Andrews Air Force Base, Dr. Moore was

monitoring the data from the spectrometer. An open phone line was connected to the White House, where Jason and Annette stood by. Jason wanted to establish a land line to another spectrometer graph, but there was no time.

Gene Moore was reporting that the X-ray output continued to build when he saw a huge spike on the graph and then several more in succession.

"The equipment must have a problem," he said excitedly, describing what he was seeing. "There's no way this could be real."

"Check the gamma indicator!" Jason shouted into the phone.

"It's spiking off the chart as well," Moore exclaimed.

"Annette, we're seeing a coronal hole forming," Jason said.

"I hope you're wrong," Moore interjected from his end. "If this is an eruption, it's the grandfather of all eruptions."

"What does it mean?" Annette asked as Jason put the phone down.

"The way a coronal hole develops is that it first puts out pulses in the X-ray range, then the gamma ray range, and after that the eruption can follow in hours — or days. We'll have less than two days to study it before the next flare hits."

12

After meeting with the president, Jason and Annette joined C.C. and Wendy and headed back to Andrews. Jason was anxious to get back to the laboratory to monitor the progress of area 403. As predicted, the media had a heyday with the announcement from President Houston. With the second solar flare less than two days away, Houston had ordered all federal facilities shut down and all air traffic grounded — much to the consternation of most Americans who still had to go to work.

Dr. Frasier and several other scientists he had lined up were interviewed regularly by every major network. Frasier continued to insist that the solar flare crisis had been significantly overplayed and that, in fact, the solar flare that was headed toward Earth would do little or no damage. He also reported that the rumor of another, larger flare was purely a figment of Professor Hobart's imagination.

Houston knew when he saw the results of the latest polls in the newspapers that his popularity with the American people was dropping rapidly. From a high of 65 percent, his approval level had now dropped to less than 40 percent. And with every poll taken, it continued to decline.

The president instructed Jason to stay in constant contact with him about any new development. And, as if the president didn't have enough problems, Congressman Gerstner was now rallying the Congress to take immediate action against him. Gerstner let it be known in no uncertain terms: If the solar flare did not develop as projected, he would support impeachment proceedings.

According to reports, there was a growing concern among legislators that perhaps Houston was mentally unstable. Even so, the president appeared to be holding his own with the public and so far had done nothing that would justify impeachment hearings. Everything hinged on Jason's predictions.

At Andrews Air Force Base, Jason set up a 24-hour monitoring system to watch over any new developments. In less than 12 hours the second wave of solar winds would strike Earth and he was apprehensive about it. Jason was resting in his room when the telephone rang. He sat up in bed, trying to shake the cobwebs out of his head before he reached for the receiver. Picking it up, he said, "Yes."

"Jason?" Annette said excitedly. "You need to come to the lab quickly."

"What's the problem?"

"You just need to hurry and see for yourself."

Jason threw on his clothes and, without

even bothering to brush his unruly hair, he hurried out the door and down the hallway, still buttoning the front of his shirt. He threw open the door and rushed into the lab. There at the spectrometer were Annette and Dr. Moore, along with two other technicians.

"What's happening?" Jason said, expecting to find that area 403 had erupted into a major coronal hole. Instead, as he looked at the graph, his heart sank into his stomach. The activity, which had been so pronounced for the previous day and a half, had dropped off by nearly 70 percent.

"It started about 30 minutes ago," Annette said. "It would appear that coronal activity is dissipating."

Jason stared at the graph. His mind was numb. He had no clue what was going on. He muttered, "I don't understand it. I just don't understand it!"

"Think for a minute," Annette said calmly. "Is it possible that the hole has collapsed again?"

Jason caught the inflection in her voice when she said *again,* and the old fears swelled up inside. He was overwhelmed with a feeling of despair. "I just don't know," Jason said dejectedly. "I don't understand it. There should be no way that 403 would just die off again."

The others, all but Annette, drifted away. Jason plopped himself down in a chair, staring at the graph. Then he suddenly asked, "Have you had a visual?"

"No," Annette answered. "Not yet anyway. We called Dr. Onera and asked him to take a look through SOHO. We also asked him to give us a visual."

Jason looked at his watch. It was 2:00 A.M. — less than four hours until sunrise in the Western hemisphere. To Jason time seemed to stand still. He was sure it had been hours since Annette had called Dr. Onera, but each time he checked his watch it had only been a few minutes. He stopped thumping his watch when he noticed Annette's grin. Finally the phone rang. Jason sat in his chair, unable to move. Annette picked up the phone.

"Yes, this is Dr. Camp," Jason heard her say. "Yes, Doctor, I understand. Thank you for the report. We'll get back with you." When she hung up the phone, Jason could see the dejected look on her face.

"I'm sorry, Jason, but Dr. Onera says SOHO shows all activity in area 403 diminishing rapidly, and the visual shows the flare is almost totally dissipated."

"I just can't believe it," Jason muttered. "It doesn't seem possible."

"We're going to have to call the president," Annette said.

Jason knew she was right, but he dreaded the thought of it. The man had trusted him so thoroughly, and he had let him down again.

"I'll be glad to call him for you," Annette offered, sensing his hesitation.

"No, it's my responsibility," Jason sighed. "I'll do it." He walked over to the phone and pressed the intercom button. "This is Dr. Hobart. Please connect me with the White House."

Within five minutes, Jason was talking with the security guards outside the president's study.

"The president is asleep," the man said. "Is this urgent?"

Jason thought, *Is it urgent? The fact is that we're not going to have a major eruption.* Then he said, "You need to wake the president. I'm sure he'd want to hear this." *Better he should hear about it from me,* he decided.

"Okay," the guard said. "Hold on, Doctor."

After what seemed an eternity to Jason, he heard a click on the other end of the line.

"This is Philip Houston. What's up?"

Jason paused. He really didn't know how to break the news to the president. *Well,* he thought, *nothing to do but to do it.* "Mr. President, I don't know how to tell you this but the activity in area 403 is diminishing rapidly."

"What does that mean, Professor?" Houston said, now wide awake.

"I wish I could tell you, but I can't. I was certain that by this time we would have had the third eruption and one much larger than the previous flares. But I honestly don't know."

"Does this mean, Professor, that the flare danger is past?"

"I just don't know. This doesn't fit any logical pattern." What he didn't have to say was, "other than my previous debacle."

Houston tried to be as polite as he could. "Well, Professor, keep me informed."

"I will," Jason said. "And, Mr. President . . ."

"Yes?" Houston answered.

"I really am sorry."

Houston paused for a minute; then he replied. "Listen, Professor, you gave it your best shot, and that's all anybody can expect. I knew the risks and I was willing to take them. Just let me know if anything changes."

"Yes, Sir, I will." As Jason hung up, a wave of depression swept over him.

Houston sat on the edge of his bed for several minutes, pondering what he should do next. *This is awful,* he thought. *The Congress will literally lynch me.* "And you know what?" he said out loud, "I can't really blame them." *I had all the warnings from all the proper people, and I chose to ignore them.* He punched an outside line and called Warren Butts's number.

When the phone rang in his study, Butts was sound asleep. Somewhere in his subconscious mind he was dreaming about the Mars lander he had worked on as a young engineer. He was halfway to Mars on what he knew was an unmanned vehicle. So how could he be on the lander? He heard an alarm going off. Instantly he thought the spaceship had developed a leak and he was going to die. Then he woke up and realized it was the telephone ringing. He was still trying to shake the sleep cobwebs out of his head when he said, "Butts here."

"Warren, this is Phil."

"Yes, Mr. President. What can I do for you?"

"Warren, you were right. Apparently, the flare activity is dropping off, according to Professor Hobart."

Now Butts was wide awake. He thought, *Oh no, exactly what I thought would happen. The worst possible thing for the president.*

"Is he sure?"

"Warren, he wouldn't have called with that kind of news unless he was sure."

He could hear the dejection in Houston's voice.

"We're going to have to contact Allen. Obviously, this news is going to hit the media and they'll crucify me over it."

"Right," Butts said. "I'll take care of it."

"I really doubt that there's any way we'll

wash this one over," Houston said. "You know, Warren, it isn't being wrong that bothers me so much. It's the crowing that I'll have to put up with from Neil Farmer and his cronies that bothers me."

"Oh, Farmer's a pain all right," Butts agreed, "but he's not your biggest problem."

"No, I understand that. My biggest problem will come from Gerstner and the Democrats!"

"For sure," Butts said. "I'll call Allen, Mr. President. We'll do the best damage control we can." Butts hung up the phone and began dialing Allen Dean. After he talked to Dean, he continued dialing, calling every friend in Congress, trying to line up allies before Gerstner could line up their enemies. What he heard sent chills up his spine. Even the most supportive members of the president in Congress were backing off on this one.

By 9:00 the next morning, every newspaper in America carried the news: "Solar Flare Fizzles. President Cancels National Alert." In fact, President Houston had not issued any further orders, but the media had already assumed that responsibility for him, and the president was virtually powerless to do anything about it.

Houston convened a Cabinet meeting that morning to discuss the issue with his Cabinet. Everyone there could feel the president's pain. He had staked his reputation and perhaps his administration on the previously discredited professor from Rockford, Illinois. He had lost, and they knew it.

In Congress, all the activity of the day was virtually suspended as the Democrats interrupted every session to discuss the solar flare issue. The Republicans tried to divert the conversation, but to no avail. The Democrats shouted them down from the floor, and the media carried every tidbit.

At Andrews, Jason was as despondent as Wendy had ever seen him. Annette had filled her in on the details of what was happening, and with every passing hour area 403 continued to calm. Activity had dropped off by more than 90 percent. It was as calm as any other area of the Sun.

The media attacks on both the president and his scientific advisor were escalating. Jason hadn't watched any television but Wendy had, and he could tell from looking at her what the latest news was. Her eyes were red and puffy from crying, so he could just imagine what the media was saying. As he thought about it, he decided he couldn't blame them. *They were right. I am a wacko. How could I have been so wrong? How could I have been so stupid again? And this time I took a president down with me.* Nothing Wendy or Annette said could help. Jason was numb from shock.

At 7:00 that evening, the second flare hit Earth, and the news couldn't have been worse for President Houston. Only two high-altitude satellites were damaged and even they were only off-line for a little more than four hours, until backup systems could be activated.

Communications were disrupted due to the static caused by the solar winds, but nothing that had not been experienced several times previously. And even though the magnitude of the second flare was higher than normal, no major disruptions were apparent — at least no major *permanent* disruptions.

Television viewers were inconvenienced as the worst of the solar winds hit the earth, and many of the GEO positioning satellites had to be shut down, due to static interference. Several power grids in the western states did drop out as surges hit the power lines but, again, nothing that would have been considered overly abnormal, except that this time some control circuits were damaged.

The next day, newspapers throughout America carried the story on the front pages: "Solar Flare Fizzles" and "Houston Fumbles." Unreported by the media was the fact that hundreds, perhaps thousands, of cars were also disabled. Either the connection to the flare was not made or it was ignored.

Jason had no further communications with President Houston, and he didn't anticipate any. It had been nearly 14 hours since the second solar flare struck Earth and, in large part, things had pretty much returned to normal for the rest of American society — but not for Jason Hobart. His life was shattered, along with his confidence. Annette and Wendy did everything they could to comfort him, but both of them knew nothing would help. He was despondent and justifiably so.

Jason went to his room and laid there for hours with his eyes shut, unable to sleep. Then his phone rang. He let it ring six, then eight, then ten times. And finally, out of sheer irritation, he reached over and snatched up the receiver. "Yes," he snapped.

"Jason, it's Annette."

"Oh, I'm sorry."

"I understand," she replied. "Don't worry about it. Jason, you need to get in here right now."

"Annette, I just don't think . . ."

"Jason, listen!" she interrupted. "We've just had another eruption from area 403. You need to get here immediately."

Jason almost leaped out of bed. Without even bothering to put on his shoes, he hurried down the corridor and into the laboratory.

"Take a look," she said.

Jason looked at the graph. He was startled by what he saw. The meter was pegged to the extremity.

"That's not all," Annette said. "I've just gotten a call from Dr. Onera. SOHO confirms the eruption."

"What magnitude?"

"Hard to tell at this point," Annette said, "but more than a level 8."

"This is it!" Jason shouted. "I have to warn the president!" Jason hurried over to the phone and called the operator.

"Yes, may I help you?"

"Yes. This is Dr. Hobart. I need to contact the White House immediately."

"Yes, Sir," the operator said. About three minutes later, the president's secretary was on the line.

"Yes, Dr. Hobart," Mary said. "How may I help you?"

"I need to talk to the president," he said nervously.

"I'm sorry, Doctor, the president's in a meeting."

"I understand," Jason said. "Can you get a message to him?"

"Probably," she said, "but it may be 30 minutes or so."

"That's okay," Jason said calmly. He realized that his alarm would be the last thing the president would respond to at this point. "Just tell him I called and that we've had a confirmed eruption in area 403. It's at least a level 8 solar flare."

Mary had learned enough over the last few days to know what Dr. Hobart was saying was important, so she said, "Hold on, Professor. I'll get the president for you." She put

Jason on hold and buzzed the president in the Cabinet room.

The president knew Mary would not be interrupting him unless it was an emergency. He told the group he was meeting with, "Excuse me for a minute. I'll be right back." He stepped outside the room and picked up the intercom. "Yes Mary, what is it?"

"Mr. President, I'm sorry to interrupt you, but Professor Hobart is on the line."

Houston had a flash of irritation. "Mary, tell the professor I'll call him back," he said sharply.

"But Mr. President, Professor Hobart said they've had a confirmed solar flare of at least a level 8."

"What?" Houston exclaimed. "Put him on, Mary."

Mary connected the lines. "This is President Houston. Tell me what's happening, Professor."

"Mr. President, I'm sorry to bother you, but I knew you would want to hear. We've just had a major eruption in area 403, and Dr. Onera at Tokyo University confirms it's at least a level 8 flare."

"What does that mean?" the president asked skeptically.

"Mr. President, I know you've lost a lot of confidence in me. I can't blame you. I've lost a lot of confidence in myself. But, Sir, this is for real. It's a level 8-plus solar flare, and it's going to cause enormous damage. We have less than three days . . ."

"To do what?" the president said sharply.

"At a minimum, you need to ground all aircraft, as we discussed earlier, and you need to power down all equipment during the daylight phase of this flare. A level 8 flare, Mr. President, could conceivably disable most of our electronic equipment. And you should warn the other nations."

"I'll take it under advisement, Professor. And thank you. I'll get back with you."

Jason heard the line go dead. He plopped himself down in the chair beside the end table. *He doesn't trust me,* he thought dejectedly. *And who could blame him?*

In a few minutes, Houston went back into the meeting. He listened to some delegations from the European Common Market, discussing issues that seemed of no importance to him at that particular moment. He mulled his way through the meeting for the next hour and then excused himself and adjourned the meeting — much to the consternation of the men and women who had traveled several thousand miles to meet with him.

He hurried to his office and told Mary, "Get Warren and Allen in here immediately."

"Yes, Sir," she said without hesitation. Fifteen minutes later, Dean and Butts were in the Oval Office with the president. He filled them in on the conversation with Jason.

"Surely, Mr. President, you're not going to listen to the professor this time, are you?" Warren Butts asked, or rather stated more as a fact than a question.

"What if he's right, Warren?" the president countered.

"What if he's wrong, Mr. President? You won't survive another wave of negative publicity. Sir, the Congress is already discussing your competency to lead the country. The opinion polls have your support level down to 30 percent. That's the lowest of any president in modern times."

"Warren, you know I'm not much into opinion polls, and Congress usually bends with the most current opinions, as you and I both know."

"True, Mr. President, I understand that. But still, this is a democratic country. And although you were elected, you still govern by the will of the majority. Can you imagine what it would do to this country if we had impeachment proceedings over the competency of the American president to lead the country?"

"Do you seriously think that could happen, Warren?" the president asked.

"It's possible, Mr. President. The mood of the country right now is very negative and hostile. Remember, you've imposed some pretty austere policies during this presidency. When you cut back on social welfare and gov-

242

ernment spending and created a lot of unemployment, the American people were willing to go along with that. But now, in the face of the things that have happened over the last few days, I don't know how they will react."

"What do you think, Allen?" the president asked his press secretary.

"Well, Sir, all I can tell you is that the media is primed and ready for blood. They've already gotten word of this latest solar flare. But, according to Dr. Frasier and several other eminent scientists, the magnitude of these flares has been greatly exaggerated. They've already primed the public to believe, based on what happened previously, that Dr. Hobart and his team are nothing but charlatans out to make headlines. I doubt that you'll be able to convince the American people that this represents a crisis, Sir. And even if you declare a national emergency, outside of declaring martial law, I doubt that most Americans are going to go along with you."

Then Dean added, "Mr. President, I don't think you have the constitutional authority to ground the airlines, and you certainly don't have the constitutional authority to shut down all the industry in America unilaterally."

"I concur with that," Butts said.

The president paused for a moment. "I'm going to defer to your judgment this time, Warren. I went against you last time and I was wrong. But issue a statement, Allen, giv-

243

ing Dr. Hobart's evaluation of this most recent flare but recommending nothing further as a result of it. However, I do want to give Dr. Hobart's recommendations a fair hearing as well. So tell the press that Dr. Hobart's recommendation is that the airlines cease operations voluntarily."

Houston thought about it for a moment. Then he said, "No, scratch that. We'll just make Dr. Hobart look like a lunatic if we do that. We'll do nothing. We'll just give the professor's evaluation of the solar flare and leave it at that."

"I heartily concur, Mr. President," Butts said.

Dean wasn't quite so sure. He had grown to respect Dr. Hobart, in spite of the current situation. But he said, "I'll get the word out, Mr. President. We'll do as much damage control as possible."

"Thanks, guys," the president said as he concluded the meeting. After Butts and Dean left, the president sat at his desk thinking, undisturbed for nearly 30 minutes, a rarity anymore for anyone holding that office. He had mixed emotions. *If this eruption had occurred even two days earlier,* he decided, *I would have followed his advice. So does two days mean that he's wrong?* He sighed deeply. *I really don't have any choice at this point. I just pray, Professor, that you are wrong.*

For the next two-and-one-half days, President Houston was skewered in the media. Only the fact that he didn't support the professor's latest warning saved him. As the public lost interest, so did Congress, but the media assault was relentless. Dr. Frasier was seen every day on every network, demeaning and undercutting the president and his chief scientific advisor, Professor Jason Hobart.

Wendy had stopped watching the television because she cried every time she did. The media now portrayed her father as nothing less than an egomaniac, out for headlines and self-promotion. She knew it wasn't true, but there was nothing she could do.

Jason was beside himself. He truly believed that the magnitude of this third flare would cause major disruptions throughout the world, but he also understood the president's position. If he were in the president's seat, he probably would have done exactly what President Houston had done — ignore Jason Hobart. He had no other choice.

Annette spent two days poring over the data coming in from around the world, and she was convinced that Jason was right! But she knew the dilemma of the president as well as Jason did. There was nothing that either of them could do about the situation.

They were collecting a tremendous amount of data that would be of great help in forecasting future solar flares, but for the moment the group at Andrews had no input into the scientific community.

At 7:30 P.M. on April 4th, the solar flare from area 403 gripped the ionosphere of Earth, and at exactly 7:32 P.M. all the power at Andrews Air Force Base went off. Forever, the world would be changed by the events of that day.

If the Sky Lab astronauts had not been evacuated, they would have died that day.

On the Russian *Mir* orbiting lab, their astronauts saw their power systems explode in showers of sparks and flames. All systems lost power and the desperate astronauts fought the smoke and flames but were no longer able to breathe. All four men were dead within five minutes of the flare hitting them.

At the South Pole, the fall sky was a flaming red and blue spectacle. The cosmic bombardment ignited the ionized upper atmosphere all the way to New Zealand.

The Earth's magnetic shield diverted the early wave of cosmic winds striking the upper regions. But as the billions of tons of charged matter continued to assault the shield, it began to bend and wobble, allowing cosmic radiation to reach deep into the atmosphere. Power grids were overloaded as lines surged. These, in turn, overloaded oil-filled transformers, which exploded into flames, showering city streets with hot, flaming oil. City by city, the lights went out as the massive solar winds struck Earth.

The instant after the lights blinked off in the White House, President Houston realized that the flare had struck. The White House backup generators were independent of any other electrical system and were well maintained. When the power failed, they cycled on automatically, then abruptly cycled off as power surges overloaded the controls. But the dead giveaway was when the TV in Houston's study flashed and acrid smoke billowed out of the cabinet.

Within minutes, Warren Butts was knocking on the president's door. "Come in," Houston said.

"Sir, all the power's out in the city," Butts said as he panted from his jaunt up the stairs.

"Has to be the flare that Jason warned us about," Houston replied. He was feeling guilty for ignoring Jason's warning.

"But even so, it shouldn't have shut down everything," Butts argued.

"Do you know of anything else that can kill all the power, including our own backup generators?" Houston snapped. Then he regretted his anger. *After all, it isn't Butts's fault.*

"Warren, I want you to contact Professor Hobart. Find out what's going on. Then, after the Sun sets, if our generators will work, I want to address the nation over the EBN, if and when the stations get on the air. Have Allen set it up for 4:00 or 5:00 A.M. I need to reach the west coast too."

"I'll get it done, Mr. President," Butts said.

"And Warren, get General Boland in here too," Houston added.

"Right," Butts replied. "And Phil, I'm sorry. The professor was right and I was wrong."

"It's okay, Warren. I was wrong too. Now let's see what we can do to recover."

Once the Sun had set, the backup generators at the White House were started. Although the automatic controls were burned out, the manual system worked fine.

The generator at the Andrews observation building was up and operating with no difficulties. Butts placed a call to Andrews only to discover that the lines were down. It was not until Gen. Boland ordered hard line patches around the AT&T electronic switches that Butts was able to finally make contact.

"The president is anxious to get a report on the flare," Butts told Jason.

"It's important for the president to tell the American people to power down all electrical and electronic devices during daylight hours," Jason said.

"Why during daylight hours?" Butts interrupted.

"Because when the country is exposed directly to the cosmic storm, any operating equipment will be destroyed. You can power up about 30 minutes after sunset. This is very critical!" Jason warned.

"Okay, I understand," Butts agreed. "I'll pass it on to the president. Anything else?"

"Yes," Jason said somberly. "I recommend that the cities be evacuated — as quickly as possible."

"Evacuate the cities!" Butts replied incredulously. "Are you serious, Professor?"

"Totally," Jason replied. "I believe an even larger flare will occur. When that happens, everything will be shut down, even during the daytime, maybe for weeks — or months."

Butts started to argue. Then he stopped. He had been wrong once because he was concerned about the political ramifications. He said, "I'll tell the president, Professor," and with that he hung up.

Evacuate the cities, he thought. *There must be a hundred million people in the cities.* When Butts briefed the president on his conversation with Dr. Hobart, he wasn't sure how he expected Houston to react.

"Let's get it done!" Houston said. "I'll make the announcement over the EBN. By sunset tomorrow we need to have a plan in place. I want people moving by midnight tomorrow."

"But, Mr. President . . . ," Butts started to say.

"No buts, Warren. I'm going with the professor this time. If he's right, the stakes are too high to wait."

"But if he's wrong?"

"Then I'll be the second president to be drummed out of office," Houston said.

The next several hours were some of the most dramatic in the history of planet Earth and certainly in the history of mankind; because, as the massive solar winds continued to pummel Earth, multimillion dollar satellites blinked out. The first to go dead were those in stationary orbits above Earth, unprotected by Earth's magnetic force field. But later, even the low-orbit satellites failed as the magnetic force field began to bend and collapse under the cosmic assault.

The solar eruption from area 403 registered a magnitude of 8.5. The flare "foot" extended out from the Sun nearly three million miles and reached a diameter that was 1,000 times larger than Earth. Without question, it was the most massive solar flare in *recorded* history and possibly the most massive solar flare ever to hit Earth directly. The initial surge from the solar flare, instead of dissipating, continued to build, pummeling Earth's magnetic shield.

Once the satellites went down, all global broadcasters went down with them. Telephone communications were the next to go, as both the deep-space and the lower-orbit satellites burned out. International communications, even by cable, were washed out by the static.

When the flare hit, aircraft pilots suddenly

found themselves with no navigation aids. The GEO satellites, the SAT COM satellites — all the navigational aids that had recovered from the previous flare — were suddenly gone. Worse than that, the aircraft commanders trying to communicate with their bases found themselves isolated with no communications. Instruments that normally were their lifeline to flight controllers were useless. Radios were out, navigation equipment was gone; even the compasses they relied on as backup were no longer reliable, because with Earth's magnetic field fluctuating wildly, the compasses were useless.

A military flight that had taken off from England on a surveillance mission had just leveled out at 37,000 feet when the communications went out. The pilot called out to his co-pilot, "My radio's out!"

"Mine too!" the copilot confirmed.

"Look at the Loran. It's gone too," the pilot shouted as his fear mounted.

"And look at that compass!" the copilot exclaimed. "What's going on?"

"I don't know," the pilot said somberly, "but I have a bad feeling. Remember that warning from the U.S. about another solar flare?"

"Yeah," his copilot said.

"Unfortunately, this may be it," the captain responded. In a calm voice he instructed his copilot, "Let's head back."

"But how, Captain? We don't have any radio, and our navigation equipment is out."

"Son, we're going to have to navigate the way it used to be done," the captain declared, with more assertiveness than he felt. It was one thing to navigate a C-47 by landmarks and another thing to navigate a jet traveling at 500 miles an hour. The smallest error could put them hundreds of miles off course.

The navigation problem suddenly became irrelevant when in the cockpit the captain saw all of his electronic indicators first blink, and then flash, as they went dead. He could smell the acrid smoke in the cockpit — the smell of electronic equipment being fried. The L22 stealth reconnaissance plane, being one of the newer breed of equipment, was a fly-by-wire airplane, meaning that it used electronic signals, rather than cables, to control the flight surfaces. Without power there were no controls.

Inside the cabin, the pilot and copilot could only sit in terror as they felt the plane plunge, roll over, and begin a steady spiral as it headed down to the ocean. The captain punched the eject button — but with no response. Then he realized that the eject system was electrically operated also. The plane continued its downward death spiral until it crashed into the sea.

★ ★ ★

The solar winds striking Earth carried billions of tons of supercharged electrical particles. The sheer mass of this flare ripped through the magnetic buffer that normally protected Earth, bending and twisting the magnetosphere until it collapsed.

At ground level, where the force field was more protective, the consequences of the solar flare were delayed but not avoided. The first to go were the power grids. As the charged particles hit the power lines, the surge of power tripped the grid breakers off line. The same scenario was repeated in every country. As soon as daylight came, the power went out.

To make matters worse, inside the power stations themselves, operators working frantically to get the grids back on line after the last flare saw the electronic monitors, control systems, and power regulators flash and burn as the shower of charged particles overloaded the circuits. The massive electromagnetic pulses created by the solar winds destroyed all operating electronic devices in their path.

Perhaps the flare in 1872 was of the same magnitude. But in 1872 there had been no electronic equipment around to be overloaded. That was not the case with this flare. Power station generators shorted and burned out. Radio and television stations saw their transmitters surge, then flash and burn. On-

253

line computer screens blossomed and then died with a smell of acrid smoke.

Water pumping station controls were fused solid. Sewage pumping stations failed, dumping raw sewage into streams and rivers. Automobiles that had been spared by the previous flare were disabled as their electronic components were vaporized.

To an observer from outside Earth, the whole scene would have appeared like a planet dying as lights flashed, then blinked out across the landscape.

13

It had been a long night at the White House. In fact, it had been one of the longest that Philip Houston could ever remember. Here he was, the leader of the most powerful nation in the world; yet there was nothing he could do. He made an announcement over the Emergency Broadcast Network, declaring a national emergency and directing Americans to turn off all electrical devices before sunrise. He also announced that mass evacuation would begin the next evening.

After making his announcement on the EBN, the president called an emergency meeting of his Cabinet and chief advisors and found several of them absent. When he asked where they were, he learned that they had either gone home earlier or had returned to their own offices and had not been able to get back to the White House.

Mobs of angry citizens were gathered outside the White House gates, and only the cordons of armed troops, hastily ordered by Gen. Boland, kept them from breaking into the White House grounds.

Houston shook his head. He never could understand people. If the solar flare had not materialized, he probably would have been drummed out of office. Instead, because the flare shut down the cities, the American people now blamed him and wanted to extract a pound of flesh.

What a crazy society we have, he reflected somberly. For the first time in his life he began to question his ability to lead people. *This reminds me of what a friend said one time about a buffalo: You can lead a buffalo anywhere he wants to go.* Houston now rather suspected the same was true with the American people: You can lead them anywhere they want to go. But, he wasn't at all sure they were wanting to go in the direction he had in mind.

As more of his staff assembled, Houston made it clear he intended to enforce Dr. Hobart's suggested ban on operating equipment during daylight hours — at least within government circles. After sunset the government facilities, those that had self-contained power, could once again power up their own generators and get back into operation. Communications could be reestablished, but information to the media would be strictly limited. The media wouldn't like it, but the decision wasn't negotiable. He wanted to control the panic, if possible, and the media would not be allowed to focus on the negatives and spread fear. He had already directed Gen. Boland to have a detailed evacuation plan drawn up and ready to implement as soon as possible.

His instructions to his military commander were clear: "General Boland, I want the military to take control of the cities. There must be no mistakes, because after dark these gangs are going to be worse than ever. I want the troops disbursed as quickly as possible. We're going to protect American citizens, and if it means armed confrontations with the gangs to do it, so be it."

Boland's countenance perked up. This is what he loved. He was trained, in fact he was born, to be a soldier, and now he had a commander in chief who was willing to take definitive action for the first time in a long time. He was ready to go. He had already contacted his security team leaders, and he had set up a relay system to communicate messages across the country.

In another 12 hours of darkness, Boland knew he could have a functioning communication system set up across most of the nation. Given two nights, he could have it established from coast to coast — much like the Pony Express, only more efficient. Electronic at night, manual during the day. *Hot dog!* he thought. *This is the way an army should be run.*

Boland's lifelong hero was Gen. George Patton. He shared many of the passions the famous general had, but action was foremost. His greatest regret in life was that he had missed all the big wars. Now he would have his chance, and he relished taking on the gangs. He had come from the inner city himself and had seen firsthand the terror they wreaked on honest people. The liberal courts had prohibited any real punishment of these thugs. But now they would get their due. And he was just the guy to do it!

Houston saw the sparkle in Boland's eyes, and his countenance lightened. *This general is all business, all military, and tough as nails. He'll have no problems with security,* Houston decided. *If it can be done, Boland will get it done.*

He directed his attention to the secretary of the interior. "Oren, I want every available working vehicle to be commandeered for transporting people out of the cities," Houston commanded. "There must be no mistakes! I want their escorts to be well armed. We're going to get as many American citizens as possible out of harm's way. Is that clear?"

"Yes, Mr. President," Blake said.

"I want everyone to coordinate all transportation through Oren, is *that* clear?"

Almost in unison the group nodded acknowledgment. At this juncture there would be no dissent, no haggling, and no political maneuvering. Each of the people in that room had families themselves, and most of them did not know the status of their own families. They were as trapped in the White House as their families were in their own communities, with no way of communicating with one another until after sundown.

Meanwhile, at Andrews AFB, Jason, Annette, and her associate Gene Moore had already discussed the situation and had concluded that the very equipment they needed to study the Sun would be destroyed if they turned it on during daylight hours. Once the initial surge from the flare had dissipated, the equipment could operate during nighttime hours, when Earth was blocking the full force of the cosmic storm; but at night they would be unable to observe what was happening on the Sun itself. It was a catch-22.

As they pondered the problem, it was Annette who came up with what turned out to be the obvious solution. "We can't monitor the Sun directly, except through visual means," she said, "but we can monitor it indirectly. We can turn our equipment on at night and measure the intensity of the cosmic radiation in the night sky. If we accept that whatever level we have right now is the baseline, then we'll simply monitor the changes. At least then we'll know whether the cosmic storm is still at critical levels."

"Good idea," Jason said sheepishly. "A little bit of common sense goes a long way."

"I agree," Gene Moore said, turning his

attention once more to the calculations he was working on.

Jason was reminded that Dr. Carrington, working more than a century before, without any electronic instruments, had come to a thorough understanding of solar flares and had developed a means to calculate their intensity and, to some extent at least, their duration. He knew that with just the solar telescopes he could work out a formula that would give them an early warning system. Along with Annette's monitoring of the ion output from the Sun, they would have a good indicator of how the coronal hole was developing.

He didn't say anything to the group at that time, but if his guess was right the current storm would last another couple of days and then diminish. The next burst of radiation, he suspected, was going to be larger and longer. They had a limited amount of time to put any plans into motion. He turned his attention to the scientific aspects, knowing that President Houston would be taking care of the political side of the crisis.

In a suburb of New York City, Kevin and Colleen O'Ryan lived in a nice, middle-income apartment complex. When they went to bed the evening before, the electricity in their home was out. Power outages for Edison Electric customers were not too unusual and, believing it to be only a temporary situation, they had not been concerned.

Kevin woke up late that morning; in fact, the Sun was already up when he opened his eyes. He glanced down at his watch and saw that it read 6:12. *The Sun shouldn't be that high*, he thought, *if it's only 6:12*. Then, taking a closer look at his watch, he noticed that the sweep hand was not moving. His watch had stopped. He glanced over at the clock beside his bed. The digital display was dark.

"Honey, the power's still off," he said, nudging Colleen. "Time to get up! I guess we're going to be late. The power's still off, so the radio didn't come on. I don't know what time it is. My watch has stopped."

Colleen leaned over to the nightstand by her side of the bed and picked up her watch. She shook it. "Mine too, Babe. It reads 6:12. Why would the power being off make our watches stop?"

Kevin sat up in bed. "Yeah, that is peculiar." They both got up. Kevin quickly slipped on his pants, shirt, and slippers while Colleen put on her robe. He walked over and flipped the light switch on the wall several times. Nothing. He went into the living room and flipped that switch. Nothing. He walked out into the kitchen to see what the time on the microwave read, and the indicator was totally blank — no indication whatsoever. *The power's definitely out, but something else must be hap-*

pening. He was as confused as he was irritated.

He walked out of their apartment and into the hallway, to see if any of his neighbors knew what was happening, but evidently nobody else was up. So, he decided to get dressed and go to the local convenience store to see what was going on. He walked back in the apartment and told his wife, "Colleen, I'll be back in a little bit. I'm going down to the Jiffy Stop to see if anyone knows anything."

"Okay," Colleen answered. "I'll have breakfast ready by the time you get back."

"I don't think so," Kevin said as he walked out. Colleen was about to ask what he meant, but by that time he had already closed the door and left. Then it came to her: *Oh yeah, I guess I can't cook breakfast with no power!*

Kevin went down the stairs to the parking lot. He crossed to his car, got in, and turned the key. He heard a click and then nothing. Not a sound. *How can my battery be dead?* he thought. *This car is almost new.*

In the split second it had taken Kevin to turn the key, the sensitive electronic equipment in his automobile had been fried. Without knowing it, just turning it on immobilized his vehicle. By this time, he noticed a couple of other people getting into their cars, all with the same effect. Not one car would start. *What in the world is going on?* he wondered as he got out of the car. He shoved the door closed and walked over to where one of his friends was standing by his car.

"What do you make of all this, Brad?" Kevin asked.

"Man, I haven't the slightest idea," his friend replied.

Another man who had just gotten out of his car walked over. "I wonder if this could be because of what happened last night."

"What do you mean?" Kevin asked.

"I was listening to the news early this morning on my Walkman. They were talking about the president's announcement."

"What announcement?" Kevin asked.

"Something about a scientist recommending that we shouldn't power up any electrical equipment — or something like that."

"Why?" Kevin said with a rising sense of alarm.

"It had something to do with the solar flare that was predicted. The commentator said it was a bunch of nonsense, so I didn't pay a lot of attention. But a few minutes later my Walkman quit. I thought the battery had run out. But, I think it has something to do with the flare."

"But why won't our cars start?" Kevin asked no one in particular.

"There's no energy left, I guess," the other man said. "I'm not an auto mechanic, but nothing in my car works."

"Mine either," said Kevin.

Brad added, "Ditto here."

"What else did you hear?" Kevin asked.

"Nothing really. That's about it. From what the commentator said, he thought the whole thing was nonsense and we should ignore it. Looks like the media was wrong — as usual."

"What are you going to do?" Kevin asked.

"Beats me," Brad said. "I guess I'll go back home and just wait."

Walking back to the apartment Kevin was thinking, *Wait? What for? What's going to happen next?* He was almost to his door when another of his neighbors walked out.

"What's going on, Kevin?" Cindy asked.

"I don't know. As far as we can tell, nothing works. The cars won't run. The lights don't work. Nothing electrical seems to work. Even my watch has stopped."

"Then it's true," she said.

"What's true?"

"I was listening this morning when the president came on. It was about 5:00 or a little after. I couldn't sleep so I tried the TV. It was out so I turned on the Walkman I use when I exercise."

"And the president was on? What did he say?"

"Just that a solar flare hit last night. Nothing else really. The newscaster said it had something to do with that nutty professor we've been hearing about," Cindy said.

"Oh yeah," Kevin said. "I remember reading something about it. What's it all about?"

"Well, from what this professor said, it has something to do with the solar flare and the radiation from the Sun. He said the energy from the flare would burn out electrical stuff — something like that. I didn't get it all. He thought the government should begin evacuating the cities."

"Evacuating the cities!" Kevin exclaimed. "Why? To where? When?"

"Oh, I don't remember," Cindy said. "I was still half asleep. Besides, right after he finished talking, the announcer said that we should ignore everything the president said. Several other scientists came on saying that what this professor was saying was nonsense — that it had nothing whatsoever to do with reality."

"Evidently it did," Kevin added.

"Apparently so. What are you going to do?" she asked apprehensively.

"Well, I think the first thing I'm going to do is tell Colleen what I know."

"Would you mind if I came with you?" she asked.

"Not at all," he said. He knew that Cindy lived alone and probably was more worried than he was — which was plenty.

As they reached the apartment, Kevin realized he had left his keys in the car so he knocked on the door. Colleen opened the door and, seeing Cindy, realized something was wrong.

"Hi, Cindy," she said apprehensively. "What's up?"

Kevin began to explain the little he knew thus far, including the suggested evacuations.

"That's unbelievable," Colleen said. "Is it possible?"

"I don't know," he replied. "Maybe." Kevin was a lot more concerned than he was willing to let on. They lived in the shadow of one of the largest cities in America and he knew any big city could turn violent very quickly. The gangs were a small minority of the population — but extremely volatile. Even in their middle-class complex, the drug dealers were active. There had been two muggings in the parking lot in the last month.

"We're just going to have to sit and wait, Babe. There's not much else we can do. What do we have to eat that doesn't have to be cooked?"

His wife replied, "Well, we have some cereal. But you were right about not being able to fix breakfast. I just wasn't thinking."

"What about the frig? Have you checked to see if the milk is okay?"

"Everything's still pretty cool, so it should be okay."

"Great," Kevin said. "Cindy, how would you like a gourmet breakfast of raisin bran?"

"It sounds pretty good to me," she said,

trying to act as cheerful as possible. But her heart was really pounding. *What are we going to do?* she wondered.

"How long do you think this will last?" Colleen asked Kevin.

"To tell you the truth, I don't have the foggiest. You know as much about it as I do."

About that time, Kevin heard what sounded like three or four backfires. Then he realized, *How can that be a backfire if there are no vehicles operating?* He rushed to the balcony door, flung it open, and looked out. There below, he saw four armed young men — obviously not tenants. Brad and the other man he had just been talking to lay bleeding in the parking lot. One of the armed group was already rifling through Brad's pockets. Kevin thought about yelling at them and then thought better of it. He wasn't armed. There was nothing he could do. He eased back into the apartment and closed the balcony door.

"What's wrong?" Colleen asked.

"Some guys with guns just shot Brad and another tenant. They're laying in the parking lot."

"Shot them?" Colleen screamed. The blood drained from her face and she thought she was going to faint.

"Try to be calm, Honey," Kevin said as he walked over and bolted the front door. He reached for the phone instinctively, but hearing no dial tone he laid it back down.

"There's nothing we can do." All thoughts of eating had suddenly vanished from their minds as more shots were heard.

Colleen and Cindy looked at each other in panic. "What are we going to do?" was on both their lips.

"I honestly don't know," Kevin said as he tried to comfort the women. His mind was reeling in confusion. "I guess we have to sit tight. What else can we do?"

"Let's get out," Colleen said. "Kevin, I'm scared."

Kevin had already decided that leaving the city was the best idea he'd heard of in a long time. He suspected it was going to get very hard to live in the city if the power stayed off very long. They had no water. They had only the food in their cabinet, and the refrigerator food would go bad very quickly with no power. And there were armed gangs roaming around, ready to kill anybody who stepped outside. The more he thought about it, the better evacuation sounded to him.

In the inner city, the scene was much worse. By 9:00 that morning the news of what had happened was spreading throughout the city. Nothing worked: no lights, no water, no elevators, no vehicles — nothing. City dwellers who were used to their catered independence suddenly found themselves trapped in their own homes as looters began pillaging the city, burning whatever they wanted and shooting at anything that moved.

After her husband left her, Noreen Ball stayed in her lovely home as long as she could, until she simply couldn't make the payments on it anymore and had to let it go. With her small surplus of money she had bought a computer to work at home, but she and her two children had to move into a low-income housing development. She had accepted the subsidized housing with great reluctance, but she had no choice.

Government housing was more horrible than she had ever imagined. Even what she saw on television had not prepared her for what she experienced. Drugs were dealt freely in the parking lots outside the building and young toughs ruled the streets at night. It was unsafe to go out, day or night, so she and her family stayed locked behind barred doors. For the first six months she had cried herself to sleep every night. She prayed for God to rescue her and her children from this nightmare. Then things began to change.

During the last five months, the tenants had started to take charge of their own lives. In total disregard for the gun ban in New York, most of them had bought guns outside the city. Soon there was virtually no tenant in her building who wasn't armed with some type of weapon.

Noreen now owned a 9mm semiautomatic

and had traveled over to Newark, New Jersey three times to take lessons in defensive arms, including shooting at least 10 clips through her pistol. She had become quite proficient and felt totally comfortable with the weapon. Just knowing it was available, if needed, gave her a sense of security. She had hidden the gun inside the drywall that had been carved out under the kitchen sink, along with three clips of ammunition hidden in another location. She assured herself that there was no way her children could get the weapon and, even if they did, they would not know where the ammunition was, so she felt totally comfortable with a gun in her apartment.

As was her habit, Noreen had planned to work through most of the night. She did the majority of her work while her children were asleep so she could spend as much time as possible with them during the day, catnapping when they napped. But before she was to start to work that evening, all the power in the apartment complex had gone out. It was the fifth time that year that the electricity had failed, so Noreen had thought nothing about it. And she was well prepared for it.

She had flashlights and even had an oil lamp that she had purchased from the Discount Mart just for this occasion, so she sat up several hours reading, waiting for the electricity to come on. She had dozed off and then was awakened by the crackle of her television at 4:00 in the morning. *Well, good! At least the power has come back on.* She was still trying to shake the sleepiness out of her eyes when the announcement about the solar flare was made.

Unlike some of the others who had heard the announcement, Noreen had believed it. She had listened intently: Americans were to turn off all equipment and stay in their homes. She had listened as the president explained about the solar flare. She didn't understand it all, but she knew enough to realize that she should stay where she was, in her own apartment, until she could be evacuated, and she intended to do exactly that.

When daylight came, Noreen was still wide awake. Sounds of gunfire erupted outside the apartment complex. She didn't have to go check it out. She knew what it was. It was the gangs that ruled the area. At the first sound of gunfire, the citizens' defense committee had mobilized. Five minutes later Noreen heard a neighbor down the hall blowing a police whistle.

She knew what to do. She went to the cabinet, opened the door, retrieved her gun; then she went into the other room and got two clips of ammunition. Sliding one of the clips into the weapon, she opened the door and stepped into the hallway. Two of her neighbors were already there, and within two more minutes the inhabitants of the other apartments stepped into the hallway. Each of them was armed. Some carried shotguns and some carried pistols; but everyone had a weapon. It had been mutually agreed that if any person was attacked by one of the gangs, *all* the neighbors would come to his or her aid.

The floor leader said to the group, "Does anybody know what's happening? Why are the lights still out?"

Noreen responded, "I can tell you what I heard this morning," and she related the entire announcement she'd heard. She said, "I believe what we're seeing is exactly what the president said: This solar flare has shut down all the electrical systems."

"I understand that the president has declared martial law and ordered the federal troops out," another neighbor said.

"Well, apparently the word hasn't reached this building yet," one of the others quipped. "It's only a matter of time til the looters come."

"Well, we know what to do," someone else said. "We're here and we're prepared to defend ourselves."

"But we want to be sure that we don't become part of the problem," Noreen reminded them. "We're not a gang. We're a citizens' defense group."

"Understood," the floor leader agreed. "Listen, what we want to do is set up a defense perimeter here. One of us will remain in the hallway at all times with a whistle. If we hear or see anything, we blow the whistle and everybody will come. Agreed?" All the neighbors shook their heads in agreement.

"What about the other floor leaders?"

"I think they're all prepared."

"One of us should go and check on them," Noreen said.

"I agree," the older woman said. "I'll do it." Noreen was relieved because she didn't want to leave her children, no matter what, and she wouldn't have gone, even if asked. But the older woman was already on her way up the stairs.

Noreen heard one of the men say, "I'll take the first watch." He was an older man, armed with a pump shotgun. "I'll cut 'em in half if they try to break in here," he boasted. "I fought in Nam. These punks are nothin' compared to the NV."

Noreen watched him pull a chair out of his apartment and into the hallway. He sat down and propped the shotgun across his knees. He had bought the shotgun from one of the gangs, ironically enough, and where they got it he didn't know. It was a well-maintained police riot gun, and he rather suspected the young man had stolen it out of a police car, but he didn't ask.

Fifteen minutes later, the older woman came back down the stairs and reported to the man on guard, "Every floor is ready. All the doors are bolted. I sure would hate to be the punk that tries to break in here," she quipped.

The older man reached down and patted his shotgun. "Me too," he agreed.

Outside the apartments the gangs were roaming the parking lots, breaking into automobiles, stealing whatever was available. They looted store after store in their paths. When they came to the tenement, they carefully avoided it. Word was that any gang member caught inside that apartment building would be dealt with severely. The gang leaders decided that the weak and helpless were a lot easier pickings without having to face angry citizens armed to the teeth.

Not content just to loot, the rioters began to set fires. They stuffed rags down the gas tanks of automobiles stranded on the streets and set them on fire just to watch the explosion and the havoc. Within a few hours, fires were raging everywhere in the city. This scene was duplicated in cities throughout America.

Police departments were doing their best, but it was hopeless. Without transportation, there was no way they could meet all the needs. The president's declaration of martial law was spreading rapidly, but about as many didn't believe it as did. Police officers, trying to deal with the rioters and gangs in the cities adopted a shoot-first-and-ask-questions-later policy.

Word spread throughout each community that armed looters would be shot on sight. City police were spread much too thin because they had to work in groups of three or four for self-protection. They were doing mortal combat with many of the gangs and looters. It was clear that mob rule was the law and that the only control available was brute force. As the day wore on, the sound of gunfire increased throughout the cities of America.

The rioting resulted in one positive aspect: The majority of honest citizens stayed home and bolted their doors; those with weapons armed themselves, and those without prayed a lot. Many of the suburban neighborhoods were spared, simply because most of the people living there were honest, hardworking people and also because most of the suburbanites had long since armed themselves. But perhaps the greatest asset of the suburbs was that the gangs had no way to get there. They were stranded on foot like everyone else. But most knew it was only a matter of time. Once the rioters had looted and destroyed their own neighborhoods, they would work their way out to the suburbs.

New York City suburbanites saw great plumes of black smoke rising from the city as more and more fires were set. It was clear to those living in the city that it was only a matter of time until rioters would destroy the city and its inhabitants. The incentive to evacuate the cities was gaining a lot of momentum.

There were a lot of converts from the liberal persuasion to the conservative philosophy that day. The media types, who had no means of communications with their flocks, found themselves just citizens once more. Those who worked in the metro areas also found themselves fearing for their lives as the marauders came closer. Expansive downtown suites became merely high-class shopping centers for the gangs and looters. In Los Angeles, as in New York, stores were looted and cars were set on fire as the frenzy grew in intensity. Anyone unfortunate enough to get in their way was killed by looters, who respected no authority but force.

At CBS headquarters in New York, support staff and news anchors alike found themselves huddled in rooms praying that the police would reach them before some of the marauders did. They could hear gunfire everywhere around them. Building security had been breached, and the minimal security force employed by the network all lay dead in the entrance hallway.

CBS anchor, Don Cantrell, was huddled in one of the editing rooms when a wild-eyed looter, brandishing a Chinese made AK-47, kicked open the door.

"Who's in here?" he shouted. "Come out, or I'll spray this room with lead."

Visibly shaking, Cantrell stood up.

"I know you," the young man said. "You're that guy on TV."

"Yes," Cantrell stuttered. "Please don't hurt me."

"I ain't gonna hurt cha," the young man said. "You're one of us. Right?"

"That's right," Cantrell agreed. "I've always supported human rights."

"Sure you have! A gang's got rights too, man. Don't cha agree?"

Cantrell, still shaking, was beginning to relax a little bit. "Yes, I do. You have the same rights as any other human being."

"Good. 'Preciate that, man, and it's my right to kill you if I want to. Right?" the young man said, as he squeezed the trigger.

Cantrell was about to scream when the first spray of bullets hit him.

"Yeah, I got rights too," the young man said as he callously walked away from the man he'd just robbed of his life. "Man, I got lots of rights. As long as I got bullets, I got *all* the rights."

At WNN headquarters in Atlanta, Neil Farmer was going nuts. Nothing worked: not the lights, the phone, the coffeepot — nothing. He gathered his technical team together to assess the options and the damage.

"Well, in the first place," the engineer said, "it would appear that our satellites are out. So, if we're ever to get back on the air, it's going to be land-line."

"Land-line," Farmer grumbled. "We're just another two-bit network if we don't have satellites. Any chance they're going to come back online?" Farmer asked.

"Hard to tell, but it doesn't look like it. Just before the last satellite went down, we switched over to backup systems and then they went down too. So, it probably means that both systems are fried."

"And the fiber optic to New York?" Farmer asked.

"Gone. By the time we were able to kill the power, nothing was operating."

"What do you mean, nothing?"

"I mean *nothing*," the engineer said. "The generators went down, the control systems went down, the cameras went down. I don't know if we'll ever get back on the air."

"We *have* to get back on the air," Farmer shouted angrily. "We cannot let Houston and his cronies control this nation."

This guy is nuts, the chief engineer decided. *The president was right, and he still won't admit it.*

"What about the mobile backup? That never was turned on, was it? Will it still work?"

"Sure, the mobile stuff'll still operate. But if we turn it on now, it's just going to fry too."

"Then we'll wait til dark," said Farmer. "Then we'll come back on."

"Who are we going to broadcast to?" the engineer asked. "All the other land-lines are out; the control systems are out."

"Do what you can," Farmer growled irritatedly. "Just get something online as quick as you can."

"Okay, Boss." Then and there he decided, *When the bus leaves from this city, brother, I'm going to be on it.* Outside the WNN building, he heard the chatter of an automatic weapon.

Farmer went back to his office. Fortunately, since he was in charge, he had one of the offices with a window, so he was able to look out over the city. He saw black smoke billowing from what appeared to be a hundred different locations. He also heard the sound of gunfire in the distance. It never occurred to Neil Farmer that what he was doing was wrong. His attitudes were so ingrained that he just took it for granted that he was right and everybody else was wrong.

Unknown to Farmer, the WNN production staff, one by one, was slipping out the door to a commonly agreed upon meeting place on the bottom floor of the WNN headquarters building. When nighttime came, if the evacuation of Atlanta was ordered, they intended to be some of the first on the bus. If Neil Farmer wanted WNN on the air, he'd have to figure out a way to do it himself.

By 6:00 that evening, much the same scene was repeated throughout the country. In the metro areas, organized gangs of young thugs were roaming the streets: some armed with knives and clubs but most with automatic weapons. Most of the honest citizens had since departed the streets for safer quarters. Rampaging rioters broke into every business, and what they couldn't carry off they destroyed. And upon leaving, they set fire to everything. They had a blood lust that kept growing.

In areas where the military already had been mobilized, control was reestablished quickly. There was no ACLU present, no federal courts to interfere, and no politicians vying for votes — only the police and the soldiers, and when they saw someone in the streets carrying a weapon, they shot first and asked questions later, if possible. The complete tally of murdered and wounded American citizens that day would never be known.

In the cities there were literally hundreds of bodies, both the good and the bad, littering every street. Police were totally occupied trying to keep and enforce the law and had no time to dispose of the bodies — victims or perpetrators.

By 6:00 P.M. the evacuation plans had been organized. Jason and his team of scientists at Andrews were poised to begin monitoring the solar flare as soon as the power was up. Gen. Boland had his security teams in place and was ready to allocate troops throughout the country as soon as communications were reestablished. Warren Butts had organized the White House staff to execute their jobs as quickly as possible.

In effect, the plan would be to power up government facilities, commandeer all government and civilian mass transit vehicles, establish control of the cities and the roadways, and begin the orderly evacuation of the cities. The designated areas were being coordinated through Secretary Blake, and the emergency food reserves that were stored in warehouses throughout America would be inventoried and then transported to various camps.

Based on preliminary calculations that Secretary Blake's people could come up with, they figured there was enough food to take care of more than 100 million people for at least four months. After that, there were no more reserves, other than current stock in grocery stores across the country. And, if what they saw in Washington, D.C. was any indication of what was happening across the country, the food reserves from the grocery stores were being stripped by looters.

No matter how many of the looters the law

enforcement agencies stopped, it seemed like there were 10 more ready to take their places. It was already decided that any food in warehouses outside the major metropolitan areas would be commandeered by the government and protected by armed personnel until it could be transported to the evacuation areas.

It was assumed that the families living in rural areas were capable of taking care of themselves for longer periods of time. So the primary efforts of the government would be concentrated on the major metropolitan areas. It was estimated that probably some 75 to 80 percent of the metropolitan population would choose evacuation, if it was possible. The remainder, it was thought, would probably stay in the cities in spite of the best warnings of the government.

Based on these calculations, it was assumed that the government would have to deal with approximately 100 million American citizens. Given the fact that they probably could transport them only during the evenings, it would take the better part of three weeks to evacuate the cities. Coordinating all of this without any nationwide communications appeared to be an almost impossible task.

President Houston sat in his office waiting for the evacuations to start. *Jason was right. He warned us, but I was too stubborn to listen. Now I hope it's not too late. Maybe if the flares die down there will be a window of opportunity to totally evacuate the cities.*

Houston knew that once communications were reestablished and transportation was possible he would need to address the nation again. Would the Congress cooperate? If not, so be it. He was the commander in chief of the armed forces of the United States and, if necessary, he would use those armed forces.

14

The second evening since the flare hit was going much better than Houston had expected. Once the cities were partially powered and the government had transportation at its disposal, Gen. Boland had allocated 300,000 troops for security, plus the National Guard reserves from every state. The real dispersal of troops began as soon as the Sun set, which meant the eastern cities would be first. Even so, 300,000 troops was a pretty meager force to control the cities.

When the troops hit the streets of D.C., the gangs, the looters, and the rioters quickly went underground. All it took was a few armored personnel carriers on the streets, raking the looters with 50-caliber machine gun bullets, to send them scurrying for cover. Once control was established, the transportation vehicles moved in with the PA systems blaring. Area coordinators instructed the residents of their districts to make an orderly withdrawal to the vehicles.

There were sporadic instances of face-to-face conflict between the military and the looters, but after the first couple of skirmishes in each area, the looters crawled back into the woodwork and didn't try to confront the armed troops again. By the time day came again, the troops would be in position to help control the looting and the rioting. Nobody, including Gen. Boland, was naive enough to believe that they could totally control the violence, but at least they could contain it with the troops they had on hand.

Throughout the evening, information flowed into the control center in D.C. and was forwarded to the White House. It was evident from the reports that massive looting and rioting had taken place nationwide. In some cities — like Boise, Idaho; Indianapolis, Indiana; Orlando, Florida; Charlotte, North Carolina — large areas had been gutted by fires. Without fire-fighting equipment available, it was virtually impossible to control the burning. The fires would rage on until they burned themselves out. It was evident also that the government planners had grossly underestimated what it would take to evacuate most of the cities.

Transportation vehicles were swamped by the huge numbers of people attempting to flee the cities, to the point that mini-riots were taking place at the loading areas. It was decided that a more orderly evacuation system would be necessary. An alphabetical lottery was chosen. Numbers corresponding to letters in the alphabet were thrown into a container and the area coordinators would randomly select five numbers. People whose last names began with the corresponding letters would be evacuated. Given this system, it was going to take a minimum of six to seven days to evacuate the moderately populated areas, and up to three weeks to evacuate the heavily populated areas. There simply was not enough transportation to do the job adequately.

As the night wore on, Gen. Boland was reviewing the reports that were flowing in. He saw the problem but was stumped about how to solve it. He only had so many buses and trucks, and there were millions of people to evacuate. Often it required moving them great distances from the cities. Then a simple solution struck him.

The big cities had the best mass transportation systems. In addition to buses, New York City had the best subway system in the world, as did Atlanta and many of the other large cities. So he instructed the area coordinators to relocate as many of the people as possible from the cities to the outlying communities using the rail systems. Not only would this remove people from some of the dangers within the cities, it also would relocate them closer to their ultimate destination.

His biggest problem was how to get the people who operated the transit systems back on the job. The president solved that problem when he went on the air that evening to address the nation. He ordered all government personnel, including those assigned to the mass transportation systems, to report for duty. Boland and his team calculated that by using this method they could evacuate the cities in about 10 days, give or take a couple.

The daylight hours of Day Two passed with the looters and rioters still in control of the inner cities. Without armored vehicles, the police and the military could only hope to control the main streets.

Just before daylight Jason and Annette had flown to the White House at the president's request to spend that day going over the data they had collected and making more specific long-term plans. Jason informed the president that area 403 on the Sun was stabilizing again.

"How long before the next eruption?" the president asked.

"It's really not possible to say," Jason said. "I pray that we'll never have another one and we'll be able to move the people back into their homes as soon as power is restored."

"I agree with you," the president said. "But be realistic, Jason. This is not a time to be timid. Give me your best evaluation."

Jason glanced over at Annette who nodded her head. They'd gone over the calculations again and again and believed area 403 was going to erupt again, and it would do so within a week. Jason said so to the president.

"How big do you think?" the president asked.

"Again, Sir, we're just using some raw calculations, but I believe we're going to see a progression upscale."

"Spell it out," the president said. "What does that mean?"

"That means, Mr. President, that you have until that flare strikes to do whatever you have to do. After that, in my opinion, nothing will function for a while — daytime or nighttime, which means we'll have no transportation and no communications for who knows how long: a week, a month, maybe more."

"The cities will be a jungle," Gen. Boland said.

"I'm afraid you're right, Floyd," the president said wearily. "We've got to get this job done as quickly as we can."

"We'll finish, Mr. President," Boland promised. "We have to."

Jason and Annette spent most of that day going over the plans with Gen. Boland and reviewing other contingencies, like the transportation of food to the relocation camps. Jason had been so consumed with his study of the flare, he hadn't given much consideration to how millions of people would be clothed, housed, and then fed once they left the cities.

"We take a lot of things for granted in our country," he said to Annette. "Like groceries."

"Not any longer. Never again will I take a hot shower for granted, or a Big Mac either, for that matter," she said with a smile.

"Time to get some rest," Jason said. Annette didn't argue; she was totally exhausted. They each went to their rooms, and after resting a couple of hours, Jason was awakened by C.C.'s knock on the door.

"It's time to go, Professor," the big man said as he opened the door a crack and stuck his head in. "I've already notified Dr. Camp."

"I'll be right there," Jason answered. He instinctively looked at his watch, but it still read 6:12, just as it had for the last two days.

On the way down, Annette met them in the hallway. "I feel like a new woman," she sighed. "I slept great on Mr. Lincoln's bed."

"It's not really . . . ," C.C. started to say.

"I know it's not his bed," Annette said, grinning, "but it's still the Lincoln bedroom."

"Right," C.C. agreed.

Jason, Annette, and C.C. walked out on the White House lawn. It was one of those beautiful spring evenings when the ice crystals in the clouds glowed a rosy color. Normally this time of year there would have been jet contrails in the sky, but on this particular evening there was nothing to mar the beauty of God's creation, because there were no jets flying anywhere in the world, including the USA.

As soon as the Sun dipped down behind

the horizon, as if on cue, things began to pop. C.C. gave the thumbs-up to the helicopter pilot, who then flipped several switches. The giant turbines on the big helicopter began to spin, and ever so slowly the rotors themselves began to turn.

As soon as the engines were up to speed and the rotors were turning normally, the pilot gave the thumbs-up sign; and, again, subconsciously ducking his head, Jason made his way to the on-ramp of the helicopter, followed closely by Annette and then C.C.

Jason was surprised, and a little confused, to discover how attracted he was to Annette. At first he assumed it was because they were both scientists and shared a common interest in astronomy. But the more he was around her, the more he realized it was something much deeper.

Annette was a witty, intelligent, and attractive woman, and although he had seen plenty of intelligent, attractive women since Nancy died, Annette was different. Maybe it was the way Wendy had taken to her and vice versa. He had watched as Annette took time to explain ideas and concepts to Wendy, treating her like an intelligent person instead of a kid, and Wendy ate it up. The two of them had an obvious mutual bond.

But what really startled him was that he had an almost overwhelming urge to reach out and touch her, to stroke her hair. He almost had once, on the evening of Day One — when he had walked up behind her while she was doing some calculations. He caught himself at the last moment. When she looked up, he jerked his hand back, turning beet red in the process. Annette had struggled to contain her amusement.

"You're a gem, Jason," she quipped. Jason had sputtered some unintelligible response. Then she reached up and touched his hot cheek with a cool hand. Nothing further had been said, but Jason felt stirrings inside that he thought were long dead.

"Keep in touch when you get to Andrews," the president shouted from the lawn as they went aboard. "I want to know what's happening."

"Right," Jason promised, focusing his thoughts once again. He grabbed Annette's hand and helped her into the helicopter. "As soon as we know, you'll know."

Shortly after sunset, federal installations throughout the East began to come alive. Back-up generators were started, and repair teams were quickly dispatched to the control centers to reestablish ground communications. With no satellite links available, old phone lines that had been used only for local service for years were tapped and rerouted.

As darkness set in, the lights in the White House blinked on as the big emergency generators roared to life. In the generator room the sergeant was barking orders: "I want those controls removed and replaced just as quickly as possible. I want these generators put on automatic backup so we don't have to keep starting them manually."

"Yes, Sir," the young airman gulped. The sergeant had ordered him again and again not to call him sir, but he still continued to do so. The man with eight stripes on his arm tended to elicit both respect and fear from the personnel under his authority.

Activity was increasing throughout the city. National Guard and regular military personnel were loaded into the carriers. Within minutes big diesel trucks and buses were rolling and troops were being dispersed according to the prearranged plan.

The same thing was happening in cities across the eastern United States. During the evening of Day One, the looters and rioters had held the upper hand in the inner cities. Boland was determined to correct that. Control was a numbers game, and he would up the ante.

In New York City alone, 5,000 armed troops were dispersed throughout the city. And gang members, who once totally ruled the streets, withdrew to the ghettos.

Gen. Boland had arranged for short-term, low-altitude hops via aircraft as well. But his instructions were that no aircraft could fly higher than 5,000 feet, thus avoiding the potential danger of cosmic radiation that would destroy delicate electronics. As the sun began to set, they set up a complex system of short hops that would disperse his evacuation leaders throughout the country. The country was divided into defense zones and troops were deployed, just as if the United States were under attack.

If the daylight hours belonged to the street gangs, the evening hours belonged to the military.

Every means of public conveyance had been commandeered by the military. Any vehicles that would run were recruited for the evacuation of the cities. The most massive transportation effort ever attempted was underway. One hundred million Americans were to be relocated from the cities to more rural areas.

Boland knew he was fighting two deadlines: one, eventually the gangs would get organized into guerilla groups that would be highly effective in the inner cities. Second, there was the specter of another flare. If the big flare came before the evacuation, millions of people could be stranded in the cities with no food and with death stalking the streets. He thought about his own family in Virginia and pushed his people even harder. His family was now safe and he would not rest until the families of others were also.

The president looked out the window at

the smoke still rising from the city and could only imagine what was happening in other parts of the world, where they would have been less prepared than the United States. He knew it had to be a nightmare in cities like Hong Kong, Saigon, Paris, London. They would be in utter disarray and panic. There were some sketchy reports coming in and all spoke of riots and anarchy.

In an effort to maximize the available communication lines, Houston had authorized Gen. Boland to set aside specific phone lines to be used only by Morse code operators. Even in a very noisy electronic environment, a well-trained Morse code operator could make out the faintest signal. It was a 1900s communication system that would prove very effective for the situation they were facing.

The military support teams had installed battery powered public address systems on the trucks, buses, and emergency vehicles that would be used to evacuate the cities. The plan was to concentrate on the highest crime areas first. Already military vehicles, with public address systems attached, were being dispensed to every city as quickly as they were readied.

The first vehicle to hit the streets of Washington was an olive drab Suburban, equipped with a PA system, and dozens more like it traversed the streets of D.C. as the sound system blared the message: **"All civilian residents are to stay in their homes until** ordered to evacuate. Military martial law has been declared throughout the city. Any civilians found on the streets are subject to arrest. Anyone found carrying weapons will be shot. Stay in your homes. The evacuation will continue tonight at 10:00. Each person is limited to one bag only. Each family will be limited to a maximum of two carrying bags. You will be notified when your block is ready for evacuation. You must be ready by 10:00 this evening," the PA repeated again and again. "You will be notified when your block is ready to be evacuated. Be ready by 10:00 P.M."

The vehicles drove slowly up and down the streets, blaring out the message. The drivers could see windows open as they came by. People stuck their heads outside to hear the message, then quickly closed the windows again. Many of the people had lived in the same area most of their lives. Now they were being asked to abandon their homes, meager as they were, and they were frightened. Many would not leave voluntarily; they simply didn't trust the police or the government. It would take another day or two of mass violence to convince them to go. For lifetime city dwellers, the shock of being pulled out of the city and thrust into a rural setting would prove to be almost as traumatic as the riots and looting.

The evacuation plans and procedures had been carefully worked out by Gen. Boland and his team. It was decided that each camp would be limited to a maximum of 100 individuals per square acre of farm land available. Nobody knew exactly how this formula was derived, but by the time it was released it had become the law of the land. This meant a wide distribution area since the population density in many cities was more than 500 people per square acre. But there were no highrise buildings in the rural farmlands.

Oren Blake's interior department team had worked out a formula whereby they calculated how widely they would have to disperse people to ensure that the population density would not exceed 100 people per acre. On average, excluding cities like Los Angeles and Chicago, it was determined that approximately 250 miles from most cities would be sufficient to relocate the residents.

Fortunately, since the evacuation was taking place in the early spring and most of the bad weather was past, housing could be provided by tents. It was discovered that the military had millions of tents stored in warehouses throughout the country. In fact, hundreds of thousands of tents from the Vietnam and Korean era were found stored in military depots around the country. A plan was soon devised to transport the tents to where they would be needed.

Why the Pentagon had stored hundreds of thousands of obsolete tents for 40 years was a mystery. Apparently, it had all been part of Lyndon Johnson's civil defense program during the sixties and, like most government programs, once it began it had never been terminated.

A summary inventory was done, and it was concluded that with the tents available in sporting goods centers throughout the country, along with those stored in manufacturing facilities and military depots, all the families being evacuated could be housed, with tents to spare.

Initially, little thought was given to ensure that entire families were relocated together; the most urgent and immediate need was to get the people out of the cities before the next solar flare hit. Consequently, if families were divided geographically, they went to different sites. Later, if time allowed, priority would be given to family consolidation.

At 8:00 P.M., still two hours before the mass evacuations would begin, Jason and Annette made their way to the makeshift solar observatory once again. By this time the power was up and most of the systems were operating again.

"What does it look like, Gene?" Jason asked Dr. Moore.

"Not a lot of activity right now, Jason. No

other sites outside of the U.S. are reporting."

"Which means they probably have been damaged by the flare," Jason said, looking at the spectrometer graph. "Maybe some will be able to get back online."

"Well, Annette, let's take a closer look."

With practiced efficiency, Jason began to calibrate the instruments. Within a few minutes the charts began to reveal the story. The level of X ray activity was diminishing as well.

"It would appear that area 403 is going into another dormant phase," Jason said as he reviewed the charts. "Would you agree?" he asked Annette.

"It looks like it. Any guess as to how long the dormant phase will last?"

"There's no way to tell," Jason replied with a frown. He was clearly troubled. Area 403 should have more activity.

It's nearly six days since the last eruption. What if I've done it again? he thought. The enormity of it all struck him. *Millions of people dislocated, billions of dollars wasted, and probably even some deaths due to the relocation.*

Annette could sense his doubt. She wanted to reach out and comfort him, but she knew the others would read her actions as condescending, so instead she said, "Do you want to halt the evacuations until you're sure, Jason?"

Jason looked at her, inhaled deeply, and exhaled slowly. He thought about it for a moment. Then he replied, "No. Absolutely not. If those people are caught in the cities they will die if . . ." Then he corrected himself, "*when* 403 erupts again."

Annette smiled slightly. *Good for you*, she thought. "Can we continue to operate during daylight hours?"

Jason ripped the paper from the printer. "Probably," he said. "When the flare activity increases again, we'll still have a three-day window of warning."

Jason was thinking about the millions of people who had to be evacuated from the cities. *This really is a window of opportunity. Evacuating people at night is very difficult and a couple of daylight cycles might accomplish more than two weeks after dark.*

"Are there any phone lines up?" Jason asked the young lieutenant.

"Yes, Sir," he replied. "We have a direct line to the White House and to General Boland's office."

"Connect me to the president," Jason said.

"Yes, Sir," the young lieutenant responded.

Jason had just walked over to get a cup of coffee when the lieutenant called out, "Sir, we have communications with the White House. The president will be on the line momentarily."

Jason normally drank his coffee with cream and sugar, but now he decided that black was the way he needed it. *This just might be a long*

299

night. More out of nervousness than anything else, he began blowing on the coffee as he walked back over to the phone. Picking it up, he said, "Mr. President?"

"Yes, what's up, Professor?"

"The activity in area 403 is falling off, Sir."

"Falling off?" Houston said, raising his voice. "Does that mean that the crisis is over?"

"No, Sir," Jason replied assertively. "At least I don't think so. I believe this is just a lull, but we should have a window here. Mr. President, I think it's possible to continue the evacuations during the daytime for the next several days." Then he added, "Assuming the solar activity continues to diminish as it is doing right now."

Houston didn't reply immediately. Inside he had a queasy feeling. *Is Professor Hobart just rationalizing?* he wondered, in spite of himself. *What if, in fact, the flare activity is dying out and we continue to evacuate millions of people from the cities?* For the first time since he began the evacuation process, Houston had some doubts.

"Professor," he said, picking his words carefully, "what if the flare activity doesn't increase? What if it continues to decline?"

The president had voiced Jason's greatest fears. His first reaction was, *Should I lie to the president and tell him I have absolute confidence that won't happen, when I have the same kind of doubts?* Jason had never been one to lie or to deceive. He considered himself impeccably honest and it had gotten him into trouble before. He paused to gather his thoughts. "Sir, I cannot guarantee this is not the end of it. I can only tell you that it would not be unusual for a solar flare of this magnitude to have several high and low periods. But, I don't believe we should take the risk of halting the evacuations."

Houston was silent on the other end of the telephone, and although the pause was no more than 30 seconds, to Jason, it seemed like an eternity. He couldn't blame the president for being hesitant. After all was said and done, he was still a discredited scientist, and the situation was still similar to his previous debacle.

Houston was not a man for indecision, and the more he thought about it, the more he concluded that, for better or for worse, he had put his trust in Jason. He replied, "Professor, we're going to continue the evacuation of the cities."

Jason sighed in relief. *So the president is still with me.* "Mr. President," he replied, as upbeat as possible, "there's one more thing."

Houston sat back in his chair. He wasn't sure he could handle one more thing. If the worst of the first solar flare was over for a while and communications, perhaps even power, were reestablished throughout the country, he was sure his enemies would have a field day with his decision to continue the evacuations. He had no doubt that the Congress would take a long, hard look at what he was doing. He sat up in the chair and took a deep breath. "Yes," he said. "What is it?"

"At most, we have a three-day window of warning when the eruption occurs. After that, it is very possible that no electrical devices will work day or night for a while." Jason didn't have to add his addendum, "If I'm right." Both he and the president knew it was there. "Sir, that is critically important, because anything that's powered up during the next flare will be destroyed. Having that equipment functional will be vital to the survival of the millions of people in relocation centers."

"Understood," the president said. "We'll shut everything down on your instruction." Houston also didn't bother to add, "If I'm still president."

"And Jason," the president said as if addressing a long-time friend.

"Yes?"

"Thank you."

Jason felt a lump in his throat, but he didn't say anything further, because the president had hung up.

Jason said to the group, "The president agreed to continue the evacuation. We need

302

to set up as much of an early warning system as possible." The whole group began to applaud. When he glanced at Annette, what he saw warmed his heart more than anything that had happened that day. Annette smiled and winked one of those beautiful blue eyes. Then she turned and went back to the instrument she was calibrating.

At the White House things weren't progressing quite so calmly. Both Warren Butts and Gen. Boland had been in the president's office when the call from Jason had come in. Both heard the president's end of the conversation and had pretty well pieced together Jason's end. The president looked at Butts. His expression mirrored his thoughts. Houston mused, *Warren never was one to conceal his opinions or his emotions.*

"I know what you're going to say, Warren," the president started.

"Then why don't you listen, Mr. President? Apparently the solar activity is dying off again. Correct?"

"That's correct," Houston said. "But the professor says it's only temporary."

"Mr. President, the man has been wrong at least once before, and you're staking your entire reputation, and maybe the lives of a lot of people, on just his word. Doesn't that seem a little irrational to you?" Butts said as bluntly as he could. He still didn't believe in

Jason Hobart, and he couldn't put his finger on why. But he did believe in Philip Houston, and he hated to see his president go down the drain because of an obvious miscalculation. Hobart had been right about that last flare, but even Dr. Morgan thought the worst of it was now over. He had already told the president so.

"Warren, I know your feelings, and I know what Dan Morgan thinks, but I've got a gut-level feeling about this. I believe that Professor Hobart is right. We've come this far and we can't stop now."

"Mr. President, we haven't come so far that we couldn't reverse things," Butts argued. "You could go on national television and say to the people of America that you began this evacuation in good faith, believing that the solar flares would cripple the cities and cause great havoc and risk many lives, and that was true. But now, based on further evidence that the solar flare is diminishing, you're going to halt any further evacuations. Leave the people who have relocated where they are and bring in more troops to establish control of the cities again."

The president waved his hand, in his characteristic way. "No," he said flatly.

"Warren, if we're wrong and this flare doesn't die out, the people in those cities would be trapped. We would have no way to get them out."

Boland had been standing by, listening to both sides. He was not a man to hide his opinions either, but he was a soldier through and through and used to taking and executing orders. He spoke up. "Mr. President, I don't know anything about solar flares, and I've only met this professor a couple of times myself. But I can tell you this: I trust your judgment. I trusted your judgment when you were a young captain under my command, and I trust you now. If you say to continue this evacuation, we'll get it done."

"Thanks, Floyd," Houston replied. The general was a longtime friend. Houston had served as a captain in the Air Force under Floyd Boland. At the time, Boland was a full colonel, in charge of an air wing. Houston had just migrated up from the F-118s to the brand-new F-121Y Super Stealth fighter. It was a mach-two Stealth fighter that had cost the government $100 million per unit. It was the first supersonic fly-by-wire aircraft ever designed for military combat, and after flying the plane only a short while Capt. Philip Houston had issued a report to his squadron commander stating that he thought the F-121 had a basic operational flaw.

Twice while flying it he had seen what he believed to be a computer glitch. But when the ground crews plugged it into the test simulator, they could find nothing. Houston had taken the plane up several times trying to recreate the flaw and had succeeded in doing it only once more. When the plane was flying subsonic at low altitude, as would be necessary during actual combat, the glitch had occurred a second time. But when he returned to base, the ground crews again could find nothing, and the flight recorder showed no glitch.

Houston refused to drop the issue, so in his flight report, over the objections of his squadron commander, he had recommended that the computer system be shielded better. It was his opinion that when he was flying at low altitude and crossed a telephone microwave beam, that was when the glitch occurred.

When Boland received the report, he had reviewed it and called in both the young captain and his squadron commander. Houston had stood his ground, and that impressed the general. He passed the report on to Tactical Air Command (TAC), and it caused quite a stir. When the press picked up on it, they made it into a major incident. A hundred million dollar airplane that wouldn't fly under combat conditions was big news. It wasn't true, Boland knew. The young captain was simply saying that he thought some preventative maintenance would solve a *potential* problem.

But nonetheless, it was blown out of proportion, and the next thing Boland knew, the head of TAC was down at his squadron, with a congressman and a senator, both of whom vigorously defended the aircraft. The politicians demanded to know why Boland had allowed a lowly pilot's report to proceed all the way up to the Pentagon. Their recommendation was to ground Houston and let the aircraft fly, but Boland had stood his ground and backed one of his junior pilots.

At the same time, the aircraft manufacturer did extensive ground exercises in simulations, trying to recreate the glitch described in the trouble report. After more than 50 simulations with no problems, it was looking bad for Boland, until one of the engineers decided to try something else. He disconnected the ground strap leading to the primary in-flight computer and then exposed the aircraft to microwaves, and, sure enough, the glitch occurred with alarming regularity.

In fact, on the tenth simulation, the entire computer system failed, causing the computer-controlled aircraft to switch over to the back-up system, which also promptly failed, leaving the aircraft commander with no way to control the airplane, which by that time would have been making 500 to 600 knots at less than 50 feet off the ground. Needless to say, it would have been a bad day for that pilot. When the report was issued by the manufacturer, the repair was relatively simple. Maintenance crews had to verify that the ground strap leading to the computer connector was in place and, as an added safety, a modification was made so that the entire computer system module was covered with a copper mesh and grounded to the aircraft's frame. Boland's hide was saved, the young captain was allowed to fly, and a friendship was created that had now lasted for more than 30 years.

"Okay, Mr. President," Butts said. "But you and I both know we're going to be knee deep in congressional subpoenas in a couple of days."

"Just do what you can, Warren," the president responded. "Keep them off my back as long as possible."

"What about a press conference?" Dean asked.

"No more press conferences," Houston said emphatically. "The people who trust me are going to continue to trust me, and the people who don't wouldn't be convinced by another press conference. We're going to make as much haste as we can. Will the military stand behind us?" the president asked Boland.

"Without a doubt," the general responded. "They know and trust you, Mr. President. They know the liberals, and they don't trust them. But, if the Congress votes to impeach, it's going to be a toss-up with several generals. They're going to go with the flow."

"Understood," Houston agreed. "Let's do it."

15

Even as the evacuations were beginning to take shape in the United States, the chaos throughout the rest of the world was escalating. Countries that three days earlier had been some of the most modern and developed countries on Earth had been thrown back 200 years in time.

In Japan the scene was chaotic. The Japanese led the world in electronic innovation and development, and essentially everything that functioned in Japan was automated: the sewage systems, the water systems, the transportation systems. The Japanese had magnetic levitation trains, totally pollution-free electric subways, office buildings with high-speed elevators, and ultramodern trains carrying Japanese workers to and from the cities at 200 miles an hour.

But all of that changed in the first few minutes after daylight on April 4th. Now the office buildings were all but deserted. Most of the early shift workers had made their way down the stairways to the streets. Others who had not evacuated the buildings were trapped in offices with no air, no means of communications, and no food or water.

Throughout Tokyo, hundreds of Japanese

workers, fearful of losing their jobs went to work as normal and refused to leave their offices. When the air circulation systems failed, many died from asphyxiation. Carbon dioxide suffocation was a pleasant way to go. As the air was used up and carbon dioxide levels began to build, they simply experienced fatigue and drowsiness until they fell asleep. A few realized what was happening and attempted to smash out windows to get fresh air into their buildings.

Unfortunately, the Japanese buildings were constructed with earthquakes in mind and the windows were shatterproof. Exhausted workers found that no amount of pounding would get the windows to yield. The few who succeeded in getting their windows to pop out injured innocent people below when the heavy panes of glass fell.

The Japanese islands contain the densest populations anywhere on Earth. Suddenly cut off from all modern conveniences, the cities could not support the masses that lived in and around them. Tens of thousands of Japanese stood at the entrances of the high-speed subways, waiting for trains that never came. On the city streets, people milled around, wondering what to do next.

On the plus side was the fact that the Japanese were very law-abiding people and, except for a few isolated instances of gang activity, the cities were still safe. But with available food supplies dwindling rapidly, Japanese officials realized that disaster was only a few days away. The lack of individual initiative on the part of the Japanese would doom many of them to starvation within a few weeks.

Japanese merchants with food stocks opened them to those in need. The Japanese people stood in long lines, waiting for the meager supplies to be handed out. Unlike America, where riots broke out and gangs robbed and pillaged, the Japanese accepted this crisis docilely, believing the government would rescue them. But Japanese officials were not prepared and, consequently, were unable to evacuate their cities. But even if they had been able to relocate the city dwellers, the limited space available on the Japanese islands left little room to put 60 million citizens. The terrifying truth for the Japanese people: Their fate was sealed.

In Frankfurt, Germany, the scene was very different. When everything shut down, millions of Germans streamed out of the buildings and onto the streets. Now they were demanding action from their government, and they already had organized into protest groups. Angry Germans were demonstrating in the streets in Frankfurt, Dusseldorf, Berlin, and elsewhere, demanding the government to do something.

Unfortunately, for the German government, there was little they could do. With transportation disabled, communications out, and riots in the streets, they were incapable of responding. In Germany, as well as most of Europe, the mood of the people was getting more and more hostile.

The German cities had fewer gangs than the American cities had, and the gangs possessed fewer weapons. But, like their American cousins, they also had a history of violence and civil disobedience. Many of the demonstrators began to pick up bricks and rocks and, when met by police resistance of any kind, they pummeled them with debris. Eventually, the police gave up and fell back to safer positions.

By the evening of Day Two, the demonstrations dissolved into riots and the rioters demolished everything in their paths. Without transportation or communications, the government was helpless. Soon the overcrowded European cities would disintegrate into anarchy. Those who survived the riots would be facing an ever-diminishing food supply and the specter of starvation, if another flare occurred.

With the effects of the first flare beginning to fade, little by little some communications began to be restored. Backup transmitters, off line during the first flare, came on, and generators were powered up. Ham radio operators in the United States began to pick up transmissions from other parts of the world, and little by little they began to piece together the pattern. In every industrialized country, the same scenario was replayed. Limited communications, little or no transportation, food supplies dwindling, and riots in the cities. The whole civilized world was being plunged back into the Dark Ages.

Gen. Boland's team pieced together as much information as possible and provided it to the president. As Houston looked over the reports, he realized how bleak the prospects were. *If another solar flare occurs, America's allies and enemies alike are in deep trouble. I have one consolation: right or wrong, I have done the best I could for the American people.*

If Professor Hobart was right about the next flare, perhaps in America alone the majority of the population would survive. The very survival of the civilized world teetered on whether to trust the instincts of a discredited professor from a small town in middle America.

Houston had been a Christian from an early age and had been raised in a Christian home with a military chaplain father who had often discussed the Bible with him. He was taught that *nothing* happens solely by chance: God is in control. Although he hadn't said so to his Cabinet or to his staff, or even to his closest friend, Warren Butts, the gut feeling or intuition he professed to rely on so much was really the leading of the Lord. He had long

314

since learned to trust it and, because of that, he felt he was capable of leading a great nation like America.

One of his great burdens was that his friend Warren was not a Christian. He was a good man and certainly a moral, ethical, honest man, but not a Christian. Very few people knew that every morning before his work day began Philip Houston, president of the United States, got on his knees and prayed that God would give him the wisdom to lead the greatest nation in the world. Houston was concerned about the moral direction Americans had taken in recent years. Most seemed to have turned their backs on their Christian heritage, even to the point of open hostility toward Christians.

Houston and his pastor often prayed that God would shake the foundations of the American people — to wake them up. Now he realized that's exactly what was happening. The self-reliant Americans were virtually helpless. If the solar assault continued, most of the world's population would perish.

Something that often had troubled Houston in his study of the Bible were the passages in the book of Revelation that describe an army of 200 million men pouring out of the East riding on horses. Living in the twenty-first century, Houston often had questioned, *Why would such a vast army be relegated to horseback in a generation of jet airplanes and*

315

rockets? A thought suddenly crossed his mind. *Of course, if the flares continue there will be no jet airplanes or rockets. If a war broke out it might well be fought on horseback again.* It could be the exact scenario described in the book of Revelation where out of the East would come a vast army riding on horses again. *Now that's something to think about,* he decided.

His attention returned to the events at hand when he heard a rap on the door. All formalities in the White House had long since been abandoned. Now staff members and Cabinet members alike simply knocked on the president's door as they came and went.

"Come in," Houston said, as Gen. Boland and Butts entered the room.

"What's the word?" Houston asked.

The general responded, "We've been able to get most of our defense groups in position, and we have limited control of the cities again. We have reestablished minimal communications, but I can contact our defense teams through our frog-leaping system. Most of the long distance lines are still inoperable, but we have a workable system in place. We can get a message across the country within an hour or so."

"Any further word on Europe and Asia?" Houston asked the general.

"Not much. Information is still pretty sketchy. A few ham operators are up and operating; and a few government transmitters

316

are back in operation. They're all asking for emergency aid. From what we're hearing, Sir, there are riots almost everywhere and the kind of chaos we saw in our cities the first few nights. Food and water are scarce. No sanitation — that kind of thing. It's like the whole world has been plunged back in time."

"Only without the morality of previous generations," Houston said grimly.

"That's for sure," the general agreed. "We all owe a great debt of gratitude to Professor Hobart. Without his warning we'd be in the same mess as the rest of the world."

"What about the evacuations?" Houston asked.

"The professor was right," Butts said. "We can operate during the daytime now. We have trucks, buses, trains — everything standing by. The evacuations should progress okay."

"What about getting food to the camps?"

"In process also. The trucks are moving the emergency reserves right now, and we've made contact with the big food suppliers about moving their stocks into our warehouses."

"Are they cooperating?" Houston asked.

"Reluctantly, but we've guaranteed them payment for everything, and that seems to have satisfied them."

"It all ultimately comes down to money, doesn't it?" the president said cynically.

"I'm afraid so, Sir. That's how the world turns today."

"Well, if the professor is correct about the rest of it, I think all that's going to change," Houston said. "Without electricity, money will quickly become the least important commodity on this planet."

"I suspect you're right, Mr. President," Butts said solemnly. "But, we're not home free yet. Gerstner is saying some pretty nasty things about you in the Congress, and Frasier has got a dozen scientists who will swear the crisis is over."

"Well, that's to be expected," Houston sighed. "Some things never change, but with most of the House and Senate scattered, they'll have a hard time drawing up a bill of impeachment. And, besides, by the time they do we'll know one way or the other."

"Well, I wouldn't put anything past Gerstner — or Frasier either for that matter," Butts said. He was concerned. He knew they had allied with his old enemy, Army Chief of Staff General Nathan Hill. Hill was an ambitious and ruthless man.

In Washington, D.C. Congressman Gerstner and Dr. Frasier had been meeting with others members of Congress, as well as Vice President Arnold Crenshaw. On the military side, Gen. Hill was feeling out the other members of the joint chiefs to see if

318

they would back a legal move to remove Houston from office.

The array of data provided by Dr. Frasier and many of his academic cohorts was truly impressive. Without exception, they all had issued written statements that detailed why they believed the solar flare crisis was over.

"It's madness," Frasier was telling the group, "that the president would continue to evacuate the cities when the solar flare threat is over."

"Doctor," the vice president said, "up until now, Dr. Hobart's predictions have been very accurate. Why should we believe that your scientists know more than Dr. Hobart and his team?"

"Two reasons, Mr. Vice President," Frasier said politely to the man he loathed. "First, Dr. Hobart made exactly the same kind of irresponsible prediction once before. And second, virtually every solar physicist of any report agrees that the worst of the solar flare is over. It will cost billions of taxpayers' dollars to continue this ridiculous evacuation."

"I agree," Congressman Gerstner said. "If we wait, at the rate this evacuation is going, in another week our cities will be deserted, except for the gangs. And to abandon the cities to these gangs means that they will loot every business in America. We can't stand by and allow this to happen. The economy of America will have its back broken."

It was clear that the vice president was beginning to waffle a little bit, as he was prone to do.

"Mr. Vice President, you have a responsibility to the people of America to stop this evacuation," Gerstner said. "It simply makes no sense anymore. The truth is, if we had waited this thing out, these people could have stayed in their homes. We could have delivered the food to them, and they would have been far better off than sitting somewhere out in the middle of the wilderness with no way to take care of themselves."

Arnold Crenshaw was by no means a decisive leader. He had been selected by the Republicans as a running mate for Philip Houston, primarily because he represented votes in the state of California, and California was essential to a successful election. Crenshaw had been in politics most of his life, having been elected to the House of Representatives for three consecutive terms, and then, when one of the more liberal senators in California was targeted by the conservatives, Crenshaw had been picked to represent his party.

He was a conservative, even if he was a wishy-washy conservative, and in a very liberal state they realized that a staunch conservative probably would not get elected. So Crenshaw had been their candidate of choice, and he had been elected. When Houston decided to run for president, the Republicans needed somebody who represented the middle ground. Crenshaw had been an articulate spokesman for compromise most of his career. Now, here he was with the most difficult decision of his life, and he simply did not know what to do.

He liked Philip Houston. He couldn't say they had become friends, because they hadn't, but he knew the president was a good man. But he had to agree that he didn't think the evacuations were a good idea either. They were dislocating millions, perhaps tens of millions of Americans. There was no way the country could afford such a huge expense. The government was just beginning to bring the budget into balance, and the Republicans had just narrowly averted a major depression. The country couldn't afford a prolonged shutdown. But what could he do? What *should* he do?

"Mr. Vice President, if you don't move right now, it's going to be too late," Gen. Hill explained. "Sir, I've been in New York City myself, and nearly half of the city is already abandoned, and the gangs are roaming wild there. Why, the president has even ordered the troops we've assigned to the cities to be pulled back." Of course, Hill knew Gen. Boland's plan, that they did not have enough people or enough transportation to continue to support the inner cities. Once they had removed all the people who wanted to leave, they had no choice but to reallocate those troops to other parts of the city that were being evacuated.

But Hill was an ambitious man. Even though he was the Army chief of staff, he had been in Floyd Boland's shadow most of his career, and he hated him. If he could convince the vice president to help remove the president, Boland would go with him. Then he, Hill, would be chairman of the joint chiefs and advisor to the president. *Crenshaw*, he thought, *is a weak man. Directing him won't be any problem.*

"I just don't know," the vice president said. "It's such a drastic step, and there seems to be no precedent for removing a president from office without a vote of the Congress."

"We have no time," Gerstner argued. "If you wait, most of the evacuations will have taken place already. Moving those people back into the cities will cost additional billions of dollars, and in the meantime the gangs will have looted what remains of the productive centers of our cities. Mr. Vice President, you can't wait any longer."

Crenshaw tried to think. His head hurt. He wished there was someone else he could talk to. There was nobody. Most of the Congress was gone, and he had no way to communicate with his old friends in California. Congressman Gerstner had gotten signed affidavits from the majority of those still available that they were in concurrence with removing the president, at least temporarily.

"I guess we'll have to do it," Crenshaw agreed reluctantly.

"Good," Gerstner said, shoving the papers at him. "Just sign these, Mr. Vice President, and we'll get this thing in motion."

"How are we going to remove a president without congressional action?"

"We're going to do it under the Incompetency Act," Gerstner said. "Remember back when President Reagan was shot, and there was no one to take leadership in the country? The Congress passed a law then allowing for the removal of an incapacitated president, at least on a temporary basis, to ensure that there would be adequate leadership in the country. Justice Andrea McConnell agrees with our position. She'll issue the order."

"But," Crenshaw protested, "the president isn't incapacitated."

"We have three signed affidavits from psychiatrists attesting to the fact that the president is mentally incompetent and therefore incapacitated," Robert Frasier said, pushing the papers toward the vice president. "It's all perfectly legal, Mr. Vice President. You have the responsibility. In fact, you have a duty to remove President Houston before more damage is done."

"I guess so," Crenshaw stuttered again. He

felt very confused. It was all happening so quickly.

"Time is critical, Mr. Vice President," Gen. Hill explained. "We have to get this done right now."

Crenshaw still had some doubts. But everything sounded right. He signed the papers. Quickly, Hill and Gerstner stepped up to witness his signature.

Good, Hill thought. *Now we'll get that incompetent out of office.* He needed to get the copies of the signed document to Justice McConnell at the Supreme Court as quickly as possible. He already had several of his hand-picked generals lined up to take control of the military as soon as Houston and his flunky, Boland, were ousted from the White House. *With a little bit of luck,* he thought, *even if this thing goes wrong we'll be able to hang it on Crenshaw, and I'll be the next Democratic candidate for president of the United States.*

In her apartment in New York City, Noreen Ball had heard the evacuation announcement. She quickly dressed both of her children in warm clothing. In fact, she'd put two sets of clothes on them and then packed two additional suitcases. She was ready to go. *There's no way we're going to stay in this city another night — not with the looting.* She shuddered at the thought of what it would be like when her food ran out.

When she heard the announcement to evacuate, she took her 9mm and tucked it inside her blouse. Being a big woman, the gun wasn't noticeable. She believed the president, and she assumed she and her children would be safe, but she had learned from experience that people were ultimately responsible for their own safety, and she felt a lot safer being armed than she did being defenseless.

"Come on, kids. It's time to go," she said. As her daughter Sierra started out she asked, "Mommy can I take Molly with me?" clasping the precious doll she had gotten two Christmases before.

"Sure, Sweetie. I'm sure they won't mind." In the hallway they were joined by six other families who were filing down the stairs.

"What about the others?" Noreen asked her friend, Maria, who lived in the next apartment.

"Two families on our floor won't leave," she replied. "I tried to get 'em to go, but they won't. They said this has been their home for 30 years, and they're not going to leave it."

Noreen felt an involuntary shudder go through her body. "This neighborhood is going to be a graveyard," she said. "When the good people are gone, only the gangs will be here. I'm not stayin' here. I can tell you that."

As they filed down the stairway, they were

met by dozens of others working their way down. It took nearly 10 minutes for the entire group to exit. Once outside, they began loading into the waiting buses and vans.

"Where are we going?" Noreen asked the young corporal standing beside the bus she was boarding.

"Don't know, Ma'am. All I know is that we were told to help you get out of the city."

"When will you be leavin'?" Noreen asked.

The young man turned and, with tears in his eyes, said, "Ma'am, I really don't know. My family's still back in Alabama, and all I know is that I've been assigned to drive this bus. I guess they'll tell me when to go."

Noreen understood the hurt look in his eyes and she reached over and patted his arm. "It'll be okay. I'm sure there's people just like you back there helpin' your family."

"Thanks," the young man said, wiping his eyes on his sleeve as he turned back to counting the people entering the bus.

All over the country, similar evacuations were taking place in every big city. Literally hundreds of thousands of buses, trucks, and vans had been conscripted by military planners to aid in the evacuations. There were thousands of other vehicles making their way to the relocation sites, delivering food and other materials — everything that would be necessary to support and sustain the millions who would be relocated. For the first time in nearly a hundred years there would be more Americans living in rural areas than in urban areas.

Hidden among the people filing onto the buses and vans were gang members dressed like ordinary citizens. The gang leaders decided that it was in their best interest to infiltrate the relocation sites.

"It's important to know where the people are," Juan Melendez, otherwise known as "Blade," had told two of his female gang members, who were now boarding the same bus with Noreen and her children. "After all, where the people are, that's where the food and money are," he said with a smirk on his face. "We'll need to know that. Who knows, we may need to go shopping one day."

Finally, most of the group to be evacuated that day were loaded into the buses and trucks. The doors were closed and the vehicles began to move out in single file. As soon as the last of the vehicles had departed, several more buses pulled up. One last announcement was made, and an hour later, after the last of the stragglers were loaded, the supporting military personnel climbed aboard the buses and were evacuated as well.

Block by block the cities of America were being evacuated and abandoned — literally left to the devices of those who remained behind. Nearly one-fifth of the city dwellers refused to leave and, instead, chose to remain behind. The deciding factor for most of them was the conflict raging in the media over President Houston's decision to continue the evacuation, in spite of the fact that many scientists believed that the worst of the solar flares was over.

At the White House, Butts and Boland were back with urgent business.

"Mr. President, we've got trouble."

Houston could see by the look on Butts's face that something was amiss. He was not a man to be spooked easily, and yet clearly he was.

"Word has it that some members of Congress met with the vice president about ousting you."

"I suspected as much," the president said. "I didn't think the opposition would take this lightly."

"No, Sir, and they haven't," Butts said angrily. "They've gotten affidavits from scientists all over the country stating that, in their opinion, the worst of the flare activity is over and that to continue the evacuations is irresponsible."

"In fact, the psychiatric affidavits described it as incompetency," Gen. Boland added. "General Hill is in on this conspiracy."

"Conspiracy is a strong word," Houston chided his friend. "I rather suspect they're using the Incompetency Act to try to oust me."

"That's correct," Butts said. "And, Mr. President, they may just be able to do it."

"Well," Houston said. "I guess this is where you guys earn your pay. What do we do?"

"You can cut them off at the knees just by stopping the evacuations, at least until we see if this flare develops further. You can preempt this scheme right now before they have a chance to act."

Houston thought for a moment; then he chose his words very carefully. "Warren, my decision has been made. I've got a strong feeling that Dr. Hobart is right. And to stop these evacuations would be to risk the lives of millions, maybe tens of millions of Americans. I can't do that."

"Well then," Butts exclaimed, "it's going to be hand-to-hand combat for the White House I guess, because if they come to evict you we're going to stand and fight."

"No we're not," Houston said firmly. "We're going to stand and wait. I will not start a civil war, no matter what. It would tear this country apart."

"But, Sir . . . ," Butts began to protest.

"No buts," the president said firmly. "I am not going to have armed conflict on the lawn of the White House."

"Then, Mr. President," Gen. Boland said. "I would assume that by this evening, the three of us will be under arrest."

"Perhaps," Houston said. "Perhaps."

By midday, as the political crisis in Washington unfolded, a different kind of crisis was developing. There were areas in many cities where it was not possible to bring in the vans, buses, and trucks to evacuate the people. Rioters had made streets impassable; and often the gangs piled debris, including old cars, in the streets, as barricades against the return of the police. With many streets blocked off, the best that the evacuation coordinators could do was to use helicopters to determine which streets were accessible.

"This evacuation is going to take a lot longer than just a few days," said the young National Guard lieutenant colonel, riding in the armed personnel carrier. "Now the gangs have set up snipers." Even now, he could hear the pinging of bullets off the APC; apparently some of the snipers had silencers. Often, one of the bullets would hit a tire on one of the evacuation vehicles and a truck or a bus would be disabled. "We need help," he told the colonel.

The colonel thought about calling in helicopter support, but he realized the narrow concrete canyons would make maneuvering a helicopter virtually impossible and likely would jeopardize the lives of the helicopter crews. Instead, he opted for more armed personnel carriers. As the word went out, APCs from depots outside the city were brought in.

The city was in ruins. It was like a scene from Beirut in the seventies. Abandoned vehicles were burning, and various buildings were burned-out hulks. Armed personnel carriers roamed the streets, stopping periodically to spray a building with heavy machine gun fire where snipers were known to operate. The gangs quickly got the message and retreated to more secure positions. Discretion was the better part of valor, particularly among those who were cowards. The gangs had little choice but to yield to the greater firepower.

As word got out to other units around the city, the pattern became clear: use APCs in front and in back of the evacuation vehicles, meeting force with force. If there were snipers on the rooftops, the helicopters would get them. If there were snipers in the buildings or on the streets, the APCs would clear them out. In a few hours, the relocation teams had control of the cities once again. With millions of frightened citizens trying to flee and with war in the streets, the evacuation was going to be a long task and, clearly, it would not be done in one week.

The decision to use the subways to evacuate people worked well until the gangs began to attack the trains. Then the tunnels became jammed. So the word went out for the refugees to walk to the outskirts of the city if necessary. The lines of people flowing out of New York City made the scene look like a page out of *Exodus*.

It also was decided that the APCs would patrol the cities to protect those who wished to leave. But no more trucks or buses would be put at risk in the inner cities. The time they lost changing tires and moving disabled vehicles was precious time that could be used to evacuate people.

With millions of people flowing from the cities, it was inevitable that many of them would be carrying weapons. An urgent message was sent back to headquarters in Washington, asking what the field commanders should do.

When Gen. Boland got the message, he immediately brought it to the president. "Mr. President, we need your counsel. Many of the evacuees are carrying weapons. Shall we disarm them?"

Houston thought for a minute. "No, General. Don't disarm them. We may need their help before this is all over. As long as they're orderly and not disruptive, tell your people to let them keep their weapons. Just be sure that you maintain control."

"Right, Sir. It will be done," Boland said, breathing a sigh of relief. The tension in his gut relaxed a little. He'd been concerned that if his people had to disarm the evacuees there would be major confrontations. With his troops battling the gangs, and a fight looming in Washington, he didn't want a third front. Without seeking the president's approval, he brought in more troops to guard the White House and began a covert probe to see where his generals stood. If Hill attempted to take the presidency by force, he would have a fight, in spite of the president's admonition, and he assumed Hill knew it too. That's what worried Boland. Hill was no fool.

Boland sent the message out immediately. Weapons were allowed, provided they weren't loaded and provided the people carrying arms were not disruptive in any fashion.

When the news reached the lower ranks, the military personnel in places like Dallas and Atlanta breathed a sigh of relief. They had seen tens of thousands of people carrying weapons and probably tens of thousands more had them hidden away. The support personnel would have been greatly outnumbered, if not outgunned, and they didn't relish the thought of trying to take weapons away from people who already had been forced to leave their homes.

Field coordinators passed the word. Loudspeakers blared out the message that those carrying weapons would be allowed to retain them, provided they were unloaded and provided there were no disruptions with the evacuations.

Throughout the country an exodus of truly

epoch proportions was taking place: Millions of Americans were streaming out of their homes, flooding into makeshift transportation provided by the government. Attempts were made to restore some semblance of normalcy to the city as power companies tried to get generators back online. But the damage to the control systems was too extensive.

"It will take days, maybe even weeks, before we can get most of the power back online," shift supervisor Maxwell Britten told the vice president of Edison Electric. "The control systems are a total loss. We probably can bring the generators up, but there's no way to control the grid system."

"Well, do the best you can!" the vice president growled, as he stormed out of the room. The generators were making an incredible noise. It was almost impossible to think. *Continue to live in New York City with no power?* he thought. *No thanks! The president might be crazy like the news said, but I'm not staying in this city.* He headed home. His family was going to be evacuated and he was going with them.

In Baltimore, Barbara Mason, a young mother of four, was frantic. She had waited two days for her husband to return from his job at the city sanitation facility. He still had not returned. Normally it was a 30-minute drive from their apartment complex to the water treatment plant. She found out from some of the neighbors that most of the streets were blocked. She knew if there were any way her husband Andy could make it home he would. She sat through most of Day Two crying, wondering what she should do. That evening when she heard the evacuation announcements she'd gotten the children ready. Still she waited, hoping that her husband would return home.

At the treatment facility, Andy Mason sat on a concrete pad, staring at the huge ponds of sludge before him. Without power, he could do nothing. He had thought about trying to go home, but without transportation it looked hopeless. As the evening of Day Two wore on and he looked out over the city, he could see fires here and there and he heard sporadic gunfire. He also heard trucks rumbling by — first on the way into the city and then later on their way out. He knew the evacuations had begun.

He would have done anything to reach his family, but it was impossible, and the ever increasing sound of gunfire convinced him that he would have no chance if he headed back into the city. He knew Barbara was smart enough to get herself and the kids out. *She probably has already gone,* he decided.

He wondered, *Should I just head in the direction of the trucks or stay and try to help get the plant back online when power is restored?* He had no idea. In two days he had had no communications with anybody in authority. He didn't know if or when power would be restored. He wished that someone in authority would show up. He was just a maintenance man. He didn't know what to do.

Andy prayed for Barbara and the children. Somewhere, somehow, no matter where they were, he would find them. As he listened carefully, he could hear the scattered pops of gunfire. It wasn't as common as it had been earlier. *The city is probably evacuated,* he decided.

He made his decision. *To heck with the sewage plant! I'm going to find my family.* He grabbed the overnight bag that usually held his basketball clothes. Working third shift left his days free and he knew he needed exercise, so he and several other employees played basketball every Tuesday morning. He doubted that basketball was high on their priority list anymore. He was the only one who had showed up for work the night the flare struck. He assumed the others had gotten the word before their shifts began.

It was time to go. His last official act as city employee was to pick up a pipe laying near the break room and smash open the candy machine. Being careful not to cut himself, he gathered everything that was left in the machine and stuffed it into his overnight bag. Andy also put the pipe he'd used on the candy machine in his bag. He knew there were some mean people out there and didn't want to encounter them without some kind of a weapon. He took off the rubber boots he wore at work, put on his tennis shoes, and left the building.

With tears streaming down her face, Barbara Mason boarded the bus. She looked out the window furtively, searching for Andy. Her two youngest children, seeing their mother cry and sensing the uncertainty of the situation, were crying too as the bus door swung shut.

16

President Houston pressed the intercom to Warren Butts's office.

"Yes, Mr. President?"

"Any word, Warren?"

"Yes, Sir. Gerstner and his group have a writ from Justice McConnell to remove you for psychiatric evaluation," Butts said as calmly as his building rage would allow.

"What does Justice think?" Houston asked.

"Gerstner was pretty slick. He filed the writ in Crenshaw's name so the Justice Department can't get involved," Butts said.

"Where does the vice president stand on this?" Houston asked calmly. He knew his vice president was pretty easily influenced, but basically he was an honorable man.

"He's somewhere in the middle. They convinced him that you really are unbalanced," Butts said angrily. "If you'll confront Crenshaw he'll back down."

"I won't do that," Houston said. "I might do the same thing in his place. You have to admit my decisions do look a little absurd in light of the current situation."

"Can we halt the evacuations?" Butts asked hopefully. "I think we can rally some support

338

at the court if we do."

"No chance, Warren," the president replied with his that-settles-it tone. "Too much risk if the flare happens."

Butts knew that would be Houston's reply. He was consistent if nothing else.

"Can you keep them off my back?"

"For a while," Butts replied. "I already have appealed to Justice Harrington for a stay. We'll be able to hang the declaration on a technicality — one justice countering another."

"Do what you can, Warren. We need more time."

"Right," Butts replied. He knew Boland had the White House sealed up tight, in spite of the president's instructions. Gerstner would need more than a small army to serve his writ. Until then Houston would have the reins.

At WNN headquarters in Atlanta, Neil Farmer was frantic. It was clear that power was being reestablished throughout much of the city, but he still was unable to get WNN back online, and most of his crew had deserted. "Where are they?" Farmer screamed at his assistant, Murray Steinbeck.

"I don't know, Sir. Most of the technical crew just took off. I assume they've gone to be with their families."

Farmer was literally in a rage. He had the

biggest story in the history of Houston's presidency and he couldn't deliver it to his public. Gerstner had informed him that Houston was being removed from office by court order for mental incompetency and he couldn't broadcast it. The more Farmer thought about it, the more livid he became. The biggest story since Watergate and no way to tell it. He could only sit idly by while the other networks pounded the story, hour after hour. It was virtually the only news the networks were carrying.

The solar flare, the reports said, was dying down, and yet President Houston was still forcefully evacuating all the cities. Vice President Arnold Crenshaw had been named interim president, and Philip Houston had been removed temporarily as president, by order of the Supreme Court, pending an investigational hearing on his mental competency.

It also was reported that the president, along with Chief of Staff Warren Butts and Chairman of the Joint Chiefs General Floyd Boland, was barricaded behind locked gates in the White House. They had surrounded themselves with military troops in an effort to keep possession of the White House. Again and again, the networks repeated the exaggerations of the actual circumstances.

ABC went even further to recommend that citizens should refuse evacuation. "There is no danger," Dr. Robert Frasier, past head of the National Institute of Science, reported during an interview. "We have confirmation from dozens of legitimate scientists throughout the world that the solar flare danger is past."

Frasier went on to explain how he had warned President Houston about seeking and taking the counsel of a discredited scientist.

"The president chose to ignore the counsel of many learned scientists and, instead, took direction from Dr. Hobart," Frasier said. "Clearly the president isn't in control of his mental faculties."

Congressman Gerstner then came on to explain the action taken by congressional leaders. He ended with an appeal for the president to obey the law and evacuate the White House. He then said that he personally prayed that President Houston would get the psychiatric help he needed. Interspersed in the broadcast were live shots from the White House, showing the cordons of armed military within the White House gates — there to defy the written order of the Supreme Court. The net result really did make the president look deranged.

At the Pentagon, Gen. Hill was addressing a session of the Joint Chiefs of Staff. "Gentlemen, I have in my hand a court order from Justice Andrea McConnell, declaring under the Emergency Powers Act that Presi-

341

dent Houston is to be removed temporarily from the office of president of the United States and appointing Vice President Arnold Crenshaw as temporary president, pending a hearing on President Houston's mental competency."

"But, General Hill," one of the others spoke up, "until that court order is executed, President Houston is still the president and commander in chief."

Hill barked at the three-star general as he might have a second lieutenant, "We can't wait until the court order is served on President Houston! If we do, millions of Americans are going to be dislocated, and their lives will be endangered and their property forfeited to the unbridled crime that's now taking place. Don't you know what this so-called president has done! He's allowed the gangs to roam freely, raping and marauding and harassing the citizens of our biggest cities."

"Actually, I don't think it was President Houston's fault that . . ." the general started to say.

Hill snapped at him again. "It *was* President Houston's idea. If he hadn't listened to that half-baked scientist, all this wouldn't be happening. The electricity would have been out for two days and then power would have been restored, and the millions of people who had been evacuated from these cities would still be there to protect their property. Don't tell me it wasn't Houston's fault!" Hill snapped. "It was. Now are you men going to follow the lawful order of the chief justice of the Supreme Court, or aren't you?"

"I understand that President Houston also secured a stay from Justice Harrington, putting aside the order by Justice McConnell."

"Justice McConnell is the chief justice of the Supreme Court," Hill countered angrily. "She is the only lawful authority in the Supreme Court as of this moment."

"But, General, in the opinion of many of the constitutional experts in this country, even Justice McConnell does not have the legal authority to remove the president. Only the Congress has that authority."

"But the Congress is not in session," Hill snapped. "And until it is, we have to do what's necessary. We cannot allow this madness to continue. The country will be ruined. I want each of you commanders to issue an order to your respective services, directing that all military personnel cease evacuating the cities immediately."

The generals sitting at the table were trying to assimilate the information and sort through it. Where did their loyalties lie? Clearly, President Houston was still the commander in chief of the United States. But the highest legal authority in the country had issued an order temporarily removing him from that position, pending a competency hearing. What were they to do?

"General Hill, I for one cannot do what you order," said Lt. Gen. Charles Riddon, head of the Marine Corps. "I've taken an oath of office to obey the commander in chief of the United States, and until that office is relinquished by President Houston, I must follow his orders."

Fire flashed in Gen. Hill's eyes. "You will submit your resignation!" Hill said. "Then I'll find somebody in the Marines who will execute the lawful orders of the new president of the United States."

"I'm sorry, Sir," Gen. Riddon said. "But you're not my boss. General Boland is. He's chairman of the joint chiefs. And until such time as he is removed from that position I take my lawful orders from him."

Encouraged by the comment from Gen. Riddon, Adm. Clayton Basinger, head of the Navy Department, spoke up. "I agree with General Riddon," Basinger said. "My immediate superior is Chairman of the Joint Chiefs General Floyd Boland, and my commander in chief is still President Philip Houston; and, until such time as he is removed from the office of presidency, my loyalty is with him."

Hill was furious, but he could see that he was losing the battle. Philip Houston was too popular a president for these men to abandon him. He decided his tactic would be better served by quietly removing them from their positions of authority. He was prepared for this kind of situation. With a snap of his fingers, he signaled the Army guard at the door. The guard turned around and opened the door to the conference room, and in poured a dozen armed security soldiers.

"Gentlemen," Hill said, "you are all under arrest for treason."

The aides who had accompanied the generals to the meeting started to go for their side arms. Almost in one motion, the armed security lowered their M-16 rifles. "I wouldn't recommend it," Gen. Hill said to the aides. "Your loyalty is admirable, but there's no point in you and your bosses dying over this."

One by one the aides were disarmed.

"I want everyone in this room to be held under close guard," Hill commanded. He turned back to the group, addressing them one last time. "Gentlemen, I'm sorry it has come down to this. But I'm acting under the lawful authority of the interim president of the United States."

"You're a traitor!" Gen. Riddon said to Hill. "I've known you for a long time, Nathan. You've always been a power-hungry fanatic. But this will not stand. The American people will not allow you to usurp the constitutional authority of the president of the United States."

"We'll see," Hill said smugly. "The people of this country will do exactly what we tell

345

them." With that, he ordered the guards to remove the others.

On his way to the communications center in the Pentagon, Gen. Hill approached the lieutenant commander in charge of communications security. "Commander," he said, "I need to issue a message to the field troops."

"Yes, Sir," the young commander said. "May I see your authorization from General Boland please, Sir?"

"Commander Gray," Hill said, "I have in my hand a court order from the chief justice of the Supreme Court declaring that Vice President Arnold Crenshaw is now interim president and appointing me chairman of the Joint Chiefs of Staff. You're under my authority now."

The young lieutenant commander was confused. He'd never faced this situation before. Falling back on the training that he had received at the Naval Academy, he decided that until such time as he had personal verification that Gen. Boland had been removed as chief of staff by the lawful authority of the United States, he would assume that authority was still in effect.

"I'm sorry sir," Gray said, "but until I am notified otherwise, General Boland is the chairman of the joint chiefs, and I cannot allow you into the code room without his approval."

Hill snapped his fingers again and two armed soldiers stepped up with their weapons leveled at Commander Gray. "You will surrender your keys and your code book," Hill barked.

Gray removed the card key from around his neck and withdrew his code book from an inner pocket of his shirt. "Let it be noted that I do so only under protest," Gray said.

"So noted," Gen. Hill responded, taking the card key and slipping it into the door. Once inside, he issued the field notice that would go out to all the units, ordering them to cease the evacuation immediately. They were ordered to reestablish control of the cities and maintain that position until further notice.

At the White House, President Houston heard a knock on his door. "Enter," he said. The door opened, and Warren Butts came in, followed by Gen. Boland.

"Mr. President, we've got a problem," Boland said.

"What is it, Floyd?" the president answered.

"Well, Sir, it appears that General Hill and his team have taken control of the Pentagon. They're issuing orders to the field troops to cease the evacuation immediately."

Houston looked as if somebody had just hit him with a two-by-four. "Aw, stupid," he said out loud. "I should have anticipated that."

"I should have too," Floyd Boland responded. "But I never thought Hill would take it this far. Until that court order is executed, you're still the commander in chief of the United States, and that makes Hill a traitor."

"Maybe so," Houston responded. "But in the absence of other authority, he represents the highest military authority in America. If we're not very careful, General Hill can become the pro tem president of the United States by virtue of his military authority. What do you recommend, General?"

"Well Mr. President, as of right now we still have communications to and from our field commanders. I would suggest that we issue a counterorder telling the troops and their commanders to continue the evacuation and that you still are the lawful head of this country."

Houston thought about that for a minute. To issue such an order was tantamount to starting a civil war within the military. They would be putting many soldiers in a compromising position. Men who weren't constitutional lawyers were being asked to decide where their loyalties were: with the president, who was holed up in the White House, or with the vice president, who had been named president by court order.

As an ex-military man himself, Houston wondered what he would do under a similar circumstance. He came to the conclusion that, lacking any further guidance, he would follow the still lawful orders of his commander in chief. He said to Gen. Boland, "Floyd, I don't like it, but I guess we don't have any choice. If we stop these evacuations, millions of people may die. Give the order."

Boland knew without having to voice it what Houston was doing, because it could potentially create the climate for a civil war within the military ranks. Some would be loyal to the new authority; some would be loyal to the old authority. But at the time, he couldn't see an alternative either.

"Floyd," the president said somberly as he was turning to leave. "You do realize that if I'm wrong about this thing and the solar flare is over, both of us will be tried for treason?"

Smiling, Boland turned to look at his old friend and quipped, "Well, Sir, I regret that you have but one life to give for your country."

"I'll bet you do, General," the president said with a grin. "I'll just bet you do."

Five minutes later, the message was going out on the Emergency Broadcast Network to military personnel all over the country. "The president of the United States, Philip Houston, has issued a direct order to the field commanders to continue the evacuation of the American cities." The message was delivered by Gen. Floyd Boland, chairman of the Joint Chiefs of Staff, United States Military.

Thus, the field commanders received two totally conflicting messages: one from Gen. Hill, commanding them to cease all evacuations, and the second from Gen. Boland, commanding them to continue the evacuations as ordered.

"What are you going to do, Sir?" Capt. Mitch Kowalski of the New York National Guard asked his unit commander, Colonel Alexander Scofield.

"As far as I'm concerned," Scofield said, "General Hill is now my authority. Justice McConnell has removed President Houston from office."

"I respectfully disagree, Sir," Kowalski said. "The presidency of this country is an elected office and, in my opinion, Justice McConnell doesn't have the authority to remove an elected president from office. I understand that only the Congress could do that through impeachment."

"You know what, Captain? You're under my authority, and I command you to issue the order to cease with the evacuations."

Kowalski, who had been an attorney for 20 years in the corporate offices of Exxon, thought about it for a minute. Then he responded. "Colonel Scofield, I'm sorry. I just cannot do that."

The colonel was reaching for his side arm when Kowalski pointed his 45 automatic in the colonel's face. He instructed the sergeant operating the telecommunications equipment to call the guard outside. When the guard came in Kowalski said, "The colonel is under house arrest. Please disarm him and hold him until further notice."

The National Guard Reserve corporal had a shocked look on his face. Much the same scenario was being replayed in command units across the country. Those who were loyal to Houston refused Gen. Hill's order. Those who disliked Houston obeyed Hill's order. It was very much a mixed message. In some units, fighting broke out. Generally speaking, the fights were limited mostly to fists, not lethal weapons. But as time went on, it was very clear that military authority was breaking down. It would only be a matter of time until armed conflict would break out within the ranks of the U.S. military.

Messages began to stream back to both Hill's headquarters at the Pentagon and Boland's at the White House, detailing the confrontations. At the Pentagon, Gen. Hill had been assessing the situation and had come to the conclusion that, at best, he could hope to rally perhaps 25 percent of the military personnel. Seventy-five percent were going to remain loyal to Gen. Boland and President Houston.

"We're going to have to isolate the White House," Hill told his field commanders. "As long as they have the ability to communicate with the troops in the field, we're never going to be able to turn the military."

"Well, Sir," Hill's communications specialist said, "all they have is land-line. There are no satellites in operation, and most air-link communications are out. They still haven't reestablished the microwave and S-band transmitters. If we break the connections at the Washington terminal, we can cut off the White House entirely."

"Can you interrupt the Emergency Broadcast Network?" Hill asked.

"Yes, Sir, I think we can. Again, they only have land lines, so they're totally dependent on the telephone links. If we cut the Washington terminal lines feeding the White House, the president will be totally isolated."

"Good. Let's do it," Hill said. "As soon as we have the White House isolated, the field commanders will follow our lead."

"General, we can do one more thing. If you will prepare a message in the name of General Boland, we can transmit it through the land lines into the Washington distribution center. It will look like a message coming directly from the White House."

Hill thought about it for a second. "Great

idea," he said. "I'll prepare a message from General Boland saying that the president has accepted the order of Justice McConnell and that he is relinquishing the office of the White House, effective immediately and that all military personnel will now take their orders directly from Gen. Hill at the Pentagon."

Superb idea, Hill thought to himself. *Once I'm in control of the military, the next step is to remove Crenshaw. Perhaps,* Hill thought darkly, *President Crenshaw will be assassinated by one of the gangs operating in the D.C. area. Too bad,* he thought with a smirk. *Crenshaw was such a loyal patriot too. I guess we'll really have to teach these gangs a lesson in the name of justice.*

Gen. Boland called the president: "Sir, we're still making the evacuation announcements but, based on our count right now, it would appear that only about 70 percent of the city dwellers have been evacuated, and the pace is nearly at a standstill. Some of the field units are in chaos, and a lot of the public are confused."

"Well, do your best, General. Let them know that it's urgent that they leave the cities," Houston said, hanging up.

"Hill has the evacuation slowed to a snail's pace," Houston said to Butts.

"He's not finished yet," Butts said somberly, chomping on his unlit cigar. "The general is an ambitious man. If I were an ambitious general with an opportunity like this, I would do two things."

"What?" Houston asked.

"First, I would want to cut your communications lines; and second, I would get rid of Crenshaw so I could take control — temporarily of course."

"Warren, I'm glad you're on our side," the president said, wrinkling his brow. "What can we do?"

"Well, I suspect Hill will try to cut our phone lines. The primary junction is the AT&T Washington junction."

"Can we protect it?"

"If our guys can get there first, we can. That building is like a fort. It was built with terrorists in mind. But the knife cuts both ways. If Hill's men beat us there we'll never dig them out. Twenty men can hold off an army once they're inside."

"Then we had better get there first," the president said.

"Our guys are on the way," Butts said with a forced grin. "A bunch of Navy Seals. I sent them, anticipating your approval."

Five minutes after Butts left Houston's study he called back on the intercom. "Mr. President, we have another problem."

"What is it?" Houston asked wearily. He had been up 30 hours now and the fatigue was beginning to show.

"We were evacuating two buses from Philadelphia when some of the gangs attacked. They killed everybody on board."

"What about security?" the president snapped.

"Our men can do only so much. They're stretched too thin now. We had APCs in front and in back, but these punks were armed with laser-guided rockets. Apparently someone supplied them with weapons from the Guard Armory."

"Supplied gangs with rockets? But what would the motive be?" the president asked incredulously.

"Chaos, Mr. President," Boland answered on the extension. "It's an old trick; Hitler used it to his benefit when he took over Germany. Create enough chaos and people will be willing to accept a temporary dictator. And, Phil, even though we have a lot of chaos in the cities right now, if these gangs are armed with enough firepower, we're going to have more turmoil than we can handle. If these punks get more rockets, they're going to shut down our security."

"What do you suggest, General?"

"I suggest, first, that we secure all the National Guard Armories with loyal troops."

"Okay. Just get it done," the president said angrily. He had a hard time believing Gen. Hill would arm the gangs.

"Good!" Boland replied. "We've already put that in motion."

If the situation weren't so critical Houston would have smiled. Boland wasn't a man to stand by and idly wait.

"What else, General?"

"Well, Sir, I think we need to treat this like it's a war. You need to go on the air and condemn Crenshaw and Hill."

"I can't do that, Floyd. Crenshaw is not a bad man — just indecisive."

"Well, at least let me send in loyal troops to clean out these gangs. They're vermin and need to be exterminated."

"I cannot authorize you to use lethal force on civilians, gangs or not. If somebody attacks you, you're authorized to do whatever's necessary to defend yourselves, but I won't go on the offensive. Once we use the army to attack our own citizens, we put this government on a slippery slope. We will protect our law abiding citizens, but we'll leave justice to the courts."

"It's hard to play by the rules when the other side doesn't have any," Boland grumbled.

"Granted, but without rule of law we're just another dictatorship," Houston said with finality.

"Maybe you're right, Mr. President," Boland sighed. And then he added, "I sure hope your God is listening to you today."

"He always is, Floyd," the president replied as he hung up.

At WNN headquarters in Atlanta, Neil Farmer was still fuming. He had finally scraped together enough crew to get the cameras on and the equipment powered up. He was online with the WNN mobile team in Washington D.C. He had missed the conference with Crenshaw and Gen. Hill, but he had gotten word that a congressional hearing was scheduled. He wasn't about to miss that.

"I want the session covered fully," Farmer commanded. "Find out what's going on, and see if you can locate Emily. Tell her I want to talk to her."

17

Emily Hart had made an unauthorized trip to Washington, D.C. when she knew Dr. Hobart had been called there by the president. She had been unable to secure an interview with anybody in the administration, and since the flare struck she had been holed up in the Rayburn Hotel.

She had been frightened out of her wits by the violence in the area. She wasn't sure how many days since the power went out, but it was obvious that the worst of the solar flare was past, because power was restored in the Rayburn. The power in her room, though intermittent, had been on for the better part of an hour; and, for the first time in three days she'd actually been able to take a shower. She decided it was time for her to get up, get out, and go to work. Since early that morning, she'd been listening intently out her bedroom window and had not heard gunfire — at least not close to the hotel. She heard what she thought might be gunfire in the distance, so she presumed the police had established some degree of control.

But Emily Hart was a different woman than when she came to Washington. She had been shaken to the bottom of her soul. When this whole episode started, she presumed it was just another story, and she had done all that she could to tear down Professor Hobart and President Houston in the process. But now she realized how stupid she had been. What Professor Hobart said turned out to be true. She had nearly contributed to the murder of millions of people, herself included. She was determined that from this point on, she was going to do honest reporting — no matter what. If Neil Farmer didn't like it, he could find himself another reporter. Based on what she had seen in the last couple of days, she suspected that WNN would have a hard time getting another reporter at this point.

She went down the hotel stairs, still fearful of using the elevators, lest the power should go out again and she'd be trapped in one of the elevators. As claustrophobic as she was, the thought of being stuck in an elevator horrified her. So she decided she would walk instead. When she got down to the hotel lobby, things had begun to assume some semblance of normality.

There were two clerks working the desk, and although there were no bellboys in sight there were three or four couples, who apparently were hotel guests. She heard one of them ask, "Is there any food?" to which the clerk replied, "We anticipate that the kitchen will be up and operating soon, but the menu will be very limited."

"How long?" the young woman asked.

"Perhaps an hour," the clerk replied.

Too long, Emily decided. *I can't wait an hour. I'll just have to see what I can find outside the hotel.* What she saw as she left the hotel made her stop in astonishment. There were smashed cars at the intersection. The drivers had abandoned them. As she turned the corner and headed toward the Rayburn Office Building, she saw two burned-out hotels. She shuddered to think how close the violence had come to her. She realized that her hotel had been spared only because of its close proximity to the D.C. police. *Three hours later in my arrival time*, she thought, *and I could have been trapped on one of the subways or trapped at the airport.* It panicked her to think about what life in the subway tunnels must be like. Underground and trapped! The thought terrified her.

As she walked toward the Rayburn Building, she noticed a WNN truck parked about a half block down the street. She turned and walked to the truck and peered inside. It was one of the big vans that WNN used, with a satellite dish on the roof and spacious enough to hold four people and all their camera equipment.

There appeared to be no one inside, so she walked around to the back of the truck and tried to see in the window, but it was too high. She climbed up on the platform that served as a bumper and strained to look in. As she did, the back door sprung open. Emily was so startled, she almost fell off the platform. A young, shaggy-headed, bearded man stuck his head out the door.

"Who are you?" he demanded, brandishing a tire iron.

"I'm Emily Hart," she answered a little shakily. "Who are you?"

"I'm Art Silver," he answered. "WNN camera crew. Say, are you the Emily Hart that does some specials for us?"

Emily responded, "Yes I am. I'm here to cover the solar flare story for Neil Farmer." She lied. She was actually here on her own, but she didn't want anyone from WNN to know that.

"I just talked to Farmer and he said for you to get in contact with him."

"Oh, is your phone still working?" Hart asked.

"Nope. It worked for a few minutes and then quit again," the young man said. "Guess the cell translators went out again."

"So how do I contact Atlanta?" Hart snapped.

"Beats me, Boss. You're the reporter. I just point and shoot," Silver said sarcastically. Then he visibly softened as he said, "I've been stuck in the back of this truck for nearly three days. Pretty scary stuff, too," he said. "For a while there, it was kind of touch and go. I thought maybe those gangs were going to get this far and I'd be trapped in this truck with no place to go. But National Guard guys headed them off. There was a pretty big gun battle a couple of blocks away."

"Yeah, I heard it too," Emily agreed. "Unreal!"

"You got that right!" Silver agreed. "Well, what are we going to do, Boss?"

"In the first place, I'm not your boss, but I thought I'd go over to the Capitol to see what's going on. Do you have any camera equipment that's still working?"

Silver replied, "Yep! The two cameras we were using when that flare hit are shot. But we have three spares in the truck, and I didn't even try to turn them on til this morning. I powered one of 'em up, and it seems to be working okay, though I don't have the foggiest idea how we'll get a signal back to headquarters. All the satellites are out and most of the land lines are down. 'Bout the best I can do is put it on tape."

"That should be good enough," Emily said. "Follow me."

"You got it, Toots," Silver said, as he ducked inside the truck.

Emily whirled, about to give Silver a piece of her mind when she thought better of it. *It's not important,* she reminded herself. *It's just not important.* She decided that such nonsense would have to take a backseat to survival, and she was still in her survival mode. When they got to the Rayburn Building entrance, they were met by a guard.

"Who are you?" the guard demanded.

"We're from WNN," Emily responded, showing the guard her credentials.

"Well, I'm sorry," he said, "but nobody's allowed in this building."

"I'm trying to find out if the Congress is in session. Is there anyone in the building we can talk to?"

"I believe there's someone in the majority leader's office," the guard replied, more cordially now.

"Does the intercom system work?"

"It did last time we tried it," he said. "Nothing's sure right now though."

Emily picked up the phone and punched in the code. On the other end she heard, "Congressman Purcell's office." The aide who answered the phone made it sound like the most natural thing in the world, even though the telephones had been out for nearly three days. It was years of practiced habit coming through.

"Hi, this is Emily Hart of WNN," she said. "Is the congressman in?"

"No, I'm sorry," she said, "the congressman is not in. He's in a meeting."

Emily was surprised. "Congress is reconvening?"

"No," the aide said. "There aren't enough representatives present to make a quorum. But there is a special session going on."

"Can you tell me where that meeting's being held?" Emily said.

"Yes, it's being held in the Johnson Room."

"Thank you," Emily said courteously. She headed out the door with Silver close behind. "We're going over to the House," she said. "They're having a meeting right now in the Johnson Room."

Once they reached the entrance to the Capitol Building and climbed the steps, they were confronted by another guard. "Could I see some I.D. please?"

They showed him their I.D. cards. "The House is still open to the public, isn't it?" Emily said, just a little sarcastically. "Right?"

The guard responded, "Yes it is, Ma'am. We're just being very careful today about security, as you can imagine."

"Yes, I understand very well. I appreciate that," she said more courteously. In the background, as she listened very carefully, she could still hear the popping sound of gunfire in the distance. The reality of the last few days resurfaced. She apologized to the guard: "I know you're just doing your job, and I do appreciate it."

"Thanks, Ma'am," he responded. "My family has left the city, but I couldn't leave this grand old building to be burned or pillaged."

Emily was surprisingly moved by what he had said. A week ago she would have labeled this armed guard a warmonger.

She and Silver made their way through the building to the Johnson Room. As she started to go in, another guard stopped her.

"I'm sorry, Ma'am. This meeting is closed to the public."

Emily replied, "I'm not the public. I'm part of the press." She showed her press card.

"I'll have to check, Ma'am. Please wait here."

In the past, she would have had a very caustic response for the guard. This time, she didn't even feel the urge to do so. She knew her attitudes had been modified over the last few days.

The guard came back out and said, "Ma'am, it's okay. You can go in."

As almost an afterthought Emily said, "Do you know if there happens to be a working telephone anywhere in the building?"

"No, Ma'am. Not to my knowledge," the guard replied. "The intercoms are back working again, and the internal switchboard is operating, but so far we've not been able to receive or to make telephone calls from the building."

"Well, thank you," she said as she walked into the meeting room.

She recognized a few of the people in the room, including Dr. Robert Frasier, former head of the National Institute of Sciences. The other man she didn't recognize, but the name in front of his seat said Dr. Henry Ostenburg, Goddard Research Center. She assumed he was a scientist. She motioned to Silver to set up his camera, and she positioned the microphone strategically on the desk to pick up as much of the conversation as possible.

"Give us your opinion of what is going on, Doctor," Congressman Dick Gerstner said, directing his questions to Dr. Frasier.

"Well, gentlemen . . . and ladies," recognizing the two women congressional representatives attending the meeting. "In the opinion of our best scientists, the worst of this solar flare has passed. Therefore, the acts of the president are totally irresponsible. The government is dislocating millions of American families, and if this continues at the same pace in another few days we will have dislocated several million more American families, sending them out to a life in the wilderness, with virtually no way to feed, clothe, or house them," Frasier added with great emphasis.

"Upon what do you base your analysis?" Congressman Purcell, the ranking Republican present, asked Frasier. "Certainly Dr. Hobart has been right — up to this point."

Frasier was still seething inside. *These idiots*

should make Houston resign. But Purcell is a loyal Houston flunkey. He decided to play his trump card: Dr. Henry Ostenburg, head of Goddard Research Center's solar observation team.

At one time Ostenburg had been an eminent scientist. Unfortunately, the ravages of age and bad health had taken their toll on him. At this point Ostenburg was looking forward to a comfortable government retirement. When he was contacted by Frasier he readily agreed to testify as a technical expert, for a promised sizeable fee.

"Describe your findings, Doctor Ostenburg," Frasier said, motioning toward the older scientist.

"Well, gentlemen," Ostenburg began in his faltering, raspy voice. "Obviously, we did have a significant solar flare, with a magnitude of at least 6. We have been observing this flare since its inception, and in the opinion of my scientific team the worst of the flare activity is over. It will continue to dissipate and, therefore, represents no further danger."

Ostenburg knew that was not the absolute truth. Several members of his team thought the solar cycle might be dying down, but others who relied on Professor's Hobart's calculations disagreed. They concluded that if the current lull was a part of a cyclical rhythm, much like other lesser flares in the past, then it was quite possible that area 403 would erupt again.

Congressman Gerstner, never one to miss a political opportunity, said, "Clearly the actions of the president are irresponsible. Shutting down the largest industrial complex in the world, based on the opinion of a discredited scientist shows that he is unfit, and the Supreme Court agrees."

Republican Congressman Stanton from Virginia spoke up. "You mean Justice McConnell agrees, don't you? Thus far, Professor Hobart has been right and President Houston has been acting in a responsible fashion. The reports we're getting from around the world verify that we're the only industrial nation still in operation. Remember that it is only because of President Houston's actions so far that we're able to be here today. We should give the president our support. *He* is the commander in chief."

Gerstner's face turned bloodred. He and Stanton had disagreed many times on the House floor, and he wasn't about to back down now. "And, if he's wrong," Gerstner said, slamming his fist on the table, "he will collapse the largest industrial complex in the world. This irresponsibility will cost billions of dollars and millions of jobs. This is insanity!" Gerstner's normal tactic was to shout down opponents whenever possible. "The Congress must back Justice McConnell.

Houston is no longer competent to be president."

Congressman Stanton shouted back, "Justice McConnell does not have the constitutional authority to order the president of the United States to step down. Only the Congress can do that. Therefore, her order is illegal, as Justice Harrington has clearly pointed out."

Gerstner exploded. "A lower justice cannot overrule the chief justice of the United States!" he shouted.

"And the chief justice of the United States cannot usurp the authority of the Congress!" Stanton shouted back.

In the meantime, Art Silver captured everything on video. The more Hart listened, the more convinced she was that Gerstner was wrong. His motives were purely political.

"Congressman, may I ask a question?" she asked, directing the question toward Gerstner.

"And who are you?" Gerstner snapped.

"Emily Hart, WNN," she responded, containing her irritation at his attitude. Gerstner suddenly lightened up. WNN was a good friend to the Democratic party.

"May I ask a question?" she repeated.

"Certainly," he replied, now almost cooing.

"Congressman, how can you be certain that you're right and the president is wrong? I've been holed up in this city for several days, with gunfire going off all around me. The lawless elements in this city, and probably every other city in the United States, have nearly taken over. If in fact you're wrong and the president is right, you will condemn millions of American families to cities that are overrun by gangs, bent on nothing less than the total destruction of our society. Can we afford to take that chance? Can you?"

Gerstner was shocked. That was not a question that a WNN reporter should ask of a Democratic congressman. It just wasn't done that way. His face reflected the anger he felt.

"Miss Hart, you're apparently an inexperienced young woman. I've talked to some of the leading scientists in America, and Dr. Frasier has confirmed this solar flare will not erupt any further."

"But what if you're wrong?" Emily pressed once more.

"We're not wrong!" Frasier blurted out. "We've got the best scientists in the world who have confirmed our observations."

"What about Dr. Onera . . . and Dr. Singer?" she countered. "Aren't they two of the foremost astrophysicists in the world? They concur with Dr. Hobart's analysis."

"Dr. Ostenburg has reviewed Hobart's data and has concluded . . . ," Frasier started to say, when Ostenburg interjected.

"Actually I haven't seen Dr. Hobart's

data," Ostenburg said. "I reviewed Dr. Frasier's report."

"Then you're making a judgment based on secondhand information," Emily said incredulously.

"We'll discuss this later," Gerstner said gruffly. "The issue here is how to force President Houston to obey a lawful order of the nation's highest legal authority."

Emily decided she had gotten all she was going to get out of Gerstner, so she closed with, "Well thank you for allowing me to ask the question."

"In my opinion," Congressman Stanton said, "it would be totally irresponsible not to consider the implications of Miss Hart's question. What if the president *is* right?"

"He is not right; and I'm going to introduce a bill of impeachment to enforce Justice McConnell's order," Gerstner shouted at his counterpart.

"A bill of impeachment cannot be drawn without a quorum," Stanton shouted back, "and the order from McConnell is *not* legal."

Gerstner shouted, "I want it noted that the House Democrats do not support the president's actions."

Stanton shouted back, "And I want it noted that the Republican side of the Congress supports the president. He's our commander in chief, and let us not forget that we are in a state of martial law at this point; therefore, the president, as commander in chief, has the legal authority to do whatever is necessary to protect American citizens."

"We're also in a state of anarchy!" Gerstner sputtered, his face strained. "Our cities are on fire and it's not safe to walk down the streets of Washington, D.C. Houston's evacuation order did that!"

"Let me remind you," Stanton said through clenched teeth, "that it's you and your friends who have coddled these thugs and gangs all these years. If you had done what the Republicans wanted to do, we would have them locked up in jails and prisons, where they would be safely out of harm's way by now. It wasn't safe to walk the streets of the capital *before* this flare!"

Gerstner was about to shout something back when the speaker of the House, who had just entered the room from the far end, said, "Enough is enough! We are under martial law. The president is the commander in chief as of this moment, and unless the Senate chooses to impeach him, he has the constitutional right to do exactly what he is doing.

"And, Congressman," he continued, looking directly at Gerstner, "I would oppose any House rule suggesting the unlawful overthrow of the presidency."

Emily captured everything on camera. She motioned to Art and they slipped out of the room. She remembered that WNN had a makeshift headquarters somewhere in the House complex, so she told Silver, "Let's find the press office. I want to get this edited."

With some help from the guards stationed throughout the building, they found the press office. There was only one person in the room: a technician from ABC.

Emily asked, "Have you seen anybody from WNN around here?"

The tech replied, "No, Ma'am. Nobody here but me, but I know there are no lines to WNN headquarters. We're having a hard enough time keeping one line up for our network."

"You still have a line?" Silver asked, his interest sparked.

"Yes, we're still able to reach our broadcast center in Washington, and some of the network is back online, though not very much."

"Could I talk with someone at ABC?" Hart asked.

"I think so," the technician said. "Hang on a second." He flipped on his phone and dialed the number. Emily could hear his end of the conversation. "Yeah, there's somebody here from WNN who would like to talk to you, Sir. Hang on." He handed her the phone.

"This is Emily Hart from WNN. Who am I talking to please?"

He said, "This is Bob Geifer, G-E-I-F-E-R.

I'm program director for ABC News here in Washington."

"Mr. Geifer, can you get me a link to WNN in Atlanta?"

"Not a chance. We have no lines to Atlanta. About the best we can do is link to our studios in Baltimore and New York, though New York is still off line. We do have a few of our affiliates back on line."

"I have a news clip that we've just recorded here in the House of Representatives."

"What's it about?" Geifer asked.

"Members of the House were discussing the actions of the president," Hart responded. "Since I can't reach my people at WNN, would you be interested in this clip?"

"Would I ever!" Geifer responded excitedly. "I can't find any of our field people. Nobody's reported in yet, and I'm desperate for fresh news to carry on the network."

"Give me about fifteen minutes," Emily said, "and I'll get back with you."

"Okay," Geifer said.

She signaled to Silver to follow her and told the ABC technician, "I'll be right back. Please keep that line open if possible."

He said, "That's what I'm here for."

Finding an empty office close by, she signaled Silver to record her.

"Rolling," Silver said.

"This is Emily Hart of WNN News. I've just attended the meeting at the House of

Representatives that you just saw. But let me add something to that meeting. For two and a half days, I have been holed up in a hotel close to the Capitol Building here in Washington, D.C., with no electricity, no water, no utilities of any kind, and the sound of gunfire raging throughout this city. As a reporter, I'm supposed to be objective; but, having lived through this, I can no longer be an objective reporter. If the president of the United States is wrong in evacuating our cities, the worse that will happen is that he will have inconvenienced a lot of people and cost a lot of money. However, if the president is right and Congressman Gerstner and the scientists you heard on this tape are wrong, the president will have saved millions, perhaps tens of millions of American lives. And my question to the American people is, can we afford to take that risk? As a reporter, I urge you to be objective. As an American citizen, I suggest you support the president. This is Emily Hart, Washington, D.C."

"You can't say that," Silver said. "Frasier will have your head."

"Let him do whatever he wants," she said. "Do you disagree?"

He replied, "Not at all, Ma'am. In fact, as soon as we dump this tape, I'm leaving."

"Me too," Emily agreed.

Within 30 minutes the camera had been connected to the high-speed transmission line, and the data had been transmitted back to ABC. When the program director reviewed the tape, he was ecstatic. It was great stuff — some of the best he had seen. And no matter what happened, it was a win-win situation for ABC. They could carry the tape and attribute it to WNN. If the president was right, they would be heroes for having broadcast the tape. And if the president was wrong, they could simply blame it on WNN and Emily Hart. He knew he could sell that to his bosses. He immediately started editing the tape down to a more usable format.

Thirty minutes later, every ABC affiliate still operating was broadcasting the WNN piece. When Farmer saw the newscast on Channel 2 in Atlanta, he was livid. "I'll kill her!" he screamed at the empty control room. "No, I'll fire her . . . then I'll kill her!"

Along with the interview, ABC aired footage showing the fires in D.C., with sounds of gunfire in the background. The intent of the message being broadcast was that the country was out of control and the president had allowed it to get that way. The effect on the viewers was mixed: Clearly, most of those in areas controlled by the gangs sided with the president; many others decided to stick it out and not evacuate.

Unfortunately, for many of the residents of these and other major cities, the confusion being broadcast over the airwaves had caused them to waffle. Even families that had packed and were awaiting their evacuation orders still had questions and doubts. But at least the WNN interview helped the indecisive to get moving.

Joel and Kelli Slife lived in the refurbished downtown area of Chicago. Joel was a programmer for the Detroit Diesel Company in Chicago. When word about the evacuation was first put out, Kelli immediately went to their bedroom and packed two suitcases. Joel had been hesitant from the very beginning, but he went along with his wife because she was so fearful.

He really didn't want to leave their apartment. They were in a safe area of the city, and he had some expensive electronic equipment to protect. He could just see looters breaking into their apartment as soon as they left and stripping them of everything they owned. He had gone along with the announcement about powering down all electronic equipment; that made sense at the time, but now that the crisis was over, he was more reticent than ever.

"But, Sweetheart," Kelli argued, "the president said we have to evacuate."

"And where are we going to go?" Joel groused. "They're going to move us somewhere in the woods to live in a tent? No thanks. I think we should stay here."

"But didn't you hear the president?" Kelli pleaded. She was close to tears. The scenes of the burned-out buildings and cars frightened her. What would they do if they were trapped in the city with no food or water? They hadn't been able to flush a toilet in three days and when the water finally came back on it had flooded all over the floor. What would it be like after a week?

"We have to go, Joel," she protested.

"Didn't you hear those scientists?" he asked irritatedly. "The worst of the solar flare is over. We can sit this thing out." *Kelli listens to anyone in authority. She never questions her doctor. If the speed limit sign says 45 mph, that's what she drives. I love her but sometimes she drives me nuts.* Joel's philosophy was, you have to take charge of your own life.

"I'm telling you, Kelli Honey, I've got this feeling everything's okay."

"Joel, I don't have any peace about it. I really believe we ought to go," Kelli said as her voice shook. She was trying not to cry because she knew how it upset her husband.

The more he thought about it, the angrier he got. How stupid it would be to leave everything they'd worked so hard for. They'd been married nearly three years, and everything they owned was in their apartment. They were saving for a down payment on a house, but it would still be a couple of years before they would have enough.

"Well, you can go if you want to," Joel said resolutely. "But I'm going to stay. I'm not giving up what we've worked so hard for."

"But . . . ," Kelli started to say, but when she looked at her husband, she knew his mind was made up. And when Joel made up his mind there was no point in arguing.

"Then I'm staying too," his wife said.

"No, you go, Honey. I'll stay. I'll bet they'll let you return in a day or two."

"If you stay, I'm staying," Kelli said firmly.

"Kelli, I want you to go. I'll be okay. I'm convinced this solar flare is over and there's no danger."

"No!" Kelli shouted in an uncharacteristic outburst. "If you stay, I'm staying!"

Joel slammed the magazine he was holding down on the table. "This is stupid! I don't want to leave our stuff. You go!"

"If you stay, I stay," Kelli said, her jaw clamped tightly. She could feel the tears coming and she fought them back. *No, I will not cry!* she told herself firmly.

Joel was really fuming by this time. He snapped at her, "You're just acting childish!"

"But I love you," she said. "Remember what we decided? 'Whither thou goest, I will go,' " Kelli said, quoting from the Bible book of Ruth.

His heart melted as he looked into her soft brown eyes. Seeing the tears did it. He walked over and put his arms around her. "Okay,

Sweetheart, you win. We'll go, but first I'm going to lock everything up. Okay?"

"Okay," she agreed with a smile, wiping the tears from her cheeks.

Joel got the suitcases Kelli had packed and put them by the door. He walked over to his neighbor's apartment and knocked on the door. His friend Bill opened the door. "Bill, Kelli doesn't want to stay," Joel said, "so I'm going with her. Can I leave some stuff in your apartment if you're going to stay?"

"Sure," his friend responded warmly. They had been good friends for more than six years and shared many common interests. "I understand," he said, winking at Joel. "Elaine would go if I would, but I won't. So she's staying too."

Joel had a knowing look on his face, but he didn't say anything. He glanced past his longtime friend to where Elaine stood. Her eyes were red from crying too. He thought about backing out again, but he didn't want to get into it again with Kelli. He shrugged and said, "Thanks, Buddy. We'll be back as soon as we can."

"We'll be here," Bill said. Then he added, "I always wanted that great CD player of yours. Bring some discs with it, will ya?"

Joel reached out his hand and Bill clasped it.

"Good luck," Bill said.

"Yeah, you too."

Kelli helped Joel carry the video equipment, as well as their prized CD system and placed them in Bill's and Elaine's spare bedroom. "We'll be back in a couple of days," Joel assured his friend. "Thanks for being such good friends."

"No problem," Bill said as he hugged first Joel and then Kelli. Before they left, Elaine and Kelli had a tearful good-bye and promised each other they'd be together again soon. As Joel and Kelli left, they could hear the bolt locking behind them. Joel thought briefly about trying to convince Kelli one more time, but he decided it was no use. So he gathered the suitcases and they headed down the stairs.

Outside, the sound truck was blaring, "Anyone wishing to evacuate should leave immediately."

Kelli opened the door for Joel as he lifted out the suitcases. Waiting at the curb was a Metro bus that was about half full of people, some of whom they recognized from their complex.

Since the bus was not equipped for passengers with luggage, there was a stake-bed truck behind them and Joel was directed to put their bags on it. Then he and Kelli climbed into the bus. The driver waited five more minutes and, when no one else came, the soldier coordinating the effort signaled to him to get going.

Joel was still irritated but, as Kelli snuggled

up next to him, he began to soften some. As far as he was concerned, anything that was important to her was important to him.

18

The president stood looking out the window of the Oval Office. There was a lot of activity going on at the east gate. He had already guessed what it was when he heard a knock at his door.

"Come in," the president said. Glancing toward the door, he saw the trio of Gen. Boland, Warren Butts, and Allen Dean enter. Butts looked at Houston. He was shocked. It was the first time he had seen the president in good light in the last couple of days. Houston looked haggard, with dark circles under his eyes, and he had been wearing the same clothes for the better part of three days. Butts also knew that the president probably had not had a wink of sleep in the last two days.

"We have a problem," Gen. Boland reported.

"Does it have something to do with the activity outside the gates?" the president asked.

"Yes, Sir," Boland responded.

"Hill and Gerstner, I assume," the president said.

"Right again, Mr. President. Gen. Hill has brought a pretty large contingent of his forces, and they've surrounded the White House compound."

"Oh really?" the president said in surprise. "Do you think they're going to storm the White House, Floyd?"

"Not a chance, Mr. President. That would be political suicide, and both Gerstner and Hill know it. Nothing you've done is illegal or warrants this kind of action. I think this is a media play."

"Then I guess the media's back up and operating, aren't they," Houston said wearily.

"WNN is still off the air, but ABC and CBS are back up, and NBC has got some of their affiliates up. Basically, I'd say they're reaching about a fourth of their normal audience," Dean responded.

"I assume they're playing up this incompetency thing pretty heavily?"

"Yes, Sir," Dean answered. "But from what we've been able to gather, the American people still support you."

"Polls are kind of irrelevant at this point, aren't they, Allen?" the president said curtly. "When it comes right down to it, I suspect that it's who holds the bigger stick that counts."

"Mr. President, I don't think the troops outside the White House gates represent a threat. If I did, I would have pulled in a whole division," Boland said. "But we have an even bigger problem."

"What's that, Floyd?"

"Hill and his men beat us to the telephone substation. For all intents and purposes, the Emergency Broadcast Network is shut down. But they don't know that some of our land lines go through another substation; so you still have telephone contact. At least we can talk to Andrews, and from Andrews we can go out to most of our own military units across the country. Just give the word, Mr. President, and I'll mobilize 200,000 troops and we'll stop General Hill in his tracks. Most of the military are still with us."

"Absolutely not," Houston said emphatically. "I told you before, I will not have a civil war in America. How are the evacuations progressing?"

"I'd estimate that we have evacuated 70 percent of the people who want to leave the cities."

"Give it to me straight, Warren. How bad is it?"

"We estimate that some 20 to 25 percent of the city dwellers are not going to evacuate. They either don't believe your warnings or they are confused. As you know, Dr. Frasier has accumulated a whole cadre of scientists who support his position."

"Frasier! We should have thrown him out two years ago."

"Probably so, Mr. President. But he's a slick politician, and he's really making us look bad. Unfortunately, a lot of people who should be leaving aren't because they believe him."

"So a lot of people won't evacuate, and we've relocated about 70 percent of those who want to," the president said. "Is that about it?"

"That's correct," Butts confirmed, and Boland shook his head in agreement.

"Continue the evacuations. I don't want anything to stop us."

"One more thing, Mr. President."

"Aw, what now?" Houston asked irritably. His head hurt and he badly needed to rest a while.

"Apparently, with more of the power being restored, the city's beginning to come to life again. The Senate is convening a steering committee right now to decide on whether to begin impeachment proceedings against you."

"As I said, I expected that would happen."

"There is some question about whether it's legal for the chief justice to throw the president out of office, but there's no question that the Senate can do it."

"What are my odds, Warren?"

"Not very good right now, Mr. President. A lot of senators are being influenced by Dr. Frasier's scientists, including some members of our own party. However, we still have some friends in the Senate, so we can slow this thing down."

"How long do we have?" Houston asked. "Best guess, Warren."

"I'd say a couple of days — maybe less. But if the Senate decides to suspend all the rules of protocol, they could rip through this impeachment hearing pretty quickly. How many senators we can count on? It's up in the air right now. Some of our friends are out of the city and some are still here. If their side has more than our side, we're going to have a real problem. They've already made the decision to suspend the rules of quorum."

"Which means that if they have only half the Senate they can hold the trial," Houston said.

"That's right, Mr. President, more or less."

"I'd like to see what's going on," Houston said. "Do we have a working TV?"

"I think so, Sir," Dean said. He stepped outside and signaled one of the security men, who came in with a small portable television. "Most of the TVs in the White House got fried. People turned them on, in spite of your instructions."

"Yes, I know," Houston said with an impish grin. "I tried a couple myself. I wasn't sure I believed what I said either."

Dean sat the portable TV down and flipped it on to the local ABC affiliate. The scene looked like pandemonium. The people gathered in front of the big gates at 1600 Pennsylvania Avenue were shouting, and some were carrying signs that said, "Impeach Houston," "Down with King Houston," "Get the dictator out of office."

Another shot showed a cordon of armed military personnel surrounding the White House. The commentator launched into a narrative about how President Houston had usurped congressional authority and had plunged the nation into financial ruin by forced evacuations. He accused the president of abandoning the cities to the gangs and looters.

The commentator said, "As a result, every major city in America has suffered significant structural damage, with private property destroyed and citizens molested by gangs — all because the president listened to a discredited scientist who created hysteria over a relatively minor solar flare."

The common theme on every channel was an indictment of the president. Then the scene cut away to a shot of Gen. Hill.

"I'm General Nathan Hill, and I've been in the military 36 years. I have to say that I've never seen anything like this in my entire military career. President Houston has chosen to ignore the constitutional authority of the United States and has assumed control of the country. No leader of an industrialized nation has done anything like this since Adolf Hitler did so in 1936."

The commentator asked, "What do you think the president's motive is, General?"

"I can only guess," the general said solemnly. "But I would assume at this point that President Houston would like to be the sole authority in the country. He has ignored the Congress, the Supreme Court, and the wishes of the American people. This situation is very dangerous."

"Thank you, General," the narrator said.

The next scene showed Congressman Gerstner standing next to Senate Minority Leader Trevor Tate.

"We're here at the Senate building with Senator Tate," Gerstner said, "where the Senate is convening a subcommittee to hear impeachment proceedings against President Houston. The president has chosen to ignore a Supreme Court order that instructs him to vacate the presidency until his competency can be evaluated. Since there seems to be some question about the constitutional authority of the Supreme Court to remove the president, the Senate is taking immediate action. Hearings will begin within the next hour on the impeachment of President Houston."

"Why the urgency, Senator?" the young female reporter asked.

Tate answered in his deep southern drawl. "We believe that if we allow the president to continue this madness further, it will totally destroy the infrastructure of the United States, and the country may never recover from it." Tate was an impressive man, nearly six foot three, with silver-gray hair, and he spoke with an authoritative tone. As Senate minority leader, he was the ranking member in the Senate available in Washington.

Alongside Senator Tate was Senator Steven Lowell of New Hampshire. In the absence of any other Republican leaders at the time, Lowell became the ranking majority senator. Lowell was long known as a liberal and often had voted against conservative issues. He was the ideal candidate for Gerstner to use in chairing the meeting.

Lowell spoke up. "As the ranking member of the majority party, I support Senator Tate's position. I will chair the committee to hear the charges against President Houston. We have decided to suspend the Senate rules requiring a quorum because of the emergency facing the nation."

"When do you think the trial might begin?" the reporter asked.

"I would assume that we'll hear arguments today," Lowell said, "and we could decide as early as tomorrow."

The reporter signed off, and the scene shifted back to the White House east gate.

"This is Zack Bowman of ABC News, and what you have heard is a live broadcast from the Senate building where the Senate of the United States is beginning hearings on the possible indictment of President Philip Houston. We have tried unsuccessfully to get an interview with President Houston, who is now holed up in the White House behind his own cordon of armed military personnel. The president has refused all our attempts to interview him."

"That's an outright lie!" Allen Dean shouted.

"Easy, Allen," Houston said. "I wouldn't have expected anything less."

"Pretty impressive show," Butts commented. "If you didn't know what was going on from the inside, you'd sure think they had things under control, wouldn't you?"

"Well, nobody ever accused the liberals of being stupid," Houston said. "They're better at politics than we are, and inside the beltway they can pretty well get their own way. But when we can take our case to the American people, they continue to vote in conservatives."

"This thing is coming to a climax," Butts said. "Mr. President, I think you're going to have to go face the Senate."

"I agree," Houston said. "We can't let this trial take place without representation. But first I have something to do. Allen, can you get Andrews on the line for me?"

"Sure, Mr. President," Dean said.

"General, can you get word to your troops to continue the evacuation, until such time as I'm impeached?"

"No problem, Mr. President. Like I say, we still have good communications through Andrews, so we should be able to get the word out."

"Good. As soon as I'm finished, you take the line."

Dean walked back in. "Mr. President, Andrews is on line one. I presume that you wanted to talk to Dr. Hobart."

"Correct," the president said.

Houston picked up the receiver. "Professor?"

"Yes, Sir," Jason responded.

"What's that flare up to now?"

"Well, Mr. President, it's a remarkable coincidence that you called. We've been monitoring the output of area 403, and we've seen a marked increase in X-ray activity over the last few hours. I waited to call you until I was sure. But, I'm convinced the next flare is building."

"How long?"

"I wish I could say, but I just don't know. It could be an hour. It could be a day. It could be a week. We just don't have enough data on a flare this size to give a reasonable estimate."

"Well, Jason," the president said, "if it's a week, I suspect you'll be talking to a new president on this end of the line."

"Surely not, Mr. President," Jason responded.

"We'll see," Houston said wearily. "Keep me informed."

"I will," Jason said, about to hang up.

"One more thing," Houston added. "If this thing pops, contact me no matter where I am. Okay?"

"You'll know as soon as we're sure," Jason promised.

"One more thing," Houston said somberly, "I may not be at the White House. The Senate is convening impeachment hearings. So I'll be at that hearing. But no matter what, you get hold of me as quickly as possible."

"Right, Sir," Jason said. His head was swimming. Impeachment proceedings against the president, and he was in the middle of it. If this flare didn't happen soon, the president would be thrown out of office.

"And, Jason . . . one last thing," the president added.

"Yes?"

"As soon as you're sure about that flare, I want you and the rest of the group there to pack up and get out of there. I'm sending some evacuation vehicles to Andrews to stand by. Do you still want to evacuate to the New Holland camp?"

"Yes, Sir, but I need to relocate all of our equipment."

"Already done," the president said. "You'll have a duplicate of everything you have there at Andrews, plus whatever you can carry with you."

"Well, that being the case," Jason said, "New Holland is the perfect site."

"Good. I'll have General Boland check the facilities and have them ready for you. And, Professor?"

"Yes, Sir?"

"Thank you. Thank you for your courage, your wisdom, and your commitment to the American people. I still believe in you, and I believe in the final analysis you will be responsible for saving millions of American families."

With that, the phone went dead. Jason couldn't have responded anyway. The lump in his throat kept him from saying anything else. He just prayed that what he had told the president was true. He hated to wish a solar flare on the world, but if it didn't happen the way he'd called it . . . well, he didn't even want to think about that.

"Okay, gentlemen," the president said to the group standing before him. "I guess we go to the Senate. Give me about 30 minutes to take a shower and change clothes, and we'll be on our way. Warren, can you call up one of the limos?"

"No problem, Mr. President," Butts said as he left the Oval Office.

Once they were out in the hall Butts asked, "General, can you give us a military escort over to the Senate building?"

"Of course," the general answered. He decided to do it himself. He already had a hand-picked crew of about 20 men, made up of Navy Seals and Army Rangers, who would escort them wherever they wanted to go. "It would be good to call General Hill's bluff anyway," Boland said. "I wonder what the media will do when we drive right through his 'steel ring' of military personnel."

"Probably say the president's escaping," Dean said, with a grin.

"I hadn't thought about that," Boland said. "You're probably right, Allen."

In less than 45 minutes, the president was downstairs, and he, along with Butts, Boland, Dean, and two Secret Service personnel, had climbed into the limo. Gen. Boland placed two APCs in front, along with an escort of three other vehicles. Boland could tell by the shocked look on Gen. Hill's face as the gates rolled back that he had not expected the president to exit the White House. As the limo rolled by, Boland gave Hill a big military salute, which was captured by the ABC camera.

"That won't make the evening news," Boland said with a chuckle as he rolled the window back up.

Houston was silent. He was thinking about the talk before him. He'd never really asked to be president, but he did enjoy the job. He always felt like he was serving the American people to be here. He would have preferred to go back to his ranch in Wyoming, although he didn't have much reason to go back anymore since his wife had died and his daughter had been killed in the car accident. His daughter's death was really what had brought him into politics. The drunk driver who caused the wreck had been released on a technicality by one of the liberal Wyoming federal judges.

Apparently the police hadn't read him his rights before they gave him the Breathalyzer test. It didn't matter that he'd had at least 20 previous tickets and three arrests for drunk driving or that he was driving without a driver's license and without insurance on the car. All that mattered was that his constitutional rights had been violated. Houston had had enough of it. He'd long been active in conservative politics, trying to help other people get elected and raising money for good candidates throughout the western United States, particularly those who were trying to combat the far left environmentalists who, through the federal government, were confiscating huge amounts of land throughout the western U.S.

When Houston had declared for governor, the conservative movement, not only in Wyoming, but throughout the whole western

United States, fell in behind him. Volunteer workers from Montana and Colorado flocked into Wyoming to help, and Houston had been elected by a landslide. In a state of only 400,000 people and about 180,000 voters, Houston had drawn three-fourths of the total vote, Democratic and Republican.

A year and a half into his term Houston had made significant progress in halting the federal government's land grab. In an unprecedented move, Houston declared federal ownership of properties in Wyoming to be unconstitutional and went to court to block further expansion. As governor, Houston had ordered the federal government to return the land it had confiscated from the state illegally.

At first, his actions were the laughingstock of the liberal movement, thinking that they had the Supreme Court locked up. They believed there was no way that Houston's petition and lawsuit could proceed. It was rejected by one lower court after another; it worked its way through the federal courts and, ultimately, to the Supreme Court. Under normal circumstances, a case like this would have taken five or six years to reach the Supreme Court, but the liberal lower court justices had shuffled it through, hoping to squash this mini-rebellion in the West once and for all.

To everyone's shock, the Supreme Court by a five to three majority vote, with one justice abstaining, sided with the state of Wyoming. All lands confiscated by the federal government without due process were ordered returned to the state or just compensation offered by the federal government. The choice was up to the Wyoming state government. In one fell swoop, the Supreme Court had reversed 70 years of federal control over states' lands and had returned to the states the right to govern themselves and secure their property from unlawful seizure. Instantly, Houston was catapulted into national attention. The media, themselves appalled by the decision, were forced to concede a major defeat.

In 1999, with the conservative trend in America continuing to swell, Philip Houston was drafted by the conservative arm of the Republican Party as their candidate of choice. And although the liberals pulled out every stop to defeat him, Philip Houston was elected president by a landslide.

That seems like a century ago, Houston thought dolefully. *Here I am now, headed for a Senate trial to impeach me. Well,* he thought, as a little grin curled the side of his mouth, *as they say, "that's show biz."*

At Andrews Air Force Base, Jason, Annette, and several technicians had been calibrating all the equipment in preparation for the next phase. They had just cycled the X-ray spectrometer back on line when it pegged to the end of the chart.

"What's this?" one of the technicians exclaimed.

"What's the problem?" Jason said.

"Uh, something's probably wrong with the machine."

Jason cycled the S-band and K-band monitors on and they pegged as well. "Unbelievable!" Jason shouted as he hurried over to the X-ray graph. "There's nothing wrong with the machine. Area 403 is developing a coronal hole!"

At that point, everybody in the building started scurrying around, turning on every graph and chart. Jason hurried over to the telescope and flipped on the automatic viewfinder. He focused on area 403.

"I think . . . ," Jason started to say, and then he exclaimed, "Come look at this!"

"What? What's happening?" Annette shouted.

Jason said, "Hurry! You won't see this but once in a lifetime."

Annette, along with several of the others, hurried over to the telescope. By this time Jason had flipped on the automatic camera and was taking pictures, one every fifteen seconds.

"Incredible!" Annette shouted as she looked through the viewfinder. "What is happening?"

"Area 403 has exploded!" Jason said. "The foot coming out from that area has to be 200,000 to 300,000 kilometers across."

"That's impossible," Annette said, but with her eye still glued to the viewer. Then she backed away from the scope and said, "Take a look, Wendy."

Wendy focused the eyepiece. "I can't believe it!" she shouted. "That's the largest flare I've ever seen."

"That may be the largest flare anybody has ever seen," Jason said excitedly. "Look at it grow." Jason was beginning to recalibrate the spectrometers that were registering the eruption, expanding the scale. "Let me look one more time," Jason said to Wendy. She backed away from the scope and Jason readjusted the viewer.

"I would say that we don't have a level 8 eruption anymore. Unless I miss my guess we're looking at about a 10 or greater."

"Is that possible?" Annette asked incredulously. "Jason, do you know what the implications are?"

"I do," Jason said, "and I need to get to the president as quickly as possible." Jason hurried over to the telephone and punched the intercom.

In the other room, the Secret Service agent answered, "Yes, Dr. Hobart."

"Connect me with the president as quickly as you can."

In a few seconds he said, "I'm sorry, Dr. Hobart, but the president has already left for the Senate. I'll try to reach him, but it may take a few minutes."

"Well, get him as quickly as you can," Jason urged.

Calling the Senate Office Building proved to be no small task from the White House. There were no direct lines, and ultimately the operator had to call back through another location in Washington, D.C., and then to another station somewhere in Maryland, then to a third station in Virginia, and then to a substation in D.C. again, until they made a link to the Senate, which had just three phone lines in operation.

The guard on the other end answered, "This is the Senate building. Who is calling?"

"This is President Houston's office. I need to talk to the president immediately."

"I believe he's in the Senate Chamber Room. I'll see what I can do," the guard said. "Hang on."

After nearly a 10-minute lapse, during which Jason thought he was going to have a stroke, the guard came back, "I've got somebody from the president's staff."

"Allen Dean here."

"Thank goodness, Allen. This is Jason Hobart."

"Yes, Professor. What's up?"

401

"I need to talk to the president immediately."

"I'm sorry but he's in the committee room, giving testimony."

"Get him on the phone right *now*," Jason said. "He said to interrupt him, no matter what, if the flare occurred."

Dean paused. "Are you saying the flare has occurred, Professor?"

"It's occurring as we speak, and it's bigger than we ever even imagined. Can you get the president?"

"Hold on, Professor. Don't leave," Dean said, dropping the receiver.

Don't worry, Jason muttered to himself. *I'll be here.*

Dean literally ran down the hall and up the stairs to where the hearings were going on. President Houston was in the witness chair facing a group of nine senators — five Democrats and four Republicans.

Senator Tate was questioning him, "Mr. President, did you or did you not order the evacuation of the cities, based on the word of a discredited scientist?"

This banter had been going back and forth for nearly 10 minutes. Houston replied angrily, "I am the president of the United States. I weighed all the information available to me and made a decis . . ."

Tate interrupted, as he had been doing throughout the entire session. "You mean you violated the Constitution? The Constitution does not give the president of the United States unilateral authority to declare martial law without consulting Congress."

"I beg to differ," the president said, just as Allen Dean burst in the door.

"Guard, stop that man," Senator Tate commanded as Dean rushed toward the president.

"That's one of my people," the president said. "Yes, Allen, what's the problem?"

Dean leaned over and whispered in the president's ear. The president turned back to the committee and announced, "Gentlemen, you will have to put this hearing on hold. I need to go take a phone call."

"But this committee . . . ," Tate started to protest.

But it was a waste of his time. Houston was already out the door. Walking quickly with Dean to the telephone, the president picked it up and said, "President Houston here. Are you there, Professor?"

Jason replied, "Yes I am, Mr. President."

"What's up?" Houston said.

"The eruption started nearly an hour ago, Sir," Jason said as calmly as his adrenaline would allow. "And, Mr. President, this flare is larger than any of us anticipated. I estimate it to be a level 10 or greater."

"Translate that for me, Professor," the president said, as he felt his anxiety increasing.

"In about three days, more or less, nothing electrical on this planet will still operate, day or night."

"Are you sure, Jason?" exclaimed the president. "How long will this flare last?"

"I'm sure, Sir, but it's impossible to say right now how long it will last," Jason responded. "We'll just have to wait and see. When this flare hits, life as we know it on Earth will be changed!"

"Understood," Houston said, slipping into his leadership role. "Professor, I want you to get your people packed and out of there as quickly as you can."

"You don't have to convince me, Sir, but can you convince the Senate?"

"I can only try. So long, Professor. We'll be in touch when you get set up again. Just follow C.C.'s advice. He'll get you through."

"Yes, Sir," Jason said as he hung up.

Houston walked slowly back to the Kennedy Room where the others were waiting. Butts was there, fielding questions in his boss's absence. Houston walked back into the room, not bothering to go to the witness chair. He said in a very matter-of-fact tone, "Gentlemen, I just received word from Dr. Hobart at Andrews Air Force Base that the solar eruption we've been expecting has occurred."

"Impossible," Robert Frasier said from his position next to Senator Tate.

"Well, impossible or not," Houston said sarcastically, "it *has* happened. Now you gentlemen can continue this meeting if you'd like. But as for me and mine, I think we're going to head out of town. It's going to be very difficult to live in Washington, D.C. once this flare strikes. Doctor Hobart assures me that nothing will work for a while."

The shocked looks on the senators' faces told Houston all he needed to know. They were now doubting Gerstner and Frasier.

"Gentlemen, you have approximately three days to get back to your families and get them bundled up and away to one of our relocation sites. I would suggest that you not waste any time."

"This is all a ruse," Frasier shouted. "There's been no eruption on the Sun. I would have heard about it."

Even while Frasier was shouting, an aide to Senator Tate charged into the room. By the look on his face, Houston knew he'd gotten the message as well.

"Well?" Tate said, glaring at the young woman.

"Sir, we've just gotten word from solar observatories all over the U.S. that a major solar eruption has occurred, in the words of one scientist at Goddard, 'of unbelievable proportions.' " The look on Frasier's face was astonishment as he collapsed back in his chair.

Houston said, "Well, as I said, gentlemen, you can continue this meeting if you'd like, but as for me and mine I think we'll depart."

Senator Lowell, who was the *de facto* chairman of the meeting, grabbed his gavel and, slamming it on the table, he announced "Meeting adjourned." With that, he picked up his briefcase, stuffed it with the committee report and headed for the door.

President Houston was almost out the door himself when he stopped and turned to the senators still sitting in their seats with shocked looks on their faces, "Gentlemen, millions of Americans who should already be relocated are going to be trapped in the cities now. Think on that while you're headed home to protect your own families." With that, Houston strode out the door, followed by Dean, Butts, and Boland.

Boland quipped to the president as they walked down the hall, "You know, Phil, this is one time when I wish I weren't able to say, 'see, I told you so' to the group."

"I know what you mean, Floyd. I know what you mean."

19

When Jason announced that they would be going to the relocation center in Lancaster County, Pennsylvania, Wendy was thrilled. Her father had been born and raised in Lancaster County, and she had heard him describe how, as a young man, he had helped his father farm side by side with the Amish farmers. Although Jason and his family used modern implements and farming techniques, he often had commented on how productive the Amish people were, using nineteenth century technology.

Wendy could envision the Amish horses and buggies sharing the highways with modern vehicles. It gave her a funny feeling, knowing that after the flare hit the Amish buggies would have the highways to themselves.

Gene Moore chose not to go with Jason and Annette but, instead, decided to return to his home in California. He had a divorced sister with children who needed his help. He would be on one of the few flights scheduled to the West Coast. Dr. Singer decided to accept the offer of a flight back to England. Jason and Annette wished them well and saw them on the shuttle to the waiting planes.

As Jason, Annette, and Wendy climbed aboard the Army-issue olive drab semi truck, the driver said, "Glad to see you, Sweetheart."

Wendy squealed, "C.C.! Good to see you too! What are you doing here?"

Jason looked up, and there behind the wheel of the big semi was a smiling friendly face.

"Hi, Professor! Glad to have you aboard."

"Well, C.C., it's good to see you," Jason said. "Are you driving semis for a living now?"

"Whatever the job requires," C.C. answered with a smile. "I'm your personal security and your driver. A relief driver will join us shortly. And, Professor, I personally want to thank you. My grandmother's already been evacuated, and she'll be waiting for us in Lancaster. I can tell you, I wouldn't want to be living in Washington, D.C. or any other big city when this thing really gets bad."

"Well, C.C., I hate to say it, but we haven't seen the bad part yet."

"How bad is bad?"

"I can't honestly say. We don't have enough data to evaluate it fully."

"Aw, Professor, now you're beginning to sound like an academic. Like the president says, just give me the bottom line. What do you think?"

Jason smiled. He liked the big man with

the warm smile. He suspected that, in a pinch, C.C. could be counted on for anything.

"Well, the next burst of solar energy is on its way now and it's going to be bad. We'll have to power down everything during both daylight hours and dark. We're going to see a solar energy show unlike anything ever witnessed in modern times. We won't be able to operate any power equipment for several weeks — perhaps even for months."

C.C. whistled. "Professor, if what you say is true, I wouldn't want to live around here when the food runs out."

Jason shook his head in agreement and glanced over at Wendy. He felt guilty. Here he was with the people he cared most about on Earth, safe within the confines of a government vehicle surrounded by government guards, with enough food to live for months, but he knew there were millions of Americans who wouldn't have that luxury, including his own sister, Karen, wherever she was. Millions of people had been relocated, but there were millions more who would be stranded in the cities. They didn't know what was coming, and by the time they did it would be too late. He knew he shouldn't feel guilty and that he had done the best he could, but somehow that didn't help a lot.

The big truck fired up and began to ease off. It had only moved a few feet when the

CB began to crackle. C.C. picked up the mike and said, "Firefly number one here. Come back."

Jason and the others heard President Houston respond. "C.C.?"

"Yes, Mr. President."

"You guys moving?"

"Yes, Sir, we are."

"Well, tell the professor that we're setting up our headquarters at Camp David, and we'll be operating out of here from now on."

"Ask him why," Jason said.

"Mr. President, the professor wants to know why you decided to stay at Camp David instead of coming to the camp."

"I think it would be better to keep a base close to Washington, D.C.," the president said. "Tell the professor that we'll be in communication with him. We're setting up land lines right now that should maintain constant contact between New Holland and Camp David. In fact, tell the professor that we've established a land-line that we're going to try when the next flare hits. We think we'll be able to maintain communications even in the worst of the flare. Our communications guys have come up with a design that's pretty ingenious."

C.C. asked the question Jason was thinking. "What kind of communications, Sir?"

"Basically it's two tin cans on a string, or something equivalent," the president quipped.

"We're going to use the same system that Western Union did in the 1860s: a press key and a battery."

"Ah," C.C. said, his eyes lighting up. "You talkin' about Morse code, Mr. President?"

"Exactly," the president responded. "Morse code. Hard line all the way — no relays, no receptors, wire-to-wire."

"Should work, Sir," C.C. responded, drawing on his military background as a radio operator. Even in the modern age every radio operator had to learn Morse code and had to be able to construct a rudimentary key system for battlefield conditions.

"Anyway," the president said, "we're going to stay around here for awhile. Tell the professor I've appointed him our national solar flare emergency director."

"Wow!" C.C. said mockingly, "That's really impressive!"

"Oh, yeah! It sure is," the president quipped. "Tell Jason what I really want him to do is to keep an eye on the Sun and tell me when we can operate our equipment and how we can feed these people we've stashed around the country. That's all he has to do. Nothing to it."

"Right," Jason muttered under his breath, with a smirk on his face.

C.C. laughed. "Mr. President, I think he got the message. Over and out."

What the group in the semi didn't know

411

was how much stock the president had put in Jason and his group. He was gambling the lives of 100 million or more Americans on their ability to find a way to survive during the duration of the solar flare, however long that might be.

Houston had heard rumblings, courtesy of Gen. Boland, that in spite of the fact that the flare actually occurred, Gen. Hill and Congressman Gerstner were still determined to oust him. It was Gen. Boland who had advised him not to leave the D.C. area, lest some of the more revolutionary minded members of the military stage a coup and overthrow the government of the United States and its duly elected authority. This prompted Houston to set up his primary headquarters at Camp David, where he could keep an eye on Washington.

In addition, Gen. Boland was bringing in two full divisions of government troops to protect the capital. He would not put anything past Hill or his cronies.

With the president at Camp David, it would be a lot easier to maintain control than if he had gone to Pennsylvania, as first planned. He shared the president's concern about feeding the evacuees, but he had an even greater concern for the survival of the nation if people like Hill and Gerstner took control.

Boland knew what it must be like in other

parts of the world, where hunger was already taking over. Guerilla warfare would be the rule of the day. The more communications he heard, even from the other industrialized countries, the more he realized how fortunate they had been to have a president who had the guts to act when he did.

He had been alarmed when he first heard about the lack of missile readiness. Virtually every missile silo, mobile launcher, and submarine in the U.S. military was disabled. Even under the best of conditions, it would take weeks to get them operational again.

Then he realized the threat of nuclear war had suddenly been erased worldwide. Every missile system that had been on readiness when the last flare hit was inoperable. One solar flare had unilaterally disarmed the world.

At the very best, the nations of the world were back to settling their disputes with small arms. Once again the Pacific and Atlantic Oceans presented a pretty daunting barrier to any potential enemy.

Boland was concerned about his daughter and son-in-law, who were stationed in Wiesbaden, Germany. He'd had no word on their situation, but one thing he knew, the U.S. military would protect its own, if it were possible, and he had a job to do here, so he tried to keep his mind clear. His biggest problem wasn't external enemies; it was the internal ones. He knew they hadn't heard the last of Gen. Hill.

The first day of travel was relatively uneventful for Jason and his group. Their caravan was two semis and four other trucks loaded with equipment and food, so C.C. knew they would be a tempting target for any organized gangs. However, in front and in back were two armed personnel carriers, one carrying a heavy machine gun and the other carrying LARS anti-tank weapons — front and back. They were as well protected as possible, given the circumstances. It would take a division of men to successfully assault the caravan.

The route had been carefully planned: They were to take I-95 down to Baltimore; turn up I-83 to Harrisburg; and then take I-78 into Lancaster. C.C. had been briefed that only the interstates were safe for travel. Federal troops had secured the interstates in and out of Washington, but many of the other roads came under sniper fire.

Unbelievable, C.C. thought angrily. *Let any kind of a crisis develop and some people revert to animal behavior. No,* he decided, *that's unfair to most animals; they're more predictable.* He knew his country was now paying the price for the breakdown in morals that started back in the sixties. Or, as his grandmother often said, "You reap what you sow."

C.C. was taking no chances. He bunched

the vehicles close together and put a scout car, one of the Hummers, way out front. He was going to run this like a true military operation. If all went well, they should be able to make the trek from Andrews to Lancaster in eight hours or less. After talking it over with Jason, he decided it would be better to leave as quickly as possible. Communication by radio was still somewhat unreliable during daylight hours, so they could be stranded on the road without communications. C.C. didn't like that prospect. He'd rather have all the odds in his favor.

Maybe he was being paranoid, but he'd seen what happened in D.C.: Even though Gen. Boland had doubled the number of federal troops in the nation's capital, the looting continued. He rather suspected that as time went on, the gangs would get bolder and bolder. He knew from past experience in both Lebanon and Yugoslavia that a well-armed group of bandits could hold a much larger force at bay just by sniping at them. He did not intend that to happen to his passengers.

Nighttime was quickly falling as the caravan moved out. Fortunately, the first leg of the trip proved to be totally uneventful. They made their way down I-95, skirted Baltimore, and turned up I-83. They were nearly 25 miles out of the city before C.C. began to ease up a little. The two semis, the APCs, and the Hummer were in constant contact

415

with each other. Now that nighttime had fallen, C.C. actually felt a little bit better. Now he knew they could maintain their communications, but also he knew that the potential danger from the gangs was less once they left the city. They should be able to make Lancaster and the base camp by morning.

It was an odd feeling to be traveling an interstate with no traffic. It had been a long time since I-83 out of Baltimore had not been filled with perpetual traffic — cars going to and from the nation's capital. As C.C. settled back in the seat and tried to relax, he noticed that his jaw muscles hurt. Then he realized he had been clamping his teeth together. He consciously relaxed the muscles. *Boy, am I ever getting uptight,* he chided himself.

Then he saw the headlights well ahead of them, coming fast in their direction. He instinctively tensed up. Then he told himself, *There's no reason to overreact. Probably another military vehicle headed back to D.C. or a truck headed back to pick up another load.* He knew that by this time there had to be thousands of vehicles transversing big cities to the country, transporting the evacuees.

The only thing was, the headlights were coming rapidly — too rapidly. He was traveling about 35 miles an hour with his caravan, not willing to risk the lives of his passengers at any higher speeds, and yet the headlights were closing at a rapid rate. *Those morons!* he thought. *Probably some young recruits driving those vehicles at breakneck speed, risking their lives and everyone else's on the highway.*

Suddenly his muscles tensed again as he realized the headlights were on his side of the interstate, coming straight toward them. He called over the CB to the other vehicles, "Headlights coming — on our side of the road!" he shouted. He told the Hummer driver, "I want you to pull 'em over and get 'em off this road!"

The driver of the Hummer complied, blinking his bright lights and turning on the blue warning light attached to the top of the vehicle. Still the headlights bore down and they were not slowing.

"Sir, I have a bad feeling about this," the Hummer driver said over the CB. "We've got our lights on and the vehicles are not slowing. What should I do?"

C.C. moved with the reflex action he had developed over the years with the Secret Service. He said in a loud but calm voice, "Arm your weapons. Block the road. I want those vehicles stopped! If you have to fire on them, do it!"

The Hummer driver complied. He stopped in the middle of the highway, and his buddy racheted a 50 caliber round in the machine gun mounted to the top of the vehicle.

Still the headlights kept coming.

The driver could see now that there were

multiple vehicles — at least two headed in his direction. The second had its lights off. He had just apprised the others when he saw the flashes leap from the front of the first vehicle. Then he heard the bullets as they smacked against the front of his Hummer. The right side windshield exploded. The corporal manning the machine gun had already reacted to the situation and pressed the 50-caliber's trigger. The first vehicle exploded in a ball of flame; the second veered to the left, went over the embankment, and into the ditch alongside the interstate.

By this time, the forward vehicle was not more than 200 yards away. Without hesitating, the young soldier trained the 50 caliber on the trailing vehicle and squeezed the trigger. One out of every 100 rounds from the machine gun were tracers so that he could see the line of fire at night. The tracers arched a path as he continued to squeeze the trigger, and the second vehicle burst into flames.

The sound of gunfire so close by startled Wendy, who was asleep in the seat beside C.C. She let out a squeal when she saw the vehicle ahead burst into flames.

Annette, asleep in the berth behind the cab was also startled awake.

"What's wrong?" she cried out.

"No big deal," C.C. said calmly. "Just some thugs out for a joyride."

"If this is nothing, I sure would hate to see

a something," Wendy said. "Wow, look at that," she exclaimed as the second vehicle was engulfed in flames.

C.C. just grinned and shifted down a gear. Although he and his group didn't know it at the time, a gang member, assigned to watch the interstate, had spotted the two semis. Knowing that semis carried valuable cargo, he had called ahead to other gang members who were waiting. Being untrained in military tactics, the one thing he had neglected to tell his comrades was how heavily armed this caravan was. Not only was the Hummer armed with a 50-caliber machine gun, but they had the APCs for backup. They would easily have been a match for a well-armed squad of military personnel but were considerably overmatched for a band of wanna-be guerrillas driving stolen pickup trucks.

C.C. signaled to speed up and they accelerated to about 45 miles an hour as they passed the burning vehicles. The first was overturned in the passing lane, but by hugging the right side of the road it was easily bypassed. The soldier in the Hummer covered both vehicles with his weapon until the semis were past.

Several men were visible, running toward the woods. C.C. rather suspected that those thugs wouldn't attack any innocent civilians that evening and probably would think twice before they ever attacked another military caravan.

Praise the Lord, C.C. thought to himself, *that those hoodlums didn't have any better armament. A couple of wire-guided LARS rockets might have stopped our caravan.* He mentally noted to himself to be more careful in the future. He ordered the Hummer to go further ahead and the trailing APC to fall back about 100 yards. He wanted to be sure he had both front and rear well covered if they were attacked again.

At midnight they were well into Pennsylvania and as they passed the towns of New Freedom and York, C.C. could see burning buildings and realized that even in these little rural communities, mob rule was the order. Just outside of York, he decided to take a shortcut when he saw the military roadblock set up on Highway 30. "Should be secure," he told Wendy, who was sitting beside him. She just nodded — still in shock from the earlier episode. The MP at the gate checked C.C.'s I.D., swung the bar back, and waved them on.

In another hour, they could see the city of Lancaster off to the right. It appeared to be completely intact, with no fires. It was clear that a different class of people lived there. It had been decided that their base camp would be located close to the little community of New Holland, right in the middle of the

Amish country. Jason, who had been fitfully catnapping after the skirmish with the road bandits, was awake. He began to feel a stirring inside as they approached the country he remembered so well. New Holland was a community where he'd spent a lot of time as a boy.

He liked the Amish people. He particularly liked the cakes and pies they made and sold, but he also had an affection for the people who still traveled in horse-drawn buggies, the women who modestly wore bonnets over their heads, the men with long beards, and the children who were always so polite. He knew these were the heart and soul of what had made America great. He languished over how much the U.S. had lost as a nation.

Industrialization should not have destroyed our value system, yet in large part we have allowed it. These people have resisted industrialization, yet they've kept their value system. I wonder, which group is the winner and which is the loser? Are the cars, airplanes, televisions, and CDs worth what we have given up to acquire them? Probably not, he decided. *Maybe, just maybe,* Jason decided, *God is going to give us a chance to recapture something of what we've lost.*

As the semis pulled up to the New Holland camp, Jason was flabbergasted. He wasn't sure what he had expected, but certainly it wasn't what he saw. A town of perhaps 25,000 people had been set up with a few permanent buildings but mostly tents — tents of every size and shape and color. They stretched as far as the eye could see under the glow of campfires. Some generators were powering hastily strung lights, and Coleman lanterns hung everywhere. It was remarkable. It was like a small city set up in the countryside — the modern day equivalent of the boomtowns that followed the trek west in the nineteenth century.

Then he realized that communities like this had been set up all over rural America, and he could only imagine what it would take to support and maintain the millions of people in thousands of camps — especially since, until two weeks ago, these people had lived out their lives in the cities, surrounded by TVs, air-conditioning, and restaurants. *It's remarkable what human beings can do when they have to,* Jason reflected. *This is what America is all about. This is what built this great nation.*

As their caravan pulled into the camp, some of the military personnel directed C.C. to their spot. Jason could see that the buildings were better constructed than most of the others. They were made of prefabricated metal, probably aluminum, with corrugated sides. In addition, there were several wooden-sided tents large enough to accommodate their entire group.

One building in particular attracted his attention because it was constructed of heavy-duty, precast materials of some kind. Later he found out the material was reprocessed tires made into logs. Essentially it was a pre-fabricated structure made of extremely durable black logs, stacked one upon the other. This building had been sized to Jason's earlier specifications and was covered all around inside with fine copper wire lattice. Jason had designed this building to be suitable for monitoring solar flares, totally shielded from outside electrical interference.

C.C. studied the building. He was impressed. *This thing would probably take a direct hit from a mortar and it would bounce off,* he mused. *If we ever go into a battle, this is the place to make a stand.*

Jason stepped down from the semi and helped Wendy down. His legs felt stiff. Even Wendy commented, "Boy, Dad, I'm about beat. If it's okay with you, I think I'm going to bed."

"Okay, Honey," he said, reaching up to help Annette down. She stepped down to the gas tank and then onto the swing steps that had been extended from under the cab. After she stepped to the ground, she didn't release Jason's hand. Instead, she squeezed it a little harder. Their eyes met, and in what seemed to be the most natural reaction, Jason pulled her toward him and gently kissed her.

The effect was electric. Jason had been a widower for almost five years. He had decided when his wife died that he could never be emotionally attached to anyone again. He and Nancy had been childhood sweethearts. Even as early as the sixth grade Jason knew that he was going to marry Nancy someday. He had never dated another girl, and as soon as they both finished college they were married.

Wendy was nine when Jason predicted the first solar flare and barely 10 when Nancy became ill. He still carried the guilt that somehow the stress of that time had contributed to Nancy's problem.

Only a few months later Nancy's first symptoms appeared: severe cramps, fatigue, missed periods, nothing definite, but lots of inconclusive tests. Then the symptoms got worse: severe abdominal pain. They were referred to a specialist in Chicago. The day they had seen the doctor had been the most painful of his life. They both knew something was wrong but had been hoping against hope that it would be nothing serious.

When the doctor told them his diagnosis, Jason felt like his life was over. Ovarian cancer: the most dreaded words that any woman could hear. The doctor had told them there was no cure.

There were treatments, including chemotherapy and radiation. They were told that with chemotherapy Nancy might live another year, perhaps two, but with some very debilitating side effects. And without chemotherapy, Nancy might live a year, maybe more. So their decision was made. They chose quality of life — without chemotherapy.

The first six months of Nancy's radiation therapy hadn't been too bad. She had taken the radiation well and the tumors actually had decreased in size, but then six months later, almost to the day when she'd had her next CT scan, the doctor said, "I'm sorry, but the cancer has spread to the liver. There's no point in continuing the radiation, and I don't believe chemotherapy will help." Nancy went downhill very rapidly after that.

Three months later she was just a shell of her former self. Her beautiful skin had turned a pale gray and she'd lost 35 pounds. In another month, she was unable to get out of bed. Jason never left her side. There were many nights, though, when Nancy needed several shots of morphine to get to sleep. Jason would sit beside her bed, his head in his hands, crying. Wendy saw her mother deteriorating and she saw the grief on her father's face.

After Nancy died, Jason totally dedicated himself to two projects — his work and Wendy. Fortunately for Jason, since Wendy was so interested in his work, it was easy. He included her in everything he did and she eventually became his assistant.

For Wendy's sake, Jason had thought about getting remarried, but he could never really get interested in anyone. Wendy was fiercely protective of her father after her mom died, and she had long since concluded that her father would be a lifelong widower — at least as long as she was still at home.

Jason closed his eyes. He had always assumed that no one ever would be able to replace Nancy, but now he realized that Annette was the companion he'd been looking for. He wondered if she could feel the same way about him. He opened his eyes, and when their eyes met he saw the same warmth he had seen in Nancy's eyes. He held Annette's hand as they walked toward the big log structure.

"Why don't you go on to bed," Jason told her.

"Are you going?" she asked.

"No, I think I'll check on the unloading of our equipment. I'd like to get it set up and be sure everything is functioning properly."

"Then I'm going to help too," she said resolutely.

"You don't have to," Jason argued. "You get some rest. I'll be glad to do this."

Annette said, "I've been told that people should never make emotional decisions in stressful situations." She squeezed his hand and said, "Let's get this stuff set up."

Much to his surprise, Jason's personal telescope had been loaded into the van. He hadn't mentioned it to anyone, but apparently in one of his conversations with Annette she had recognized his attachment to it and had ordered it put into the van for him.

"Thanks, Annette. That was very thoughtful." She just nodded.

It took nearly five hours to unload and assemble all the equipment. Inside the big structure were two generators vented to the outside: one that had electronic controls and a second, older diesel generator with a manual starting system, including a hand crank. Although it wouldn't power all the equipment, Jason was certain it would at least run all the critical instruments he needed. Shielded as it was, inside the log structure, he hoped it would still be operable, irrespective of what was happening on the Sun.

Silently, Jason thanked President Houston for his courage and integrity.

At the New Holland camp, most of the people were still familiarizing themselves with the camp routine. Daily life began by standing in line to take a shower: men would take showers on even days of the month, women on odd. If you happened to be at the end of the line, by the time your turn came there would be no hot water. In fact, worse than that, it would be icy cold.

There was a lot of grumbling in the camp. Morning after morning everyone had to stand in lines to get meals prepared by camp personnel. One thing about Gen. Boland: he was an organizer. He had the camps laid out in evenly spaced rows with families housed together in large tents, wherever possible. Singles were housed individually in smaller tents. The unattached children, and there appeared to be many from the inner cities, were housed in large prefab barracks under the supervision of married "dorm parents."

Because of the enormity of the dislocation program, there were not enough federal troops to adequately protect the camps. Each camp was provided several military personnel who would oversee security and transportation. But beyond that, it was the responsibility of the evacuees to protect themselves. To that end, each camp elected one overall leader, who usually had either a military or civilian police background.

At Gen. Boland's suggestion, a unit commander was assigned for every 1,000 people and, under the commanders, deputies were assigned for every 100 people; then lieutenants were assigned to every 10 people. It was, in a loose sense, a military arrangement. Gen. Boland knew this structure had worked very well for most military camps, and it was likely it would work well for the civilian camps.

As soon as the majority of the people were settled into the camp, an assessment was made of what weapons they had brought with them. Usually it was a mixed array that ranged from switchblades to fully automatic machine guns. In most instances the armed civilians presented more of a danger to themselves than any potential attackers. It was clear they needed training.

Back at Camp David, as Gen. Boland began to get reports from the camps, he was astounded to see how many weapons the refugees had. He decided he wouldn't want to be an enemy trying to invade the U.S., especially the South and Southwest. The camps from Florida to Texas seemed to have three weapons for every person. He had established a training schedule to organize the civilians, many of whom were ex-military, into defense groups.

Once the basic task of transporting people settled down to a routine, the next task was to get the camps set up. By using the camp residents, setup had been accomplished efficiently. The flimsy structures, such as tents and makeshift buildings would be good only for the spring and summer. By fall, more permanent structures would need to be erected.

An assessment of all available food supplies was made. To date, Boland's teams had secured most of the emergency reserves available throughout the country, including those stored in grain warehouses — both public and private. By his calculations, they had enough food to make it through the first winter — that is, if everything was rationed properly.

But since things rarely go as planned, he had a backup plan. The backup plan was fairly simple: Each community would be required to raise its own food. They could not count on transportation, once the next solar flare hit, so seed and fertilizer was being distributed to the camps as quickly as possible. Doing this in the three-day window required a huge nationwide effort.

Another problem was how to teach people to farm who had only seen bread in a bag and beans in a can. It was a daunting task and one that Boland wasn't sure could be solved. The best he could do was to find a way to train the refugees later.

America had become highly efficient in growing food on huge farms owned by megacorporations, which then processed it, packaged it, transported it, and sold it to the American consumers. That would no longer be possible. Now people were going to have to feed themselves from small, relatively inefficient plots of land. If this plan was to succeed, everyone would have to work. But many of the ex-city dwellers were unaccustomed to real work. Anarchy could easily break out in the camps, as it had in the cities.

It was already the beginning of spring and crops would have to be planted quickly if any food were to be harvested before fall, particularly in the more northern camps. The growing season was short and to miss it, even by a few weeks, could mean starvation or, at the least, hunger in those camps.

Boland also had to deal with another growing problem. As the military relaxed its hold on the cities, the gangs became bolder and bolder. Very soon the authorities would have to abandon the inner cities altogether — and the people in them.

He also realized that as the gangs got bolder and the cities offered slimmer pickings it was only a matter of time until they would try to raid some of the camps. Out of necessity, many of the camps were located within just a few miles of the cities. These people needed to learn not only how to feed themselves but also how to protect themselves — and quickly.

Gen. Boland made the decision to take selected personnel from special forces, like the Navy Seals, Army Rangers, and Green Berets, and assign at least one military advisor to every camp. The thought was that if one highly trained coordinator who understood military tactics was assigned to each camp, they could help organize the civilian personnel into self-defense groups.

The civilian defense coordinator at the New Holland Camp was C.C., a graduate of the Naval Academy who had joined the Seals immediately after graduation. In the manner and style of the Navy Seals, he had been a marvelous physical specimen. Standing six-foot-five, and weighing 242 pounds, C.C. could bench press more than 300 pounds. He could hold his breath under water for nearly three and one-half minutes and, when dropped into a pool at the Seal Training Station with both arms and feet bound tightly, C.C. had been able to stay afloat for more than six hours.

In addition to his assignment as personal security for Jason, his task at New Holland was a very simple one: train the civilian personnel to protect themselves in the event they were attacked by marauding gangs.

The solar flare struck just as the camp was waking up the next day — nearly 24 hours ahead of schedule — catching the camp unaware. The explosive force of the coronal eruption was so massive that it had accelerated the cosmic winds to nearly 1.5 million miles an hour.

20

At Camp David, it was instantly clear that the solar flare had struck prematurely. Nobody had guessed, nor could they have known, that the eruption on the Sun was so violent it accelerated the solar winds to nearly 1.5 million miles an hour.

When the lights blinked out, President Houston jerked upright, as if lightning had just struck the building. "The flare!" he said in astonishment.

Allen Dean and Warren Butts, who were in the room, just looked at each other. "How could that be?" Dean said. "I thought the flare wasn't due to strike Earth until tomorrow."

"That's what I thought too," Houston said. "But it's here. Look out the window."

In the dim, early morning light the multicolored display could clearly be seen. Streaks of red and orange flashes lit up the sky. Never before had the northern lights been seen this far south, but here they were.

"Wow!" Dean exclaimed. "That's unbelievable."

"Believe it!" Houston muttered. "Are we ready?"

Butts responded, "As ready as we can be, Mr. President." In the dim light he made his way over to the closet and removed some lanterns that had been stored there. "We have lights, water, and gas for cooking. And the telegraph system is ready."

"What's this going to do to our evacuation schedule?" the president asked.

"Not a lot," Butts responded. "We thought we had another day, but we think most of those who wanted out have been relocated."

In New York City, the very last evacuation buses, which had just been loaded, were on their way out of the city when the flare struck. The bus driver found himself in a vehicle with no power. Steering the big bus with no power steering proved to be a little tricky, but fortunately the brakes were pneumatic and independent of any electrical system, so he was able to bring it to a stop. It was half full of adults and children — families that had waited until the last minute to evacuate the city.

"What happened?" one of the women cried out. "Why did we stop?"

The driver responded, "I don't know *what* happened. It just quit." He shifted the transmission into neutral and tried the starter. There was no click, no sound — nothing. A veteran of the previous flare, the driver had been through this once before, so he could guess what had happened. "Of course! Another flare!" the driver announced. "This bus is not going anywhere."

"What are we going to do?" a young mother cried out, clutching her daughter next to her.

"I guess we're going to get out and walk," the bus driver replied. By this time, the young Marine lieutenant driving the support vehicle in front had come around to the door just as the driver opened it.

"Bus went dead too, huh?" the young lieutenant shouted.

"Yep," the driver answered. "Dead as a doornail." He glanced in his mirror and saw that the trailing vehicle was also stranded in the middle of the road.

"What now?" the bus driver asked the young Marine.

"Beats me. My orders said to lead you out of the city and link up with another convoy."

"How far to the rendezvous point?" the bus driver asked.

"A good hundred miles — maybe 125," the Marine lieutenant said, looking at his map.

"Well, we sure can't walk that far," the driver quipped. "Now what?"

The lieutenant replied, "Tell your people to get out and stay close together. About all we can do is head out of the city and see if we can find a place to hole up."

The bus driver relayed the instructions, and

a few minutes later a group of frightened passengers had assembled at the roadway.

"We don't have any food or any water," a young Hispanic mother cried out, clutching her six-year-old daughter close to her. "What are we going to do? We would have been better off staying where we were."

"You're probably right about that, Ma'am," the bus driver said. "I would have been a lot better off where I was yesterday — a long way from this city."

"Calm down folks," the lieutenant said with as much authority as his youth would allow. "It's going to be okay. I'm sure the authorities considered this possibility and will do something."

"Yeah, right!" the driver responded sarcastically. "When pigs fly."

The young Marine, though he had put up a good front, was shaken. He had all these people on his hands, no transportation, and no real way to protect them. He didn't have the slightest idea how he could get them out of the city. All he knew was they had to find shelter before nightfall. He didn't want to be on the streets with this group of unarmed civilians, with thousands of armed homicidal maniacs roaming the city.

He got the group moving by hoisting a little girl on his shoulders and heading out. After some grumbling the driver said caustically, "Well, come on people. This young lieutenant is the only one who knows the way."

The group had walked nearly an hour and had barely covered two miles. But at least they were out of the worst part of the city. The lieutenant heard a loud sound behind them and looked around to see the strangest sight he had ever seen in his young life.

A hansom cab, being pulled by two wild-eyed horses, was coming toward them. The driver was whipping the horses for all they were worth.

The Marine stepped in front of the carriage and signaled the driver to stop. It was obvious he was not going to. The lieutenant fired his side arm in the air twice, and the driver pulled back on the reins, bringing the frightened horses to a skidding stop.

"Wha . . . what do you want?" the terrified driver stuttered.

"Where are you going in such a hurry?" the lieutenant asked. "What's wrong?"

"What's wrong? A gang just tried to kill me. That's what's wrong," the man yelled hysterically. "Get out of my way. I'm gettin' outta here."

"Not without these people you're not!" the lieutenant growled, brandishing his weapon menacingly.

"I can't haul that many people," the man protested. "I've got to get away, man. The power's gone out again."

"Yeah, we know. We're not out here just

taking a stroll. I've got to get these people to a relocation camp."

"You mean you know where one is?" the driver said more calmly now.

"Yes, and if you help I'll get you there too."

"Well, hop on," the driver said with a big grin. "Polly and Molly will get us there," he said, pointing to the two big horses.

Two minutes later the whole group was packed into the Central Park horse-drawn cab headed out of the city. The others trapped in the cities would not be so fortunate.

At Camp David, the emergency plan was being activated. The president walked outside and was surprised to see an antique four-horse carriage pulling up to the front of his cottage. "Is this transportation?" he shouted to the young officer.

"Yes, Sir. This is the way Mr. Lincoln got around. We took it out of storage."

"Out of the museum, you mean," Houston chuckled. "Well, I guess if it was good enough for Abe, it's good enough for me. Let's take a tour, soldier," he said as he climbed into the carriage.

"Yes, Sir," the second lieutenant responded, smacking the horses with the reins. The horses plodded away as if it was the most natural thing in the world for them. They could have cared less that the biggest solar flare in recorded history had just struck Earth.

When the carriage got to the communications building, Houston stepped down and went into the building, where he was met by Air Force Colonel Ron Coulter. The president knew Col. Coulter well, having met him several times previously during his weekends at Camp David.

"Is the land line set up?" Houston asked.

"Yes, Sir, it is," Coulter responded.

The president walked over to the sergeant at the ancient telegraph key. "Is New Holland on the line?" he asked.

"Yes, Sir," the sergeant responded with a big grin, as he tapped out a message. "Works like a charm too." Pausing for a few seconds, he got the response he was expecting.

"How is this thing operating?" the president asked.

"Well, Mr. President, it's battery powered and, so far, the flare doesn't seem to have affected the batteries."

At New Holland, the situation was not quite so bad. Although all the power had failed in other parts of the facility, inside the solar observation building the main generator was still operating.

"The shield is working very well," Annette said.

"Apparently so," Jason agreed. "With that copper shield covering every square inch of this building, we're totally isolated from the

439

outside world electrically. But who knows what will happen if this flare continues to intensify?"

"Intensify? You mean it may get worse?" Annette asked.

"It's possible. I think the reason it struck prematurely is that the first wave of lighter particles were accelerated out in front of the main flare. If that's true, then it's going to get worse — maybe a lot worse."

Even as he spoke, the lights flickered slightly. *Not a good sign,* he thought. *If Earth's magnetic field collapses, who knows what effect it will have. There is no data on that particular phenomenon. We may lose our power too.* Jason heard the telegraph key activate and the young corporal operating the key tapped out a message in response.

"Professor," the corporal said. "We've got Camp David. The key works fine."

"Great," Jason said with a sigh of relief. At least he was still in contact with the president, for whatever good that would do. At Jason's instructions, the young soldier tapped out a message that told the president that they were all well and that inside the shielded building they still had power.

The operator on the other end sent a response, confirming the message had been received. Jason went on to tell the president what he had just told Annette — that, in his opinion, they had just caught the leading edge of the flare and over the next 12 to 14 hours the electrical storm probably would increase.

"What is the current status of solar activity?" the president asked.

Jason sent back, "No change in activity at present. Anticipate another flare occurring within 72 hours."

Houston's response: "Understood. Keep me informed."

As the two operators signed off, Jason returned to check some of the newer equipment that had been set up. This equipment was designed to monitor Earth's magnetosphere, the magnetic force field put out by Earth itself. Since the magnetosphere was Earth's primary defense against cosmic storms, Jason knew it would be essential to monitor how it was functioning.

Both he and Annette looked first at the graph, then at each other. Jason shook his head from side to side slowly. The initial findings showed that the magnetosphere was fluctuating wildly. In his mind's eye, he could envision what was happening. Billions upon billions of magnetic lines of force were extending from the North to the South Pole. Every one-millionth of an inch of space was penetrated by one of the magnetic lines. Normally, though invisible and unseen, they were very stable, acting like a huge permanent magnet surrounding the planet.

Many times in his youth, Jason had simulated the magnetosphere to demonstrate Earth's giant umbrella to others. He would draw a picture of Earth and then sprinkle a few ounces of metal filings over the picture. Then he would take the big permanent magnet that his father bought at a surplus store (the magnet had come out of a power generator that had been dismantled), and he would place the magnet behind the image of Earth. Instantly the iron filings would line up to simulate the magnetosphere, covering Jason's world with a magnetic shield. In effect, he was showing that Earth itself is a giant magnet, created by its liquid core churning and twisting.

He could envision what was happening to that magnet now. The lines that normally were curved symmetrically were bending and twisting as the force of the solar flare winds struck Earth. As they bent and twisted, not only did they disrupt the electrical power grids, but other more fundamental changes were taking place.

Animals, whose internal direction finders relied upon the stability of the magnetosphere, were disoriented. Carrier pigeons, for instance, could not get their bearings. Ducks, geese, and other fowl that relied on these invisible lines of force lost their direction. For humans, these fluctuations meant that finely tuned instruments that normally had relied on the magnetosphere for their headings — instruments like inertial guidance systems on nuclear submarines — would no longer function. For all intents and purposes, the submarines were blind under water.

Whether or not the submarines were still functional, Jason could only guess. But he knew that unless the commanders responded quickly, the submarines and all the men aboard would be lost in the depths of the ocean. Although President Houston had commanded all U.S. nuclear submarines to either return to their U.S. base or put into port, it was unlikely that all the submarines had made it back to port. He shuddered to think about nuclear submarines with no power. With no manual way to blow their ballast tanks, they would sink into the deep trenches of the Atlantic and Pacific Oceans, to be crushed by the depths, their nuclear reactors fully charged and operating. They would leak nuclear waste for the next thousand years.

In many ways, Jason couldn't help but be awed by what was happening. It was a unique event in history. Billions of man hours had gone into transforming Earth into an industrialized planet and now, in a span of a little more than one week, most of man's greatest technological achievements had been neutralized. Electricity, perhaps the greatest invention of mankind, was canceled on planet Earth and, along with it, most of man's modern conveniences.

As if reading his mind, Annette spoke up.

"Twenty-first century America has suddenly become nineteenth century America."

Jason corrected her with a smile. "What you really mean is, the twenty-first century *world* has become a nineteenth century world."

In the capital the scene was typical of that being played out in cities across the nation. The city had just begun to come alive again, with about 10 percent of the normal street traffic active once more. Most of the traffic lights were still out, so drivers were exercising extreme caution, with the exception of a few foolhardy individuals who persisted in speeding across intersections, often with disastrous results. But then everything stopped again. Vehicles stopped en route. All the traffic lights quit. The city was dark.

In her hotel room at the Rayburn Hotel, Emily Hart was taking a shower, only her second in almost a week. She'd just been thinking how wonderful it was that she actually had hot water for a shower. Then suddenly all the lights went off. The shower continued to operate for a few seconds, and then the water quit as well.

Oh no, she thought in alarm. *Not again.* She got out of the shower, dried herself off, and dressed quickly. *At least this time,* she thought, *I was smart enough to stash some water.* She had gotten several two-liter bottles and stored water in them. She took one of the bottles and used part of its precious contents to brush her teeth. With the toothbrush sticking out of her mouth, she glanced up at the mirror, and she stifled a gasp. She didn't recognize the person staring back at her in the mirror.

In her early 40s, Emily was still a young woman, but the woman in the mirror looked older, with deep wrinkles in her brow, crow's-feet at the sides of her eyes, and eyelids that were dark even without makeup. *I've aged almost ten years in the last week,* she thought somberly. *Now it's starting all over again. I can't believe how stupid I've been. Professor Hobart was right. President Houston was right. All I've ever done is ridicule and demean these men who were trying to save lives, including my own.* She had intended to leave the city today on the 10 o'clock evacuation bus. Now, she knew there would be no bus.

Suddenly she burst out crying. She hadn't really cried in nearly 20 years. Emily was a shattered woman. She looked in the mirror again and decided, *I look awful.* Her big brown eyes had dark circles around them, and her hair, which was normally meticulously groomed, was a mess. *What am I going to do?* she thought fearfully. *I'm trapped in this city with no way out now. Oh God,* she cried out. *Please forgive me, and please help me.*

She recalled the one time in her life when she had felt completely secure: when her mother and dad were still together. She and her mother would go to the little community church in their neighborhood every Sunday. Emily had spent many hours at the church in various youth groups and camps throughout most of her early years, and she had felt comfortable and secure there. She also remembered that she had felt comfort in the knowledge that God was real and that He cared about her. When had she lost all of that?

She realized it was after her mother and father had divorced. She and her father had never been close, but she had loved him dearly. However, when he had walked out on his family, it had shattered her — not only her belief in her father but also her belief in God. Now she realized that God wasn't to blame for her father. Maybe it was too late for her. She had done so many bad things she didn't think God could ever forgive her.

"Get a grip on yourself, Emily," she said aloud. "You're not a kid anymore. You're a 41-year-old woman trapped in a city that's being overrun with gangs and thugs, and if you don't get out of here, you're going to die. God will help you get out of this situation."

She hurriedly put a few things into her backpack and got dressed in her warm-up suit and sneakers. She knew if she was going to get out of the city, there was only one way:

She would have to walk out. She hated to leave her other things behind, but she knew there was no way she could carry more than the backpack. She didn't even know where the camps were. All she knew was that they were somewhere west of the city. *Anywhere,* she decided, *is better than D.C.*

She decided, *Well, if I walk far enough, I'll eventually hit the Pacific Ocean. Surely I can find one of those relocation camps before I get there.* She threw her backpack over her shoulder and took the stairway to the lobby. Just as she entered the lobby, she heard the gunfire outside and saw the big plate-glass window in the front of the Rayburn Hotel shatter.

Outside, four members of a local gang were in a fire fight with three D.C. police officers. The police officers were hopelessly out-gunned. The gang members had machine guns, and the officers had only their side arms. Emily stood paralyzed as she saw a blonde policewoman attempt to run through the door into the hotel. Then she saw the glass in the side panels explode as one of the thugs turned his machine gun on her.

The rest of what happened was just a blur. She started screaming uncontrollably. Within 30 seconds, the fight was over, and three police officers lay dead, along with one of the attackers. An evil-looking thug brandishing an AK-47 burst into the hotel. Stepping over the dead bodies, he walked over to Hart, who

447

was still screaming hysterically, and slapped her.

"Shut up!" he commanded. "Who are you?"

Emily stopped screaming when she was struck but, being paralyzed with fear, she was unable to answer. The burly thug struck her again, this time with the back of his hand, knocking her to the ground. "Who are you?" he commanded, bringing his foot back to kick her in the side.

She stuttered, "I . . . I'm Emily Hart," she said, "with WNN."

"WNN!" the gang leader spat. "There ain't no WNN no more lady. Get up." He reached down, grabbed her by the hair, and jerked her to her feet. She was afraid to scream again, but she felt like she was going to faint. As the thug shoved her outside, what she saw looked unreal — out of place.

It was one of the D.C. horse-drawn carriages loaded with all kinds of contraband the gangs had pillaged. The thug pushed her into the back of the carriage and signaled to the other two, who were now in the driver's seat, to get going. One of the men grabbed the reins, whacked the horse on the rump, and away they went. A nineteenth century conveyance being used by thugs with automatic weapons.

Even though terror gripped her mind, she almost smiled at the paradox. *What a great story this would be,* she thought. *Unfortunately, I don't have a camera; nor do I have a network.* The humor of it faded as she remembered where she was and what was going to happen. She trembled, realizing that she was in the hands of men with no morals, no compunction about killing, and no restraints.

In Chicago, Bill and Elaine had just watched as Joel Slife's stereo equipment, which they were playing, went up in smoke. They realized instantly that the solar flare had struck. Trying to lighten the moment with humor, Bill commented, "Joel's going to kill me when he sees what's happened to his equipment."

Elaine screamed at her husband, "Bill, don't you understand what's happened — what you've done?"

"What do you mean — what I've done?" Bill replied defensively.

"We're trapped!" Elaine sobbed. "We have no way out now. What are we going to do now? What happens when the food runs out?"

"But Elaine, it'll just be a little while until the power comes back on — just like last time."

"Bill, you don't get it do you?" Elaine screamed. She was scared out of her wits. "The power isn't coming back on. I told you what that professor said — that when this flare hit, it would shut down everything, and it might be weeks or months before the power comes back on."

"Surely not," Bill said hesitantly. He hadn't really thought it was possible. He thought it was all hype. *All the power out for months?* he thought. *Impossible.* He heard a frantic pounding on the door, and he yelled, "Who is it? What do you want?"

It was their neighbors from down the hall. Ken and Ruth were another young couple who had decided to stay behind when the others left. "It's Ruth . . . and Ken," the woman screamed. "Let us in, please. Let us in. They're coming." The next thing they heard was the sound of gunfire outside their apartment. Elaine rushed over to Bill and put her arms around him. She was sobbing. Bill hugged his wife. He was scared too. They were totally defenseless.

He heard the sound of more gunfire and saw his front door shatter as two men carrying machine guns kicked it in. Bill was reaching back to get the andiron from the fireplace, to defend himself. The last thing that Bill or Elaine heard was the sound of the automatic weapon and the despicable laugh of the two men as they sprayed the apartment with gunfire.

In Atlanta, Neil Farmer was cursing at the top of his voice. "The power is out again," he was screaming maniacally. "Where are my engineers?"

"What's going on?" a studio technician shouted through the darkness. Not even the dimmest glimmer of light came into the tightly sealed studio. Even the emergency lights were out. He had stayed on when most of the others left. He reached into his pocket, pulled out a cigarette lighter, and struck a flame. The small glow sent an eerie reddish-orange light across the room.

"Another flare must have struck," he said. "All the power's out again."

"It can't be," Farmer said hysterically. "It's impossible. I talked to Frasier. He told me there wouldn't be a big flare."

"Well, Boss, I guess he was wrong," the engineer said.

Another studio employee said, "I guess you listened to the wrong person, huh, Neil?"

Farmer screamed back, "Who said that? You're fired."

"I've got news for you," the woman shouted back. "There's nothin' to be fired from here. WNN is history."

In the meantime, the technician found a newspaper, rolled it up, and lit the end of it. It gave off enough light for the crew to find their way to the outer door. With the door opened, daylight streamed through the front windows. There were several more employees in the lobby and the entire team, including Neil Farmer, rushed out of the building and into the streets of Atlanta.

An ex-cameraman asked his friend, "What are you going to do?"

"I'm going to get out of this town as quick as I can. I've got some food and a couple of guns stashed in my apartment."

"I'll go with you," the other man said. "Let's get out of here."

"Come back here!" Farmer screamed. "You've got to get the studio up and operating," he shouted. Both men turned and looked at Farmer, and one of them said, "Farmer, you're insane!"

Farmer shouted back, "You'll never work again! You'll never work at another studio again!"

One of the men turned and, in a sarcastic tone, said, "Promises, promises."

The other man commented, "He really is crazy, you know."

"Yeah, I know. We've seen it for a long time."

Five minutes later Farmer was standing alone outside the WNN building. Dejectedly, he walked back into the building and plopped himself down in a chair in the enormous lobby that at one time had hosted hundreds of guests. Now there was nothing.

Houston! Houston did this! Farmer thought bitterly.

★ ★ ★

Until that flare struck, Gen. Hill had been preparing for the ouster of Houston and Boland. Once word of the new flare reached him he panicked. He knew if he didn't act quickly he would lose any chance of getting rid of Houston. He nearly panicked. He was involved with a conspiracy to oust the president. He would be finished if it failed. He had to act quickly. Then he thought, *Houston will be back at Camp David. It'll be easier with Houston at Camp David . . . away from the city.*

Hill was at the Pentagon, trying to convince his senior staff that President Houston was incompetent and incapable of leading the country. He was saying, "Houston is holed up at Camp David. We could take 300 men and place him under arrest."

The imbalanced Hill had already decided that once he had Houston in custody the president would never see the light of day again. Earlier he had played his trump card: He had made a deal with one of the toughest gangs in D.C. Once Houston was under arrest, the gang would attack the squad escorting the president back to Washington. He hated to sacrifice the soldiers, but it was necessary.

In exchange, Hill had promised the gang leader modern weapons from the D.C. Army depot. He had given him a few shoulder-fired rockets but had no intention of delivering the heavy armament they had demanded. Instead, he would have the military wipe them out after they killed Houston. Using Crenshaw as his front, Hill intended to take over the government. By the time order was reestablished, he would be firmly entrenched. Then, with Houston out of the way and the conservative movement crushed, it would be a small step for him to be nominated for the next Democratic president of the United States. It was just a small step.

But he needed the support of his senior staff to make the plan work. Houston's arrest had to be legitimate. He could not be seen as a rebel leader. Most of the men in the room had begun to waffle. Although many of them liked Houston, they also thought the president was out of line by declaring martial law and evacuating the cities. The general assured them that the new flare threat was just another attempt by the president to buy more time.

Hill had just asked for a show of hands from his senior staff. All but two of the 12 men in the room raised their hands in support. *More than enough,* Hill thought. Hill was a pompous little man. At five feet, four inches tall, he had always been self-conscious. As a boy, he'd been the brunt of a lot of jokes and the target of a lot of bullies.

But now, as a four-star general, he wielded

the power of the strongest army in the world, and soon, as president of the United States, he would have the authority that he had always sought. He didn't hate the conservatives, or even Houston. After all, Houston had helped to rebuild the military. They were very simply an impediment to his lifelong goals. Houston was an unnecessary roadblock that had to be eliminated.

When the lights in the Pentagon went out, Hill shouted to the orderlies to get some backup lights on. Under normal circumstances, the emergency lighting would have activated automatically. But when the main power went out, the emergency lighting failed also.

One of the orderlies said, "General, another flare has struck."

"Impossible," Hill said. Frasier had assured him that the flare wouldn't strike for at least another day. Fortunately, the room was totally dark, because if he could have seen the look on the faces of his senior staff, he probably would have court-martialled them. Only minutes before, Hill had stood before them and told a bold-faced lie. He had assured them that there was no flare headed toward Earth. He swore it was a contrived lie of the president and his staff.

Hill's mind was racing. His plans would be wrecked, and he would be disgraced. He had to get away. If he could kill Houston everything would be okay. His plan would still work. It had to. *The gang,* he thought. *I can use the gang to kill Houston. Then after I get the power, I'll straighten out everything. I'm still a four-star general. That should get me anything I need.*

He bolted for where he thought the door was. Instead, he tripped over a chair and crashed to the floor, striking his head on the concrete. The last thing he knew was the taste of warm blood.

21

Neil Farmer wandered throughout the WNN building looking for anyone he might command to do his will, but nobody was left. All the staff had evacuated the building. He was totally alone. He wandered back down to the lobby, his mind in a daze. *How could this have happened?* he thought woefully. Then he got angry again. *It's Houston's fault! It's all part of that stupid conservative agenda.* His hatred for Houston and the conservatives clouded everything else. *Worst of all,* he thought, *I can't do anything about it now.*

Farmer plunked down on one of the chairs in the lobby. Outside he could hear gunfire, and it sounded like it was getting closer. Suddenly he came back to his senses, and he was frightened. Here he was alone in that big building, in a city that was being overrun by wanton killers. He decided to turn the alarm system on and find out what his resources were. *Food,* he thought. *How much food is there left in the building . . . and what about water? How long will this thing last?* he wondered. *What was it that the professor said? He thought this solar flare might go on for months?*

Farmer was fast waking up to the reality

of his situation. In months, he would be dead of starvation; in fact, maybe in weeks or even days. He had no idea what his resources were. Going to the security panel behind the receptionist's desk, he attempted to arm the security system in the building, which would lock all the doors. He knew that he had access to the security areas and thought he could hole up in these areas — at least for some period of time. Unfortunately, without power, the security system was disabled. Farmer cursed at his misfortune.

Behind him, he heard a loud crash. He swung around to see the double glass doors in the WNN building exploding. Then he heard another sound: a heavy caliber machine gun. It was trained on the WNN building doors. The last thing Farmer saw was the two thugs breaking through the security door with their automatic weapons pointed in his direction. He started to scream, but never had the chance because, even while he was turning to run, the bullets from their weapons were on the way. Neil Farmer, head of WNN news programming, crumpled behind the shattered security desk.

At the Pentagon building, Gen. Hill, after tripping over the chair and cracking his head on the corner of a desk, was taken to the infirmary, where his wounds were treated and he was placed under guard. Col. Newsome,

Pentagon security, decided that the general should be held until Gen. Boland could be contacted. Hill woke up in the infirmary, his head splitting. He lay very still and glanced over at the orderly who was busy going through some documents on his desk. Hill reached up and touched his head, where he had a very large bandage, and he winced at the pain.

As his senses returned, he knew he had to get out of the Pentagon. He still had a plan, but to execute it he had to get away. Laying on the cot, he feigned unconsciousness and groaned loudly. The orderly looked up. All he knew about the situation was that he had a four-star general in his care and there was an armed guard outside. He wasn't sure about the politics of the situation and could not have cared less; his job was to take care of the patient. Hill groaned again, and the young corporal went over to the cot.

"Are you all right, Sir?" he asked with genuine concern.

The general groaned again, with his eyes still shut. The young orderly reached over to feel the general's head and, in the process, exposed his vulnerable chin to what he thought was an unconscious patient. As he was moving forward, Hill was moving up. Hill had a lot of upper body strength for his five-foot, four-inch height, and when his fist connected with the orderly's chin, the young man dropped instantly. As he went down, he hit the plastic pitcher of water sitting on the stand by the general's cot and sent it sprawling across the floor with a great racket. Hill sprung to his feet like a cat. Even if he was 55 years old, he was a veteran combat officer and he knew what he had to do.

When the guard in the hall heard the commotion, he opened the door and stepped inside. Even as he was stepping through, the general attacked. As he delivered a blow to the guard's face, in one motion he reached down and pulled the man's nightstick out of his belt loop. The guard whirled around and reached for his side arm. However, the flap on his holster was still buttoned, and the moment of hesitation that it took to unbutton the flap was enough for the general. He swung the nightstick, catching the soldier on the temple, and down he went.

Hill paused long enough to retrieve a weapon from the downed soldier. Stuffing it into his belt, he retrieved his shoes, hastily put them on, and hurried out the door. Hill had spent many years in and out of the Pentagon and knew the layout of the building. He had little difficulty evading detection. With the power off, the only lights inside the building were a few candles spaced strategically along the hallways. The security systems were immobilized, and Hill quickly found an emergency exit.

Once outside, even though he was weak from the loss of blood and unsteady on his feet, he was free. When somebody finally discovered the guard and the orderly, they would have a difficult time spreading the word without any communications. Hill knew what he had to do. *Houston has to be eliminated.* To do that, he would need the gangs. *After Houston's eliminated, I'll deal with the gangs. They're a bunch of punks. They'll be no great problem.*

Hill had made contact with Carlos Chevara, a local gang leader, several days earlier. Hill had met Chevara when he had been picked up by one of the security teams in the city. Chevara had been caught trying to break into the National Guard Armory, was arrested, and was brought to the military detention center. Normally, it would have been a routine arrest and Chevara would have been booked and jailed, awaiting the military tribunal. However, Hill knew that in order to execute his plans to eliminate Houston he would need a scapegoat, and Chevara was perfect.

It was Hill's intention to use Chevara's gang to attack the envoy transporting Houston after his arrest. Chevara had been instructed that if he ever wanted to get out of jail, he'd better learn to cooperate. Now Hill would modify the plan and use Chevara and his men to attack Camp David. Chevara's men would be assigned the task of assassinating President Houston and anyone else who was found with the president, especially Gen. Boland. It would be risky, but with the current turn of events Hill knew that he would never be able to command the military troops necessary to take over the camp.

As he left the Pentagon, his intent was to locate Chevara and plan the assault on the Camp David complex. Hill had worked it out, even in the few minutes since he had made his escape. He would provide Chevara and his men with military uniforms and the proper documents. With his help, they should be able to get through the security at Camp David, and once inside they would locate the president very quickly, assassinate him, and then Hill would take control of the temporary government.

Hill had promised Chevara money, food, and weapons in exchange for his help. But once the president and Gen. Boland were eliminated, once again Hill would be the ranking military authority. And once he had control, it would be a simple plan to eliminate Carlos Chevara and his scum. Hill had no intention of sharing his power with anyone and certainly had no intention of leaving anybody behind who could testify.

Hill was counting on the lack of communications and knew that no one would have had the opportunity to warn Houston yet. In fact, with the other members of the joint chiefs still under the assumption that he was under house arrest in the infirmary, he would have some time.

The first thing Hill needed was troops, and Chevara's men, though they could not realistically be considered troops, were at least warm bodies with an attitude. Once outside the Pentagon, Hill made his way through the virtually deserted streets of the city. He knew Chevara was holed up less than three miles from the Pentagon. The gang leader would have no way to know that Hill's planned military assault had fallen apart. He'd been able to get Chevara released from custody and had provided the obnoxious gang leader with a few anti-tank weapons, which pacified him for the moment.

Hill could hear sporadic firing but couldn't locate the source. From time to time he would hear the sounds of military security; then he would duck back into an alley or side street. Twice before he saw armed soldiers, two by two, patrolling the streets. Each time he ducked back out of sight. He wished he could have found a lone soldier, because he preferred to have an automatic weapon, but he couldn't take the chance, so he relied on stealth instead.

He was surprised at how many of his skills returned after all these years. He hadn't been in combat himself for nearly 25 years, and yet his training came back as if it had been yesterday. His head was still pounding but, to avoid drawing attention to himself, he unwound and removed the bandage. He was easily able to evade the few patrols that he saw, as the soldiers were looking for larger numbers of armed gang members — not lone individuals. In another 30 minutes, he was out of the patrolled area of the city. Once he stepped onto the side street, it was like stepping out of civilization and into a war zone.

Burned-out hulks of cars lay all along the street. The apartment complexes looked like the war-torn streets of Beirut from the 1960s. Windows were smashed and several of the buildings were burned. Seeing the lack of restraint on the part of the inhabitants of this area, he thought to himself darkly, *These people are animals*. He was determined that when he ran the country, he would eliminate these lower classes of people that couldn't be trusted; they didn't deserve to live in America.

He picked his way around the twisted shells of vehicles in the streets. The area had been a residential district at one time. Low-income housing provided by the government had now been turned into smoldering ruins, and for nearly 10 minutes Hill didn't see another living soul. It was quite obvious that the soldiers weren't patrolling this area. They had their hands full just trying to keep the main arteries of D.C. habitable, and they weren't about to patrol what now was nothing more than burned-out ghettos. Hill knew this was the territory run by Chevara.

Hill grew more cautious. He figured that if he were spotted by the soldiers he could probably reason with them. However, if he were spotted by roving gangs, he suspected there would be no reasoning with them. So he got even more cautious. He made his way through the neighborhood cautiously, building by building. He had the stolen 45-caliber weapon in his hand, ready for whatever might confront him.

One thing Hill was not was a coward. He'd risked his life in battle several times. He was surprised to know, after the first combat, that he was not frightened. In fact, he looked forward to it. He felt he was born for war, so even in this situation he felt comfortable. He was alert, and he was alive, and he loved it. Although his head still pounded from the crack on the skull he'd gotten earlier, he had experienced a lot more pain in his life.

As Hill got closer to Chevara's hideout, he got more cautious. He slowed down his pace and moved quietly from one building to the next. He knew from his earlier meeting with Chevara that the gang leader's hideout was in what once had been a fashionable hotel on the outskirts of a housing development. Over the last 20 years, the hotel had continually run down, until it had become little more than a fleabag and a meeting place for pimps, drug dealers, and prostitutes. But Chevara called it home.

Hill became even more vigilant as he approached the building. *These gangs can be very dangerous, and Chevara is a highly unstable ally. It's better to use him to get the deed done as quickly as possible and then get rid of him.* The longer he stayed exposed to these dopeheads, the greater danger he would be in.

He reached the entrance to the hotel and started up the staircase. At one time there had been a landing area with a rail around it, but that had long since been demolished. Little was left of it now but a few splintered remnants of the handrail. Hill slipped down beside the staircase. "Chevara? . . . Chevara?" he said softly. In a few seconds he heard a response.

"Yeah, who's there? And whatta ya want?"

"It's General Hill," he replied.

"Who's Hill?" the gang leader asked.

"General Hill. Don't you remember? We made an agreement."

"Oh yeah," Chevara said through his drug-dulled brain. He really wasn't sure what was going on in the city. All he knew was that his lights were out again and none of his vehicles would run. He wasn't scared though. Chevara wasn't scared of anything except sleep. It was only when he closed his eyes and started to dream that he became frightened. It was always the same dream. He was a little boy again, and one of his mother's boyfriends was there and was beating him with a clothes hanger — always the same dream . . . and always the same ending. Chevara would wake up in a cold sweat. He could still feel the welts on his face and back where the brutal man had beaten him night after night.

In his dreams, he was never able to get rid of his tormenter, and he woke up in terror. He used drugs to cover his fear, but there were never enough. Awake, however, Carlos Chevara was afraid of nothing or nobody.

"Yeah, come on up, General," Chevara shouted.

Hill, clutching his weapon in front of him, cautiously began to climb the steps to the hotel. Close to the top, he cautiously said, "Chevara, I'm coming in."

"C'mon, General," Chevara shouted back. "It's okay."

Hill, still clutching his gun, cautiously pulled the door open. He looked around and, seeing nothing, stepped inside. Once inside the building, almost immediately Hill felt the familiar sensation of cold steel pressed against his temple.

"Hand over your weapon, General," Chevara demanded, keeping his AK-47 pressed against Hill's temple.

"No way!" Hill said angrily.

"Then I'll have to kill you, General," Chevara said.

"Then do it," Hill commanded, "but you're not going to take my weapon. And if you kill me, you'll never have a chance to kill the president."

Chevara laughed, lowering his weapon. "You're okay, General. You're my kinda guy," the gang leader said. "Where are your troops, General?"

"I've run into a small problem," Hill replied. "There's a change of plans. How many men can you muster?"

"How many do you need?"

"At least 20."

"No problem. We can get you 25 or 30."

"No, 20 will be enough, but they have to be clean and sober and be able to look like military personnel. Can you do that?"

"Ah, sure," Chevara quipped. "All my men look like soldiers."

"Yeah, right," Hill responded sarcastically. "What you want us to do, General?"

"First, we're going over to the National Guard Depot, and we're going to equip your men with uniforms and military weapons."

"All right! They'll like that," Chevara said. "They always like to play soldier."

"Cut the chitchat," Hill snapped, "and let's get on with it. We need to get through with this as quickly as possible."

"Then let's get goin'," Chevara said as politely as he could muster under the circumstances. He didn't like the general, and he would have been delighted to kill the pompous little man, but he wanted to kill the president more. After all, very few people ever get the chance to kill a president. That would make him KING of the gang leaders.

Chevara was feeling no pain at the time; he had taken his daily dose of heroin, and he knew that he was invincible. He was bulletproof. He could do whatever he wanted. *I could fly if I really wanted to*, he thought.

Then they heard a shrill scream from below.

"What was that?" Hill demanded.

"Aw nothing, General. Just a little trinket we picked up along the way."

Chevara shouted for his men to come up. A dozen of the meanest-looking men Hill had ever seen stumbled up the stairs. They were wearing all kinds of assorted clothing. It was obvious they had stolen most of what they had, and they represented the style for looters in D.C: some wore jackets from thousand-dollar suits; others were wearing expensive leather jackets; some had exclusive ostrich-skin boots; and there was jewelry — lots of jewelry — and tattoos of every description.

"You see . . . my men look just like your Army. Right, General?" Chevara laughed.

Hill shuddered in spite of himself. This band of criminals easily could have been pirates from the sixteenth century, except that these guys were drug addicts: their eyes fixed and glazed. Many of them had a gleam in their eyes that Hill knew was a lust for blood. He had seen it in combat: men, even out of good families, when exposed to the killing, developed a lust for it. They lived only to kill more people.

Hill was surprised when he realized these thugs were not much different than the soldiers he commanded — less disciplined and more disorderly, but in different circumstances, the same. After some 25 of the gang members staggered in, the last two came, dragging a captive with them. Hill looked at the woman. Somewhere inside there was a faint note of recognition. *I think I know her. She looks familiar.*

"Who is she?" he demanded of Chevara.

"Aw, General, she's just a chick we found."

"She looks familiar," Hill said. "Who is she?"

"Uh, we think she used to be a TV announcer."

That's where Hill had seen her! Television.

As Emily Hart looked at the general, he could see sheer panic in her eyes. She had been held captive by this gang for nearly 24 hours, and she was terrified. Four other captives had been brought along with her: three women and one man. The man had been killed almost immediately by the gang, and the other three women had been divvied out, much like a commodity, by the fearsome gang. She wasn't sure why she hadn't been molested, but she felt it had something to do with the gang leader. He told the others that she was "his girl."

"What is she doing here?" Hill demanded.

"Aw, she's my girlfriend, Señor," dropping the formality of even referring to Hill by his rank. Chevara saw no need of showing any respect for the general.

"This is crazy," Hill said. "She's a witness to what you guys are doing. Get rid of her."

"Oh, no, Señor," Chevara said. "She's much too pretty. Besides, she's a celebrity."

Speaking to Emily, he said, "Aren't you a big celebrity? Tell the general your name."

Emily was so scared she couldn't even think who she was. Her lip was trembling.

"Tell the general your name!" Chevara commanded.

One of the men holding her reached up and slapped her as hard as he could on the side of her dirty, tear-stained face.

"Emily . . . Emily Hart," she stuttered. Then she burst into tears.

"Emily Hart?" Hill said. "With WNN? Chevara, you're crazy. Why are you keeping her?"

Anger flashed in Chevara's eyes. No one challenged his decisions. He started to lift his weapon to Hill's face again. He was ready to pull the trigger, but then he thought better of it. He remembered, *No, I get to kill the president.* He answered, "She's my girlfriend, General. I can't kill my girlfriend. At least not right now."

"Get rid of her," Hill ordered.

"No, General. She goes where I go," Chevara said.

"She can't go with us," Hill declared.

"Okay then, you'll have to go by yourself, General, because where I go, she goes."

Hill was furious. If Chevara had been a soldier, he would have had him court-martialled and put in prison for the next 30 years. But he wasn't a soldier; he was a criminal, and Hill knew he needed Chevara. "Well, just keep her out of sight."

"Certainly, General. Don't worry about her. Everything's under control."

"Do you have any transportation?" Hill asked the gang leader.

"Sure, General. We've got that under control too. We got horses and buggies." And in fact, Chevara did. He had two of the carriages commonly seen throughout Washington, D.C. in normal times, transporting tourists around the city. With those, Chevara could move as many as 30 of his men anywhere he needed them. As such, he had as much mobility as the authorities did. *It's my city,* he reasoned. *With the weapons we'll get, I'll run the police right out of town. Then I'll become the mayor of D.C.* In his drug-fogged brain, Chevara had moved up several notches on the scale of gang leaders. He envisioned himself the leader of Washington, D.C.

"Okay, okay," Hill finally relented. "Get your men together. We're going to raid the local armory. I'll get the door open. You be sure that your men are ready to go when that door opens."

"Si, General. My men will be ready," Chevara said sarcastically.

In New Holland, Jason, Annette, and Wendy were in the solar observation building. Jason was ecstatic to see that they could still operate the generator and that the spectrometers were operating normally. They calibrated the equipment as well as they could and settled down to analyze the data from the previous flare. It was astounding. The flare that was bombarding Earth was in excess of a level 10.

"I'm amazed that we're still able to function," Jason said. "The electromagnetic pulse is almost constant. It's like living inside a nuclear furnace — only without the radiation."

"I know. It is unbelievable. Jason, what will happen to all the people in the cities . . . and to all the people out here? How are they going to survive?" Annette had thought about it many times. Millions, perhaps billions of people, would die before this ended.

Suddenly Wendy cried out, "Daddy, come quick!"

Jason was startled and rushed over to where Wendy was standing by the spectrometer. As he crossed the room, he asked, "What is it, Honey?"

"Daddy, something else is happening. The short-range spectrometers just went off the scale again."

Jason looked at the indicator and, sure enough, both the X ray and the S-band spectrometers were pegged off the chart again.

"Oh my word," Jason said. "Not again!" He hurried over to his telescope. Quickly shifting the filter over the lens, he pointed it directly toward the Sun. "Look at this, Annette. It's unbelievable." He stepped back from the telescope and let Annette put her eye to the viewer.

"Incredible!" she exclaimed. The foot of the solar flare was rapidly expanding out from the surface of the Sun. "This one's bigger than the last one!" she exclaimed.

"Yes," Jason said. "I think it's going to be much bigger."

"Jason," Annette said, stepping back from the viewer and reaching her hand out to him. Jason took her hand. She said, "What's going to happen?"

"It means we need to power down everything, including this building, before that flare hits. Let's not take a chance."

"But, the building is shielded," Annette said. "Why should we have to power down?"

"Yes, Daddy, what's the problem?" Wendy asked, catching some of her dad's and Annette's emotion.

"Unfortunately, the laws of physics, at least where they apply to electricity, may not apply when a trillion tons of supercharged cosmic matter strikes this planet," Jason said. "What we have seen so far is nothing compared to this next flare."

Wendy was frightened, and she said so. Jason reached out and pulled Annette and Wendy close to him. "We need to contact the president immediately," he said. Then he paused. "You know, at least President Houston won't have to worry about being impeached," he quipped.

22

The attack on the Armory was well planned. Gen. Hill, in his full military attire, strode up to the front gate, where the armed guard asked him for his credentials. The guard had heard nothing of the episode at the Pentagon and he assumed, logically, that Gen. Hill was operating with full authority of the U.S. military. The guard pressed the button and the gates rolled back, allowing Hill to enter the compound. Once inside, and as soon as the guard turned his back, Hill drew his side arm and shoved it in the small of the soldier's back. The startled young private was so astonished he couldn't even respond when the general asked, "How many more people are in this compound?"

"Uh . . . uh . . . uh . . . three, Sir . . . I think," the private stuttered.

"Hand me your weapon," Hill commanded, "and do it very slowly. I don't want to have to kill you."

"Yes, Sir. Is this some kind of a test, General?" the young man asked.

"The only test is whether you live or die," Hill said.

As soon as Hill had control of the entrance,

Chevara and his band moved through the open gate. Hill glanced up as the men went by and was angered to see that the two men still had Emily Hart in tow. He started to shout at Chevara but changed his mind, lest he alert the other guards, but he made a mental note to chew out Chevara as soon as he had the opportunity.

Hill signaled to Chevara and his men to get out of sight quickly. Then with the young private in front of him, they moved toward the armory. Once there, Hill had the young soldier pound on the door. After what seemed an eternity, they heard a voice through the door.

"Yes, who is it?" the voice commanded.

"Private Myron Cohen," the young man responded to Hill's prodding him with the gun.

"Yeah, what do you want?"

"Let me in. General Hill is here from the Pentagon, and we have an authorization to remove some of the weapons."

"Slide his credentials under the door," the man on the other side commanded. Hill took his plastic I.D. card and shoved it under the door.

"Stand in front of the viewer," the man inside commanded once more. Hill stood in front of the optical opening that allowed the person inside to view what was going on outside. A few seconds later they heard the bolts inside being withdrawn, and in another 10 seconds, the door was flung open.

"Now what's this all about?" the sergeant asked gruffly as he swung the door open. He never had a chance to say more because, in the next second, he had a 45 automatic pointed at his nose. The diminutive Hill commanded him, "Hand me your side arm, Sergeant." The sergeant complied, Hill snapped his fingers, and Chevara and his men poured through the door. Once inside, they locked and bolted the door again.

"Anyone else here?" Hill asked the sergeant.

"No, Sir," the sergeant said out of conditioned response to the general's rank. "There was another man, but we didn't need him so we sent him off for security duty elsewhere."

"Give me your key, Sergeant."

"General, these men look like common criminals. Why are you doing this?"

"None of your business," the general said. "And if you want to live, you'll shut up." Hill commanded two of Chevara's men to take their belts and tie the two soldiers.

Chevara said, "No, General. It's better to kill them."

"These men have done nothing," the general responded coarsely. "I will not kill innocent men."

"Oh, it's okay to kill an innocent president but not to kill innocent soldiers? I see," Chevara said. "Makes sense, General."

"Shut up," Hill snapped at the gang leader.

The sergeant said, "What's he talking about, General? Kill the president?"

"Shut up, I told you," Hill commanded. "One more sound, mister, and you won't have any more worries."

The sergeant turned beet red but kept his mouth shut. He was seething inside. He calculated whether he could grab the smaller four-star general and snap his neck before the other gang members could kill him, but experience told him that he probably couldn't. So he just bided his time.

Two of the gang members pulled the belts from the two soldiers, tied their hands behind them, and shoved them roughly to the floor. In the meantime, Chevara's men were going through the armory. A couple of them came back lugging anti-tank weapons and anti-aircraft missiles. "Drop those," Hill commanded Chevara. "They don't work anyway; they fire electrically, so they won't do you any good."

Chevara started to argue but then held his tongue. As he thought about it in his drug-dulled fog, he decided the general was probably right. Nothing electrical worked.

Hill said, "Tell your men to get M-18s and at least two pouches of ammunition. And we want uniforms."

"Si, Señor General," Chevara said in a mocking tone.

Once the armory had been looted of what

was needed, the two guards were tied securely with telephone wire ripped from the walls. The door to the armory was relocked and the outer gate locked. Hill studied the men as they came out of the armory dressed in the blue uniforms of the Air Force National Guard. They were a pathetic-looking group. They might pass muster as a military unit from a distance, but up close even a casual observer would have no difficulty identifying them. The scraggly beards and long unkempt hair sticking out from under the caps was a dead giveaway.

Hill had a deceptively simple plan in mind. Having been to Camp David many times, he knew that getting into the compound was the major difficulty. Once inside, they would meet with very little opposition, even with the additional security that Boland was using inside the compound.

"What now, Señor General?" Chevara said, still exercising his mocking tone. Hill was raging inside. He was not used to being mocked by anyone and certainly not by a scraggly, drug-laced punk like Chevara. But he held his tongue. He needed Chevara and his thugs; but, once he was rid of Houston, he would no longer need any of them. Then he would be in control.

The men loaded back into the carriages, still shoving and pushing Emily Hart with them. It was a long and difficult journey to

Camp David, constantly having to dodge military patrols and the burned-out shells of vehicles that littered the streets and highways everywhere — as well as perpetually keeping a lookout for rival gangs. But they were well armed and, even in their drugged condition, this band of guerrillas probably could hold their own with anyone — except a military unit. During the trip, Chevara and his men had twice dipped into their ready supply of drugs. Hill had argued with the gang leader about laying off the drugs until the operation was over, but Chevara just ignored him.

It was well after midnight before they reached the outer gates of the Camp David compound. Hill stopped well away from the security shack that was illuminated only by two small fires at either side of the gate. Chevara, dressed in a blue uniform and baseball cap, and sporting a military police armband, was to accompany Hill to the gate. Hill was thankful that there was no better lighting than the two fires, because in anything other than minimal light, Chevara would have been pegged for what he was — a dirty inner-city gang member, sporting a military uniform.

Hill was about 60 feet away from the gate when the guard spotted him in the flickering light, and he cried out, "Halt, who goes there?"

The general replied, "General Nathan Hill

and Sergeant Carlos Chevara."

The young MP guarding the gate was confused. At that time, a second guard, an older man wearing four chevrons — the mark of a staff sergeant — came up to the gate. "General, what are you doing here?" the man asked, recognizing Gen. Hill's name.

"I've come at the request of the president," Hill lied. "May I approach?"

"Yes, General," the sergeant said. "But please keep your hands in sight. Do you have any weapons?"

"Naturally," the general shouted back.

"Please put your weapons down and approach the gate," the sergeant commanded. He wasn't taking any chances, not with the kind of violence and crime he had seen taking place over the last several days.

Hill hadn't expected that. He was hoping to get close enough to get a drop on the guards. Chevara whispered, "Get me inside that gate, General. I won't need any weapons."

After considering it, Hill decided he really didn't have any alternatives. So he put his weapon down, as did Chevara.

Squinting his eyes in the bad light, the sergeant commanded once more, "The side arm too, General."

Hill thought about dressing down the sergeant but then thought better of it. The last thing he wanted to do was alert the entire camp. *Better to play along with the sergeant at this point.*

He and Chevara withdrew their side arms and put them on the ground. They approached the gate slowly. Chevara had his hands in the air, but the general simply raised his hands out to the side. Hill whispered to the gang leader. "Stay well back behind me in the shadow and out of the light. If they see you, they'll know this is a ruse."

"Si, Señor," Chevara chuckled, as if it were all a game.

Now Hill was frightened. If the drug-laced Chevara decided to do something crazy, Hill would be right in the line of fire. But Chevara immediately dropped back about three paces directly behind Hill. As they approached the fence, the guard could clearly see it was a four-star general in full uniform — a little disheveled perhaps, but who wasn't these days?

"General," the sergeant said. "Did you come all this way with just one soldier?"

"Yes," Hill lied.

"That's very dangerous, Sir," the sergeant said.

"You don't have to tell me, Sergeant, but these are unusual times. You and I both know that."

"Yes, Sir," he responded.

"Will you let us in?" Hill asked.

"Well, Sir, we've been instructed to keep

these gates closed."

"Sergeant, I doubt that two unarmed men, one of them a four-star general, really represents much of a threat to the compound, do you?"

The sergeant thought about it for a minute and then agreed, "Yes, Sir, I guess you're right." He ordered the private to roll back the gate. As the big gate swung back, Hill stepped through, followed by Chevara. As soon as he was as close to the private as he could comfortably get, Hill sprung at him. Swinging his right hand, he struck a blow, dead center on the chin, and the young man crumpled like he was made of papier-mâché.

The sergeant was so startled by the action that he hesitated a second before responding. His hesitation was just enough for Chevara, who rushed through the opening and kicked the sergeant as hard as he could in the solar plexus. The sergeant was bent over by the force of the blow, but he was a trained soldier and he knew his only chance was to fight off his attacker.

As he was bending from the force of the blow, he brought the butt of his rifle up to catch Chevara as he charged. Had the sergeant been another inch to the left, Chevara would have had the lower part of his face caved in by the stock of the weapon but, instead, the butt merely glanced off of the gang leader's shoulder. Chevara was spun to the right, but he still crashed into the sergeant. By that time, Hill had joined him, and both men were on top of the sergeant, pummeling him with blows.

In less than 10 seconds, the first skirmish was over, and the two guards lay unconscious on the ground. Chevara had taken the weapon from the sergeant while Hill was retrieving another weapon from the ground. Chevara whistled softly back to where his men were standing waiting. They moved forward, still dragging Emily with them.

"We need to dump her," Hill said to Chevara. "This is insane. You're risking the lives of all of your men."

"She goes with us," Chevara growled. By this time, it was more than just a woman he desired; it was a test of wills between this gringo general and a gang leader who now considered himself to be the leader of Washington, D.C.

Once the men were inside the compound, Hill had the big gate swung shut once more. The two guards were tied securely, then dumped well beyond the reach of the bonfire's light. Chevara would have killed them both, but Hill wouldn't allow it. Somewhere inside Hill there was still a small spark — not of decency, but of duty. He simply would not kill an American soldier unless there was no alternative.

Two of Chevara's men were stationed at

the gate to play the role of guards, while the rest of the ragtag band began to weave their way through the Camp David compound — over to the old lodge that served as a temporary headquarters for the president and had served so many presidents before this one. Hill knew exactly where it was, and he knew the trails and roads of Camp David as well as he knew those in his own neighborhood.

Hill noticed that, amazingly, there was very little security. They'd seen only two outpost squads of four men on their way to the lodge. His mouth turned up in an evil grin. *Houston's so stupid,* he thought. *This is going to be the easiest thing I've ever done. Once we're rid of Houston and Boland, the rest is going to be easy.*

By this time Hill was already planning what he was going to do about Chevara. He would let Chevara and his men attack the lodge, kill the president and all the men with the president, and then he would slip away in the confusion and melee and commandeer a squad of military police. In the confusion he was sure they would not disobey a four-star general. A squad of trained military police could easily wipe out Chevara's gang. He would make certain that not one man stayed alive to testify against him. He would swear that Chevara and his men forced him to go along with the robbery and breaking into the compound. With the gang all dead, it would work. After all, he was a full general. He, himself, would be extremely distraught over what had happened to the president and his staff and, as the ranking senior military officer, he would then assume temporary authority.

Getting rid of the weak-willed Vice President Crenshaw would be relatively simple after that. Perhaps he also would meet with an "accident," and then Hill would establish a military government to operate during this interim crisis. Of course, when the crisis was over, by that time he would be well entrenched in his position. It was a simple but effective plan but, first, he had to kill the president.

They slipped across the compound to the presidential lodge. Inside, everything was totally dark, which was what Hill assumed it should be. It was now well past 12:30 A.M. Everybody would be asleep, with the exception of the guards. Hill stopped a good 40 feet away from the lodge, still hidden by the shrubbery. He signaled Chevara to get his men down and also signaled to keep them quiet.

Looking over the compound, he spotted the guards, one at each door — a total of six. *Stupid,* he thought disgustedly. *Houston's the president of the United States and he's only got six guards.* Hill knew the Secret Service would be inside, but they also would be asleep. They needed one swift attack. Hill huddled low to the ground and went back to Chevara.

"There are six guards," he said. "I want you to take two men per guard, surround the building, and when I give the signal you kill the guards."

"Si, Señor General. We kill the gringo guards."

If Hill could have seen the evil grin on Chevara's face, he might have thought better of this whole escapade. But they had come too far anyway; the fat was in the fire. If he were caught on the Camp David compound, he would be held as a traitor. He had no doubt of that.

For the next 10 minutes, Chevara worked his men around the lodge. When they were in position, one of the men signaled and Chevara nodded to Hill.

"My men are ready, General. What now?"

Shouldering his M-18, Hill told Chevara, "Give the order."

Chevara whistled softly. Instantaneously, the whole scene changed from one of tranquility to fury. Chevara's men charged the lodge, their weapons blazing. Caught without any warning, the guards crumpled. One of the guards managed to squeeze off several rounds and cut down one of Chevara's men. And then another guard, after being hit, squeezed off a round as he was going down and cut down another gang member.

Within fifteen seconds, that battle was over. Chevara and the rest of his men charged the old lodge screaming and shouting at the top of their lungs. By this time, the men who had shot the guards were reaching for the doors to break into the president's temporary residence. Like a feeding frenzy of sharks, the drug-laced guerrillas had gone totally mad — Chevara included.

Hill hung back in the shadows. He wanted all of the guerrillas inside the lodge. As soon as he was certain the president had been killed, he'd mingle among the other military personnel who would be coming. By this time, they would have heard the shots. Hill knew that the president had to be located and killed within the next three minutes or the compound would be swarming with military personnel. He'd instructed Chevara how to find the president.

Chevara had expected Hill to be right behind him, and once inside the lodge they would go immediately to the president. He didn't see Hill, but it was simple enough, he felt. They would just kill everybody they met. By this time, the guerrillas at the door were smashing through safety glass to reach inside and unbolt the doors. Then all of a sudden, from inside the lodge, machine guns started blazing; soldiers stationed inside the lodge were firing into the startled guerrillas. The effect was instantaneous and disastrous. Every one of Chevara's men was cut down where he stood. Those who weren't killed instantly attempted to turn and run back to the cover of the shrubbery, but they were cut down as they ran.

Only Chevara, who was following his men, wasn't killed. He wheeled and ran back toward the shrubbery he had just left. Two 30-caliber bullets struck him, one in the left shoulder and one in the right side.

Hill was aghast as he watched the scene. His mind was numb as he tried to sort it all out. They had been ambushed! The lodge was full of armed military personnel. Hill stood there for several moments looking at the scene, trying to take it in and evaluate what had happened. Somehow, they had been detected. When his senses returned, he wheeled to run, but by this time the mortally wounded Chevara was almost on top of him. He saw Hill and rage filled his mind.

As Hill turned to flee, Chevara raised his weapon and, with his dying gasp, pulled the trigger. The M-18 is capable of firing 90 rounds per second. The clip Chevara had in the weapon held only 68 rounds. But as he was dying, he held the trigger down and emptied the entire clip in the direction of Gen. Hill, who was hit by at least six 30-caliber bullets as the weapons sprayed through his area. Hill never had the chance to take his first step. He died where he stood, crumpling to the ground. The guards that had been shot by the guerrillas were just getting up. Bulletproof vests had saved their lives.

Inside the lodge, Gen. Boland was smiling. *Well, welcome to Camp David, General Hill,* he thought darkly. Boland had recommended to the president that he move his location, and the president had agreed. He had set up his temporary office in the bachelor officers' barracks, and Gen. Boland, anticipating some scheme by Hill, had laid a perfect trap.

He had assigned minimal guards to the gate and a minimal number of patrols inside the camp to make it look to an intruder like the camp was extremely vulnerable. And then Boland had ordered more than a hundred trained military personnel secreted inside the lodge, just for this contingency. They had heard Hill and his little gang coming for nearly 15 minutes, and they were ready.

The firing had stopped, and there was a deadly silence, except for one sound. Boland, now outside, was on alert. He signaled two of his military police to follow him, and they very quietly made their way toward the sound. To his total surprise, he found a young woman bound and gagged, lying in the shrubbery where the gang members had left her. Once more Emily Hart was in the protection of the United States government.

23

It had been two days since the attack on Camp
David. President Houston was still having a
difficult time believing that a general of the
Army had attempted to overthrow the U.S.
government. *What a crazy world we live in,*
Houston thought. *Maybe the Lord is simply tired
of all this mess, and He's taking control now.*

The reports that were filtering back to the
president were pretty dismal. Life in the cities
had deteriorated to the animal level, people
preying upon people as armed gangs and looters took over every major city — at least the
ones that the president had reports from. He
presumed that if they had taken over cities
like Miami, Orlando, Jacksonville, Charlotte,
Atlanta, D.C., New York City, Chicago, and
Baltimore, it was logical to assume the same
was true everywhere. The reports of violence
and destruction kept flowing in. Whole sec-
tions of cities had been gutted by fire, and
there was nothing that could be done about
it. People attempting to flee the cities found
themselves confronted by ruthless gangs who
stripped them of everything they owned —
often committing needless slaughter.

Houston shook his head. He wished there

was something he could do about it, but it was beyond his control now. It was truly in the hands of God. They had sent as many of the military patrols into the cities as they could, trying to evacuate anybody who had wanted to leave the city: on foot, horseback, or horse-drawn carriage. He really appreciated Floyd Boland's organization skills. Even now, Boland was out with his troops, rounding up every four-legged creature he could lay his hands on — some for milk, some for food, and some for transportation.

Houston remembered hearing from someplace that there were more horses in America in the twentieth century than there had been in the nineteenth century, and apparently the report he was getting back confirmed that. There were literally millions of horses around the U.S., and most of them were being pressed into service. Boland had established a modern-day equivalent of the Pony Express so that messages could be relayed back and forth to the command center at Camp David.

A few of the manual telegraph lines were operational and, hopefully, more would be established as time went by. Houston was particularly thankful for the line that connected Camp David to New Holland. He was evermore appreciative of the humble professor's skills. As Jason's daughter Wendy was prone to say to anybody who would listen, "My father's a genius." Houston now believed it.

He'd been able to keep his solar observation equipment in operation, although periodic shutdowns were getting more frequent now.

The fourth big flare was scheduled to hit Earth momentarily. Houston didn't know what to do in preparation; his people had done all they could. Clearly, the estimates from some of his staff demonstrated that this flare would bring with it high exposure to cosmic radiation. Nobody, including Jason, could agree on the net result. Cancer, pestilence, a change in the weather — nobody really knew what was going to happen.

On the morning of April 12th, the fourth solar flare struck Earth. The cosmic winds that had been hurtling across the vast void of space between Earth and the Sun struck the upper atmosphere with such force that not only did Earth's magnetic shield collapse but, in a matter of seconds the magnetic poles reversed, and compasses that once pointed north made a 180 degree about-face and now pointed south.

At the New Holland facility, Jason heard the change in the backup generator's output. The machine had been left running as a test when the flare hit. First it was a humming sound, and then it sounded for all the world like someone had thrown sand in the gears. The effort of the centrifugal force of the machine trying to reverse direction was literally tearing it apart.

Jason yelled above the melee to the corporal standing by the generator.

"Shut it down! Shut it down!" he shouted. The young man, who himself had been startled by the racket coming out of his smoothly tuned machine, quickly hurried to the kill switch. Grabbing the handle, he slammed it down, shutting off the flow of diesel fuel to the engine.

"Switch the generator off line," Jason yelled again.

The young man, already sensing what was happening, had started the shutdown. He quickly reached the decoupler and shifted it to the off position. That decoupled the diesel motor from the electrical generator, allowing the generator itself to freewheel, or at least it should have freewheeled. Instead, the big motor continued to put out a variety of sounds that varied from a horrible screech to a grinding rumble.

As the machine continued to protest, Annette rushed over. "What's happened?" she yelled over the noise.

"I don't know," Jason shouted back. "The generator sounds like it's trying to reverse." Suddenly a thought struck him. "I think something has happened to the magnetic poles. Maybe the storm has caused the poles to reverse." Even as he said it, he wasn't sure he believed it himself.

"The poles reversed?" Annette said with a

495

stunned look on her face. "Is that possible?"

"Remember earlier, we discussed the theory by Dr. Carrington that at some time in the past it appeared that the magnetic poles had reversed? Well, apparently they had," Jason said. "Look at our compass."

They glanced over to the compass, which was nothing more complicated than a large floating needle — the kind used on nineteenth century sailing ships. Normally a dependable instrument, it was fluctuating wildly; but it was obvious that what once had been north was now south, plus or minus a few degrees.

"What will this do?" Annette asked as the noise began to die down.

"Who knows?" Jason answered. "Apparently our motors are not going to run in the same direction, so it's not possible to generate electricity. For all intents and purposes, we are now back in the eighteenth century, electrically speaking," he quipped. "Nothing electrical will work anymore, even inside this shielded facility."

"What about our link to the president?" Annette asked.

"Good question," Jason said, walking over to where the telegraph operator sat. "Do you still have contact with the president?" he asked.

The young man removed the headset from one ear and looked up. "Yes, Sir, we do," he said. "Apparently a battery's a battery, and it doesn't care about the polarity of the poles."

"Very good," Jason said. "At least that's a plus. Tell the president what happened."

"What do you recommend, Sir?" the young man asked Jason.

"Tell the president that we'll need to assess what's going on. Then we'll get back to him just as quickly as we can," Jason responded.

Wendy, who had just come in, asked, "What's going on, Daddy?"

"Well, Honey, apparently this fourth solar flare caused a reversal in the magnetic poles. If you don't mind, Dear, I'd like for you to stay inside the building."

"But why, Daddy?"

"Because, this solar flare is bombarding Earth with massive cosmic radiation. I believe Earth's magnetic shield has collapsed."

"Then why are *you* going outside?" Wendy asked matter-of-factly.

"I need to go outside. We can't advise the president unless we know what's happening."

"Then I'm going too," Wendy said firmly.

"I'd rather you didn't."

"I know, Daddy, but what about all the other girls and boys who are outside? Are we going to bring them all inside this building? And what about those around the world?"

Jason saw her point. "I guess you're right, Honey. We're all in this together, and, come what may, we're going to have to live with it."

Jason glanced down at the dosimeter that Wendy was wearing. It was still green, as was his and Annette's. Apparently, they had not been bombarded with any significant gamma radiation. He wondered what it would be like outside.

To the few souls at the North Pole, the cosmic display was truly spectacular. Great bolts of multicolored lights were streaking their way through the atmosphere, providing the most magnificent display of the aurora borealis ever seen by mankind. The sky, even during the daytime was a multicolored hue that was both frightening and fascinating. People as far away as Georgia could clearly see the northern light display. Unfortunately, for those at the North and South Poles, it was a deadly display, because when the poles reversed even the shielded generators quit. Everyone living at the North and South Poles would eventually freeze to death. For a time they could burn the fuel in stoves and heaters, but inevitably the end would come.

As Jason opened the door to the observatory and they walked outside, his attention was riveted to Wendy's dosimeter. He breathed a sigh of relief when, after more than 10 minutes outside, the indicator still read green. *Good*, he thought. *There is no gamma radiation tracking the solar flare, so at least in the short run we're going to be okay.*

Jason heard a commotion in the compound, and a large group was gathering. He hurried over. "What's happened?" he asked, pushing his way through the crowd. An older man was laying on the ground, and another man Jason recognized as a doctor was working on him. "What happened?" Jason asked.

The doctor pulled the stethoscope away from his ears and put it around his neck. "It would appear that his pacemaker just quit," the man said. "I wonder why? He made it through the last flare without a problem."

"The poles reversed," Jason said. "And apparently the device, as shielded as it was, cannot operate with the magnetic North now at the South Pole."

"Unbelievable," the older doctor said. "I guess it's just one more thing in a whole series of unbelievable events, isn't it, Professor."

"To be sure," Jason agreed. "To be sure."

Although he didn't say so, Jason's biggest concern was the ultraviolet radiation they were now exposed to. Normally the ozone layer would deflect much of the ultraviolet radiation, but with the magnetic shield collapsed and more cosmic storms on the way, there was no way to tell what the effect would be on the weather or crops or even the air they needed to survive.

Jason wrote a message for the telegrapher to transmit to Camp David. It was simple and direct: **Latest storm caused reversal in magnetic poles. Systems not functional under these conditions. Suggest all camps prepare for extended duration. Imperative food sources be expanded before winter. Will keep you informed. Jason.**

When the president read the message, he had a thousand questions, but obviously Jason had told him all he knew at the time. He sent back his response: **Thanks! Phil.**

Winter, Houston thought somberly. *A hundred million people in tents and short rations. God help us!*

Three days had passed since the flare had struck and life in the camps began to return to a routine, of sorts. The poles remained reversed, but little else seemed to change. Some of the engineers in the camp set about trying to manufacture a water delivery system so the camp would have a regular supply of fresh water.

It was simple enough. They located some plastic pipe and diverted the streams running through the property into a variety of reservoirs. Using mechanical ram pumps in the streams, they were able to pump water uphill to a series of storage tanks. Simple boilers made of 55-gallon drums were used to heat the water to suit the needs of the camp inhabitants. The problem of running out of water during morning baths or showers was not completely solved, but at least most of the people didn't get a cold bath every time.

Gen. Boland's camp coordinator at New Holland was Col. David Davenport. Davenport had established very stringent rules, in accordance with what Gen. Boland had prescribed. There was virtually no crime in the camps, except for some petty thefts, apparently perpetrated by some of the wayward teenagers in the camp. But there were lots of domestic and interpersonal disputes as people began to rub each other a bit raw.

Davenport realized immediately that the people needed something to do to keep them busy. They had to be organized. They had to be helping themselves, or the whole system was going to degenerate into a chaotic mess.

It was clear that they had to organize into work groups to start planting food. It was almost May — time for spring crops to be planted. Now the task was how to teach city dwellers to feed themselves. He started by having the group leaders take an inventory of their supplies.

There were nearly 25,000 people in the New Holland camp, and they had more than two tons of seed that primarily consisted of corn, beans, and a whole variety of northern climate vegetables. The tools they had were more than adequate. They had thousands of hoes and rakes and shovels. Davenport had the people organized into work groups, following the pattern used by the local Amish farmers. The younger men would break the ground, using the hand tools that they had at their disposal. The older men and the women and children would then plant the seed and take charge of the weeding and irrigation for the crops. Initially, there was a lot of grumbling about the jobs assigned, especially among the teenagers. But Davenport ruled the camp with a stern hand, with the support of Jason and the other camp leaders.

Davenport assessed their situation as being similar to what the first governor of the Massachusetts Bay Colony, William Bradford, found when he arrived. The colony, established in 1672, had suffered a disastrous first winter. Made up primarily of criminals and rejects, many of the colonists refused to work. When it came time to break ground and plant the crops, only a few families were willing to do the backbreaking work. The few could never provide for the many, so the crops were meager. During the winter they had run out of provisions, and nearly half of the entire colony died.

Bradford, who had come from solid Dutch Protestant stock, took command of the situation. He issued an edict that all colonists would work. To enforce that law, he drew from the apostle Paul's writings in 2 Thessalonians 3:10: *"If anyone will not work, neither let* [that person] *eat."* Bradford posted that warning on the town hall door, and he enforced the principle behind it with a stern hand: If anyone did not work, that person did not eat.

Several of the slackers in the group tried to test Bradford's resolve. They found it to be strong and inflexible. After several days with no food, even the worst slacker in the colony did his share, showing up every morning to work the fields until the crops were grown, harvested, and stored for the winter. Davenport applied the same principle. Drawing from the same Scripture Bradford used, he brought the group together and shared the rule: *"If a man will not work, neither let the man eat."*

The New Holland camp was instructed that those who refused to work would not eat from either the storage provisions or from the produce grown in the fields. The majority in the camp saw the wisdom of the rule and abided by it. But, as always, there were some troublemakers who felt that society owed them a living.

Those who could not work in the fields were assigned tasks suitable to whatever physical handicap they had; but all able-bodied men, women, and children were required to work a regular shift. Those who didn't work were relegated to stealing food, as best they could, from others. This proved to be a very risky practice.

In one instance, a 19-year-old sluggard named Larry Pink was caught stealing food from one of his neighbors. He'd slipped into their tent when they were out working the fields and was greedily consuming their emergency provisions. A neighbor had seen him sneak into the tent and called two other men, who caught him in the act, with his mouth full of food.

The three men grabbed the kicking, screaming young man and dragged him outside. They brought him before Davenport who, according to the rules established in the camp, called together the board of elders to hear the case. The man who had seen Pink go into the tent testified and the other two men who'd gone in with him to capture Pink also testified.

Davenport asked Pink, "Do you have anything to say for yourself young man?"

Pink said sarcastically, "Yeah, I'm hungry."

Davenport turned to the board of elders and asked, "What's your verdict?"

The three men and two women on the board agreed unanimously, "Guilty!"

Davenport turned back to Pink and said, "Well, young man, you've been found guilty of stealing food from your neighbors. What do you think ought to be done?"

He grinned. "Well, give me more food and I won't have to steal."

Davenport replied, "Mr. Pink, you'll find

out that in this camp it doesn't work that way."

"Oh yeah?" Pink said. "What are you going to do about it, old man?"

"I suggest we use a punishment that was used in some of the first colonies," Davenport replied. Turning to the five elders he said, "What would you think about putting young Mr. Pink in stocks?"

They paused for a moment, huddled together very briefly, and came back. "Well, Colonel, we think it's a judicious idea."

Pink, with a shocked look on his face, said, "What do you mean stocks? What is that? What are you talking about — stocks?"

"Well," Davenport said, "we really don't have any stocks, but I think we could probably improvise just for you, Mr. Pink."

With that, Davenport directed some of the men to erect a structure according to his instructions. They took two logs, about four and one-half inches in diameter and buried them in the ground so they measured about three and one-half feet high. Then a third log was laid over the top and nailed solidly to the two vertical logs, forming an inverted "U" in the ground.

Then Pink was brought out, struggling and cursing. He was placed facing the structure, bent over the horizontal log, his head in the middle and his arms stretched out to his sides; then he was tied firmly. The rope, tight

505

enough to hold him but loose enough to let him breathe, was tied around his neck and then to the stock, and ropes were tied around his hands and wrists. Because of his height, he was forced to stand in a semi-crouched position, unable to move.

He shouted and cursed at the group, "You can't do this!"

"Oh sure we can," Davenport said. "If you don't like it, why don't you appeal to the ACLU? Maybe they'll listen to you."

The large crowd gathered around Pink heard the comment and laughed. "Mr. Pink," Davenport said, "the terms of your punishment are that you will stay in this stock until you are genuinely repentant of your crime."

"You don't have the right to do this!" Pink shouted. "It's not human!"

"Sure it is, Mr. Pink. You're just not used to justice," Davenport said. "You will serve as an example to the others who might be tempted to follow you in crime and when you're willing to repent, just give us a shout."

Pink stayed in the stocks throughout that entire day. Davenport assigned one of the younger children to periodically give him a drink of water. He wanted the young man punished, but he didn't want him to die of dehydration. Pink shouted and screamed and cursed for the first three hours and then, after getting so hoarse he could barely make a sound, he stood silently in the stocks.

Every time he tried to drop to his knees the rope around his neck tightened and he had to go back up into the crouched position. His arms hurt and his neck hurt and his back hurt and his legs hurt. His legs felt like they were on fire and they were getting rubbery. Then Pink stopped shouting and cursing and began to cry.

People passed by on their way to and from their jobs and Pink cried out for help in his hoarse voice, but nobody would stop. His parents avoided that path past their son, but both approved Davenport's actions. They had realized long ago that their son was headed down the road of self-destruction.

Pink had been tied to the stock at about 9:00 that morning. By 6:00 that evening, Larry Pink was a changed young man. He had shouted and screamed until he was hoarse. He'd cried until all of his tears had dried up and still nobody stopped to do anything about it. He began to realize that nobody was going to stop. Even more than that, the awareness that came to Larry Pink was that he was where he was because of what he did.

Around 6:30 that evening Col. Davenport came by. He stopped in front of Pink, who looked up at him through bloodshot eyes. "Well, Mr. Pink," Davenport said, "what do you think?"

Pink, in a weak, raspy voice replied, "Sir, I was wrong."

"What do you think I ought to do about it, Mr. Pink?" Davenport said.

"I think, Sir, that I need to work and pay off my debt to the family I stole from."

"Well," Davenport said, "perhaps you can be redeemed after all." And with that, Davenport signaled for two men to come and release Larry Pink.

After cutting his ropes loose, and with one man on each side supporting him, they walked Pink over to where a kitchen had been set up. They sat him on a bench. Pink felt like his legs were going to fall off. His skin was parched from standing out in the sun all day and his throat was so dry that he could make no more than a whisper.

Davenport instructed the men to bring him some water. "Only a half a cup," he said. "Don't let him drink too fast."

Pink gulped the water down immediately. Davenport instructed the men to bring the docile young man a small cup of soup and some bread, and he told Pink, "Eat very slowly. Soak the bread in the soup and just suck on the bread. You need to give your system time to adjust." Pink never even thought about arguing. He did exactly as he was instructed. Nothing in his life had ever tasted as good as that soup.

Life in the camp settled in. Many similar

events were to happen. But very quickly the dissenters and troublemakers in the group discovered that the punishment would be fair, swift, and stern, and there would be no appeals to the ACLU or to the federal courts or to the Supreme Court. As far as a criminal in that camp was concerned, the Supreme Court was the elders of the camp.

In the city of Indianapolis, Indiana, the situation had gone from desperate to disastrous. Rioters had totally decimated what had once been the beautiful metropolitan community. Two-thirds of the buildings in Indianapolis had been burned to nothing but shells, and those that were left were all but uninhabitable. The few families that were left in Indianapolis found themselves without food or water, and starvation was beginning to take its toll. Disease and pestilence were running throughout the city. The situation was so desperate that even the gangs themselves were looking to escape.

One of the gangs, calling themselves "The Green Hats," were a collection of malcontents and mental defects who had banned together after the solar flare, for self-defense but also to establish control over the other smaller gangs in the city. Gang wars were a commonplace event and very soon the ranks of the opposing gangs had been thinned out. The Green Hats now had a contingency of nearly

150 members. The head of The Green Hats was a scrawny, pimple-faced homicidal maniac who called himself "El Diablo," or "The Devil." Prior to joining the gangs of Indianapolis, his name had been Gary Molinari.

He was from a middle-class family in Indianapolis, but through the influence of drugs and alcohol had become a social dropout. He quit high school in the tenth grade to join a lesser gang in Indianapolis and had spent the next five years learning his trade: selling drugs, using drugs, and generally wreaking havoc upon the honest citizens of Indianapolis. He truly had a warped and twisted mind, and to look into his eyes was to look at El Diablo.

Molinari's pupils, through the overuse of drugs, were fixed and dilated most of the time. He had a fanatical desire to kill or control everything he came in contact with. As his gang roamed, murdered, and burned, less and less of the city was available to support them. As food began to wane, he realized they were going to have to abandon Indianapolis.

Molinari was diabolically cruel and, through one of those circumstances that often happens, one of the drivers from the New Holland camp, returning to Indianapolis to get another group of citizens to relocate, had been captured by The Green Hats. Molinari had tortured the driver until he revealed the location of the New Holland camp.

Ever since that time, Molinari had been planning a raid on New Holland. It was obvious to him that there were greener pastures just over the hill: plenty of food, plenty of water, and a virtually unprotected group of people ready to be assaulted. He gathered nearly a hundred of his ragtag band together and, after collecting whatever means of transportation could be rounded up — consisting mostly of old wagons, a couple of buggies, and some makeshift carts — he was determined to attack the New Holland camp.

The gang leader gathered his band of cutthroats around him. "Brothers, as you know this city is no longer any good. It's totally wasted. We're going to have to move out. The driver of that government bus told me where he'd been. It's in a community called New Holland. It's got everything we need — food, water, guns, and women — and, it's ours just for the taking."

One of the saner gang members known as Bumper spoke up. "How many people in that camp, El Diablo?"

Molinari answered, "I don't know. A few hundred maybe. Why? They're just a bunch of sheep. We're gonna shear 'em."

"Are they armed?" Bumper asked.

"They've probably got some guns, but we've got more guns than they do. Are you scared?"

"No, I'm not scared, but I'm not stupid

neither. I hear some of those camps are pretty big, and they outnumber us, maybe a hun-nerd to one."

"Don't argue with me!" Molinari warned. "Sounds like you're scared. Ya wanna go home to mama?"

Bumper said, "I'm not scared, but I'm not ready to die neither."

"Come up here, Bumper," Molinari said. "I like your spirit."

The young man stood up and cautiously looked around. He gripped the AK-47 he was holding and started to move forward. He wasn't afraid of Molinari. He was following him, but he wouldn't commit suicide for him. He stood defiantly before Molinari.

"I think it would be crazy to attack one of those camps," Bumper said bravely.

"Well, you could be right," Molinari agreed. "What did *you* have in mind?"

"I know that country," Bumper said. "There's a bunch of Amish farmers around there. They have food and water and they've got women . . . and they don't carry guns. Why don't we go get them instead? It'd be a lot easier pickin's than going into one of those camps . . . specially since we don't know what's there."

"Good idea," Molinari agreed. Originally he'd called the rebel forward with the intent of having somebody cut his throat when he wasn't watching, but the more he thought about it the more he liked the idea. "Yeah, I like that. A bunch of Amish. They're some kind of religious group ain't they?"

"Yeah," Bumper replied. "They're a bunch of farmers that still use horses and buggies like they did a hunnerd years ago."

"Man!" Molinari said, "that's just what we need: horses and buggies — then we'd have transportation. We could even live on their farms. They got lots of food stored up, you say?"

"Yeah, the Amish are always puttin' aside stuff so they can feed theirselves."

"Good idea!" Molinari said. "We'll go kill ourselves some Amish. You just made your way to the head of the line, Bro."

"What's that mean?" Bumper asked cautiously.

"You're gonna become my lieutenant. You get to lead this raid. You game?"

"Sure am! I'm tired of this city. I'm ready for some action."

"Good," Molinari said. "Listen, I want everybody who can travel ready to go. We're going to leave first thing after daylight. Those who can't get a ride, walk. It'll take us about 12 hours to get there in the carts, and if you're walkin', maybe a day. We'll go case the place and wait for ya."

Molinari had it all planned. He would transport the first 30 or 40 men, and the rest of them, those dragging the women along, could walk. In the meantime, he'd have the whole area cased, ready for the assault. *Yeah, it's a good plan,* he thought. *We'll live off the fat of the land.*

The next morning Molinari and his ragtag band loaded in the wagons and headed toward New Holland and the Pennsylvania-Dutch area known as Lancaster County. Unknown to Molinari, or anybody else, Gen. Boland had at least one government plant in every gang, and The Green Hats were no exception.

One of the young men, who looked very much like the others in the gang — with the dirty clothes, tattoos, and earrings, was Lt. James Hardy, of the U.S. Marine Corps. He joined the gang weeks earlier as they had been combing through the streets looking for recruits. Hardy was part of a unified effort by Gen. Boland to infiltrate the gangs themselves. It was his job to keep an eye on the gangs and to ultimately bring them to justice when the government was able to reestablish control. To do that, he needed firsthand information.

Hardy had followed the gang as they raped, pillaged, and burned their way through the city. When an attack occurred, Hardy would simply slip away, often firing his gun into the air to make the others think he was participating. He realized that the plan El Diablo had adopted would be very effective. The

Amish people would have no defense against these thugs and killers. It would be open slaughter. He had to get word to the New Holland camp.

24

When the gang fell asleep, Hardy, who had made his bed near the edge of the encampment, sneaked away. Slipping through the burned-out city, he located the headquarters of the military coordination unit. Picking his way through the rubble, he found the staircase that led down to the basement.

The structure appeared to be nothing more than a burned-out hulk of a building, but when he reached the bottom of the stairway one significant feature was noticeable: the door was a steel, fireproof assault door, totally intact. Hardy knocked on the door — three fast raps, two slow, and then three fast. An instant later, the door swung open. He was greeted by a very menacing sergeant, brandishing an M-18 that was pointed directly at his nose.

"Relax, Sergeant. It's Lieutenant Hardy."

Sergeant Fulkam, stepping out of the way, said, "Welcome, Sir."

"Sergeant, I need to get a message to the New Holland camp. Can you do it?"

"Yes, Sir, I believe so. We've got our telegraph link open to Camp David, and from Camp David they can contact the New Holland camp."

"Good. I want you to give them this message for me: **Armed group approaching Amish country, Lancaster county. Close to New Holland camp. Advance group of approximately 40 armed men, to be followed by the rest of the gang: 60 to 80 armed members — men and women.**"

As soon as Hardy delivered his message he hurried back to the gang's location. Because order and discipline were in short supply in The Green Hats gang, it appeared that Hardy was able to slip away and come back without being detected.

However, nothing was lost on Molinari. He had noticed that Hardy was missing and then, when he saw him return, he made a mental note. *If anything abnormal happens on this raid, Hardy will pay the price.* Molinari had a question about Hardy from the beginning. He was just a little bit too perfect, a little too well-conditioned, and the fact that he didn't use drugs had made Molinari suspicious.

Once the message had been received at Camp David, the word went out quickly. When the operator at New Holland began receiving the transmission from Camp David, he immediately sent an orderly to find C.C., who was in the observation building talking to Dr. Camp when the messenger arrived.

"Sarge has a message from Camp David," the orderly told C.C. "He needs you to come."

C.C. quickly made an apology to Annette and then followed the orderly out the door.

He had been talking to Annette about some of the things he missed from the city life. Being single, he missed the singles' clubs. He also missed his CDs. He didn't miss television because he didn't watch it much, but he hadn't realized how hooked he was on music until it was no longer available. But the more he discussed it with Dr. Camp, the more he realized there were a lot of things about city life he didn't miss at all.

He didn't miss the traffic, and he didn't miss the telephones, and he didn't miss the angry people who were always taking out their resentments on others around them. Come to think of it, he concluded as he left the building, he wasn't all that sure he missed city life all that much. Music? Maybe, but the rest of it he could probably learn to live without.

By the time C.C. got to the communications center, the message from Camp David was complete. It had an ominous tone. An armed gang from Indianapolis — 100 or more strong — was approaching their location. From the information the agent had been able to provide, it appeared they were going to attack the Amish farmers in the New Holland area.

C.C. took the message from the sergeant. His mind was going over a plan of action.

This was not totally unexpected. He knew that eventually the gangs, once they had looted their own communities, would leave the cities. C.C. also realized that the gang leaders, if they were smart enough, probably had some "plants" within each of the relocation camps, but who they were was difficult to ascertain. There were a lot of strange-looking people who had followed them out of the cities. *But strange-looking people seemed to be the norm,* he concluded.

C.C. decided that the one thing they could not do was abandon the Amish people to the gangs from the city. They would have no chance at all.

He wasn't sure he agreed with their passivity, but he did agree with their ethics and Christianity. They had already been of great help to the New Holland camp. Many of them had volunteered time to help the camp members learn how to prepare the ground and plant their seeds. Without their help and encouragement, he wasn't at all sure that the New Holland camp or any other camp would have been able to survive.

He went to the building that served as the community center, courthouse, church, and anything else the camp needed. In accordance with a prearranged plan, he had the young man on duty ring the big church bell that had been relocated to the top of the building. The young boy, about 12 years old, began ringing the big bell with great fervor. All the boys who rotated duty at the community center loved to ring the bell. It was rung at the start of each day, then for lunch, and later to stop work; but in each of those instances it was never rung more than 12 times.

Now the boy began to swing the big clapper back and forth. The big brass bell rang 12 times and then continued as the youngster swung faster and faster. When the workers in the field heard the bell, they gathered up their tools and began to hurry toward the community building. Others within the camp also stopped what they were doing and hurried toward the community center.

Within 10 minutes, virtually every member of the camp was gathered, and C.C. made the announcement: "We have received word from Camp David that an armed gang is on its way from Indianapolis. Their target is the Amish farming community. We can't allow that to happen." Almost as one, the entire group shouted in agreement.

C.C. explained, "We need to separate into our prearranged defense groups. Half of the defense team will remain here in camp for security, and the other half will follow me."

In an earlier meeting it had been decided that all weapons would be collected and stored in one location. The most secure building on the facility was the armory and, other than the weapons needed by camp security, all other weapons were stored there. Within a few minutes C.C. had the weapons distributed among the defense team.

C.C. had been able to procure several hundred automatic weapons from the Army Depot, as well as an adequate supply of ammunition and an assortment of other small armament.

He realized there was no way to know exactly where the gang would attack, but he also knew that they greatly outnumbered the attackers, so he divided his group into units of 200 and began to disperse them across the countryside. At first, the Amish farmers objected. They didn't like the idea of having armed men on their property, but once it was explained to them what was happening, they reluctantly agreed.

Abraham Johnstone, the elected leader of the New Holland Amish community, knew that his people would have no chance against an armed band of marauders, and although they themselves had taken a vow of passivity, he readily accepted the services of the New Holland defense team.

Against C.C.'s better judgment, it was decided that the defense team units would not lay in ambush for the gang but, instead, would confront them as they reached the Amish community. C.C. didn't particularly like that idea. He would far rather have laid in ambush and attacked the gang before they knew what happened. He felt that to do otherwise would expose members of the defense team to needless risk. But since it was either that or have the Amish people kick them off their land, he reluctantly agreed.

His men had been in position for hours and still no sign of the gang. What happened was that the gang was totally disorganized, wandering off whenever they saw anything of interest. Although most of the communities had been razed by previous gangs, some of his men went off in pursuit of easier, closer prey.

By the time they got well out of the city, Molinari's advance group was down to 30 or less. All he could hope was that his lieutenants following behind would be able to keep the largest contingent in line. Even Molinari was not sure now that leaving the city was the great idea he'd originally thought it was. He was tired, hungry and, more than that, he was very thirsty. Instead of packing water, as they should have, the poorly organized city gang had packed alcohol. Molinari quickly discovered the last thing a thirsty man needed was a drink of whiskey.

The further out of the city he got, the less comfortable he felt. He was out of his element, but he was committed now, and to back down was to admit weakness. He knew what he needed was in the hands of some soft-shelled Bible toters, and he meant to have it.

For his part, Lt. Hardy tried to discourage as many of the gang members as possible. He complained about how good it was in the city and how bad it was out in the country. By the time the gang had gone less than 40 miles, he had been able to discourage several of them. As opportunity would allow, they peeled off and headed back to the city, one at a time.

By the time the ragtag band was approaching the New Holland area, Molinari's head was hurting, and he was raging mad. He intended to take his anger out on the first human beings they made contact with. As the disorderly unit made its way down highway 391 toward New Holland, any trained observer could have heard them coming at least two miles away. Every time one of the gang members saw something move or even thought he saw something move, he would cut down on it with an automatic weapon. It served to warn any residents along the way of the gang's presence, and they were able to slip away into the woods. They were able to observe the gangs, but they were not seen by Molinari and his group.

Molinari tried in vain to silence the shooting. Once, when one of the men in his own cart fired his weapon, Molinari turned, fully intent on silencing the young punk personally;

however, when he raised his weapon he was met by a dozen other weapons pointed in his direction. He could see his control diminishing the further out of the city they got.

He was determined to push on. They needed the food and water; but, more than anything else, he needed something to preoccupy his men. To be sure, the Amish women would do that.

C.C. had established roadblocks on every highway in and out of New Holland. He had correctly assessed that the gangs would not trek across open country but would stick to the paved roads. As a second precaution, he set up barriers and kept about 50 men behind each one. He took at least 100 defenders and hid them in the woods opposite the barricades. He had promised Abraham that he wouldn't ambush the gangs. However, he had not promised that he wouldn't set a trap.

It was nearly evening when the first contingent of Molinari's ragtag army made its way over the hill and down the last slope into New Holland. Molinari knew so little about open country that he didn't realize he had passed more than two dozen farms on his way into the city. His whole mentality evolved around city living and, therefore, he just naturally assumed that the people and the things he needed would be located in the city of New Holland itself.

He was startled to find a roadblock in his

way and an armed contingent blocking his path. He had expected to see Amish farmers who would simply collapse at the first shot and allow him to take whatever he wanted. He was not expecting this. He also was not expecting to see someone as imposing as C.C. standing in his way carrying an M-18.

"Whatta ya want!" Molinari shouted as he stepped down from the cart he'd been riding in. "Get out of my way!"

C.C. merely pulled the bolt back on the automatic weapon, ratcheting a shell into the chamber, but the effect was electrifying. In the dwindling light, Molinari was assessing the strength of the band before him. He knew that he had about 30 men, all armed, but he wasn't sure how many of them he could depend on in a one-on-one fight. Before him he saw 40 or 50 men, well-armed and well-positioned. He decided that his best method of attack would be ambush.

C.C. spoke up. "Who are you and what do you want here?"

Molinari countered arrogantly, "Who wants to know? We got a right to be here just like you do."

"You've got *no* rights except the ones I give you, punk," C.C. said in a threatening tone. "I want you and your men to turn around and get out of here."

Molinari was furious. Nobody talked to him like that — at least nobody who lived to tell about it. He heard the murmuring behind him as his men also assessed the odds and didn't like them. Molinari knew, if he lost face he would also lose his command. He wasn't about to risk that.

He told his men, "Okay guys, turn it around. Let's go. We don't want any trouble." His intent was to catch C.C. off guard and then attack with all the fury his band of wanton killers was capable of.

C.C. had already thought two steps ahead of Molinari and assessed the situation. He signaled to someone in back of him, who reached down and took a firebrand out of the fire and began to wave it above his head. On that signal, 50 men from each side of the road moved in on the gang. At the same time, those behind the barricade ratcheted shells into the chambers of their weapons.

The one thing Molinari was familiar with was the sound of bullets moving into the chambers of automatic weapons, and the sound was riveting. He wheeled around, weapon in hand. At the same time, the men in the carts looked around and saw the movement to the left and right of them. Armed men — more than 100 of them moving in on their position. They were trapped.

"Throw down your weapons!" C.C. commanded the gang leader. "Throw down your weapons, or I'll have my men attack."

Molinari was panic-stricken. His eyes

darted to and fro. They were big and wide in the glow of the fire. He knew he was hopelessly outmanned. He also knew that if he didn't do something, he would cease to be the leader. He slowly began to move his weapon into position. *If I can cut down the big man, maybe we'll have a chance,* he thought.

But he had hardly moved when he felt the cold steel behind his right ear. Lt. James Hardy said coldly, "Put your weapon down. It's all over." Molinari stood there for what seemed like an eternity — not moving. He could feel the cold steel of the weapon behind his right ear and beads of sweat on his forehead.

"Okay," Hardy said coldly as he cocked the hammer of the weapon.

Dropping his weapon, Molinari cried out, "No! No! Don't kill me! Please don't kill me!" Then the other gang members followed his lead, and one by one the weapons clanked to the floor of the cart or to the asphalt outside. Hardy led Molinari down from the cart and, still holding his pistol behind Molinari's ear, led him over to where C.C. was standing.

"Lieutenant James Hardy, U.S. Marine Corps," he said to C.C.

"Glad to know you. Just call me C.C. I'm a member of the president's Secret Service staff."

"Secret Service out *here?*" Hardy said incredulously.

"Yes. We have the solar observation team and Dr. Hobart at a nearby camp," C.C. answered. Hardy just nodded in agreement. "Now, what are we going to do with these guys?" C.C. asked the young lieutenant.

"Well my suggestion is that you take their weapons and their transportation and head them toward D.C., where they'll be more comfortable, I'm sure."

A cold chill went through Molinari. It was the last thing he wanted to hear. It would have been better for him to die in battle.

C.C. chuckled. "You know, Lieutenant, I think you're right." He ordered his men to gather all the weapons. Then he ordered them to search the gang members for additional weapons. Once they had done that, he quipped, "Well, that's a neat little addition to our armory. Now," he said, looking Molinari straight in the eyes, "get back to your holes."

Molinari snarled at the big man, but his courage was broken. He turned, and with the rest of his band, except for Lt. Hardy, began to head toward the city. It had been a 12-hour ride to the New Holland community. It would take twice that long to walk back.

Walking back to his gang, he ordered, "Let's go. The rest of our gang will be coming up behind us. When they catch up, we'll have plenty of weapons. We're gonna come back here and teach these people a lesson."

One thing about Molinari, he was a bully but he wasn't a leader, and he certainly didn't read his gang very well. As soon as they were out of sight of the camp, they began to grumble.

"You led us into a trap," one of the gang known as Snake said. No one knew his real name but called him Snake because of tattoos that ran the length of both muscular arms.

Molinari, who was much shorter than most of the other men, was used to leading by intimidation, and in the city he might have been in his element — but no longer. He made the mistake of lunging at the bigger man and striking him with an open palm. "Nobody talks to me like that," Molinari snarled at Snake.

But instead of drawing back, as he would have before, the man came around with the back of his hand and caught Molinari on the cheek. The force of his blow slapped the smaller man to the ground. Like a wounded animal, Molinari jumped to his feet. He reached down inside his boot where he normally kept a knife, only to realize that he'd been stripped of the weapon at the roadblock.

He looked into Snake's eyes and what he saw terrorized him. There was a smirk on his face and a glint in his eye as he approached Molinari. He grabbed Molinari by his shirt, pulling him forward and, at the same time, punching him in his solar plexus. Molinari collapsed like a sack of potatoes and let out a moan. Snake snapped him to his feet again and slapped him twice across his face.

"Listen, punk," Snake said, "you're no longer in charge."

"Yeah," several of the others growled.

Molinari, who was just beginning to recover his breath, gasped, "You can't do this." The big man shook him, like a terrier shaking a rat. He slapped him across the face three or four more times.

"Shut up, punk," Snake said, slapping him again. Molinari began to whimper.

"Pick up my stuff," the bigger man said as he released Molinari, who collapsed to the ground. He started to protest again when he saw Snake draw his leg back.

"Wait . . . okay, okay!" Molinari cried out. "Don't hurt me anymore."

"Pick up my stuff!" the big man commanded again. Molinari, totally broken now, reached down and picked up the backpack. It was so heavy, he could barely lift it, but Snake showed no sympathy. He'd been waiting for his chance to show up Molinari and the time had come.

"You can either carry it or stay here," Snake growled. "Either way, don't matter to me."

Molinari hoisted the backpack to his shoulders and, shifting the weight as best he could, staggered down the road after what had been his gang.

Back at the roadblock, C.C. was talking to Lt. Hardy. "Glad to have you, Lieutenant. Think you could take over this roadblock?"

"I'd be glad to," Hardy said. With that, C.C. transferred his weapon to the Lieutenant and headed back to the camp.

This is just the first, C.C. thought. *Once the food runs out, there will be others, and they may not be as stupid as this bunch.*

25

Two days passed and no further sign of the gang appeared, so C.C. assumed they had withdrawn to the city. It didn't mean that they wouldn't return again; they well might. If they did, he knew he wouldn't catch them unaware again, but the crisis was over — at least temporarily.

The New Holland community, as with many other of the camp communities across the country, began to settle into a daily routine, with most of the people working the fields to grow the food they would need to survive the winter. But alarming reports from other camps began to come into Camp David.

Some of the camps, like New Holland and half a dozen others, were well organized and were right on schedule. Theoretically, all the camps had enough food to last through the winter, but for those who didn't grow enough food it meant drastically reduced rations. And if the winter was more severe than normal, it could bring disaster.

Gen. Boland would have liked to reallocate some of the food stocks, but it was impossible. Nothing except horse-drawn equipment was available, and that would not do the job.

Interior Secretary Oren Blake was doing the best job he could but it was woefully inadequate.

Blake had located virtually every means of transportation available and had pressed it into service. There was not enough transportation to make any significant impact on the problems the camps would be facing.

The cities were virtually abandoned. There was no alternative. As the gangs grew bolder, it was clear that even the armed military personnel wouldn't be able to hold out. The gangs themselves were fighting one another for the remaining supplies that were still available in the cities.

Relief centers were set up where possible, but what the gangs didn't destroy, the rioting tenants, desperate for food, did.

The reports from every major city in America were basically the same: Life in the cities was unsustainable.

Even in Miami, where the climate would not be a factor during the winter, there were almost no supplies left. Gang members and citizens alike stole and looted. With all utilities inoperable, people were relegated to drinking dirty water and gathering coal or wood for cooking.

Disease was rampant within the cities. With virtually no medical supplies left, diseases that had once been eliminated in the U.S. erupted again. Diseases like scurvy and typhus and even tuberculosis were again on the upswing. It was only a matter of time until one of the ancient plagues — like bubonic — would break out; perhaps they already had in other parts of the world. Rumors were now filtering into Camp David that in other parts of the world total anarchy existed. Rich and poor didn't exist, because as supplies ran out material wealth meant nothing.

In lower Chicago, Kafu Mafumi, a gang leader there, called a council meeting of what was left of his gang. The whole organization had fallen apart. At best, it had been a loosely knit group, unified only by their common goal: to spread drugs throughout the city of Chicago. At one time Mafumi had controlled an organization that did $25 million a year in drug traffic, but now the drugs had run out and the kids they had once supplied were either gone or dead. The gang had fallen upon hard times.

Lately their days consisted of getting up cold and dirty, to no running water, and scouring the streets of lower Chicago, looking for anything they could find to eat. They had long since stripped all the existing drugstores and pharmacies of whatever drugs were available, and many members of the gang had died trying to take what they thought were narcotics, but which turned out to be poisons.

Mafumi was not only losing control, he was

losing his contact with reality. He'd gone through the withdrawals of drug addiction and had come out the other side, but several members of his gang had not survived the ordeal. Some had committed suicide, and others had been driven crazy by their craving for the drugs that no longer existed. Mafumi's organization now was down to 14 men and women.

"Man, we're gonna have to do somethin' different," Mafumi said angrily to the group. "Every one of ya bring in everything ya got. We're gonna put it all together and see what we got. We're gonna have ta get outta this city 'fore it crumbles on our heads." What Mafumi didn't recognize was that the 14 men and women he was addressing were no longer under his authority. Those who had survived were clear-headed, the drugs having worn off. They saw the city for what it was: a jungle, a burnt-out hulk of a jungle, in which they were trapped.

Dora Shine couldn't remember the last time she'd been able to think clearly. She was only 19 years old, and yet she looked more like 39 years old. She'd been on the streets for almost six years. She'd been prostituting herself for drugs since she was 11. Her brain had not been drug-free since she was a kid, but now she was clean, and she never intended to get hooked on drugs again.

"I'm finished. It's all finished," she declared. "I'm gettin' outta here."

Mafumi was furious. "You ain't goin' no place," he shouted. "You belong to me. All of ya belong to me, and you'll do just what I say."

Dora responded defiantly, "I don't belong to nobody but myself. You don't control me no more. I'm gonna find my family."

As she turned to leave, Mafumi reached behind him and produced the 9mm automatic he always had tucked in his belt.

"Stop!" he commanded her, "Or I'll shoot."

"So, shoot!" she said calmly. "Do me a favor and shoot. Look around ya," she said to the onetime gang leader. "You have nothing. The city's in ruins. There's no food. There's no water. Even the people left around here are eatin' rats. Is that what you want? Give it up, Mafumi," she said coldly. "It's over."

Mafumi ratcheted a cartridge into the chamber of the weapon he was holding. "Stop!" he commanded as he raised the weapon. But even as he did so, he realized the futility of it all. For the first time in as long as he could remember, his brain was drug-free as well. He suddenly realized, *It really is over. Dora's right.* The demon that haunted him every night was back again; and with no drugs to dull the fear, he lived on the edge of insanity. He wasn't afraid to die. He was afraid to live.

Mafumi lowered the weapon, looked at the other members of his gang and said, "Get outta here!" With that, Mafumi turned away, raised the weapon to his head, and pulled the trigger.

After a few moments of stunned silence, Dora opened the door to leave, and the other gang members turned to follow her. She took the AK-47 she was carrying and leaned it against the wall as she walked out. Inside she could hear the clatter of weapons as gang members dropped them beside where Dora had left hers. The fight was out of them. All they wanted was to get out of the city.

As Dora walked down the alley, a young woman in ragged and filthy clothes bolted from behind a pile of boxes.

"Wait!" Dora said, grabbing the woman by the shoulders.

She screamed, "Please don't hurt me! I got nothing. My children are starvin'."

"I'm not gonna hurt ya," Dora said gently. "I wanta help ya. You gotta get outta this city. Winter's coming, and if we're caught here we'll all die, includin' your kids."

"Oh, God, help me," the young woman cried. As the tears came from her eyes, they streaked the filth caked on her face. It had been three days since she or her children had eaten. There was practically nothing left and if she found anything, as she had a couple of times before, she couldn't make it home without somebody taking it away from her.

Her two-year-old daughter and four-year-old son were holed up in the basement of one of the burnt-out buildings, and they were near starvation. She'd been able to catch one of the rats in her building a few days earlier, and they had cooked it over the charcoal grill using bits of wood from the building, but now even the rats were scarce. They should have evacuated when it was possible, and now she and her children were trapped in the city.

"Don't worry," Dora told her. "I'm gonna stay with you. We'll get your kids out of this city. I promise you." She had a small stash of foodstuffs hidden in her room. It would last them a few days — hopefully long enough to get well away from the city. She felt alive again. She was a human being helping another human being, instead of acting like an animal. With the gang she had stolen and pillaged until there was nothing left. Now at least she could give something back.

The summer months passed quickly in the camps, and most of the evacuees looked toward winter with fear and apprehension. When possible, trees were felled and sturdier, more permanent structures were erected.

In New Holland, C.C. often joked about the avid environmentalists in the camp who chopped down trees right along with the loggers. "A little self-preservation seems to lower our resistance to eco-pillaging," he told Jason with a chuckle.

"Well, fortunately, the trees will grow again," Jason said. "We just need to manage the natural assets, not worship them."

"Right you are, Professor," C.C. agreed. "What's the latest on the flares?"

"They appear to be less frequent . . . and weaker," Jason said, "but there's no change in the magnetic poles. So that means still no electricity."

"How long do you think this will last?"

"Who knows, C.C," Jason said a little wearily. "Maybe tomorrow; maybe forever."

"Wow," C.C. said. "I guess we'd better plan like it's forever and pray it's tomorrow. Right, Professor?"

"Right you are," Jason agreed. "Right you are."

Five months had passed since the evacuations had begun. Summer was nearly over, and soon the colors of fall would be settling upon the land. A few families were still escaping the cities the best they could. Every so often one or two would stumble into the camp with horror stories about what was happening in the cities.

Even outside the big cities, the situation was getting desperate. The available food stocks were almost depleted. The few families that were able to find food were subsisting on meager rations. The supplies consisted mostly of canned goods and dehydrated foods supplied by the government.

President Houston knew it would be difficult, if not impossible, for those still in the cities to survive through the winter, and he made a determined effort to evacuate those remaining in the cities if humanly possible.

He called in Oren Blake to discuss the situation. "Oren, how much transportation do we have available?"

"Not enough, Mr. President. We estimate that there are still at least 10 million people in the cities."

"Including the gangs?" Houston asked.

"Yes, Sir, although you can hardly call them gangs anymore. Some of them still control the inner-city areas, but others have laid down their weapons and are begging to be rescued from the cities."

"Well how about that!" the president said.

Gen. Boland spoke up. "Mr. President, we've begun a systematic disarming of the gangs who want to leave the cities. We've told them if they want to get out, they have to walk out with no arms."

"How much success are you having?" Houston asked.

"Pretty good, Sir. I would estimate that at least half of all the gangs are willing to lay down their arms."

"What are you doing with them?"

"We're trying to relocate them to some of the closer camps, but it's been pretty difficult."

"How so?" Houston asked.

"Many of the camp members remember these gangs, and they're not willing to take them in."

"Can't say I blame them," Houston said. "What alternatives do you have?"

"Well," the general said, propping his feet up on the table in front of him with the informality that had developed over the last few months, "my suggestion is that we divide them up and spread them out across all the camps. The discipline in most camps is pretty good, and the people there won't tolerate any nonsense from these guys. Without the drugs involved, I think they can be rehabilitated — at least some of them can."

"Floyd, do whatever you have to do," Houston said. "I just want to move as many people out of the cities as we can."

"Understood, Mr. President. We'll do our best."

"Good. Just keep me informed."

At the New Holland camp, as with many of the camps across the country, things were proceeding pretty well. Thanks to the Amish farmers' training, the ground had been tilled and planted in a timely fashion, and now the crops were ready to be harvested.

It was a beautiful autumn evening. Jason and Annette were sitting on the steps of the observation building. Other than observing the Sun through the telescope, they had not been able to do a great deal of work. None of their equipment was operable. Jason was convinced that the solar activity was diminishing.

The huge solar flare that had erupted several months before had been followed by several big but lesser flares — almost like aftershocks. Most of these had dissipated and no more visible flares had occurred for nearly a month. The Earth's magnetic poles were still reversed, but he was convinced that the activity from area 403 was dying out.

However, without electronic instruments he had to rely on guesswork. They had tried to start the manual diesel generator a few days earlier and the engine ran fine. But when the generator was coupled to the motor, sparks flew everywhere and the shaft snapped. Jason assumed the laws of physics were still not functioning on planet Earth. Every time he talked with the president, Houston always asked, "When?"

Jason could only tell him, "I honestly don't know."

One thing he did know: The more time he spent with Annette the more he fell in love with her. He was trying to work up the courage to ask her to marry him, and he had decided that this would be the night.

Annette was getting more than just a little impatient with Jason. Although she didn't show it, she had already decided that she was going to marry Jason Hobart, if he would ever ask her. And contrary to the modern philosophy, she was not going to be the one to propose. She knew Jason was a shy man and needed to be the leader in his home, and that lead had to start with *him* asking *her* to be his wife.

"What are you thinking about, Jason?" she asked, glancing over at him.

Jason, who had been lost in thought about how he was going to ask Annette to marry him, glanced up, and as their eyes met Jason reached over and took her hand.

"I was thinking about how much I love you," he told her in a very matter-of-fact tone.

"I know," she responded just as matter-of-factly, imitating him. "I love you, too."

"You do?" he said in surprise. "Then will you marry me?" he asked.

"Why certainly, Professor Hobart," she said with a grin. "I've already been waiting nearly two months for you to ask me."

"You have?" It hadn't occurred to Jason that she felt the same about him.

"Why naturally. Wendy and I have already decided that we want to have a fall wedding — Thanksgiving, we think. I was afraid you were going to wait until winter to ask me," she said with a teasing tone.

Jason's face lit up and a big grin crossed his face. "You mean, you and Wendy both have been plotting this?"

"Why certainly," she said. "What would you expect of the two favorite women in your life?"

Jason reached over and gave her a big hug and then kissed her like he'd been wanting to for so long. "We need to tell Wendy," he said.

"I agree," Annette replied. "Where is she?"

"I don't know," Jason said, "but she'll be somewhere close."

The two of them walked hand in hand over to the assembly building where C.C. was meeting with a group from the camp. They were discussing where the harvest would be stored and how they would prepare for the winter. Special storage sheds had to be built before the first snows.

Jason had seen a tremendous change in C.C. — a kind of softening. The gentle man had given his testimony several times to different groups within the camp about how, when he was younger, his grandmother told him that she had prayed that he would go into the ministry.

His grandmother, a committed Christian, had prayed for him since his birth. C.C. had accepted Christ one summer as a young man in a church camp, but over the years his relationship with God had grown cold; and although he still considered himself a Christian, C.C. had drifted away from the Lord. But since being in the New Holland camp, he had recommitted himself to the Lord. Now he actually led a Bible study within the camp. Attendance at the Bible study had grown to more than 500.

The influence of Christianity on the camp was profound. The assembly had voted to adopt biblical standards of law. A woman who was skilled in calligraphy had written out the Ten Commandments and they were posted throughout the camp. Others within the community had written other Scripture verses that were prominently posted throughout the camp. It was clear that the pilgrims of the twentieth century had no difficulty with the somewhat theistic form of government within their own community. Without interference from the federal court system and the ACLU, Scripture noticeably adorned every building and every wall in the camp.

The few people within the camp who had initially objected had been won over, because as a result of the Christian influence in the camp, crime was virtually nonexistent, and the crime that was committed was dealt with swiftly and fairly by the camp leaders. It had been decided that no prison walls would ever house one of the New Holland family. Instead, those who stole were required to apologize publicly and make restitution. Those who assaulted another person, were required to apologize publicly and spend time in the stocks.

With each crime there was an equitable punishment being meted out fairly — but firmly. Those who refused the punishment and refused to apologize were put out of the community to fend for themselves. After the first five or six people had been evicted, there were very few violations of the camp laws.

Jason searched until they found Wendy in a women's Bible study being led by Dixie Raye — a beautiful woman, easily recognized by everyone in the camp because she had been a major Hollywood star prior to the solar flare. Her Christian testimony had been well-ignored by the media during her film career, but her roots were solid. She had made a commitment to Christ as a young girl and had stayed true to that commitment all of her life. When others in Hollywood were drinking and carousing and sleeping around, trying to get ahead, she'd never compromised her value system. Her looks and talent had carried her to the very top of stardom in Hollywood, as more Americans supported films with good family values.

Now, with no films, no videos, and no movies, her true character had come out once again. She had been a blessing to many people in the camp. She worked as hard as anyone else in the fields by day. And then in the evenings she taught Bible studies and shared her faith with many of the young girls in the camp.

This evening she was in Wendy's part of the camp. For over an hour Wendy had been listening to Dixie share her testimony about how God had allowed her to have a great career and to make millions of dollars, most of which she had given away. She told how grateful she was that God had allowed her to be a part of the New Holland community. She knew that many of her friends in Hollywood had decided to stay in the city and very likely had lost their lives trying to protect their possessions.

She quoted the Scripture where Jesus said, "[The one] *who is faithful in a very little thing is faithful also in much.*" And she told the girls how material things, money, fame, success, and beauty were the smallest of things because all of them could disappear. "Only the love of Jesus will last forever," she said.

Dixie was nearing the end of her testimony when Jason and Annette walked up behind the group. There were nearly 200 young girls listening intently to this beautiful actress as she shared her faith.

"In conclusion," she said, "if there's anybody here who would like to know Jesus Christ as their personal Savior, I invite you to come forward and invite Him into your heart today."

Jason was a little startled when he saw Wendy jump up and go forward, along with about 60 other girls. At the front, Wendy bowed with the other girls as Dixie shared with them the saving message of Jesus Christ and prayed the prayer of salvation. Jason and Annette stood in the back for nearly 20 minutes, until the session was over.

The minute Wendy spied her father and Annette, she ran back to where they were, her face beaming. Jason had never seen her so radiant.

"Daddy!" she shouted excitedly, "I just accepted Jesus Christ as my Savior. I've become a Christian!"

Jason mumbled a bit, not knowing exactly what to say. His daughter clearly had experienced something meaningful to her, because there was an undeniable change in her demeanor. "Well, that's great, Sweetheart. I'm really happy for you."

Annette reached out and hugged Wendy. Jason was startled to hear Wendy say, "You were right, Annette. It's the greatest feeling I've ever had."

Jason looked at Annette. "Annette?" he said in a questioning tone.

"Jason, I wanted to tell you, but I . . . I didn't exactly know how. A few weeks ago, I accepted Christ as my Savior as well. You're a good man, Jason, and I know that God wants you to be one of His own as well. Wendy and I have been praying for you, and now that Wendy's a Christian, we know you'll be next."

"She's right, Daddy. God wants you too."

"You could be right. Tell me about it," he said, directing his remark to Annette.

For the better part of the next hour Wendy and Annette alternately shared with Jason what they had learned and what they had found in the Lord. That evening, Jason knelt with his daughter and his future wife and accepted Jesus Christ as his Savior.

Later that evening as they were walking back to the living quarters, Jason said, "Now we've gotta work on C.C."

"I don't think so," Annette responded.

"Why is that?" Jason asked.

"Because it was C.C. who told me about Jesus," Annette said.

26

The president woke up to a beautiful fall morning and the sound of birds chirping outside his window. As he pushed the covers back and sat on the edge of the bed, he thought, *It's funny. The birds don't know and don't care that anything has happened. Here I am — the president — the leader of the strongest nation on Earth, and I don't even have a way to communicate with the people of America. It's really amazing how puny we are when it comes right down to it. There are billions of stars in the universe, and among those billions of stars I understand that our star is fairly insignificant as stars go. Yet one little burp from our star and this planet is virtually shut down. Amazing how we human beings tend to think more highly of ourselves than we should.*

Houston had heard the day before that the final efforts to evacuate the cities were going better than expected. They didn't have a lot of transportation, but the people who were left in the cities were desperate to leave now and brought with them tales of horror — of people turning against other people. Not only were the gangs preying upon the people of the cities but, as the food ran out and civilization broke down, neighbors began to prey upon neighbors, the stronger upon the weaker.

We haven't really done much to improve civilization over the last several thousand years, Houston concluded. *Even the gangs are now willing to evacuate the cities.* The gangs were coming out unarmed, begging for food, but Houston didn't know what to do with them.

During the last few months he had often reflected on the early pilgrims and how they must have suffered. They traveled thousands of miles from home. Often half of them died on the boats; then they landed on the shores of America, only to starve to death during the winter because so many of them refused to work. Houston had read and reread the works of William Bradford, governor of the Massachusetts Bay Colony, and how Bradford had relied upon biblical wisdom to save the people from starvation.

Houston got angry every time he thought about what the Supreme Court of the United States had done to America: declaring God to be dead, prohibiting prayer in the classrooms, removing morality from the courts, allowing sexual filth under the banner of free speech, and killing millions of unborn children in the name of convenience. *It's no wonder we are where we are,* he thought somberly. *I just hope some of the liberal justices stayed in the cities to witness firsthand their own handi-*

work. After thinking about it briefly though, he decided, probably not. They would have been the first ones to run.

He vowed silently, *Well that's all over. No longer will the federal court system in America dictate to the American people what they should or should not believe and what they should or should not hold as right and wrong. Never again will the people allow that to happen.*

For the last several weeks, members of the Congress had been coming to Camp David, as transportation would allow, and he knew the sentiment in Congress was exactly the same — Democrats and Republicans alike. They had experienced the horror of society at its very worst, and they were committed to raising society from the moral morass into which it had sunk over the last three or four decades. Many of them had confessed their part in the demoralizing and dehumanizing of America, all in the name of free speech, personal rights, or social justice. Never again, they had decided. From this point on, right is right and wrong is wrong. Most agreed that allowing the Ten Commandments to be displayed again was the starting point.

The contrast between life in the cities, where society had broken down, and life in the camps was startling. For the first few months there had been a lot of groaning and griping in the camps — more by the teenagers than by anyone else, because they had lost their entertainment source. No longer did the boob tube dull their minds every night until they went to sleep; nor did the rock music and rap scream out obscenities and discontent. They were not able to feast on sex and violence on the big screen or waste countless hours on violent video games — all to the joy of most parents.

Other things had slowly begun to fill their lives. During the day when the adults were working the fields, the children were organized into study groups. Most of the people in the camps, being nonprofessional educators, relied upon commonsense teaching. They went back to the basics — the ABCs of learning. They concentrated on teaching the children to read and write and to add and subtract, without the use of electronic calculators. With the calculators and computers gone, most of the youths in the camp had to learn how to think on their own.

Afternoons, when the families came back from the fields, games were organized — games that many of the older people remembered from their youth: kickball, dodgeball, softball, and soccer games that involved adults and children together. At night, with no television and no distractions, families ate their meals together. In fact, groups of families would often eat together. Later, the more proficient readers in the group would read stories, and the children would sit around enthralled as they learned to use their imaginations instead of being spoon-fed a lot of slick programming.

The rules in the camp were fairly simple: no stealing, no lying, no violence; and for the unmarried couples, particularly the teenagers, no sex. To be sure, early on there were some problems, including several pregnancies. The consequences were harsh by twenty-first century standards — lenient by nineteenth century standards.

Both the boy and girl were publicly confronted. The families of both were held responsible and required to administer the discipline. The boy forfeited one-third of his daily ration to the yet unborn child. For the teens under 17, the child was offered for adoption, first to the grandparents and then to others in the community. No unwed mothers were allowed to raise children. The rules were stern, but they were designed to promote the community.

Rules that had been lost for generations were reestablished. There were rules of courting that were strictly enforced. Boys and girls were not allowed to go out unescorted. Those who did spent time in the camp kitchen washing dishes and mopping. Repeat offenders spent time in the stocks. The net result was that teen pregnancy dropped to zero.

In closely knit societies, such as the camp,

everybody knows their neighbors' business. This helps to maintain order. At New Holland, a married man and woman were caught in adultery, so a meeting of the leadership was held, and the couple was brought before them. The shame of being caught probably would have been punishment enough, in and of itself, but having been caught, tried, and convicted before the committee, it was the decision of the committee that both the man and woman should spend one full day in the stocks, with signs naming their indiscretion. And they did.

After that, the incidence of infidelity dropped dramatically. Of course there was some grumbling and mumbling from some elements of the camp, particularly those who once had been of a more liberal persuasion, but the majority of the camp population agreed with the public punishment. It was clear that most people were sick and tired of the lack of responsibility on the part of their fellow Americans. And now that each person depended upon the others for their very survival, community rights superseded personal rights.

As life in the camps began to grow more commonplace, so did religion. Various religions were represented in the camps, including Judaism, Catholicism, atheism, and Islam, and all competed for the hearts and the souls of the people. But, in the end, it was Christianity that prevailed. The religious heritage of America was Christian, and the majority of the population associated with it.

Once people understood the role religion had played on the ethics and morality of early America, there was a renewed interest. In the New Holland camp, a true revival broke out. In one month more than 17,000 residents accepted Christ as their Savior or recommitted their lives. By majority vote, it was decided to reestablish religious studies for the children. The Bible became a text that once again was acceptable to teach children, because it taught them right from wrong.

In the New Holland camp, a major crisis arose. Late one evening in mid-September, a ten-year-old girl named Journeyah Walker was missing from the camp. Once it was discovered that she was missing, the entire camp spread out to find her. Two hours later they discovered her body in the woods about three miles outside the camp. An investigation was started immediately and C.C. and several members of the leadership began to question people. Within a few hours a pattern was pieced together, and it was discovered that the girl had last been seen playing outside her hut. The last person who had been seen talking to her was a 39-year-old unattached male named Donny Harbor.

Harbor was brought before the committee and questioned thoroughly. As more and more evidence was pieced together, it was obvious to the members of the committee that he had abducted Journeyah. A further check into his background revealed that he had been convicted previously as a child molester. The man was held under close house arrest while a jury was formed. Judge Benjamin Holt of the Fifth District Appellate Court was appointed to hear the trial.

Before the flare, Judge Holt had been known as one of the more liberal judges in the federal judiciary. Holt had been a strong advocate of civil rights, especially the rights of the accused, and many times he had been responsible for releasing convicted felons and convicted murderers, because of technicalities.

C.C. told Jason, "I don't think Judge Holt should be allowed to hear this case."

"I understand your feelings," Jason said, "but if we only choose the judges and juries that fit our profile, we'll be just as guilty as the liberals of trying to stack the deck."

"But Holt's likely to let the man off on a technicality."

"I don't think so," Jason said. "I've gotten to know Judge Holt over the last few months, and he understands that he and others like him were part of the problem in America. We've had many discussions, and Judge Holt told me that now he realizes that the judicial system was out of control. He admitted that judges were trying to make law rather than interpret it, and the rights of the accused were put above the rights of the victims."

"Well, I sure hope you're right," C.C. said, "because if we let this murderer off it will encourage others who might be thinking the same way."

"We're going to have to trust God on this one," Jason said. "I want a true operating democracy — not a dictatorship."

Sentiment inside the camp was running very high. One group that was close to Journeyah's family was trying to stir up the crowd to form a vigilante committee.

"Holt's going to let him off," one of the women said. "He's one of the liberal judges that ruined this nation."

"I agree!" somebody else shouted.

"Harbor shouldn't be allowed to live!" another shouted back.

Soon there was a crowd of about 50 people, their angry voices rising as they headed toward the assembly building. Lt. James Hardy, who had become the adjutant general of the camp and as such was responsible for law enforcement, met the crowd in front of the assembly building.

"Bring him out!" someone shouted. The crowd roared with agreement.

Hardy stood in front of the group unarmed. He addressed them, "Friends, listen. I abhor what this man is accused of as much as you do, but mob rule is not the answer. If we dissolve into mobs, this community will fall apart. You have to be willing to trust the legal system."

The little girl's mother cried out, "This killer's a product of the legal system. Twice before he's been convicted of molesting young girls and was let off. If they had punished him the way he deserved, my Journeyah would still be alive today."

"I can't disagree with what you're saying," Hardy said compassionately. "But vigilante justice will not solve this problem. Trust the system. Remember that Judge Holt is not some elite member of the judicial system anymore. He's one of us. Every one of you has seen Judge Holt working in the fields. He's worked side by side with all of us."

"He's part of the liberal federal judiciary!" someone shouted.

"He *was* part of that judiciary," Hardy corrected them. "Judge Holt is now a member of the New Holland community. I believe he'll do what's right. Give him a chance."

C.C. walked up beside Hardy. "Friends, remember this," C.C. said. "You're here with your families, with enough food to eat and places to sleep, because someone in the federal system had the courage to make some difficult choices. So give the system a chance. If we're to ever create the kind of community that God wants us to have, each of us individually have to be willing to give up our rights to a greater cause collectively."

The arguments by Hardy and C.C. turned the tide. The crowd began to simmer down, and although from time to time somebody would shout an objection C.C. knew they had won.

The interesting phenomenon within the camp community, C.C. noticed, was the lack of profanity. In a society where at one time four-letter words were considered commonplace, even acceptable, they were virtually unheard in the New Holland community. It was one thing to shout obscenities from a movie screen or from a passing car and quite another thing to shout them at a neighbor you were working side by side with in the fields.

"All this society needed was a little hard work," C.C. once commented to Jason.

"Pretty profound," Jason said. "I think you're probably more right than anybody would suspect. Americans had become lazy, and in their idle time they had become pretty profane as well."

For several hours, prospective jurors were interviewed. It was going to be difficult to get an impartial jury of 12 people, because most of the people in that camp knew Journeyah Walker or her mother and already had firm convictions about the crime. But after enough people were interviewed, both the defense and the prosecution felt that a fair trial was possible. The defense attorney was Andrew Mallory, an ACLU attorney who had been a close associate of Judge Holt before the flare.

C.C. expressed his concern to Jason, but Jason said, "Harbor has the right to the attorney of his choice."

The next day, Wednesday, October 3, the jury was impaneled, and the trial began. The prosecution first presented its case. At least five eyewitnesses testified that the accused had been seen with Journeyah the night of the crime. Next, the man who used to work in the records department of Washington testified that the accused was in fact a convicted child molester. The defense attorney objected and, much to the surprise of all, Judge Holt overruled. The background of the defendant was pertinent to the case, contrary to what federal law had decided previously. With that one decision, Judge Holt had overthrown the liberal federal judiciary from which he had risen.

All the facts of this case would be brought to the jury, and the jury would be allowed to make a decision based upon the evidence, not legal maneuvering. The prosecution's case was presented in a little over four hours and the defense began to call its witnesses.

One of the witnesses testified that the accused had been with him when the crime was committed but, even before the witness was off the stand, someone in the crowd spoke up. "It's a lie, your Honor. I was with the witness, and the accused was not with us."

Mallory objected, and again Holt overruled and said that if the testimony was pertinent to the trial it had to be brought forward. The witness was temporarily excused while the new witness was sworn in. Under sworn statement he testified that the accused had not been with them on the night of the crime.

When the first witness was brought back to the stand, Judge Holt decided to question him directly. Mallory objected and was overruled once again. He stomped back to his chair, fuming and muttering about the lack of legal protocol.

"I want a straight answer, and I want the truth," Judge Holt said to the witness, "and remember, you are under oath. Was the accused with you the night of the crime?"

The witness, with eyes pointing to the floor, replied, "No, Sir, your Honor. At least not at that time. He had been with me earlier."

Judge Holt said to one of the bailiffs that had been assigned to the court, "I want this man placed in contempt. He will serve three days in the stocks."

"Yes, Sir," the bailiff said, escorting the man out.

That decision set the tone for the rest of the trial, and witnesses that had been lined up by the defendant, when placed on the stand, refused to corroborate the defense's position.

By 5:00 that evening the trial had ended, and the jury had been sent to deliberate. Thirty minutes later the jury came back with the verdict: guilty of murder in the first degree. The recommendation of the jury was execution by hanging.

When the sentence was announced, the defendant broke down and started screaming and crying, begging for mercy. He confessed to the crime and asked for forgiveness. Judge Holt pounded his gavel several times to quieten the crowd. Then looking directly at the defendant, Judge Holt said, "The only mercies you'll get from this court are from God Almighty. The crime you committed is so heinous it deserves no mercy. May God have mercy on your soul." With that, Holt said, "It is the sentence of this court that you be hanged by the neck until dead at 6:00 tomorrow evening." The prisoner was led out of the court.

The next day the perjured witness was seen strapped in the stocks outside of the assembly building, and at 6:00, Journeyah's molester was hanged. The trial might not have passed the muster of the ACLU or the former federal judiciary system, but it satisfied the need for justice in the camps.

After that, those in the New Holland camp who had prior convictions for child abuse, child molestation, or murder were required to register with Judge Holt's court. An objection was raised by some of the more liberal members of the New Holland leadership committee, and a vote was brought before the entire committee two weeks later. The decision was made by a vote of 7 to 3 that all convicted felons would be registered with Judge Holt. As a result, or at least as a consequence of that action, there were no more kidnappings, molestations, or murders in the New Holland community.

It was November and all the crops had been harvested before the first hard freeze. "Well, C.C.," Lt. Hardy said, "it's been an interesting year, hasn't it?"

"You can say that again," C.C. agreed. "And in many ways, you know, it's been the best summer of my life."

"Yeah, me too," Hardy said. "I've discovered a lot of things about myself that I never knew before."

"Oh, yeah? Like what?" C.C. asked.

"Like I make the best canned tomatoes you ever tasted."

C.C. chuckled. "Yeah, I've learned a lot about cooking and canning that I never thought I would know."

"Well, at least we've laid in enough food for the winter and, along with the emergency rations provided by the government, we shouldn't have a problem."

"Yeah, I think you're right," C.C. agreed. "When are you and that girl going to get married?" C.C. asked his friend.

"Married? I'm not sure I'm ready for marriage," Hardy said. "Remember, I'm still a member of the Marine Corps, and we never know where we're going to be stationed."

"Ha!" C.C. laughed, "I rather suspect you're going to be in New Holland, that is at least until we get some lights back on."

"Yeah, I hope so," Hardy said. "Rachel's a great girl. I'm looking forward to having a family of my own, but in all honesty I think, until we're out of this situation, it would be better for me to remain single."

"Well, everybody's entitled to his own opinion," C.C. said, "even if it's wrong." He chuckled as he nudged his friend in the side. "But one thing's for sure. We're going to have a big wedding when the Professor and Dr. Camp get married."

"Yeah, I can hardly wait. I understand they're getting married around Thanksgiving. Is that right?"

"Yeah, I think so. I don't think they've actually set the date yet but, according to Wendy, she'd like for them to get married on Thanksgiving Day."

At the observation building, Jason turned to Annette and said excitedly, "Look! The compass is pointing north again. Sometime during the day the magnetic poles must have reversed again."

"That's wonderful, Sweetheart," Annette responded, "but what does it really mean?"

"Well, I hope it means we can crank up the generator again. I believe the last of the cosmic storms have passed Earth."

Jason motioned to the sergeant in charge of maintenance in the facility and said, "Nick, fire up the main generator again."

"Are you sure, Professor?" the Sergeant said.

"I'm as sure as I can be. Fire it up and let's see what happens."

"Yes, Sir!" Nick said excitedly.

They were getting power back again. Civilization! Within 30 minutes the first of the diesels was up and running, and the output was holding steady for the first time in nearly eight months.

Once the power was up and stable, Jason said to Annette, "It's time to bring the spectrometers up and see what's happening on old Sol up there."

Annette was standing by. She flipped the spectrometer power switches on. Wendy, standing by the S-band spectrometer, flipped hers on as well. They gave them a few minutes to stabilize. Then Jason asked, "Well, how are we doing?"

"On and steady," Annette answered.

"Same here, Dad," Wendy responded.

Jason was monitoring the spectrometer outputs and, clearly, area 403 had stabilized. There was virtually no activity.

"Does this mean it's all over?" Annette asked.

"I believe so," Jason answered. "Let's contact the president and let him know," Jason said to his wife-to-be and daughter.

It took Jason about ten minutes of monitoring to convince himself that area 403 was stable. Jason hurried over to the communications hut and told the sergeant, "Contact the president and tell him it's okay to bring the generators back up," Jason said.

"Yes, Sir!" the sergeant said enthusiastically. "Does that mean that we're going to get something besides the key for communications?"

"I should think so," Jason responded. "We should be able to bring the telephones back online as soon as we get the power up."

It took a few moments for the sergeant to make contact with Camp David, and he conveyed the good news to his counterpart on the other end. The corporal taking messages that day hurried to the Camp David information headquarters. He gave his message to the sergeant in charge, who gave it then to the captain. After reading it, the captain stuffed the note in his pocket and hurried out the door. He went immediately to the presidential residence, where he conveyed his message to the Secret Service agent in charge. Within another three minutes, President Houston had the message in his hand.

"Tell them to fire up the generators," Houston ordered.

"Yes, Sir!" the agent said and hurried off to find the maintenance officer.

It was about 30 minutes before any visible effect could be seen, but at 10:00 A.M. on November 14, the lights at Camp David came back on. Houston hadn't said anything to his staff about the report. Within 15 seconds of the time the lights came back on, there was a knock at his door.

"Come in," Houston responded. It was Warren Butts and Allen Dean at the door.

"Mr. President, did you know the power is back on?" Butts asked.

"Yeah. The professor called and said it's okay to fire up the generators."

"Wow! We're back in civilization again!" Dean exclaimed.

"Yes, unfortunately, with all of its assets and liabilities," Houston sighed. "Warren, I want to concentrate on getting communications operational as quickly as possible. Let's establish the phone link to New Holland and to our other camps and find out what's going on.

"Allen, I want you to contact the press and

let them know that Dr. Hobart has given approval to start powering back up."

"Yes, Sir!" Dean exclaimed.

"Also, Allen, tell them that Professor Hobart cannot guarantee that the solar flares are over, so we're operating on a three-day window. If another flare erupts, we will have three days to power everything down, so we're going to operate with minimal power at first."

"Right. Understood," Dean said as he turned to leave.

Houston thought about the last eight months and what they had meant to his country. The biggest cities in America were in total shambles. By the best estimates his staff could come up with, there was perhaps $5 to $6 trillion worth of damage. He knew that eventually he'd have to begin thinking about what they were going to do with the cities: how they were going to get the people back in to repair them and where the funds were going to come from. But, right now he had more pressing problems to think about. *Winter is coming, and there will be millions of Americans without heat, power, water, and basic foodstuffs.* He called Gen. Boland into his office.

"Floyd, we've gotten the signal to power up and we're operating on a three-day window, but I want you to assume that we're up and operating for awhile. Come up with a plan to get minimal power back on in the cities — at least in some of the buildings that aren't destroyed — and I want to get food and water to the people who are still living there."

"Yes, Mr. President," Boland said. "But it's going to be difficult in the inner cities where the gangs are still in control."

"Understood," the president said. "Establish an area where you can maintain control, and we'll bring the people to us. And Floyd, I want you to begin working on a plan for holding the gangs accountable. I want everyone who was involved in gang activity during this crisis brought to justice."

"Yes, Sir," Boland said with the enthusiasm that he felt inside. Finally, the tide was turning, and they would be able to function normally again. He was anxious to get at the gangs. "A lot of them won't need trials," he vowed.

27

By Thursday morning some parts of America were beginning to wake up again. Power had been restored throughout the Camp David facility and the New Holland camp. A few other camps had minimal power but, since some of them had attempted to operate their generators during daylight hours, many of the generators were inoperative.

Houston sent word to all the power company officials that he wanted to get as much power back online as possible. Many of the military personnel were pressed into service to repair the power systems. It was discovered that parts of the telephone system could be functionally operable within a day or so. Virtually all of the line power amplifiers and regulators had to be replaced, and many of the power generators needed to be refurbished before they would function. But, overall, things were beginning to normalize a little.

Houston was hopeful that within 30 days they would have much of the power and communications back online once again. It wasn't much, but it certainly was a lot better than they'd had for the previous eight months.

As the information began to flow into

Camp David, it was obvious that conditions in the cities were worse than anybody had imagined. In New York, Chicago, and Los Angeles, as well as many other big cities, like Atlanta and Miami, 75 percent of the buildings in the city were structurally unusable, and the other 25 percent were in varying conditions of disrepair. Those that were still serviceable were in the hands of the most resistant of the gangs. Ferreting them out was going to be a long and bloody task for the security forces.

Nobody was sure of how many hostages the gangs had taken, but it was certain that in many areas the gangs had taken prisoners. Already Houston had heard grumblings from the contingent of ACLU about the rights of the gangs.

"Rights!" Boland sputtered as Houston relayed the information. "Rights! Those criminal scum have terrorized people in the cities for the last seven months. They're responsible for tens of thousands, if not hundreds of thousands, of deaths. Rights!" he spat out.

"Take it easy, Floyd," the president said. "You knew we'd be faced with this once the power was back again."

"We're still living on the edge, Mr. President. Winter is coming, and there are millions of people in the cities who will starve or freeze if we don't do something for them, and the camps are not out of danger either. Some of the camps, like New Holland where the leadership is good, are in great shape, but in other camps they either weren't willing or able to grow enough food, and the supplies that we provided them won't last the whole winter."

"I want a plan to get more supplies into those camps, Floyd."

"It can't be done, Mr. President. The stocks have been depleted. There is no more food."

"Then I want communications with those camps," the president said. "If they don't have the right leadership, we want to get new leadership in there. They need to start rationing right now if they're going to make it through this winter alive."

"Already done, Mr. President. It's in process right now. I'll give a report as soon as it's available."

"Thanks, Floyd," the president said. "I appreciate your efficiency."

"Warren, what do you hear about the Congress and the courts?" Boland asked.

"Well, so far we've located six members of the Supreme Court. Unfortunately Justice McConnell was murdered by a gang that attacked her neighborhood."

"That's too bad," Houston said, and he meant it. He disagreed with McConnell, but she deserved better.

"Gerstner was attacked in Richmond, but it looks like he'll pull through. But he lost an eye and may have some permanent brain damage," Butts said. "Neil Farmer was murdered at WNN headquarters in Atlanta."

"How long before we have to deal with the politicians again?" Boland asked.

Houston brushed at some invisible flecks on his desk and took his time about answering. "I knew that's what you were after, Floyd. Well it's hard to say, but I can tell you this: Martial law will stay in effect through this winter, and no matter what anybody says we're going to maintain discipline. After that, we'll just take it a day at a time."

"Great!" Boland replied. He was afraid that Houston, being a consummate constitutionalist, was going to turn the government back over to the few politicians that were clambering to get their hands on it. He had his arguments all ready. He was glad to find out that he wouldn't have to use them — at least not yet.

Gen. Boland left, and the president studied the reports coming in from the cities across the country. It really was bad in the cities — worse than he had realized. It would take years, maybe decades, to rebuild the cities. It was clear that there was going to have to be a major readjustment of priorities in America. America was going to concentrate on itself for a while and not worry about the rest of the world.

There was a knock at the door. "Enter,"

Houston said. A security guard pushed the door open and Emily Hart walked in. "Emily," Houston said with a smile, "how are you doing?"

"Very well, Mr. President," Hart replied. She was dressed in an Air Force jumpsuit, and she really did look like she was doing well. It had been nip and tuck for a while after she was rescued. She had been through a real battering, and she had a lot of emotional scars that wouldn't be healed for a long time.

On her part, Emily was a changed woman. The liberal attitudes that had permeated her whole mind-set were now totally erased. She was a realist. She realized that government had a function and the function was to protect the people — not to provide for their every want and desire. She wasn't sure what the future would hold for her, but the one thing she was sure of, President Philip Houston and the conservative party had an ally in Emily Hart.

As she walked into the president's office, Emily's heart melted once again. She had grown not only to admire but to love this gentle man that represented the sole buffer between the terrorism of the lawless element and the rights of honest citizens. What had impressed Emily more than anything over the past few months was that Houston never had a selfish thought. It was never what he could do for his own future or how he could build an empire out of this, which she knew he could have very easily done. In every discussion in which she participated, Houston's primary concern had been for the safety of the American people and the return of power to the legitimate government of the United States once this crisis was over. Everything she'd ever heard about Houston had been proved wrong.

As she thought back over the years she'd spent in the media, she was ashamed of so many things she had done. Looking back she couldn't believe how thoroughly she'd been duped by Neil Farmer and the other liberals she'd been around for such a long time. They professed to be caring people, but when it came right down to it, they cared mostly about themselves and not about the rights of American people.

"Emily, I called for you because I wanted you to know that we're reestablishing some communications around the country. If you're willing, I would like for you to be my media coordinator. You'll be working closely with Allen Dean. We need to start informing the American people of our plans. We have fairly good communications within the camps, but we're going to need the help of the media if we're to do a coordinated effort. This is extremely important, Emily. If we don't do this thing right, there may be millions of people who will starve or freeze this winter."

"I understand, Mr. President," Hart responded warmly. "I'd be honored to be your media coordinator."

"Thank you," Houston said, walking over to where Hart was standing. Looking directly into her eyes, he said, "Emily, you've become very special to me." He reached out and held both of her hands in his. "I would really like for us to remain friends." Suddenly tears welled up in Hart's eyes and she couldn't contain herself. She began to cry. Then she began to sob. Houston reached out and pulled her to him. "It's all right, Emily. Everything's going to be all right. Why the tears?"

"Oh, Mr. President . . . ," she started.

Then Houston corrected her. "Please call me Phil, at least in private. You make me sound so stuffy when you call me 'Mr. President.' "

Emily smiled through her tears. "Okay, Phil. You just can't imagine all the things I've done in my life that I'm so ashamed of."

"You know what?" Houston said, holding her by the shoulders and looking into her eyes. "It really doesn't matter anymore. Emily, one of the things I've learned over the years is that today is the first day of the rest of our lives. Jesus said a long time ago that we should remove the beam from our own eyes before we look for the speck in someone else's. I've found that to be pretty helpful."

Houston pulled out his handkerchief and dabbed the tears away from Emily's face.

She said, "Thanks, Mr. President."

"Phil," he reminded her. "I'm really not old enough to be your father," he said, "but I also don't want to be considered your brother. I wouldn't like that."

"Neither would I . . . Phil," Emily responded.

He gave her hand one last squeeze and then said, "Well let's go to work and see if we can put this country back together."

During the next few days, more and more utilities were being restored. Although power couldn't be restored throughout the cities because of the downed power lines and burned-out buildings, at least power was being restored to the emergency facilities. Most of the hospitals had their own generators up and running. Telephone companies had their generators back online, and telephone service was being reestablished on a very limited basis. Calls were being limited to official communications only, but families who were worried about other family members were given priority, and messages were being routed from camp to camp.

Jason sent out a message over the official communications line along with hundreds of others from his camp. He was concerned about his sister Karen and, unknown to Jason, his communiqué was given special priority. A thorough search was begun in camps throughout the country in an attempt to locate Karen Hobart. Joel Slife sent out a message to see if he could locate his former neighbors, Bill and Elaine Nowland, but as of this point had received no response. Obviously it was going to take a while, not only to locate the people, but to get communiqués back and forth.

Jason's sister was located in a camp about 200 miles south of Chicago. She had been held captive by a Chicago gang and freed during a daring raid led by an ex-Army ranger, Roger Webb, only a few weeks earlier. When the camp officials learned she was Professor Jason Hobart's sister, she was treated like royalty. Karen was flabbergasted to learn that Jason was the president's science advisor. She had heard nothing about Jason except what the media had released — all negative.

A phone connection was arranged between Karen and Jason. When he came on the line Karen started to cry. "I'm so ashamed, Jason," she said. "Can you ever forgive me?"

Jason responded, "Karen, it's okay. God used this time to mature me. Wendy and I both have become Christians, and I've got some more good news! I've met a wonderful woman and we're going to be married. I wish you could be here."

"I do too," Karen said through her sobs.

"I know she must be a special person."

"She is," Jason agreed. "We'll see you as soon as we can. Take care of yourself. I love you."

Karen couldn't reply. Her tears choked out the words, so she just hung up the phone.

In Washington a very unusual meeting was taking place. The meeting was between the leaders of four rival gangs. Constant fighting between the gangs had narrowed their numbers so that all the gangs together had less than 200 "soldiers." "Big Tony" Garcia, the leader of the largest gang, the Blue Crypts, had called the meeting with the other gang leaders.

"Listen," Tony said to the others. "There ain't but about 200 of us left in this city. If we keep up this constant fightin' and snipin', there won't be none of us left. I don't know about you guys, but my guys are gettin' kind of hungry. We've pretty much picked the bones of this city."

"What do you have in mind, Tony?" one of the other gang leaders, Scar, said. "Get to it!"

"I say we throw in together. If the four of us work together, we got a gang big enough to be a force in this city again. Otherwise, we're just gonna to kill ourselves until there ain't nobody left."

To that one of the other gang leaders

growled, "That's for sure. They ain't hardly nothin' left in this city worth havin' anymore. But, supposin' we work together, what are we gonna do?"

"I got information that might be useful," Big Tony said. "Is it agreed that if we have a plan we'll work together and not try to cut each other's throats?"

"Yeah, if you've got somethin' worthwhile," Scar said, the others nodding in agreement.

Garcia snapped his fingers. When he did, one of the other gang members dragged a thin balding man in by the collar. Robert Frasier was terrorized. He had made contact with the gang members because he had a plan. When he saw the power being restored, he knew he had to act quickly. He hated Houston, but most of all he hated Jason Hobart, and he had a plan to get even with the haughty professor. But, in the few days that he had been with the gangs, he'd been more afraid than ever before — and Frasier was a weak man who'd been afraid many times.

"Who's this?" Scar asked gruffly.

"This here's the head of the National Institute of Sciences," Garcia announced.

"Yeah, big deal. We ain't got no sciences," the others said.

"Tell 'em what you told me," Garcia demanded of Frasier. He signaled his man to release Frasier, and when he released Frasier's collar, he almost collapsed. Then he caught himself and straightened up.

In a whiny subservient voice Frasier said, "I know how you can get all the food and other supplies you need."

"Oh yeah? How's that?" one of the gang leaders said.

"Do any of you remember the professor who predicted the solar flare?"

"Yeah, I remember. I remember seein' that guy on TV. What about it?"

"I know where he is, and I know how you can get control over the camp that he runs. He's the president's number one man right now, so if you have control of him you will also have control over the president."

"Oh yeah? And where is he?"

Frasier began to outline what he knew — that Jason and the other scientific team had gone to a camp in New Holland, Pennsylvania. He knew how large the camp was and what kind of security the camp had.

"Those camps are pretty well armed," one of the gang leaders said. "A lot of gangs tried them and failed. They got thousands of men. We only got a few hunnerd. How we gonna attack that camp?"

"Don't have to attack the camp," Frasier said. "Hobart has a daughter." When he said that, he could see the light come on in the gang leaders' eyes. "If you get control of his daughter, Hobart will do anything that you want," Frasier said authoritatively.

"Yeah, and what do you want out of this?" Scar asked.

"Nothing," Robert Frasier lied. "All I want is to get even with Dr. Hobart."

"Ya got a plan, Tony?" the other gang members asked Garcia.

"Yeah, I do. If we all agree to work together, this thing'll work. Listen, if we don't, we're gonna starve this winter. We ain't got no more food, and we all know how cold it's gonna be here in D.C. Unless we're willing to do like the ducks and head south, it's gonna be a tough winter for all of us."

The other gang leaders shook their heads in agreement. "Okay. What's your plan?" they asked.

What none of the other gang members knew was that big Tony Garcia had a plant in the New Holland camp. As a matter of fact, Garcia had plants in five of the relocation camps. He had not been able to make contact with his people for the last seven months, but he knew they were there, and when he needed them they would be ready. All he needed was to be able to get a message to Tina Riosa, his plant at New Holland.

Word quickly filtered through the streets about the power and communications being restored. Garcia knew it had to be true because he had seen crews working on the substations in D.C. Heavy security surrounding the crews precluded the gangs from any action. Also, the word around the street was that the government was searching the cities, trying to locate families that had been separated. He decided to use another one of his girls to send a message to Riosa at the New Holland camp.

The woman he chose, Destiny, was another one of the street girls who had worked for Tony for several years. If Destiny had a last name, nobody remembered what it was, including her. She and Riosa had worked the streets together for a long time. Destiny was sent to one of the police stations outside of the gangs' territory. When she got to the station, she asked to see the person in charge.

"What do you want?" the sergeant demanded. He could tell by looking at her that she was a gang member, but their instructions were clear: no arrest unless provoked. After the policewoman searched Destiny and found no weapons, she was allowed inside the building.

The sergeant asked her again, "What do you want?"

Destiny responded, "I'm tryin' to locate my sister, and I think she might be in the relocation camp in New Holland, Pennsylvania. Can I send a message?"

"Yes," the sergeant said. "We'll put it on the queue, and it should go out sometime today or tomorrow. What's the message?"

Destiny handed him a note. **"Attention: Tina Riosa. Dear Tina, Tony and I are alive and doing well. We hope to see you soon. We hope everything is working out for you."**

"That it?" the sergeant said.

"Yes."

"Okay, like I said, it'll go out — sometime today or tomorrow. Where can we reach you?"

"I'll be back day after tomorrow," Destiny said, "to check my messages."

After Destiny left the building, the sergeant went to the captain in charge. "Sir, I just got this message from a street girl here in D.C. Name's Destiny, but it's a little suspicious."

"How so, Sergeant?" the captain asked.

"Well in the first place, Sir, she didn't ask us to relocate her. Second, she didn't ask us for any food, which would be highly unusual unless she's attached to one of the gangs — which I suspect she is."

"Okay, Sergeant," the captain said. "I'll take it from here."

"All right, Sir. Should I send out the message?"

"Yes, it may be legitimate. She could be a gang member looking for some of her family. Send the message."

"Okay, Sir. I'll do it," the sergeant said.

After reading the message again, the captain decided that it didn't amount to anything. After all, what could a gang in D.C. do even if they knew somebody in the New Holland camp? It seemed totally irrelevant to him. He took his copy of the message and put it in his desk drawer. *There are bigger things to worry about,* he told himself.

When the message was received at the New Holland camp the next day, Tina Riosa was surprised. She hadn't heard from Big Tony or anybody in the gang since she'd left D.C. nearly seven months ago. So Tony's still alive . . . and Destiny too. Destiny had been her closest friend when she was working the streets. She immediately sat down and wrote an answer to send back to the police station in D.C.

"I'm alive and doing well. Look forward to seeing you. Tina Riosa."

When Destiny relayed the message two days later, Tony knew he had the contact within the camp they would need. He got the other gang leaders together and told them, "Listen, we got what we need. I got a plant inside the New Holland camp that can get me information about Hobart's daughter. If we're gonna snatch her, we'll need a diversion."

"What kind of diversion?" one of the other gang leaders said.

"We need to get a hunnerd men together and attack the camp. While they're busy tryin' to defend their camp, we'll snatch the girl."

"How we gonna to do that with an armed camp?"

"You leave that to me," Garcia said. "I'll get the girl. Can you guys pull off the diversion?"

"Sure," the others agreed.

"It will be dangerous, though. That's why we all have to work together," Garcia said. "Any one gang couldn't do this job, but all four of us together can handle it easy."

"How we gonna get there?"

"The government's got things up and runnin' again. They've got the vehicles. All we have to do is snatch a couple."

"Oh yeah? How're you gonna snatch vehicles from one of them military depots?" one of the gang leaders asked.

"Simple enough," Garcia said. "We need another diversion. Rico, I want you to take 20 men and attack the police substation near the Capitol. That oughta bring the military runnin'. Can you handle that?"

"Sure," Rico responded. "No problem."

"In the meantime, I'll take 20 men and we'll go to the Army depot. When they break out the soldier boys to defend the police station, the place'll be left with no guard. That's when we'll move in and get our trucks." Garcia had to admit his plan had a few holes, but he believed in doing things the simple way. If everybody did what he was supposed to do, it should come off without a hitch.

The women didn't much like it when he told them their job would be to stay there and guard the supplies while the men were gone, but they knew better than to question Big Tony.

Four hours later 20 armed gang members surrounded the police substation near the Capitol. On command, they all cut loose. The guard at the door was cut down immediately. He never saw what happened. Inside the building men were scurrying for cover as hundreds of bullets shattered windows and ricocheted through the lobby of the old building.

The sergeant on the desk put out an emergency message that was picked up by the Army Depot less than three miles away. At the Depot, the word came through loud and clear that the police substation in Capitol Square was under attack. At any given time, the depot housed about 100 personnel. Two assault teams of 50 each were on constant alert and had been for the last several months. When the call went out, within three minutes the two assault teams and two armored personnel carriers were rolling. They would reach their destination in just under six minutes.

As soon as the last of the vehicles rolled out of the compound, Garcia and 25 armed gang members struck the complex. With only 12 guards left on duty in the compound, the outcome was a certainty. The battle was fierce, but very short, as Garcia and his men overwhelmed the remaining guards. Garcia lost five gang members, and two guards from the army depot were wounded. As the guards fell back to a more secure position, Garcia and six other men jumped into the remaining trucks, fired them up, and drove them out of the compound under a constant hail of bullets from the guards, now secure inside the main bunker. Twenty other gang members had loaded 10 drums of diesel fuel aboard two of the trucks and beat a hasty retreat before the soldiers returned.

In five minutes it was all over and Garcia and 20 other men were loaded into trucks and headed back into the inner city. He now had his transportation to New Holland.

At the Camp David headquarters, word of the attack on the police substation in D.C. and the Army Depot nearby quickly made its way to Gen. Boland's office. Attacks of that magnitude were rare these days. Although seven months ago they had been a commonplace event, this attack caught Boland's attention. He quickly put the pieces of the puzzle together. The attack on the substation was obviously a diversion for the purpose of stealing the transport vehicles.

"Now what would gangs want with transport trucks?" Boland asked himself. "There's only one logical explanation: They're planning to go someplace and need trucks to get there."

As he reviewed the reports, he discovered that not only were six trucks stolen, but ten 50-gallon drums of diesel fuel also were taken.

So they've got six trucks and ten drums of fuel. Wherever they're going, it's not going to be a short trip, Boland decided.

He took out his maps and began to look at the territory surrounding D.C. "Well let's see. They sure wouldn't be going to Philadelphia, and they're not going to New York. Might be headed south for the winter," Boland decided. He made a note to check on that. "What else is around here?"

Within a radius of 500 miles, there were three camps. Just within the perimeter was the camp at New Holland. A second camp was located in northern Virginia within easy access of the city, and a third much smaller camp, which had been used for relocating some of the ex-gang members, was up in Maryland. Boland quickly discarded that one. There would be no purpose in the gang members attacking that camp. It had minimal resources, but the other two camps — the one in Virginia and the one in New Holland — had significant resources.

He concluded that either the gangs were headed for one of the camps or they were headed south. If they were headed south, he should be able to pick them up on any of the main highways. It would be very difficult for them to work their way down to Florida without getting on at least one of the major highways. However, if they were smart enough, they could work their way to the camps without ever using a major highway.

Boy, do I wish we had some helicopters, Boland thought.

But so far none of the avionics would operate. Almost all the electronics on their aircraft were still disabled, and even though the solar activity had died off significantly it was still impossible to operate aircraft without risk of disaster. The professor thought that within another few weeks they should be able to get some aircraft back in operation, but for now they were limited to ground transportation.

What are these creeps after? Boland asked himself.

Obviously food and other supplies had to be their main objective. He realized he didn't have the resources to go into the city and look for the trucks, and he doubted that his people would be able to locate them anyway. The burned-out hulk of the inner city was the territory of the gangs. It was on their turf. He would have to wait until they came out and got on his turf.

At New Holland, Jason began to sense that life in the camp was beginning to normalize. They had been there a little over seven months and some of the old ways had begun to fade — certainly in the minds of the children. They seemed to adapt the best. They loved the games and the interaction with the adults. The parents knew that they could let the children play outside all day, without fear of them being molested or kidnapped.

As the months went by, more and more of the old fears began to fade. Some of the oldtimers told stories of how it was back in the '40s and the '50s, when parents were able to let their children stay out all day without any concern for their safety, knowing that all the neighbors would watch out for the children. The same attitudes were being restored in the camp.

Once the basic standards had been established for the camp — the standards of conduct in terms of theft and other types of crimes — more social standards began to evolve. Jason and the other leaders decided that they would not extend their authority beyond the basics: that of securing the property rights and the rights of life and freedom from physical harm. The other social constraints had to be established by the people themselves.

As the months went by, more social constraints became apparent. It was no longer acceptable to use four-letter expletives in public, and those who did were ostracized by the rest of the group. In large part, jokes in bad taste also were eliminated — not by government edict but by social acceptance. The barriers that once had been artificially established by the society around them — barriers of race, age, and gender — were virtually nonexistent. People were accepted on the basis of who they were — not because of their color, their religion, or their gender.

C.C. was gratified to see the growth and the outreach of the Christian community. With all religions represented within the camp and all given equal access to the people, it was the Christians who quickly stepped forth, sharing their faith through helping other people, not just by their words.

When the morning services were held, it was the Christian groups that continued to grow. Soon, over 90 percent of the camp population were attending the services. Every group had an opportunity to meet for 15 minutes prior to the workday, and then in the evenings voluntary Bible studies were offered throughout the camps. Initially, the Bible studies drew about 10 percent of the people. Now they were attended by 70 to 80 percent of the community. The message of Christ spread, not by government edict but by the free choice of the people.

C.C. was a great influence on the group. This huge man with a big heart spread the love of Christ wherever he went, and people flocked to him as they would have the pied piper. In another time, C.C. might well have become the best-known evangelist in America. As it was, he simply became the best-known evangelist in the New Holland camp and could count hundreds of people as converts to Christ as a direct result of his efforts.

The Amish farmers in the New Holland community had become an integral part of camp life. Their expertise and patience in training the New Holland people to farm, using nineteenth century techniques, had won over the hearts and minds of the people. During the preceding seven months, the difference between the Amish and their new friends had faded. Soon, members of the New Holland community were as welcome in the Amish homes as the Amish were in the New Holland homes.

As the city dwellers adapted to a more rural way of life, they became deeply committed to the community. It was rare now to hear complaints from the children about the lack of television, CDs, or movies. If the truth were known, many parents in the New Holland community prayed that the solar flares would continue because they had no desire to leave their new life.

In D.C. Garcia began to put his plan into motion. "Look," he told the other gang leaders, "the cops and the military ain't stupid.

They know we got these trucks. We're gonna have to be extremely careful. It won't take 'em long to figure out that we're not gonna use 'em to take kids to Sunday school. If they find out where we're headed, they'll be waitin' on us."

"Yeah, well whatta ya want us ta do?" Scar asked.

"I say we travel at night and stick to the back roads. Load a coupla hunnerd men into the trucks and all the weapons and ammunition they can carry. If we're gonna attack the New Holland camp, we better be prepared. I hear they got about 12,000 in their defense group there."

"How'd ja know that?" Scar asked.

"Just picked up bits and pieces — mostly from Frasier," Garcia said. "But with a camp that size they'll have an awesome force. We won't be able to hold out against them very long."

"Yeah, well, what are we gonna do then?"

Garcia sat down at the table and began to outline his plan. "I'm gonna need about 20 minutes after we reach the camp. Then, you start the diversion. If you keep 'em distracted for about 15 minutes, I'll have the girl and be gone."

"Yeah? What happens to us then?"

"Get back in the trucks and head out as quickly as ya can. If I got the girl, they won't come after you."

"And what if ya ain't got the girl?" one of the others growled.

"Then ya don't have to worry 'bout it. We won't need nuthin' to eat this winter," Garcia quipped with an evil grin on his face. "Besides," he said, "what choice we got? Are you willin' to give up?"

Each of the gang leaders looked around at each other. They weren't. Based on what they had done, retribution from the government was going to be swift and severe, and they all knew it. Their only chance would be to hold what they had and keep control of their part of the city.

At the New Holland camp, Tina Riosa was thinking about the message she'd received from Destiny. She knew Big Tony wouldn't have contacted her unless he needed her help. That's why she'd been put in the camp in the first place. She figured that he was coming. The gang probably needed food and other stuff. Life in the cities had been pretty bad when she left. She could only imagine how bad it must be now.

What would Big Tony be wanting? she asked herself. She began to think, *Surely he wouldn't attack a camp this big. All the gangs together wouldn't be enough, so what else? Could he just slip in steal some stuff? Nah! That's not Big Tony's style. He would never do that. What then?* Then it came to her. *Ahh. He wants to* snatch somebody from the camp and use 'em as a hostage. Then he can get what he wants. *Now who would Big Tony snatch?* she thought hard. Then it became clear. He had to snatch the professor. He was the big shot in camp, and everybody knew it. Word had just recently come down that President Houston was going to give the Distinguished Service Medal to the professor.

Yeah, he's the big shot. Tony's after Hobart. Or, she thought to herself, *maybe his fiancee. What was her name? Camp, yeah Dr. Camp. Maybe he's after his fiancee. Yeah, that's it. She'd be easier to snatch.* Or, she thought, *the kid — yeah, the kid. She'd be the easiest one to snatch.*

Big Tony will need information, she decided. *I'll need to start watching the kid. Look for some kind of pattern, some easy way Tony can snatch her.*

28

Garcia knew that the trickiest part of his plan was getting out of the city undetected, but he also knew the city better than anyone else. They weaved their way through the broken and ruined streets, around the burned-out hulks of automobiles and trucks. Garcia looked at what had happened to the city much as he did everything else in life: him and them. He felt no remorse and no guilt — and certainly no responsibility. His job was to survive and to control, and if that meant killing and maiming, stealing and burning, that's what he did.

Garcia was from a generation of young men who had been raised with no conscience. They were taught not to feel guilty for their actions but to always blame somebody else, and Garcia blamed plenty of people. He blamed the rich, because he wasn't born rich; he blamed the Anglos, because he was born Hispanic; he blamed the government, because it wouldn't give him what he wanted when he wanted it; and he blamed his parents, simply because he had been born — it had to be their fault.

As the trucks weaved their way through the

shattered city, Garcia's advance guard spotted a few military patrols, but they were easily avoided. Once he was out of the city, he felt uncomfortable. He was now out of his own element. No longer was he the hunter; he was the hunted. Several days earlier, he had led the group that attacked a military patrol and stolen vehicles, one of which was a Hummer. He made that his personal vehicle.

Garcia really had no intention of sharing the spoils of his conquest at New Holland with any of the other gang members. He simply needed their help to accomplish his plan. Once he got back in the city, he would have to be extremely careful, until he could take over the unified gangs. There could be only one leader, and "Big Tony" Garcia intended it to be him.

For the better part of two days, the trucks weaved their way across the countryside, avoiding any main roads. Often when the side roads were blocked, they'd have to backtrack several miles until they found a way through. The smaller towns had long since been evacuated, and there was a minimum security watch over those towns. Usually it consisted of three or four soldiers on the main roads in and out, so it was easy enough to avoid them.

Garcia wasn't sure how good the communications between the outlying villages and the main headquarters were, but he wasn't about to take any chances either. He traveled only at night, holding up during the daytime to rest and recover.

At Camp David, Gen. Boland had taken the precaution of sending a message to each of the camps, warning them about the potential of a gang attack, but since the trucks had been stolen, not another word had been received about them. The general was sure the gangs had not given up, but he was not sure when or where they would launch their attack. He would have given 10 years pay for just one helicopter he could put in the air, but with communications being what they were and the lack of air support, his capabilities were pretty much on a par with the gangs. Only time would tell.

Robert Frasier, in the Hummer with Garcia, was still terrified, as he had been for the past week and a half. Against his will, he had been forced to go with Garcia. He argued that he would be of no value to the gang leader, but Garcia would not listen. Where he went, Frasier went with him. He didn't want the back-stabbing little weasel left behind. Garcia had a warped sense of loyalty, but it was his conviction that if somebody would rat against friends, they would eventually rat against him as well, and he was taking no chances with Frasier.

The timid and weak-kneed Frasier was horrified by what went on in the camp every night. Life inside the gangs was like a perpetual orgy. Frasier had never even imagined that such a life existed, and now he was a part of it. He began to doubt his own resolve. He hated Houston and he hated Hobart, but he wasn't sure that he hated them enough to risk his own life in the process. And yet here he was, and he had no way to get out of it.

It was nearly midnight when the caravan approached the town of New Holland. Garcia got out his maps. The route around New Holland to the south would take them directly into the camp. He ordered the others to stay back while he took his scout vehicle and went ahead to reconnoiter the terrain. Garcia had no military background, but he had an instinct for ambush. Although he felt distinctly uncomfortable outside the city, the closer he got to his quarry the more excited he became. He drove up to the knoll overlooking the camp, and at first he was taken back.

The size of the camp, in itself, was impressive. Tents were strung out for what looked like miles, and in some places more permanent structures had been erected. Although there was no fence around the camp, it was clear there was a barrier. The trees had been cleared for 40 or 50 yards around the camp, many of them obviously used for fuel or building materials in the camp itself. But he could see that a clear firing zone had been arranged around the camp. Although he didn't see many armed guards, he knew they had to be there somewhere.

Since C.C. had received the message from Gen. Boland, he had doubled the security in the camp but kept it very unobtrusive. Most of the guards carried no weapons — at least no visible ones — and they went about their business as if it were normal camp activity.

C.C. wished he had some infrared scanners. He would have set them up around the perimeter of the camp; but, so far, that was impossible. So he did the best he could. Lt. Hardy had strategically located the weapons around the camp within easy access of the men and, at any given time, he kept at least 1,000 of his troops on emergency alert. If the alarm was sounded, meaning the church bell, 1,000 armed men could be mobilized in less than a minute. C.C. knew it would take a pretty formidable force to confront that defense team.

Tina Riosa had been watching Dr. Hobart, Annette, and especially Wendy for the past three days. Their routines were very predictable. Dr. Hobart was up by 5:00 in the morning and by 6:00, after eating breakfast, he was in the observation building. Shortly after that, Dr. Camp would join him and they would stay there until the noon meal. They would eat lunch with the group from 12:00 to 12:30, and after that they would take turns working at various jobs around the camp, the same as everyone else. Riosa had heard many times that the camp committee had asked Dr. Hobart and Dr. Camp not to work, but they felt it was their responsibility.

Tina Riosa was torn between loyalties. She had been with Big Tony a long time, and though she wasn't sure whether she feared him or loved him, she felt loyal to him. On the other hand, she'd only been in the camps for seven months, but she'd never been treated better in her life than she had been at New Holland. She was accepted as a member of the group — an equal. Her past didn't matter. All that seemed important to the others was how she worked and interacted with them. Because of this, she didn't want to see them hurt. But she realized that in a few months she would likely be back in the city. She shuddered to think what Big Tony would do to her if she betrayed him.

Garcia was looking over the camp with his binoculars. It was pretty obvious that the big building in the center of the camp was the main meeting building. With a camp this large, he wasn't at all sure how he would make contact with Riosa. He wished now that he had sent a message ahead telling her to meet him, but it was too late. He'd had no concept of just how large the camp would be.

He worked his way down the knoll toward the camp until he was about 150 yards away.

He scoured the camp with his binoculars. Only a few people were moving around. He spotted only two guards. *Stupid,* he thought to himself. These people should have more guards out. If I were in charge, that's what I'd do. As he panned the binoculars, he suddenly stopped. There was a familiar figure: Tina Riosa.

By a stroke of luck, Tina had just left her tent and walked toward the main assembly building, where she could keep an eye on the solar observatory. Dr. Hobart, Dr. Camp, and Wendy were still inside. She had discovered during the last three days that they often worked very late at night, and so she made a habit of checking to see when they left the building. For the last two evenings, they had left between 12:00 and 1:00 in the morning.

Inside, Jason was still going over the graphs and charts. The level of activity from area 403 was now nearly normal. He had done some calculations and had come to the conclusion that the worst of the flares were now passed; perhaps they were finished. It wouldn't be long before things could begin to develop a semblance of normalcy.

The cosmic assault on Earth's magnetic field had ceased, but the magnetic field itself was still fluctuating wildly. It was as if the molten core was readjusting. It was these fluctuations that made air travel very risky. From time to time, Jason could sense a power surge, even on the short lines within the New Holland compound. Since most of their equipment was either manual or relay operated, the power surges had no real effect on them. But he knew it was going to be impossible to power up across the country until these surges ceased. It also would be impossible to operate most of their communications equipment and aircraft, at least for the foreseeable future.

Drawing again upon Dr. Carrington's nineteenth century observations, he calculated that it would be another two to three months before all the fluctuations died down to the point that normal operations would be possible again. He and Annette had dedicated the last few nights to an intense study of this particular phenomenon. Wendy had been working alongside them, and Jason was impressed with how much help she was. At 15, Wendy was more mature than most 20-year-olds. She had a good head on her shoulders; she learned very quickly; and she was totally dedicated — not just to the project but to her father and to the woman she now considered to be her mother.

It was Tuesday, and Thursday would be Thanksgiving, and that's when Jason and Annette would be married. Wendy was so excited she could hardly contain herself. She was excited for her father but also for herself as well. She loved Annette, and they were great friends. She was the happiest she'd been since her mother had died.

Big Tony snapped his fingers as a signal to the man known as "The Rat." The Rat was a good name for Booker Tee Jones, who was a small, thin, scheming, 30-year old with a pockmarked face, a hatchet nose, and beaded, ratlike eyes. Rat had a talent, and that talent was the ability to get in and out of places without being detected. Garcia had brought him along just for that purpose. Looking over the small mound where they were hiding, Garcia pointed.

"It's Riosa," he said. "I need you to contact her. Find out what she knows, and bring the information back here. Can you do it?"

"No problem," Rat said, and he immediately scurried out of sight. Garcia was always amazed at how quickly the man could move and yet make so little noise. Garcia scanned the entire area with the field glasses, but could see nothing. The Rat was moving through the woods and the grasses so smoothly that he had hardly left a ripple behind and he was impossible to see in the dark light. Then Garcia saw a movement across the open field; The Rat was hunched down so that he was slightly higher than a dog. He moved swiftly across the open area and slid in behind one of the buildings.

The building The Rat had chosen was a smaller structure made of logs. It had no windows and only two stacks coming out of the roof. The Rat figured that even if anybody was inside they couldn't hear him. He moved around to the darkest side of the building, careful to keep to the shadows. By that time, he was a mere 15 yards away from Riosa. He whistled lightly, as he had thousands of times before in the city when they were on patrol. Tina looked up. She thought she'd heard something — a familiar sound.

She glanced around slowly and carefully but could see nothing. Rat was hidden in the shadows; not even one inch of him was visible. He whistled again. Tina knew the sound. It was The Rat. She'd heard it many times before when they worked together in the city. She looked around to see if anybody was watching, but there was nobody in sight.

In the camp, people were accustomed to other people getting up in the middle of the night and wandering around as they wanted, and nobody thought anything about it. Crime was virtually unknown, and they felt as safe at night as they did during the day, which gave them the liberty to move about comfortably. Riosa's movement had gone unnoticed. She walked slowly toward the area where she heard the sound, and it was only when she got within three yards of The Rat that she saw him.

"Rat, what are you doing here?" she whispered.

"Riosa! Commear!" he snapped.

As she stepped into the shadows, The Rat moved around the corner of the building once more. "Big Tony sent me for information."

Tina took a minute to fill him in on what she had been doing: watching Dr. Hobart, Dr. Camp, and Dr. Hobart's daughter Wendy. She told them they were all in the observation building and would be there until probably 1:00 in the morning or later; and she filled The Rat in on their schedule. She told him that she had assumed Tony was planning a kidnaping and would use a hostage to get what he wanted. The Rat filled her in on Big Tony's plans, including the diversion.

"He needs to be very careful," Tina warned. Her loyalties were still confused. She had known Tony for many years, had been his girl for a while, and had worked for him, and he had always treated her pretty good — a lot better than she had been treated at home. But now she also had a loyalty to the people of New Holland. They had treated her well. They took her in and treated her like one of their own. They trusted her.

She told The Rat, "I don't want to see any of these people hurt. They're good people."

"I'll tell Big Tony," The Rat said with an evil curl of his mouth. He cared for nobody or nothing. He had no loyalty to Garcia or to anybody else except himself. His main purpose in life was to eat and to stay alive. Tina told The Rat about the wedding that was coming up in two days. She also mentioned that the entire camp would be focused on the wedding. It was the biggest event to take place since the camp was formed.

The Rat slipped away, again moving from corner to corner, building to building, until he got to the clearing. He stopped, looked nervously both ways, and then scurried across the open area. Garcia barely saw him, even though he had been looking intently through the field glasses. Once in the tall grass and woods, The Rat simply disappeared. Three minutes later, not even panting, he was standing beside Garcia. He quickly gave his report from Riosa.

That's my woman, Garcia thought. She had anticipated what he would want, and she was absolutely correct. Now the question was, when would be the best time to snatch the girl? Then it came to him. *I'll snatch her right after the wedding when no one will be expecting it.*

As they approached the place where the Hummer was waiting, well out of sound range of the camp, the driver saw them coming and fired up the vehicle. He backed down the ravine and drove to his camp. Garcia called the others together and told them of his plan to kidnap Hobart's daughter.

"How you gonna do it . . . and when?" one of the gang leaders asked.

"We'll attack the camp when everybody's at the weddin'. They won't be expectin' nuthing," Garcia said. "And remember, I don't want nobody killed, if possible. We don't want 'em trackin' us down."

If Big Tony could've read the other gang leaders' minds, he might have thought better of the whole idea. They had in mind a more direct approach to getting what they wanted: mainly, taking it. They had already talked it over.

"Let Garcia do his thing with the girl," one of them said. "In the meantime, we'll take what we want and get outta here." They had done that in the past, and it had worked pretty well. They saw no reason to change now. They would lay low for a day, but on Thursday they would make the rules.

The wedding was scheduled for 4:00 in the afternoon on Thursday, and the preparations involved the entire camp. C.C. and the other camp leaders had already decided that they would have a banquet. They didn't bring Jason in on the decision, because they were sure he wouldn't agree, especially since it was his wedding. They figured, what the heck, they had enough food, and one meal more or less wasn't going to make a difference.

Both Jason and Annette had gotten to be good friends with an Indian missionary pastor by the name of Light Horse Harry. Light Horse had been an inspiration to everybody in the camp. He traveled from family to family, caring for anyone who was sick or hurt or depressed. There were many times when Light Horse had worked for three or four straight days without sleeping to care for those who were sick or injured.

The doctors in the camp considered his services more important than their own. He was so spiritually uplifting that they had seen several seriously ill people recover as a result of Light Horse calling on them and spending days praying over them during their recovery period.

Light Horse had an imposing presence. He was bigger than C.C., and to hear him pray was like standing in the presence of Moses or Abraham. Few people, other than C.C. and Lt. Hardy, knew the history behind the scars on the Indian's face and arms. Light Horse Harry (named after Robert E. Lee's famous father, Colonel Light Horse Harry Lee of the revolutionary army) had been a ruthless soldier of fortune until his conversion five years earlier. Now he was a totally dedicated servant of God.

For his part, Light Horse was excited about the upcoming wedding. He'd grown to love Jason and Annette, and Wendy was one of the most special people in his life. She was a delightful young lady, always laughing, always happy, and always willing to share whatever she had with someone else. Light Horse tried not to envy Jason, but for many of his 48 years he had been looking for the mate God intended for him. So far he hadn't found her. He had reconciled himself to life as a bachelor. Jason often reminded Light Horse that even though he was a bachelor he was an adopted brother of many of the families in the camp.

Thursday morning the entire camp was up early. Thanksgiving Day was a special time at New Holland, a time when the entire 25,000 members of the camp were to gather together to give thanks and praise to the Lord, just as the early pilgrims had done and just as Abraham Lincoln had requested the entire nation to do in the midst of the Civil War. Now they had even more reason to be thankful. They had survived the greatest crisis the civilized world had ever experienced. Millions, perhaps billions, of people across the globe had surely died as a result of the massive solar flares. But because of Jason Hobart's wisdom and President Houston's courage, their families were safe, as were millions of other families across America. They truly had reason to be thankful this day.

By 2:00 a small temporary wedding chapel had been erected in the middle of camp, in the space normally reserved for camp assemblies. The clearing was large enough to hold more than 25,000 people. By 2:00 in the afternoon, it had begun to fill up.

Jason, who had no dress clothes with him, had borrowed a full-dress military uniform from one of the officers in the camp, stripped of all of the insignias, of course. Annette, who had no wedding dress, had planned to be married in a conservative blue suit — the only one she owned. But as she was getting ready several of the women came into her hut. One of the Amish wives was carrying a beautiful white dress with inlays of tiny tucks and delicate lace.

"This is for you, Dr. Camp," the woman said. "It was my mother's. I was married in it, and my daughter will be married in it one day. I would consider it an honor if you would wear it for your wedding."

Annette looked at the dress and at the simple, humble people around her, and her eyes filled with tears. She loved this place, and she loved these people. They were really the closest thing to family she had now. She wished that her mother could have been here to see her married, and she missed her parents more today than she had since the two of them had been killed in the automobile accident five years earlier. Her mother had longed for grandchildren, but when her only daughter remained single she had consoled herself by becoming a surrogate grandmother to many of her friends' children.

Wendy was scurrying back and forth between Annette and her father. Jason was pacing nervously, and when Wendy entered his hut she said, "Daddy, you need to sit down and relax. You look a little pale."

Jason smiled faintly. "I think you're right, Honey. With a little bit of encouragement, I just might pass out."

"Daddy, you just sit right down there and take some deep breaths," his daughter scolded him.

Jason looked at his daughter and obediently sat in the chair. She reminded him so much of her mother it was startling. That was something Nancy would have said to him. And he did take several deep breaths. "Ah, that's much better," he said. "Thank you, Honey. I appreciate that. How's Annette doing?"

"Oh, Daddy, you should just see . . . ," Wendy started to say, and then she checked herself. "Never mind, Daddy. You'll see."

Jason started to ask her what she meant but decided against it. It was obvious she wasn't going to tell him, and no amount of coercing would get Wendy to reveal a confidence to anyone, including him. The next hour was the longest in Jason's life. He glanced at his watch every few minutes.

Then C.C. knocked on the door and said, "Time to go, Professor."

Jason paused. "C.C., would you please just call me Jason? There are no doctors, no professors, no judges out here. We're just people. We have different skills but no titles. Right?"

"Right, Profess . . . I mean, Jason," C.C. stammered out with a big smile. "Well, let's go. You don't want to keep your bride waiting, do you?"

"Absolutely not," Jason said. He took a deep breath and followed C.C. out of the hut.

When they entered the clearing, Jason did a double take. Somebody had erected a huge double arch, and a platform had been raised in the middle of the clearing. "Why, none of that was here a couple of hours ago," Jason said. "How in the world . . . ?"

"Cooperative effort," C.C. told his friend. "Don't worry about it. It's all paid for — in cash," he laughed.

Jason smiled and said, "C.C., you're a wonder."

"I sure hope so," C.C. countered. "You know, I've really never been a best man at a wedding before. I hope I'll do okay." His dark skin shone against the snow white of the shirt he was wearing.

"You're going to do fine," Jason said. They had talked about rehearsing the wedding, but then decided not to. Jason wasn't much for formality and neither was Annette. They just wanted to have a simple ceremony and then get on with their lives. *Yeah, a simple ceremony,* Jason thought as he looked out — except the crowd that had gathered numbered several thousand.

When the crowd saw Jason, they broke out

in a tremendous roar, and the hand clapping sounded like thunder. A blushing Jason was embarrassed by the show of admiration, the shouting, the whistling, and the clapping, which continued for a good five minutes. Finally, when Jason climbed to the platform, he turned and waved to the crowd and then raised his hand. The crowd began to quiet down.

From somewhere over to his left, Jason heard an unbelievable sound: a pipe organ. He looked as hard as he could and could barely make out the big organ. It was the prized possession of one of the Amish pastors. Manufactured in the early 1800s, it had been transported across Europe and half of America before it reached Pennsylvania. It had been located in the same church for more than 100 years. The Amish men had dismantled the organ into transportable pieces and brought it to the camp, reassembling it for the wedding. It was a sign of solidarity and love on the part of the Amish people, who acknowledged their debt to Jason.

As the organ began to play, Annette walked out of the assembly building, followed closely by Wendy, the maid of honor, and 10 other young ladies who were all carrying brilliantly decorated baskets full of colorful fall flower petals. Each of the girls was wearing a beautiful off-white dress. The fabric had been provided by the Amish women, and several seamstresses in the camp had made the dresses.

Jason caught himself staring and wondered if he had his mouth open. He was stunned. He could not believe it. The thing he really couldn't believe was Annette. Here she came down the longest aisle he'd ever seen, between rows of people, wearing the most beautiful white gown. He was startled by what a vision she was. Over the last several months he had grown accustomed to being around Annette, and almost always she had been wearing slacks or shorts with either a pullover sweater or the equivalent, much as everybody in the camp did. Jason had not even envisioned what she would look like in a wedding dress.

C.C. reached over and patted him on the shoulder and said, "Man, she is really something. You're one lucky dude."

Jason would have agreed with C.C., but the big lump in his throat kept him from making any sound at all. It took a while for Annette to reach the podium. By that time, Light Horse was in position with his big black Bible open. As Annette approached the stairs, Lt. Hardy offered her his arm.

Once they were all assembled on the stand, Light Horse began to speak in his booming voice. Those in the back who couldn't hear clearly still understood what he was saying. He welcomed the assembly and the bride and the groom. Then he asked the entire assembly to pray with him. In the big booming voice that must have sounded to those in the front like the voice of God, he began to give thanks to the Lord Almighty for the many blessings that He had bestowed upon the group. And he closed with a prayer for Jason, Annette, and Wendy — that God would use them in a mighty way as witnesses for the Lord Jesus Christ in a world of chaos.

Having completed that, Light Horse cut directly to the ceremony. He asked, "Do you, Jason Edward Hobart, take Annette Renee Camp to be your lawfully wedded wife?"

Jason responded with a hearty "I do."

"And do you, Annette Renee Camp, take Jason Edward Hobart to be your lawfully wedded husband?"

Annette, looking into Jason's eyes, responded, "I do."

Jason hurriedly recovered Annette's ring from C.C., while Hardy handed Jason's ring to Annette. They exchanged rings, crossed hands and looked up at Light Horse, who then said, "By the authority vested in me by God Almighty, I pronounce you man and wife."

29

The crowd let out a tremendous roar and began to applaud. Jason lifted Annette's veil and gently kissed her. The crowd roared a second time.

Just then, a tremendous explosion was heard from the far end of the camp. C.C. looked up and said, "What . . . what was that?" Then another explosion ensued from the same area.

At the farthest end of the camp nearly 200 gang members had attacked the storage depot. The two lone guards at the depot had been easily overwhelmed. Even before they could fire their weapons, a half dozen members of the gang were on them and knocked them unconscious. Complying with Garcia's order, they didn't kill the guards, as would have been their norm in the city. Two explosive charges were applied to the door of the storage building, and it was blown wide open.

C.C. was already shouting for the men in the audience to quickly get their weapons. He chided himself for being so stupid. The defense team would lose precious time. After some momentary confusion, 1,000 men broke into a dead run back to their assigned locations. Explosions continued to erupt from nearly half a mile away at the end of the camp. By this time, the armed gang members had begun to fan out across the storage facility. Trucks were backed into the food depot, and two dozen men began to load sacks on the trucks, grabbing everything they could.

It was clear that the first section of the depot had been totally demolished by the enormous charges that had been used. The inexperience of the gang had led them to blow the whole front end of the storage building off and, with it, a good portion of the food that was stored there. The gang leaders decided they would load the trucks with as much food as they could steal before the defenders could arrive — several months rations, they calculated. Garcia, holding Wendy, could negotiate for the additional supplies they would need, if he survived.

Jason grabbed Annette's hand, Annette grabbed Wendy's hand, and down the stairs they went. C.C. had already bolted down the stairs before them and was running as fast as he could toward the sound of the explosion. Along the way, Lt. Hardy met him, carrying the Browning automatic rifle C.C. preferred and shifted it over to him, along with two full belts of ammunition.

"What's going on?" C.C. asked.

"Looks like gangs attacking," Hardy replied.

"Aw, my stupidity," C.C. muttered. "General Boland warned us, and I just got lax. I got caught up in the wedding."

As they ran, Hardy said, "Too coincidental to be an accident, C.C. Somebody in this camp sold us out."

"Yeah, I know," C.C. said.

Jason was down off the podium. His first thought was to get Annette and Wendy safely inside the observation building. Once inside and the door locked, it would take a direct hit from a 500-pound bomb to get them out of there. Then he would go to his own defense team as quickly as possible.

They headed down the platform and across the opening toward the observation building. Before they could get there, however, a figure stepped out from behind the building and Jason saw the evil-looking face of Big Tony Garcia. He was carrying an automatic weapon and was surrounded by four of the most sinister-looking men Jason had ever seen. One of them looked for all the world like an overgrown rat. Behind them, Jason saw something that made his skin crawl: Dr. Robert Frasier.

Annette saw Frasier as well, and she cried out, "Dr. Frasier, what are you doing here?"

"Shut up!" Garcia warned her and pointed the weapon directly at Jason.

"Stop right there," he commanded.

Jason stopped. "What do you want?"

"Shut up," Garcia said. He nodded to The

Rat, who ran forward and grabbed Wendy by the arm.

Wendy screamed and Jason lunged toward the small man. "Leave her alone," he said. But he didn't reach Wendy. Garcia stepped forward and smashed Jason beside the head with the butt of his rifle. Jason staggered, but he went for the small man again. He grabbed The Rat by the hair. Rat screamed, and Garcia stepped forward again and gave Jason another nasty crack from the butt of the rifle.

Big Tony Garcia was an experienced street fighter. He knew the blow would not kill Jason, but he wanted him down and disabled. By that time, Annette was screaming, and without any thought for her own safety, she attacked the big gang leader. Garcia took one hand and shoved her as hard as he could. She fell back against the side of the building, hit her head, and went down, unconscious. Wendy was screaming as The Rat dragged her off. Two of the other men grabbed her and hoisted her off the ground, one of them carrying her across his shoulder as they ran across the compound.

They were nearly to the edge of the opening when four armed camp militia spotted them. When they saw Wendy, they immediately knew what had happened. They fired their weapons in the air. Garcia turned as if to fire his weapon and then stopped, as he yelled out, "Stop! Don't come any closer, or the girl will get hurt."

The men halted in their tracks.

"Drop your weapons," he commanded. They slowly lowered their weapons to the ground, as instructed.

"Now run," Garcia told them, firing his weapon in the air. The men began to back away from their weapons.

"I said run!" Big Tony repeated, lowering his weapon menacingly in their direction. The men then started to scamper off in the direction from which Garcia had come.

"If anyone follows us, the girl dies," Garcia yelled out. "Tell the professor we'll be in touch."

The men, glancing up, saw two figures laying on the ground by the observation building. They sprinted across the opening, and by the time they reached the building, Annette was beginning to rouse. One of the men took her by the hand and patted her softly on the face.

"Dr. Camp," he said. "Are you okay?"

"Yes, I'm okay. He didn't hurt me. Just knocked the breath out of me."

"Jason?" She looked over to where Jason was lying. His head was bleeding profusely. One of the men was bending over him. Jason's eyes fluttered slightly, and then he opened them.

"Wendy? Where's Wendy?"

"Doctor, stay still," the man commanded. "We have to bandage your head. You're bleeding pretty badly."

"No, he's got Wendy," Jason said. "We've got to find him," Jason argued as he struggled to get up.

"Don't worry, Doctor. C.C. will find your daughter."

Wendy was frightened nearly out of her mind. Everything had happened so rapidly, she didn't have time to think. Now she was being dragged through the bushes. The branches were whipping at her face and tearing at her beautiful dress. She realized right away that these men were the bandits, the gangs, that she had heard so much about in the cities.

Her mind was freewheeling, *How did they find their way to our camp? Why did they take me? And where's Dad?* She almost panicked as she thought about her dad. He'd been struck twice by the big man leading the group. *And Annette? I wonder if she's all right?* Wendy had seen her crumple to the ground as the evil man called Rat had pulled her away.

She was sobbing and struggling as she was carried along by The Rat on one side and another man on the other. Her feet were not touching the ground. Rat looked over at her with an evil grin. His dark brown eyes glinted with the evil that was inside him: pure lust.

"Don't worry, little lady," he whispered.

"You'll have plenty more to cry about before this is over."

Wendy let out an involuntary shudder. Rat reached over and caressed her arm with his free hand. Wendy tried to jerk her arm back, but the little man had muscles of steel. He held her hand firmly, and she could hear him chuckling under his foul breath.

They made it through the woods and were heading up a very steep ravine. The big man put Wendy down and she kept stumbling and falling in the flimsy little shoes she was wearing. The men on either side of her held her up and dragged her along until she could catch her footing. Then she started half running and half stumbling. Meanwhile The Rat kept whispering, so low that no one else could hear it, "You're mine, you're mine, you're mine."

Wendy continued to pray as the tears flowed down her face.

Back at the camp, C.C. directed Lt. Hardy to take control of the fight. It was clear that there were only about 200 attackers — at the most. At first C.C. had thought, *How stupid they must be to attack a camp of thousands*, but he decided, *Things must be so desperate in the city that these rats are coming out, no matter what.* Now he realized it had been a diversion. Four of the big trucks had been stuffed full of whatever the group could steal and were already pulling out of the compound.

"Let them go," Hardy cried to his men. "We can get those provisions back later. Besides," he yelled, "those idiots mostly stole our seed for next year." He would have laughed if the situation hadn't been so serious. Obviously, the men knew very little about reconnaissance. They'd broken into the wrong warehouse: the seed storage warehouse — the seed they were storing in the event they had to plant crops the next year.

They're going to have a hard time cooking up seed for breakfast, lunch, and dinner. The dopes, Hardy mused.

In the meantime, C.C. was already running across the compound back toward Jason. By the time he got there, Jason and Annette both were up on their feet, although Jason was still groggy from the blows he'd received. A doctor was peering into his eyes.

"A slight concussion," he said. "Jason, you're going to have to take it easy."

"I've got to go get Wendy," Jason exclaimed. "They've got Wendy."

C.C. said angrily, as he caught his breath, "Don't worry, Jason. I'll get Wendy back."

In the meantime, Light Horse had joined them. Somebody was explaining to him what had happened. Light Horse was already taking off his jacket. "Give me five minutes to get dressed. I'm going with you, C.C."

"Okay," C.C. responded. "I can use your

help." Then one of the others explained to Jason, "Light Horse used to be one of the best scouts in the Army Rangers. Right before he got saved, he was a real holy terror. We can use his help. I don't know how much tracking we'll have to do, but Light Horse can track an ant through the rain forest, if necessary."

In the meantime, a group of men were gathering, all volunteering to go with C.C. He looked out over the crowd and picked out five of the men he knew to be ex-military and experts with their weapons. He said to the others, "I only need five men. Too many will just hold us back. Thanks for volunteering, but you're going to be needed at the camp."

A few minutes later, Light Horse was back, dressed in Army fatigues with the sleeves ripped out. He had a band wrapped around his head to keep the hair out of his eyes. He also was carrying a compound bow and a quiver full of the strangest-looking arrows Jason had ever seen.

"We've reverted to the past," C.C. said to the big Indian.

"No, Sir!" he said. "I'm combining the best of the two. A full-blooded Osage Indian and a born-again Christian with the wisdom of God."

"Yeah, me too. A Christian, I mean . . . not an Indian."

"Really?" Light Horse said smiling. "I

wouldn't have known."

C.C. chuckled. "Let's not waste any more time," he told Jason. "I'm going to need the Hummer we brought with us."

"It's yours," Jason said groggily. "Take whatever you need. But please bring Wendy back."

"You can count on it," C.C. said.

A couple of minutes later, the door to one of the storage buildings swung open, and C.C. drove the Hummer out. Looking over the terrain before them, C.C. said, "These guys are city dwellers, so they're not going to hang out in the forest. I know where they're headed."

"Yeah, back to the city," Light Horse said.

"Well let's get started. You guys go up the hill," pointing to Light Horse and two other men, "and the rest of you get in the Hummer. Light Horse, I'll meet you on the top of the hill."

"Right," Light Horse agreed, "but if I'm not there, don't wait." With that he started across the open field in a trot. The other two men fell in behind him.

"I wouldn't want to be those creeps they're going after," one of the men in the crowd said. "Not when C.C. and Light Horse catch up with them." Several other men in the crowd murmured in agreement.

Somebody else said, "Let's pray," and the entire group dropped to their knees. Annette went over to Jason and they put their arms around each other, closed their eyes, and prayed with the men.

One of the men led in prayer, "Great God Almighty," he said. "Maker of Heaven and Earth, you promised that if we lacked wisdom, you would give it to us liberally, and we claim that promise, Father. Give us your wisdom and your discernment and your courage. We pray for our sister Wendy, that you would protect her and bring her back safely to us. In Jesus' name. Amen."

And all the others said in unison, "Amen."

The doctor who looked at Jason was already instructing two of the men to escort Jason over to his tent. "Somebody will have to stay with him until he's alert," the doctor said.

"Don't worry about that," Annette replied. "You couldn't get me away from him if you wanted to. I've got a brand-new husband, and I'm not about to leave him. Where would an old maid like me ever find another?"

Jason looked over at her and smiled. Even through the pain that was surging through his head, he felt his heart soften. This was an ordeal he didn't have to experience alone. God had indeed provided him with a helpmate.

At the other end of the compound, Lt. Hardy and more than a thousand of the defense team were now in position. The attackers, though ferocious, were terribly inaccurate. The men had reported only four casualties from the defense team, and those were minor injuries, caused more from ricocheting bullets than from direct hits. In the meantime, Hardy had his main group of men advancing on the attackers. The two other groups flanked them left and right. He thought to himself, *Those idiots have no idea about tactics. Nobody in their right mind would stay in that defensive position.*

The main force in the middle continued to fire a fusillade of bullets at the attackers, bringing them down where they were. Unable to advance, the gang began to withdraw. In the meantime, the two flanking groups had nearly connected behind them. And on a signal from Hardy, they began to pour fire into the attackers. In less than five minutes, it was all over. The attackers, faced with a superior force in front and now a superior force in back, threw down their weapons and raised their hands. Hardy had his men move in and disarm them.

The four gang leaders with the assault group, seeing that it was hopeless, had long since split. And they, along with their lieutenants, were now running across the fields in an attempt to catch up with the trucks at the rendezvous. They knew that Garcia had crossed them up. The attack had been planned so that they would all be caught and Tony would get away with the girl, along with the supplies that had been stolen from the depot. It might not be enough to sustain 200 to 300 people, but it would be enough to sustain 40 or 50, they reasoned.

In the meantime, Big Tony and The Rat, along with several of the others, had made it to the rendezvous site. By the time they got there, the four trucks were already there. He ordered Rat and one other man in the back of the Hummer with the girl. He signaled the others in the truck to follow them. One of the drivers, who was a member of the rival gang, spoke up. "But we're gonna wait here till the others come."

Garcia, still holding his automatic weapon, shot him without warning. As he rolled out of the truck, the gang leader commanded, "Get me another driver." That settled any further dialogue. A few minutes later, with the Hummer in the lead and the trucks following, they headed toward the highway.

The four other gang leaders were within a couple of hundred yards of the rendezvous site when they heard the trucks gunning their engines. They ran as fast as their tired legs could carry them. They weren't used to physical exertion, and they were weary to the bone. They had almost made the clearing when they saw the last of the trucks heading down the road. They fired their weapons and cursed, but to no avail. The trucks just kept moving.

"Garcia sold us out," one of the men spat out.

"We'll get him," the other said. But one of the men in the group asked, "What are we gonna do? We're stranded out here in these woods with no transportation, and you know somebody from the camp is gonna be lookin' for us."

"Aw, they're gonna be lookin' for the girl," the one called Lobo said. "Come on, let's get goin'. Just stay off the road. Stick to the woods, and we'll be okay. Remember that little town we came through? There should be some easy pickin's there. All we have to do is get us a vehicle and some food and we'll be okay. We'll make it back to the city and take care of Garcia." He turned and headed into the woods.

Light Horse had no problem following the men who had taken Wendy. They left a trail clear enough that a blind man could have followed it with no difficulty. Every several yards there were pieces of Wendy's dress caught on a bush or bark of a tree. Each time he saw the fabric, Light Horse got madder. He'd been a Christian now for nearly six years, and during that time he had diligently tried to control his temper. He had always been known as a bad actor and, as a believer, he'd worked hard to restrain himself. Now he found himself reverting to old habits. Surprisingly enough, it wasn't the uncontrolled rage

632

he had felt before; he was just very angry. And then he suddenly realized, *You know, that's okay. God made us as human beings to get angry. We're just not to let the Sun go down on our anger.* He was determined that he was going to catch the men ahead of him before the Sun went down. That was simple enough.

He was still moving up the hill at a trot, and although the men behind him were in excellent shape, they were not in the same condition as Light Horse, and they began to huff and puff. He kept moving on steadily, and he suddenly found himself in the clearing where obviously the transfer had taken place. He looked at the Hummer tracks and then saw the tracks of the big trucks following the Hummer. The dead man on the ground was clearly a casualty of a gang conflict.

In the meantime, he heard the Hummer carrying C.C. coming. A few seconds later, it pulled into the clearing. Light Horse looked around the clearing for a few seconds more, and then he went over to C.C. He reported, "There are 12 men. Eight of them are now in the trucks and the Hummer. Four others are headed out through the woods. Apparently, the others left them.

"C.C., you go after the ones on wheels, and I'll go after the ones on foot," Light Horse said.

"Do you want to take somebody with you?"

"That won't be necessary. They'd just slow me down. Take them with you," he said, pointing to the two men who had followed him.

"All right," C.C. said, not wanting to lose any time. "How are you going to catch up with us?"

"Don't worry about me. You just stay on the trail of those kidnappers. I'll catch up."

"Right," C.C. responded, and knew that his friend meant exactly what he said. A smile curled at the edges of his lips. He wouldn't want to be the four men who had taken to the woods, not with Light Horse after them.

Shortly after C.C. took off in the Hummer, Lt. Hardy returned. Some of the men filled him in on what had happened and he said to one of the Army personnel, "Go over to the communications hut and contact Camp David. Let General Boland know what's going on. According to the guys we captured, these thugs came out of the city. Maybe Boland can put up a road block going back into the city, just in case C.C. doesn't catch up with them."

"Right, Sir," the corporal said, jogging off toward the communications hut.

Light Horse headed into the woods, following the four men. Again, he had no difficulty tracking them. Not only were they inexperienced woodsmen, they were just plain stupid. In their haste they were breaking down brush and tripping over rocks. He thought about the many years he'd spent in the Army as a member of their special forces.

For Light Horse, his stint in the special forces helped him to realize that to continue what he was doing would dehumanize him. He went back, resigned from the Army, and starting looking for the truth. Three years later he found it.

While surfing through the television channels on a beer-drinking binge, he came upon a Luis Palau Crusade. Hearing the message of Christ clearly presented for the first time, he turned his life over to Jesus. Since that time, he had dedicated himself to being a man of peace and to saving lives, not taking them.

Here he was, though, plodding through the woods once again. He had to confess that he felt good, and it felt normal to him. All of his ancestry boiled up inside. He was a man of the forest; he was home once again. He had trekked about half a mile when he heard the sounds of the gang members ahead of him. They were arguing and grumbling. He could see from his tracking that they had been stumbling over rocks and stumps. One time they had wandered into a thicket of brambles and had left pieces of clothing and drops of blood in the bramble field.

He thought to himself, *These men are really stupid. They have no idea about how to survive in the woods.* Once he got within about 60 yards of the men, he slowed down. He flanked them and, hidden behind a very large tree, he shouted, "Throw down your weapons."

The gang leaders and their lieutenant stopped, raising their weapons as they looked around. They heard a voice, but they didn't see anyone.

"Lay down your weapons," Light Horse said in a more commanding tone. He'd developed a technique using cupped hands of throwing his voice so it sounded like it was coming from another direction. In response to the sound, the gang members turned, pointed their weapons, and cut loose, emptying entire clips where they presumed the voice had come from. Light Horse moved his location and shouted out again.

"Drop your weapons." He could hear the empty clips being dumped and new clips coming down. The gang members fired once more, this time shorter bursts. Light Horse took out one of his steel-shafted arrows with a small knob on the end that looked like a miniature pine cone. He put it into his bow and aimed at a big limb in a tree 20 feet away from where the enemy stood. Pulling the bow back, he let the missile fly. The small cone on the front of the arrow had a whistler attached to it. As it flew through the air, it made a screaming noise, not unlike what the Luftwaffe had used on their dive-bombers in World War II.

The four gang members hit the ground. The shaft moved so fast it was unseen until it struck the limb in a huge fireball. The limb, nearly eight inches in diameter, was split off the tree and hit the ground. The very tip of the limb reached the gang members and slashed them with its thin fingers. Looking out through the foliage, Light Horse saw the gang members again turn their weapons and fire indiscriminately in every direction. By mere chance, one of the bullets pinged off the tree where Light Horse was hiding, but it did no damage to him.

As soon as the firing stopped, he eased out of his position and circled around one more time about 30 degrees from where he had once stood. He shouted out again, "This is your last warning. Throw down your weapons."

By this time the gang members were terrified. They had no idea what had happened. As far as they knew lightning had struck the tree. They never saw the arrow and could only guess what kind of a demon they were facing.

"What is it?" Scar asked the others.

"I don't know," Lobo replied. "Some kind of a rocket was launched at us, I think."

"Do you see anything?"

"No, I don't see nothin'. Why don't we surrender?" Scar said.

"He'll kill us," Lobo whined.

"No. We need to get him out in the open. Then we'll kill him," Scar countered.

Scar shouted, "Come out where we can see you."

Right, Light Horse thought to himself. *He must think stupid is in this year.* He called out one more time. "Drop your weapons. This is your last warning."

But instead, Scar, the most defiant of the gang leaders said, "When I count three, we'll fire. Keep your weapons waist high and just spray in a circle. We'll get him. He's hiding in the bushes somewhere." And he started, "One . . . two . . . ," but he never made it to three, because before he could pull the trigger, another steel-shafted missile with a finely honed pointed shaft struck him in the right thigh. Light Horse had only pulled the arrow back halfway. Otherwise, he was afraid that it would shatter the bone, and he would end up having to carry the man out of the woods.

The aim was nearly perfect. It penetrated the outer part of his thigh and passed all the way through. The man screamed, dropped his weapon, and grabbed his thigh. The other men, seeing their comrade down, threw their weapons down and raised their hands in surrender. Light Horse stepped into the open, another steel shaft ready in his bow. But the fight was out of them.

"Help him up," he ordered. The man on the ground was still writhing in pain. Light

Horse went over and ripped the bottom of his trousers open to look at the wound.

"He'll be all right," he said. "It's just a flesh wound."

But to listen to the man scream, you would have thought he had been mortally wounded. Taking out a piece of the steel wire, Light Horse tightly bound the hands of all four men behind them. Then he took a piece of the man's trouser, tore it off, and wrapped it around his leg to stop the bleeding. Taking them to a small clearing near where they were, he plunked the men down in the middle of it and told them to sit.

"What are you going to do?" Scar asked, his eyes big in terror.

"I'm going to leave you right here," Light Horse said. "I'm going after your boss."

"You can't leave us here," Lobo pleaded.

"Sure I can," Light Horse said. "And let me tell you something. There's things in these woods that will eat you if you move, so I would suggest you stay right where you are. You will not be able to get your hands free. And it isn't a good idea to go wandering around these woods with your hands bound. I'll send somebody back for you. In the meantime, you stay right here."

"Hey wait. Don't leave us."

But Light Horse was already gone. He'd gathered the weapons the gang members carried and dumped them in the bog as he headed out to the road. His bow was stowed and arrows secured in their quiver, and he was jogging at a pace that would cover a mile every seven minutes. It was two miles into New Holland and 14 minutes later a big Indian clad in an Army Ranger's uniform, less the sleeves, appeared on the edge of town.

Forty-five minutes had lapsed since he had left C.C. in the clearing, and Light Horse knew he needed a means of rapid transportation. He found what he needed at a farmhouse on the outskirts of New Holland. The Amish farmer who lived there was a connoisseur of horses himself, and he had two beautiful Arabians. Light Horse had made friends with the man over the last few months, as he was a lover of horses himself. When he approached the front door and knocked on it, the Amish farmer's startled wife saw a huge bronze-skinned man carrying a bow and arrows looking in through her door.

He said, "I'm Light Horse. I'm a friend of your husband. Is he home?"

"Yes," the woman replied. "Everybody in town heard the shooting from the camp and wondered what was going on."

In a few brief minutes, Light Horse filled in the details of what had happened and asked the couple, "May I borrow a horse?"

"Certainly," the big farmer said. "Take whatever you need."

A couple of minutes later, Light Horse was

heading away from the farm. He loved horses. They were his favorite animals. They were big and strong and totally loyal, and he had made friends with this big Arabian over the last several months, carrying him bits of food every time he went to visit. The big animal was in superb shape. Light Horse knew the trucks would be moving faster, but by heading across open country he hoped he might be able to catch up with the trucks before they reached the main road.

In fact, when the gang members had headed out, one of the men driving a truck had neglected the most important part: putting fuel in the tank. Before they had even gone 10 miles, his truck stopped. Garcia came back shouting and screaming obscenities at the man, and while they rolled one of the drums of diesel fuel over to the truck he ordered the other trucks to proceed, telling the man, "When you get it started, catch up with us."

The man had pleaded for him to wait, but to no avail. Garcia wasn't about to wait for the pursuers he knew would be after them. The driver and another of the gang members connected the hand pump to the 50-gallon drum and began to pump diesel fuel into the truck. When he thought he had enough in, he tried to start it. It refused to start. Once the injectors had air in them, it was going to take several minutes before the engine would start. In a panic, he kept grinding and grinding until finally all he heard was a click out of the starter. He had worn down the battery.

He was near panic when a vehicle pulled up behind him and one of the biggest men he had ever seen stepped out of the Hummer, carrying a Browning automatic rifle. As with most bullies, he had no stomach for a fight. He opened the door and threw out his weapon. He commanded the man on the other side to do the same. When C.C. leveled the BAR at him, he complied immediately.

One of the men with C.C. produced four huge plastic ties, normally used around air conditioning ducts, and instructed the men to put their hands behind their backs. Then he bound them tightly with the ties. Next he overlapped their legs and bound them together securely with the other ties. Convinced that these men would go nowhere, C.C. and his men piled back in the Hummer and roared away.

While tying the men on the ground, C.C. had learned the name of the gang leader: Big Tony Garcia. *Well Mr. Big Tony Garcia,* C.C. said silently, *you and I have a date.*

30

Driving furiously, C.C. pushed the Hummer across open fields. He knew the trucks had to stick to the highway, but the Hummer was a great all-terrain vehicle. He told the men inside to hang on as he crossed fields and smashed down fences on his way. He was determined to catch up with the kidnappers, no matter what.

At speeds of up to 70 miles an hour, everyone inside was hanging on for their lives as the Hummer bounced and skidded its way across ditches and underbrush and even over small trees. Nothing would stop C.C. from catching the slime that had Wendy.

And catch them he did. He saw the trucks on the opposite side of a big open area leading across State Road 93. He headed for the highway, pushing the Hummer for all it was worth. He skidded onto the highway not more than 300 yards behind the trucks. As he entered the highway, the lead vehicle, an older Hummer, was just making the left-hand turn onto State Road 16.

One of the gang members looked back and saw the dark gray Hummer entering the road behind the trucks, and he yelled to Garcia,

"Somebody's following us!"

Big Tony Garcia looked around and saw the Hummer closing in behind them. "Don't worry," he said boastfully. "It's just one vehicle. We can take care of 'em."

He signaled the driver to turn his Hummer around. Deftly the man swung the vehicle out across the road, across the ditch, and back onto the road, headed back in the opposite direction. Garcia already had his weapons out and ordered the others to be ready.

C.C., seeing the maneuver, floored his Hummer and quickly caught up with the three slow-moving trucks. As Big Tony's Hummer went by on the left side of the road, C.C. swung his vehicle over into the grassy area on the right side, using the trucks to block Garcia's line of fire.

Garcia swore at his driver and ordered him to swing around again. In the meantime, as C.C. passed the trucks on the right side, he ordered two of the men in the back, "Shoot the tires out as we go by!"

As the Hummer sped past the trucks, two of the men in the back cut loose on the tires with their weapons. The first truck swung out of control, careened off the road, and rolled to a stop in a ditch beside the road.

The second driver, seeing what had happened, attempted to sideswipe C.C. as he came past, but C.C. anticipated the move and slowed his vehicle as the truck swung wildly over to the right side. C.C. then whipped his vehicle back onto the highway and, as he passed the truck on the left side now, he ordered the men on the right side of his vehicle to shoot out the tires, which they did. The driver of that truck, already off the road, lost control and the truck careened over on its side.

The driver of the third truck, seeing what happened in his rearview mirror, pushed his accelerator to the floor, but the slower moving truck could not outrun the Hummer. As C.C. started to pass on the left, the driver swung the wheel hard to cut him off. Anticipating that move, C.C. swung his vehicle back to the right and passed the truck once more on the grassy knoll.

Abreast of the truck now, two of the men in the back cut loose with their weapons on the back tires. The blowout caused the vehicle to veer sharply. C.C. let off the gas, allowing the truck to cross in front of him, then skidded the Hummer back onto the highway again and, as he did, saw the truck do a full 180° stem to stern and flip upside down in the ditch beside the road.

In the meantime, the Hummer carrying Garcia and six of the gang had turned and was in hot pursuit of C.C. The two vehicles were some 200 yards apart when C.C. whipped his vehicle around and headed back in the direction of Garcia and his men.

Inside Garcia's Hummer, The Rat still had a firm grip on Wendy's arm. She guessed who it was in the other Hummer. It would be her dad or C.C. coming to rescue her. Her heart swelled with excitement.

"Get your weapons out!" Garcia shouted angrily. He had seen all three of the trucks disabled and he was mad with rage. But he knew he had a trump: the girl! "They're not going to hit us — not with the girl in the car," he shouted, readying his weapon.

C.C. had already concluded that Wendy was in the other Hummer. He was pondering what he should do as his vehicle screamed toward the other vehicle at nearly 60 mph.

As the two vehicles approached each other, C.C. shouted to the men in his vehicle, "Hang on! I'm going to try something."

He was judging the pace of the two Hummers. Garcia was confident that whoever was driving the other Hummer would not crash his. His intention was to wait until the two vehicles passed and then open fire, hopefully killing everybody in the other vehicle.

C.C. continued racing toward the gang leader's Hummer, hoping he had judged correctly. Just before the two vehicles were about to crash, C.C. put his vehicle into a full skid. Stopping on the right shoulder, the vehicle blocked all but a small portion of the right lane from the oncoming Hummer. In the ditch and blocking most of the apron of the road was one of the overturned trucks.

The other Hummer, now up to nearly 50 mph had no place to go. If he veered to the left, he'd lose control of his vehicle, because there was a deep ditch on that side of the road. He had no choice but to try to squeeze between C.C.'s Hummer and the wrecked truck on the right. Seeing C.C.'s move, the driver slammed on the brakes. The unexpected move caught The Rat off-guard, and he was thrown against the seat in front of him. The blow knocked the wind out of him and he released his grip on Wendy.

The Hummer was decelerating rapidly. All four wheels locked and it started to slide. By the time it careened off of C.C.'s Hummer and then off the truck, the speed was down to 30 mph. The impact ripped the right front wheel off of C.C.'s Hummer and almost ripped the left front wheel off of Garcia's. It bounced hard, and at first C.C. thought it might go end over end, but the rear end set down and it skidded to a stop. The impact had dazed The Rat, but his body cushioned the blow for Wendy.

Wendy didn't hesitate. She jumped out through the open window. Hitting the ground, she rolled three or four times, but her young, strong legs quickly gathered under her and she came up running — toward C.C.'s Hummer.

C.C. was a little dazed from the blow of

the second Hummer as it came by, and he asked the men riding with him, "You guys okay?"

"We're okay," they all responded. Most of them had minor cuts and bruises from being banged around inside the vehicle, but otherwise they were in good shape.

"Well let's go get 'em," C.C. said as he leaped out of the vehicle.

C.C. and the other three men bolted from their Hummer a few seconds before the gang members began to pour out of theirs. At first he thought it was going to be a fire fight, but the punks in the other car had no stomach for it. The big man in the right front seat came out with his weapon ready, but the gang was already covered by C.C.'s men. The others could see the futility of resisting because it would have meant sure death.

"Drop your weapons!" C.C. commanded. "You don't have a chance."

Garcia momentarily thought about cutting loose with his weapon, but then he saw the hopelessness of it. He ordered the men with him, "Drop your weapons," which they did.

In the meantime, Wendy had come up to where C.C. stood. She hugged him and said, "Thanks, C.C. I knew you would come."

"You're right, Sweetheart. There wasn't a chance these worthless punks were going to get away with my favorite girl."

"Big talk when you've got the weapons on

us," Garcia said, "but you'd be nothing without your guns."

He cursed at C.C., using racial slurs. C.C., with his adrenaline pumping and his anger piqued, walked up to the gang leader who towered a full two inches above him and said, "Hey punk. How would you like it if I put the guns down?"

An evil grin crossed the face of Big Tony Garcia. He'd been a street fighter all his life. He'd never been beaten in hand-to-hand combat. And as big as C.C. was, Garcia was a full 40 pounds heavier.

"Yeah, let's see whatcha got!" Garcia screamed at him.

C.C. turned to give his weapon to the one of the men close to him, and when he did, Garcia struck, bringing his fist down on the right side of C.C.'s head, behind the ear. The blow was calculated to cripple an opponent, or at least to stun him. It dropped C.C. to his knees.

As he dropped, Garcia brought his knee up to meet C.C.'s nose. The intent was to shatter the nose bone, driving it back up into the brain and killing the opponent. But when the knee came up, it met nothing but air. C.C. had rolled to one side and come up in a defensive position.

The shock on Garcia's face was apparent. He'd always been able to disable an opponent with a single blow, but now he saw his opponent still standing. Garcia was no slouch as a fighter himself; he had been conditioned through years of street fighting. He struck at C.C. Again, to his surprise, his fist just whistled through thin air. C.C., anticipating the blow, ducked it and came up with a hammerlike blow under Garcia's right ribs, knocking the wind out of him. The shock on Garcia's face told the story: Big Tony was not used to fighting an equal. In fact, C.C. meant to prove to the gang leader that he was not only his equal but his superior.

Garcia was spun around by the blow and, in one swift motion, C.C. came back with his left and caught him in the back just above the kidney. Garcia screamed in pain and dropped to a knee.

Without waiting, C.C. moved in quickly. When the gang leader looked up, all he saw was a dark ham-shaped fist coming directly at him. C.C. smashed him in the right eye. Garcia went down, but he was strong as a bull and as mean and vicious as one. He kicked hard at the onrushing figure. C.C. anticipated the move however and deflected the kick.

As Garcia attempted to get up, C.C. smashed him in the face again. Garcia roared in anger and it sounded for all the world like the growl of a wounded bear. Snapping to his feet, he shook his head; blood was streaming down from his broken nose. When he reached up and touched his nose, the pain made him wince. It was clearly broken and had shifted to one side. Garcia screamed obscenities and charged at C.C, who sidestepped and stuck his foot out, sending the larger man sprawling. Garcia went headlong into the gravel beside the road. Looking around for a weapon, he found a piece of broken headlight glass from one of the Hummers. Wielding it like a scalpel, he went for C.C., intending to slash him across the face.

C.C. smiled. "Listen punk. This is the last time you're going to harass innocent people." Then he backhanded Garcia across the face.

Roaring, Garcia rushed in. This time he anticipated that C.C. would step out of the way, so he made a quick move to the right, hoping to catch C.C. ducking and slash him with the glass. But instead, C.C. stood his ground this time and, as Garcia made his move, C.C. stepped forward and smashed the big man just below the heart with a thundering blow that sent him to the ground. The piece of glass he'd been holding fell from his hand.

C.C. stood over Garcia, arms down at his side and said, "Come on, big man. What's the matter?"

Garcia sprung to his feet, a little less rapidly than he had before but still with plenty of fight left in him. Now he circled his adversary with a great deal more caution, trying to find a weakness. He feigned to the left and feigned to the right. C.C. stood absolutely still, arms down at his side. That threw Garcia off. He'd never seen a man who wasn't afraid of him, and clearly this man not only was not afraid of him, he disdained him.

Garcia rushed in, intending to grab C.C. and squeeze the life out of him. As he did, C.C. stepped forward and swung a big fist into the face of the gang leader. That stopped the big man's momentum in his tracks. C.C. smashed another right into his stomach and heard the wind go out of him. Garcia looked up to see another fist coming at him, and then another, and then another, and the last thing he remembered was C.C. catching him right behind the ear, where he had struck the first blow. Down he went, with his head bouncing off the asphalt pavement in front of C.C.'s Hummer.

As C.C. looked around, he could see the shock on the faces of the other gang members. Their leader had never been beaten in hand-to-hand combat, and now he not only had been defeated, he'd been humiliated. The other men in C.C.'s group gave him a small cheer.

Wendy rushed up and hugged him again. C.C. hugged her back. Pulling her out in front of him, C.C. said, "I don't think that dress is going to make another party, Sweetie."

Wendy looked down at her torn and tattered dress and began to laugh. Then, as a release for some of the pent-up emotions, she began to cry, and C.C. hugged her to himself.

"Well, now what?" C.C. said as he looked around at the wrecked vehicles. "It's going to be a long walk back to New Holland, Miss Wendy."

"Maybe we can get the one truck going," one of the men who was with C.C. said. "If we take some tires off a couple of the overturned trucks and put 'em on that one, we can probably get it running."

"Good idea," C.C. agreed. "Let's get started."

When Light Horse had heard the shooting, he'd kicked his horse in the ribs and urged him into a full gallop. He'd covered the three miles across the open pasture in record time. He got there just in time to see the last of the fight between C.C. and the big gang member. In some ways, he pitied Garcia. He himself had tangled with C.C. many years before, and he had never forgotten the experience. C.C. was hard as a rock and quick as a cat, and Light Horse learned by personal experience that he could take anything anybody could hand out and keep standing. As he watched C.C. take the big gang leader apart, he could only chuckle.

He'd better try to pick on somebody his own size next time, Light Horse chuckled to himself as he rode across the field.

When he rode up, C.C. said, "Well Light Horse, how'd you make out?"

"I left them all sitting in a clearing a couple of miles out of the camp," Light Horse said. "What are you going to do with these guys?"

"As soon as we can get one of these trucks moving, we're going to load them up and take them back to the camp."

"Yeah, it looks like they made a mess of some of our seed," Light Horse said.

"Well, some of it's salvageable," C.C. responded. "We'll send a crew back later to collect it. Right now we need to get word back to Jason that Wendy's safe."

Light Horse swung down from his horse and walked over to where Wendy was standing. "Well, Little One, you doing okay?"

"I sure am," Wendy said confidently as she rushed over to her other big friend and gave him a hug.

"Well, are you up to riding back to camp with me?" he asked.

"Can I? Cool!" Wendy said enthusiastically. "I've still got a wedding celebration to go to."

"Right you are," Light Horse said as he swung back up onto the horse.

C.C. reached down and grabbed Wendy by the waist and hoisted her onto the blanket in back of the big Indian.

"See you later, Amigo," he said to C.C. as

he headed toward the camp.

"You take it easy now, Indian," C.C. said with a grin.

"Later, Kimo Sabe," Light Horse replied as he kicked the horse into an easy trot. The horse was hardly winded from the heavy riding Light Horse had put him through but, even so, for the first half hour he held him to a slow trot. Once he was sure the horse was rested, he kicked the pace up a little bit. Thirty minutes later, Light Horse and Wendy rode into the New Holland camp. They immediately went over to Jason's hut, and Light Horse hoisted Wendy to the ground. Then he turned the horse and started to ride away.

Looking back, Light Horse said, "Tell your dad I'll be around later. I need to go clean up a little bit."

"Right," Wendy replied. "And, Light Horse . . . thanks."

"Anytime," Light Horse responded. "It's really been a good day." With that he nudged the horse to a trot.

Wendy burst into the hut. Jason and Annette had been sitting on the side of the bed praying when she entered.

"Daddy!"

Jason turned to see his daughter rushing toward him, and the pain in his head was all but forgotten. He jumped up to give her a hug but then eased back down on the bed.

"Still a little woozy I guess," he said.

"Are you okay, Daddy?" she asked.

"Yeah, pretty thick skull. It'd be hard to hurt me by hitting me in the head," he joked.

Wendy sat down beside him and hugged him. Then she looked at Annette and winked.

"Are you all right too . . . new mom?" Wendy asked.

"I'm fine, Honey," Annette said. "Praise God you're okay. What happened?"

Wendy took the next half hour to explain the entire ordeal, embellishing every little detail about the rescue and C.C.'s fight with the big gang leader.

"That evil little man with him made my flesh crawl. They actually called him The Rat!" Wendy said.

"Well, Sweetheart, it's all over now."

"Okay, let's get on with the wedding celebration," Wendy said.

"Oh, Honey, I don't know if that would be appropriate now," Jason argued.

"Why, sure it would, Daddy. Otherwise, those guys will have won. We can't have that."

Jason chuckled. "Well I guess you're right, Sweetheart, but I think you'd better change your dress. You can see through that one in a couple of places."

The tally for that day was four members of the defense team were wounded, one with a shoulder injury that would disable him for a few weeks and the other three with fairly superficial wounds. Twelve members of the gang were killed; another 20 were injured to varying degrees. In total, 161 gang members were captured, including Big Tony Garcia and The Rat.

After communicating with Camp David, Gen. Boland assured them that he would send an Army MP team to collect the gang members. This particular group would do time in the maximum security facility set up by the military. A military tribunal was being planned to try individuals for crimes committed during the last year.

After hearing about the crisis at Camp New Holland, the president called.

"Jason, how are you doing?"

"I'm doing fine, Sir," Jason assured him.

"Congratulations on your marriage."

"Thank you, Mr. President. This is the most exciting day I've had in a long time."

Houston laughed a little bit.

"Jason, based on what I've heard, I think you need to get out more often."

Jason chuckled. "Yes, Sir, you're probably right."

"What's the status of the flares?" the president asked.

"We'll let you know just as soon as we have a final analysis," Jason said. "Probably in the next week or so."

"Good," the president responded. "I appreciate you, Jason. We're looking forward to having you back here. Do you think you could return to Camp David after your honeymoon?" he asked. "We've got some important preparations to talk about."

"One second, Mr. President." Jason cupped his hand over the phone and looked at Annette and Wendy. "The president would like for us to come back to Camp David. What do you guys think?"

He got a nod from Annette, but Wendy's face wrinkled into a slight pout. "I'd really rather stay here, Daddy," she said.

"Mr. President, Annette and I will be at Camp David in two weeks. Wendy would like to stay here."

"That'll be fine, Jason," the president said. "I kind of suspected that. Do you know what's happening? We've polled the people in the camps all over the country and 95 percent of them don't want to leave. I don't know where we're going to get the people to populate the cities again." Then he added, "See you, Jason . . . in two weeks . . . right?"

"Right," Jason said, hanging up the phone.

For the rest of that evening, the biggest Thanksgiving celebration ever held in any single community took place. Twenty-five thousand members of the New Holland camp spent that evening eating, singing, and dancing, and generally giving praise to God for being alive and being together.

Jason and Annette spent the next three days

isolated, except for the time they spent with Wendy; then, almost simultaneously, they decided it was time to go back to work. The next morning, the members of the camp saw the Hobart trio enter the solar observatory at 6:30. They continued to monitor area 403, leaving the spectrographs on 24 hours a day. It had been nearly two months since they had seen any major interference from solar activity. Jason was convinced that the worst of the solar activity was over. They had a long, hard winter yet to go through, but if everything went well, they should be able to begin evacuating the camps the next spring.

He reported his findings to the president and assured him that he and Annette would head back to Camp David in another 10 days.

At Camp David, the president had assembled most of his Cabinet, as well as several members of the House, the Senate, and six members of the Supreme Court. The others were in various stages of returning to Washington, D.C. Gen. Boland told Jason about their plan to control the gangs in the big cities. With the exception of a couple of cities in Florida, southern Texas, and southern California, he knew the pressure on the gangs to surrender would be very strong, once winter set in. Winter in New York City, Chicago, or even Indianapolis with no food, electricity, water, or heat was going to tame the toughest members.

Military tribunals had been set up in four areas across the country to try the riotous criminals, gang members included. Much like the trials at Nuremberg, these tribunals had absolute authority during martial law. The six members of the Supreme Court all agreed that while the country was still under martial law the military had control over the justice system. Gen. Boland referred to it as a time to do a little "house cleaning." The uniform rules of military justice would apply in this situation, and those rules were very simple and direct, much like the original law intended by the framers of the Constitution. Crime and criminals would be dealt with swiftly and sternly.

A preliminary appraisal of the big cities showed that 70 percent of the structures were unusable as they stood. It would take trillions of dollars to restore them.

There were two big surprises in store for Professor Jason Hobart. The first was when the president announced that he and the members of Congress had agreed to present Jason with not only the Distinguished Service Medal, which is usually given to civilians for outstanding service, but they had also agreed to give Jason the Congressional Medal of Honor, an honor normally reserved for full-time military personnel in times of combat.

The president had convinced Congress that because Jason had been drafted into the service of his country while the country was under martial law, he did qualify. He would be the first civilian in history to receive the nation's highest award. The vote was unanimous among the members of Congress who constituted the quorum.

The president had requested and received permission to make the office of science advisor a permanent member of his Cabinet. Jason's second surprise was that he had been named to that position, and it had been approved by the Senate — at least those present.

Jason was flabbergasted. When Houston asked if he would accept the post, he replied, "Mr. President, I'm humbled and honored, and I would be proud to serve in your Cabinet."

"Well thanks, Jason," Houston said with a big grin. "I would hate to have to draft you into the military under martial law to have access to your services."

Houston added, "I also would like for Mrs. Hobart to serve as the head of the National Institute of Sciences, if she would consent to do so."

The look on Annette's face showed that she was even more surprised than Jason had been.

"Mr. President," Annette said.

"Please call me Phil, Mrs. Hobart."

"Then address me as Annette," she corrected the president. "I would be proud to serve as the head of the National Institute of Sciences. But Mr. President, there are some changes that need to be made."

"I understand, Annette. You just do what you have to do to clean up the mess over there."

"What ever happened to Dr. Frasier?" Jason asked.

"Well, unfortunately, Dr. Frasier was involved with an ill-advised raid on Camp David," Gen. Boland explained. "Right now, he's in a prison camp. He'll be tried by the tribunal and I suspect he'll do 20 years in Leavenworth — that is, once Leavenworth is up and going again."

"Too bad," Jason said as he shook his head. "Frasier wasn't really a bad man."

Boland corrected him. "A man who lies, cheats, and steals and then tries to kill his neighbors is a bad man by anybody's definition, Jason, and let's not forget that. That's one of the problems with this country. We've rationalized sin too often."

"You're right about that, General," Jason said. "I stand corrected."

"Mr. President, if it's all right with you, Annette and I will go back to New Holland. We'd like to continue our observations, but I'm as sure as I can be that the solar flares are over."

"That'll be fine, Jason. I'd like to have you

back here in the Spring, so we can try to get this country back up and running again."

"Right," Jason responded. "I'll see you in April, Mr. President."

"Take care of yourself, Jason," the president said. "And you too, Annette."

31

To say that winter was difficult would be an understatement for the families living in the camps. The majority of their dwellings were still mostly tents made of canvas and nylon. Although winters in New Holland, Pennsylvania are very harsh and unkind, at least everyone had adequate winter clothing. The key to staying warm was to dress properly, indoors and out. Other than the occasional cases of frostbite for those who ventured outside without the proper attire, winter was more of an inconvenience than a disaster.

For those remaining in the cities the situation was drastically different. Most buildings had no electricity, water, or gas. Survival consisted of wearing what clothing could be scrounged from the ruins. The only heat available was usually from makeshift wood burners that belched smoke and emitted deadly carbon monoxide, which killed those who made the mistake of sealing their rooms too tightly.

Fuel was scarce, and to burn a fire hot enough to warm a room was to risk a raid by looters who would steal everything. Life was a living nightmare. Food was almost nonexistent inside the city, so the government established food drop areas where people could come for necessities like bread, jam, peanut butter, water, and medical supplies. But since the gangs couldn't use the drop zones without fear of arrest, they would wait until the others retrieved their supplies and then attack them. The cities truly had become jungles with ruthless criminals at the top of the food chain.

There were startling contrasts in society. In the camps life was hard but rewarding. Disputes were settled by mutually agreeable rules. Work was a community effort. Rotating work teams regularly cleared the snow off the paths so people could move around and get outside. There were arguments among families and neighbors as cabin fever set in, but they were settled without violence, and best of all there was enough to eat. Friendships grew stronger as mutual respect was practiced.

Days were mostly consumed with clearing snow and fixing problems like frozen water pipes, collapsed roofs, and mud — lots of mud. Evenings were crowded with Bible studies, parties, and fellowship among the thousands of families housed at New Holland.

In one fellowship group meeting, Bonnie Escobar, a single mom who had lived in government housing most of her life, was chatting with the others in her group. Bonnie was a third generation welfare recipient who had three children: the first child was born out of wedlock; the other two were fathered by her husband Clyde, whom she hadn't seen in over three years. She had tried to escape the welfare life by marrying Clyde; then one day he just didn't come home. She always assumed that he had taken off with another woman.

Bonnie was forced back onto government welfare and into government housing. For the previous three years she had seen her children terrorized by drug-dominated gunfights by the gangs. The gangs ran the tenements, and the police, what pitifully few there were, were either bullied by the gangs or actually were working for the drug dealers.

Her best friend at the camp, Dee Meriweather, had two children about the same ages as Bonnie's oldest two: 12 and 10. Dee was talking about how glad she would be to go back home.

"What do you mean home?" Bonnie asked.

"I mean back to the city. I really miss so much of our life."

"Exactly what do you miss about it, Dee?"

"Well, I don't know exactly. I miss the traffic and the people. I miss television and movies. You know, all the things that made life good."

Bonnie laughed. "Dee, I don't know about you, but I can't remember anything about my life in the city that was good."

Several others in the group agreed.

"Yeah, I ain't left nothin' back there but a lot of misery," one of the other women said.

Dee spoke up defensively. "Well I don't like all the rules around here. It's like they want to dominate my life. I don't like that. There's no TV, and you can't have alcohol. I want to be free to live my own life again."

Bonnie said, "Dee, I hope you'll think this through, for your sake and for your children. How many nights were you able to go out and walk the streets in your neighborhood like we do here?"

Dee said defensively, "Obviously we didn't walk the streets after dark."

"And why was that?" Bonnie asked. "It's the nation's capital, the heart of America. Why couldn't you walk the streets?"

"Well . . . the danger," Dee said slowly.

"Danger! The dangers were from the drug addicts, drug dealers, dopeheads, rapists, burglars, molesters, all the rest. Dee, can't you see what we have here? We have a new life. We have people who care about us. We have people that care about our children and watch out for them. My daughter could walk out of here right now and go anywhere in this camp without fear of being molested or kidnapped or raped. Don't you understand what that's worth?" Bonnie said passionately.

"When I was 16 years old my mother had been on welfare 15 years. A drug dealer in our community gave me free crack — until

I was hooked on it. For seven years I sold my body every day on the streets to buy enough crack to keep high. Then when I had my first baby, I went on government welfare and continued prostituting on the side just to have enough food to eat and keep myself in drugs.

"Then I married Clyde. He had been a street kid himself. We both tried to get ourselves straightened out, but it didn't work. Clyde got back into drugs and started dealing. I told him I was going to turn him into the police, so he took off. There I was, left with three kids, no husband, and no way to support myself, so I got back on government welfare and back into the tenements. I was afraid to let my kids outside, afraid they would get killed or kidnapped.

"It seemed like every day in our neighborhood there was a drive-by shooting. Every night we'd go to sleep to the sound of gunfire. Everyone in my neighborhood had double bolts on the doors and bars on their windows. Two of my neighbors died in house fires, trying to get out of their apartment that had burglar bars on the windows to keep the thieves out.

"Dee, I'm telling you, there isn't any life back there that I want to go back to, and I'll stay here if one other person will stay with me. I'll starve before I'll go back to the life I had before. I didn't know this kind of life was possible. And you talk about missin' television? I made a vow to God that I won't ever own another television. And I won't ever let my kids see another filthy Hollywood movie. And, my children are goin' to be raised with the fear of God — rules we have in camp: rules like, 'Love your neighbor and care about them,' 'Don't steal,' 'Don't rob.' "

One of the others in the group said, "Same here. I'll die here before I'll go back to the city again." Others nodded in agreement.

"How will we make a livin' here?" Dee asked. "How you goin' to survive?"

"Well, with God's help, I'm going to buy a tract of land here, and I'm going to raise my family like they were raised 100 years ago. I'll scratch out a livin' somehow. At least I'll have some good neighbors who'll watch out for my kids. I want children who obey their parents and respect their elders. I want children who can grow up without seeing their friends killed on the streets."

"You mean you want to live like some of these backward people who live on farms around here, who travel in buggies and wear black clothes and black, brimmed hats and cover their heads? No thanks," Dee said.

"That's fine, Dee," Bonnie said. "You go do whatever you want, but I'm tellin' you, I've gotten to know some of these people, and they have something that you and I have never had before. They have faith, and they have friends, and they have family, and that's what I'm after. In fact," Bonnie said, "I'm going to ask the leadership of the camp if we can keep it in operation, even after electricity is back on."

A murmuring went through the crowd and several others said, "Yes, I agree. Let's do it."

"I want to stay too," someone shouted.

"I'm not going back!" another said.

Dee just sat there shaking her head as she listened. She couldn't understand Bonnie. She thought she'd had a pretty good life before the camps. She didn't like camp life, and she wanted to get a *real* life. But as Bonnie spoke, her mind began to wander back to a time before they were evacuated, to the time when she also had been terrorized by the gangs. She remembered how, when the power went out, the gangs had immediately moved in, pillaging and burning everything in sight.

Maybe, she thought, *I didn't have it so good after all. Maybe Bonnie's right. Maybe there is a better life here, at least a better life for my children.*

As the winter dragged on, plans were being made in Washington for the transition back to the cities. It was clear that most of the people would not be able to move back immediately. With 70 percent of the buildings damaged or destroyed, it was going to take years to get everything operable again.

As communications began to be reestablished around the world, it was learned that most other countries had fared far worse than the United States.

In Europe, an estimated 30 million people had died from a combination of riots, starvation, exposure, and the pestilence that had swept across the land during the winter.

In Japan, 20 million people had died. Disease was running rampant throughout Japan as the Japanese government organized crematoriums to get rid of the bodies.

In Russia, 40 million or more were dead. Most had starved to death during the cruel Russian winter. With little or no heat available and virtually no food, those who survived had just barely hung on.

And so it went throughout the world. Another 50 million people had died in Asia and Africa as the food ran out. People, who a century before had been able to feed themselves, had been unable to eke out the barest necessities. The devastation in Africa had made wildlife nearly extinct.

Some of the countries in the Southern hemisphere had fared better. Australia, like the United States, had prepared their people and had moved as many people out of the cities as was possible, and since winter in the Northern hemisphere was summer in the

Southern hemisphere, they had fared much better over the last seven months. The sparse population and huge open country had served the Australian people very well.

President Houston had called together the members of his Cabinet. "I want an assessment of our options," Houston said to Oren Blake.

"Well, Mr. President, most of the cities are in ruins. We're not going to be able to move all the people back in, but we can begin to relocate perhaps half of the people by summer. The power grids are slowly being restored and some basic utilities are back in operation. The manufacturing plants on the West Coast tell us they'll be back in operation in another month or two, and we should have the supplies we need to get the rehab started. I would say that we'll probably have the country operating again, at least on a limited basis, by late summer — that is, if we have the money to rebuild."

Gen. Boland spoke up. "According to Dr. Hobart, we should be able to reestablish most of our land-line communications before summer, and we'll have aircraft flying pretty shortly, Mr. President. Without the geo-positioning satellites, it's back to the Dark Ages, as far as air traffic is concerned, but at least we'll be up and operating on a limited basis."

"Okay," the president said. "Now gentlemen, I'd like a recommendation about what we need to do to get this government in operation again; and, where are we going to get the resources to rebuild this country?"

"Well, Mr. President," Warren Butts said, "it's kind of like starting all over again. We need to expand the debt if we're going to rebuild."

"Warren," the president said, "I'm just not willing to do that. We made the mistake of thinking the government could do everything for the people before. I won't make that same mistake again. The government's responsibility is to preserve the peace and protect the people but, from this point on, the American people have to do for themselves. If a building is to be rebuilt in New York City, then the people of New York are going to do it, and the same will be true in Chicago, Los Angeles, Atlanta, Orlando, and any other city in this nation.

"The government's responsibility is to preserve and protect freedoms and give the people an equal chance. The people have to decide for themselves what standard of life they want. We're truly going to enforce equal opportunity," Philip Houston said. "That means every one in this country will have equal opportunities to do whatever God calls that person to do, but the government will neither prohibit nor promote one individual over another. Period!"

"Uh, that sounds pretty heavy, Mr. President," Dean joked. "It almost sounds like you're going to enforce the Constitution."

"You've got it, Allen. That's exactly what I'm going to do. We'll maintain martial law until we're sure that crime is under control and the criminals have been punished; then, we'll turn this country back over to its duly elected authority. If the people of the United States decide they want me to be their president, they'll keep me in office and, if not, they can vote me out. I'm ready to relinquish authority any time they tell me."

"You may get a little flack from the Congress," one of the other staff members said.

"That's okay," Houston said. "That's democracy at its best. If that's what the American people want, that's what they'll get. I'm going to give them the opportunity to choose.

"Warren, I want to take whatever cash reserves this government has in gold and whatever we have in borrowing ability, based on collateral we own — land, buildings, cars, and whatever else — and that's what we'll operate on. There will be no more unfunded mandates from this government, and there will be no more borrowing without adequate collateral."

"Wow, that's kind of a revolutionary thought too, Mr. President," Butts said.

"Yeah, it almost sounds like what the founding fathers intended, doesn't it Warren?"

"Sounds like it to me, Mr. President."

As Winter ended and Spring began, a sense of normalcy was beginning to permeate American society. Someone had located a large screen TV and had set it up in one of the community buildings at New Holland. Somebody else located a VCR, and then eventually some old videos made their way into the camp.

Most of the camp personnel were out getting the fields ready to plant once again. Although the rumor had it that the government was going to relocate some of the camp members back into their own communities, they couldn't take a chance. Spring had arrived and crops had to be started. One afternoon Bonnie came in from the fields and found her children were not home, so she asked one of the neighbors about them.

"Someone set up a television over in the assembly building," she said. "I think that's where the children are."

Bonnie hurried over to the building as fast as she could. When she walked inside, she saw several hundred of the children, sitting mesmerized in front of the television — something they hadn't seen in nearly a year. She was furious. She grabbed her three children and told them to follow her. The youngest complained, "Mommy, we were watchin' telvishun."

"Not anymore, you're not," Bonnie said. "Television was a lot of the problem we had before, and we're not going to watch television, at least not in this family."

That evening Bonnie made a decision. She drafted a petition that she began to circulate throughout the camp. Actually she drafted two petitions. The first one was a petition to have the television removed from the assembly building. The first day or so she collected about 200 signatures. Then volunteers copied her petition and began to circulate it. Before the week was out, Bonnie had two-thirds of all the camp members' signatures.

A meeting was called and the issue of television was debated. It was decided by majority vote that within the community buildings there would be no television and no movies. The next day, the big television set was removed from the camp.

Bonnie started a second petition, one that was going to have a profound effect on American society. It requested that the government continue the New Holland camp and allow residents to homestead federal lands. In the New Holland camp, nearly 22,000, out of 24,000 members, signed the petition. Once the word got out to the other camps, others started petitioning. In less than a month, over

40 million Americans had signed petitions, requesting the president not to disband the camps but to make resettlement an option for those who did not want to return to the cities.

The petitions flooded into the White House, where President Houston and his team had relocated.

"This is unbelievable, Warren. Are you sure this is accurate?"

"Yes, Sir. I've checked and double-checked it. A large percentage of the people in the camps don't want to go back to the cities."

"Did they say why?"

"Yes, Sir. They say they have discovered a way of life that's far better than the one they left," the chief of staff said.

"Well, Warren," Houston said, slapping his old friend on the back, "maybe there's hope for America after all! Let's find a way to do it. From what I hear about life in those camps or, more correctly now, those communities, I think I may just move out and join them when I'm out of office."

The employees of Thorndike Press hope you have enjoyed this Large Print book. All our Large Print titles are designed for easy reading, and all our books are made to last. Other Thorndike Press Large Print books are available at your library, through selected bookstores, or directly from us.

For information about titles, please call:

(800) 257-5157

To share your comments, please write:

Publisher
Thorndike Press
P.O. Box 159
Thorndike, Maine 04986